A Love That Saved Us

Also by Erin Cornia

The Chicago Series

If It Can't Be Us

The Most Perfect Wrong

The Broken & Bound Duet

A Love That Broke Us

A Love That Saved Us

Key Characters in A Love That Saved Us

- **Main Couple**
  - Jensen Adams
  - Alley Evans/Adams
- **Jensen and Alley's Family**
  - Matt - Jensen's lifelong best friend; like a brother
  - Megan - Jensen's sister
  - Kevin - Megan's husband; brother-in-law
  - Jeff - Jensen's brother
  - Amber - Jeff's wife; sister-in-law
  - Christy - Jensen's mom
  - Tom - Jensen's dad
  - Michael Evans - Alley's brother; Leo's friend
  - Stella Evans - Michael's wife; sister-in-law
  - Craig Evans - Alley and Michael's dad
- **Alley's Friends**
  - Scarlett - Alley's best friend in New York
  - Zach - Alley's close friend from work
- **Crossover Characters from The Chicago Series**
  - Leo Weston - MMC in *If It Can't Be Us*
  - Vivian Weston - FMC in *If It Can't Be Us*; Leo's wife
  - Adam - Michael's best friend from childhood
  - Ryan Brooks - MMC in *The Most Perfect Wrong*
  - Cooper Bradley - FMC in *The Most Perfect Wrong*

 Formatted with Vellum

Content Warning
Your mental health matters

A Love That Saved Us explores deep emotions and themes, and contains the following content:

- **Strong Language**
- **Mature Content**
- **Explicit Romance Scenes**
- **On-Page Anxiety and Panic Attacks**
- **Depictions of Drug Addiction, Withdrawal, and Recovery**
- **On-Page Drug and Alcohol Use**
- **On-Page PTSD Symptoms**
- **Emotional Trauma**
- **Mentions of Relapse and Cravings**

If these themes are triggering for you, please read with care.

This book is not intended for public schools or readers under the age of eighteen. **Reader discretion is advised.**

For anyone who's loved someone through the darkness.
Who's forgiven even when they were hurting.
Who's believed in someone when they were broken.
Who's lifted someone when they were falling.
For second chances.
For redemption.
For Jensen and Alley.
And for every broken heart after A Love That Broke Us.

** * **

To my friend, Courtney—thank you for walking through the hard parts with me while I wrote this duet. For sharing the grief and pain, and for inspiring me to believe that love after addiction can still end in forever.

A Love That Saved Us Playlist

Music always plays a huge role in the writing process for me, and *A Love That Saved Us* was no different. I hope you enjoy this playlist as much as I do.

- *It'll Be Okay* – Shawn Mendes
- *If You Love Her* – Forest Blakk
- *Notice* – Thomas Rhett
- *Love Is Gone (Acoustic)* – SLANDER & Dylan Matthew
- *Hold On* – Chord Overstreet
- *If You Want Love* – NF
- *Guilty* – Jelly Roll
- *When You're Gone* – Shawn Mendes
- *The Night We Met* – Lord Huron
- *I Hate That It's True* – Dean Lewis
- *Hold Back the River* – James Bay
- *All That Really Matters* – ILLENIUM & Teddy Swims
- *With You* – Dean Lewis
- *Love Me Anyway (feat. Chris Stapleton)* – P!nk
- *I Saw Love* – Forest Blakk
- *Rewrite the Stars* – Michael Gerow
- *Falling* – Harry Styles
- *Lover (Remix feat. Shawn Mendes)* – Taylor Swift
- *This Love (Taylor's Version)* – Taylor Swift
- *Fall Into Me* – Forest Blakk

A Love That Saved Us

The Broken & Bound Duet

Book Two

Erin Cornia

Prologue

JENSEN

September

THE COUPLE beside me starts making out.

There goes her shirt.

And bra.

I barely blink. I'm too numb to care—or be turned on. Hell, it's more irritating than anything. Just another reminder of what I've fucking lost. And what I'm about to do to forget her.

I sit up abruptly. *Where the hell is Seth?*

I sink back into the sofa with a sigh, glancing at my watch. My jaw aches. I open and close my mouth a few times, trying to ease the tightness. Shit. It's locked up again.

Cupping my chin, I press my thumb and ring finger into the muscle. My pulse hammers in my chest, and I take a deep, slow breath... but it doesn't help. My heart won't settle.

Exasperated, I pull out my phone and text Seth.

> Dude. Where the hell are you? I've been at this fucking party for over an hour.

My text immediately turns to read, and I stare at the screen. Nothing. The bastard leaves me on read.

Figures.

The guy lifts her skirt as she straddles him. I push up from the couch when he unzips his pants and she slips her hand inside. *Jesus Christ.* I'm about to witness full-on penetration. *What the hell is wrong with people?*

I pull at my shirt, airing it out from the sweat dripping down my back. I open and close my hand a few times. Everything's tense. Someone laughs behind me and I wince, feeling wired and dead at the same time.

I shove my way through the bodies crowding the hallway. I don't want to be around any of these fucking people right now. I'll just have to meet up with Seth tomorrow.

I'll need a bump, though, if I want to get home.

This penthouse is big. It reminds me of Matt's. It's dim, low music thumping in the background. Each beat grates across my nerves like a blade.

Everyone's fucked up here, and the sexual tension is thick in the air. I've already had to push two girls off me. God, that's the last thing I need—or want. All I care about is Alley.

And she's gone.

It's just pure survival at this point. Though, I'm not sure I even want that. I've been going from one hit to the next, overlapping, drinking, combining—anything to black me out, keep me from reliving the nightmare of her leaving me. I'm barely breathing. Just a walking pulse.

I took a leave from work. I don't know if it was accepted. I don't even know if I still have a job. It doesn't matter.

Nothing does.

I stumble into the back room, the fog of smoke settling over me. There's a couple on the bed having sex.

Nope, not a couple. I squint, bringing them into focus. A threesome—two naked chicks and one lucky bastard.

One of them glances over her shoulder, noticing me. She doesn't stop. And neither do I.

I head straight to the dresser by the oversized window. Everything I need is right there. A tray, a cutting blade, a candle, foil, sanitation wipes—not that anyone gives a shit about that when they're desperate.

I clench my jaw, pull the bag of coke from my pocket, and shake a fat line onto the tray. After zipping the bag, I shove it back into my jeans and roll a bill tight between my fingers. I press a finger to one nostril, about to lean down when I catch movement in my peripheral.

I glance over. There's a guy about my age, slumped in the corner of the room. He's curled up on his side, arms wrapped around his stomach. He twitches, a low groan falling from his lips.

His shirt's soaked in vomit and his skin's slick with sweat. He looks like he hasn't eaten in days.

My brows furrow. *Fucking loser.* He looks one hit away from dead.

I turn back to the tray, shaking my head. Junkies like that end up on the streets with nothing and no one.

Pressing my finger against my nostril again, I lean down, but the thought slams back into me, loud and disturbing and impossible to ignore. It wedges itself into the hollow parts of my brain—the parts that used to be filled with something real. Memories. Meaning. Alley. Work. Family.

My hand falls to my side. *That was me.*

I whip back around, eyes locking on the guy again, heart pounding in my chest. *Holy fucking shit.* This was me two weeks ago. The night Alley left. *Is this what she saw when I came home?*

A cold wave of clarity knocks the breath from my lungs, and I lean against the dresser, needing something to hold me up. I close my eyes, scrubbing a hand over my face, like maybe the haunting image will disappear when I open them.

It doesn't.

For the first time, it's like I'm seeing myself through Alley's eyes. And I hate what I see. I can't take it.

I squeeze my eyes shut, and freeze—the bill still in my hand. The line still waiting.

Swallowing, I look down at the coke, then back at the guy. I clench my fist, opening and closing it again.

Fuck. Is this who I've become?

Is this what she sees when she looks at me?

I drop the bill onto the tray, stepping back like it's a loaded gun. Because it *fucking is*.

Sweat beads down my forehead, and I swipe at my brow, nausea rising, feeling sick as hell.

What the hell happened? I'm not this guy. No fucking way.

Do I really want to be the guy who lost his wife to drugs? Is that my story? My legacy?

My stomach knots, chills following.

I don't want this. I don't want to be this guy. I'm successful, smart, motivated—hell, I'm a good time. I'm the guy that Alley Evans fell in love with. She'd never fall for this guy on the floor. She *left* that fucking guy.

I'm so much better than that. So much better than *this*.

I back away from the line. My heart pounds in my head as I take one last look at the guy on the floor. I turn and walk toward the door, shaking my head as moans echo behind me.

I push through the crowd again, my shirt clinging to my skin, anxiety climbing. I need to get the hell out of here. Fear grips my chest as I step into the elevator, exhaling slowly. I'm not taking another hit. My mind's made up. But the second I think it, my hand slips into my pocket and wraps around the coke.

Just one more.

Fuck.

No.

I grip the coke, the sting of tears threatening. *I can't fucking do this. I need it. Just one more.*

I clench my jaw so hard it aches. *I'm stronger than this. I have to be.* I press my back against the elevator wall and sink to the floor, forcing myself to think of one thing.

Alley.

I want her back. I *have* to get her back. I won't lose her.

I can't.

A few minutes later, I stumble outside and manage to get a cab.

It's only ten minutes. Only ten more minutes, I repeat as I stare at the coke in my hands. I'm this close to pouring a line onto my jeans and sniffing it in the backseat.

We pull up to my building, and I practically roll out of the taxi.

Suddenly, I've changed my mind. I'm not strong enough. I can't do this. I'm seven floors away from relief. As I approach my elevator I picture Alley again. But this time I picture her looking at me on the floor, covered in vomit, and I veer to the left—to the private elevator.

"Hey, Mikey," I say, barely able to think straight. I'm a mess. My shirt's drenched, and I know I look like hell. "Matt home?"

"He is..." He hesitates, like he's deciding whether he can trust me or not—like Matt's told him not to.

It stings.

"Is he expecting you?"

"Jesus. Come on, man. You know me. Just let me up." My hand opens and closes again, and I can't make eye contact. My head's a buzzing mess.

He calls up to Matt instead. My patience is running thin, and I feel myself giving in. I don't even hear what he says to Matt. I'm too focused on keeping my shit together—on not punching Mikey in the face.

Alley. Just think of her face. Think of her eyes when she looks at me.

Matt's voice finally comes through, bringing me back. "Let him up." I let his words pull me into the elevator. They wrap around me as I ascend with a flicker of hope. He hasn't given up on me. Not completely. Not yet.

The doors open, and I lock eyes with Matt. His brows are raised, arms crossed, already bracing for whatever bullshit I'm about to dish out.

I step into the penthouse. "I want her back," I say, my voice cracking like a fucking twelve-year-old boy. "Please... help me get her back."

Matt stares me down as I drag a hand through my hair. "I need help. For real this time. I'm done. I'll do whatever it takes."

"Yeah?" he asks. "Are we just not going to talk about the last time you were here? When you fucking swung at me?"

"I didn't mean it, man. You know I didn't mean it. I lost her." I fall back against the elevator doors, the sturdy steel barely holding me up. My head tips back as I take a shaky breath. "I lost her. I fucking lost my wife." My eyes flutter closed, and a tear slides down my cheek.

I swallow the lump in my throat, feeling Matt's gaze on me. Then his hands grip my shoulders, steadying me.

I open my eyes, vision blurred from emotion and fear.

He's silent for too long, and panic strikes. *I'm too late.* He's given up on me too. There's no hope.

Then his face softens, and finally he says, "I'll help you. Of course I'll help you."

I collapse, sliding to the floor. Sobs break out of me, and my body shakes as I crumble.

This is it.

Rock bottom.

I'm not sure what took me so long—to realize I lost her. To admit I'm no longer the kind of man she can love. But I can't go on knowing that.

So I fix one image in my mind, and one image only.

My wife.

Alley.

Chapter One

JENSEN

Eight Weeks Later

I SWALLOW the lump rising in my throat, blinking back the tears that threaten to fall.

"Jensen? Did you hear me?"

The words hit harder than they should. It's not like we haven't talked about this being a possibility—a reality. But still...

I'm stunned.

She filed. She fucking filed.

"Jensen?"

I clear my throat, my eyes flicking between Tobias and Nina. "I heard you," I say, my voice rough and thick with emotion. Then, because denial's my default setting, I ask, "Are you sure?"

Tobias nods. "I spoke with Matt last week. He asked if we should tell you now or wait. We talked as a team. Decided you were strong enough to hear it. Someone attempted to serve you six weeks ago... a few days after you arrived."

I don't say anything.

"What are you feeling?" Nina asks. Her voice is calm and comforting, but laced with concern.

I close my eyes, pinching the bridge of my nose as I lose the battle and let the storm of emotions rip through me. Tears spill freely now, and I sniff hard, struggling to get a grip.

"Like shit," I manage. "Hurt." I inhale, the breath ragged. "Fucking defeated." A sob breaks loose.

"I'm going to leave you two to your session," Tobias says gently as he stands. "If you need me later, Jensen, my office is always open."

He leaves, and it's just me and Nina, my therapist.

She doesn't speak right away. Just sits there quietly, giving me space. Letting me process.

"I know this is a blow, and not one you were ready for. But we've talked about this. We've explored the possibility of Alley filing." Her voice is steady but soft. "I'm sure you don't want to talk about it... but I really think we should."

My thoughts race in a hundred directions, but only one stands out.

She filed for divorce. She actually filed.

She gave up on us.

She gave up on me.

I stare at the floor, my chest burning, each breath shallow and tight.

I tried. Right after detox, I called her. Texted. Begged her to wait—to give me one more chance. I told her I was getting help. That I was finally serious. That I was done using.

She picked up once. Told me it was too late. That she wasn't coming back. That she was done. And after that, nothing. No replies. No answers. Crickets.

Matt's the only one I've been able to talk to here. Everyone else is off-limits. No texts. No voicemails. Just me, my thoughts, and the silence Alley left behind.

I don't blame her. I really don't. But God, it still hurts.

I reach for my water and take a sip, trying to swallow down the thick lump in my throat. "What am I supposed to say? This fucking sucks? What's it all for if she's not there when I get home?"

I really thought she might come back. When she left ten weeks ago, I knew something had shifted. That this time, she was serious. But I still thought I had a chance.

I had that bad night—the last one we ever spent together before she left. I must've been really fucked up because I don't remember much. All I know is I went home, and Alley was there. We didn't fight—at least, I don't think we did. I don't remember any yelling, and the next morning is fuzzy. I got high and left, and when I came back, she was gone.

Not gone to the store or out to lunch. Gone, like... gone. Bags packed. Out of our life.

I thought maybe she just needed a break, like the time she went to Chicago but came back a few days later. This time, she didn't.

I crashed, worse than ever before. I was doing shit I'd never done. Smoking or snorting anything put in front of me. I didn't give a fuck what it was. It wasn't even about the pain in my knee anymore, it hadn't been for a long time. I wanted the escape.

Because that feeling of losing Alley—it was unbearable. Like Jack and Rose on the Titanic, only I'm not even sure which one of us was Jack and which one was Rose. Either way, I couldn't breathe without her.

I was drowning. Sinking straight to the bottom. And I think she knew if she didn't let go, I'd take her down with me.

Leaving me was her raft.

I had to lose her to hit rock bottom. Something had to give for me to change. And Alley gave—she gave up.

Fuck.

"What's the point of all this if the one person I care about is gone?" My voice is hoarse, bitter. "Why am I even here?" I look at Nina. "She gave up on me."

She holds my gaze. "Let's explore that. Why don't you tell me what matters to you?"

My eyes drop to the floor. I don't want to talk. Not right now. I'm too emotional, too deep in it. My thoughts won't stop spiraling.

Goddammit. I'm fucking sad. I'm devastated.

When I don't say anything, Nina flips back through her notebook. "I have a list here," she says gently. "Things that you've told me matter to you."

She starts reading, "Matt. Megan. Kevin," then continues, naming every member of my family. "Your job. Your clients. Your apartment. Weekends in the Berkshires. Ski trips. Your health…"

The list is long—an entire page. And I listen, because I need to hear it.

When she finishes, she meets my gaze. "This is hard. And I feel for you. I really do. I know Alley's been a driving force in your recovery, but she's not the only reason you're here. Remember the guy on the floor?"

I press my lips together and nod.

"You didn't want to be him. Are you that guy, Jensen?"

I shake my head. "No," I say quietly.

"Then who are you?"

These are the questions I hate—the ones that crack me open and make me feel vulnerable. I've done surprisingly well in therapy, considering it's my first time, and that I've always believed it to be pointless. I resisted it in the beginning, pushed back hard. But little by little, I've started to open up.

Still, these are the questions that make me squirm. The ones that dig beneath the surface and make me face who I really am.

They keep telling me to get comfortable being uncomfortable. Because staying clean isn't some walk in the park. It's resisting when your body craves. When your ego whispers lies you almost believe. It's standing at parties and not drinking. It's saying no when everything inside you screams yes.

It's fucking uncomfortable.

"Who were you when you met Alley?"

I let out a bitter scoff. "I don't know… I was fun. Successful. I could always make people laugh. I made *Alley* laugh. All the time. We always had fun together."

Nina nods slowly. "Tell me more about that. What did you two do together that made her laugh?"

I glance at the wall, eyes stinging. "Everything," I whisper. "We didn't even need plans. We'd go for walks and end up on some random bench eating ice cream. Or stay in and watch movies or football. I'd mess with her just to hear her yell at me and start smacking me with pillows. She'd try not to laugh… but she always did."

A smile tugs at the corner of my mouth, but it fades just as quickly.

"I miss her laugh so much," I say, the words breaking something loose in my chest. "It's the best sound in the world." I rake a hand through my hair. "I can't lose her, Nina. I know I already have, but... I don't know how to exist in a world where she doesn't want me anymore."

Nina's quiet for a beat, letting the moment settle.

"You existed before Alley. And based on our conversations, I take it you were quite happy before you met her. You'll learn how to exist and be happy again... with or without her."

I shake my head. "No. You don't get it. I thought I was happy. But I didn't know there was this whole other level of happiness. It's probably like what my sister tells me about having kids. That you think you understand love and purpose, but you don't really get it until you do."

I pause, my voice breaking as I try to explain.

"That's what Alley is for me. She gives happiness a whole new meaning. She brings a purpose I didn't know existed." I scrub a hand down my face. "Now that I've had that, how the hell am I supposed to go back? Losing her feels like death. Going back to the way things were before? That's not happy. That's not meaningful."

She waits a moment, giving my words space to breathe. Then, calmly, she says, "I imagine she felt something very similar, watching the person she loved slip away."

Fuck. That one stings.

I swallow, trying to push back the truth of her words, but the ache's too strong—lodged in my throat, heavy in my chest, and sharp in my gut.

Nina doesn't let up. I like that about her. She's smart and genuine, a really great therapist. But she's also a hard-ass. She calls bullshit— and often.

"You're grieving, Jensen. And it's okay to feel like this. It's normal. But you're not trying to exist in a world without her. You're trying to rebuild your world so that, regardless of who's in it, you can stand on your own."

Her voice stays gentle but firm. "You don't have to give up on her.

Maybe she'll come around someday. But I don't want you clinging to that as your lifeline." She pauses, letting the words sink in. "I don't want you holding on to false hope—the kind that keeps you stuck or stops you from healing. Because you didn't come here just for her. She might've been the push, but you're the reason you stayed. You're the reason you're still here."

My throat tightens again.

"You've got your whole life ahead of you. And you get to decide how big the prize is at the end of all this. Whether she's there or not, *you* have to be. You can't give up on yourself—not anymore. Not ever."

I close my eyes.

She's right.

I know she is. And while I don't want to imagine a life without Alley, I can't keep believing she's my only path to happiness.

Nina gently closes her notebook. "We're going to hold space for both: the man who misses her, and the man who's trying to come back to himself. Okay?"

I nod, barely holding it together.

"Can you keep showing up for him, too?"

I nod again—firmly this time, even as my lips tremble.

"Good." She offers a soft smile, one that says she's proud of me. I'm not sure why it matters so much, but God, I need that smile. Like maybe, buried beneath all my failures, I've done something right. Like she sees some good in me.

I let her words soak into me like a sponge. I am doing this for me.

I still have a life to live, and I refuse to live it the way I was.

But that doesn't mean I have to stop wanting Alley.

I know my purpose. I know my end goal. When I go home, I'll be clean, strong, and better than before.

And I'll have done it for me.

It hasn't been easy—not even close. And I've still got six more weeks to go. I just have to keep remembering who I am, who I was, and who I want to be.

I want to be the kind of man Alley might fall back in love with.

The kind of man she'd be proud of.

The kind of man I used to be.

A smile tugs at my lips as a memory sweeps in, Matt and me on the couch, talking about Alley. About the first time I saw her. God, I couldn't stop thinking about her. Matt looked at me and said, *A hospital unit's never stopped you before.*

And dammit—neither will divorce papers.

He was right. Nothing's ever stopped me.

I'll stay clean. For me.

But I'll be damned if that means I give up on Alley. I'll show her how much I've changed. I'll prove it. She just needs to see me.

Fuck the divorce papers.

We'll find our way back.

Chapter Two

MATT

December

I MAKE my way up the long, winding roads. It's beautiful—snow-capped mountain views and trees blanketed in white. I wish I could enjoy it, but I'm not present. My mind's spinning—thoughts of Jensen, Alley, and the past two years cloud everything. It's been insane. Never in a million years did I think I'd be picking up Jensen from a rehab facility in fucking Switzerland.

It's been a rough year. Watching my best friend destroy his life. Getting calls from Alley—hearing her cry, watching her crumble because of him. I'm not a judgmental person by nature, but fuck, there were moments I wanted to pummel his ass. We almost came to blows after she left. He showed up—completely fucked up—asking if I'd talked to her, where she was.

There was no reasoning with him when he was high. And when I didn't give him what he wanted, he snapped. Shoved me. Accused me of lying. I shoved him back. He swung and missed, and ended up against the wall with my arm pressed to his throat and tears in his eyes.

It wrecked me. We've never fought before. Ever. I remember my own eyes burning as I stared into his and didn't recognize him anymore.

He left after that, and I didn't see or talk to him again until he showed up two weeks later, pleading for help.

No one ever talks about this shit. How addiction's like a poison that seeps into every corner of the addict's life. It stains everyone in their path. Everything they touch. Alley's taken the brunt of it, that's for damn sure. I don't know if anyone comes back from the kind of hell he put her through.

The tires crunch over gravel as I pull up the rehab's long driveway. I'm excited to see Jensen and to have my best friend back. His counselors say he's doing great, and when I talked to him last week, he sounded like himself again. He seemed... happy. And knowing that, it feels like I've been given an extra tank of air.

I just wish Alley were here with me.

Alley. Definitely not a topic I'm looking forward to. And I know it's all he's going to want to talk about.

I haven't shared much with him since he got here. Only what's necessary, and only recently, to avoid setting him back.

I texted her before I left yesterday to let her know I was picking him up. She replied with, *Thanks for letting me know.* That's it.

What the hell am I supposed to do with that? What am I supposed to tell Jensen? *Sorry, man. She doesn't fucking care?* He's her husband for Christ's sake.

I shift into park, staring up at the massive building. It looks like a resort. It was impressive three months ago with all the fall colors, but something about it now gives off the impression that if you're staying here, you're rich as hell and better take this seriously.

Good. Because it was expensive as fuck.

I open the car door and step into the bitter cold, zipping my coat as I begin the hike from guest parking to the front entrance.

The building's modern, set high and tucked into the mountain, with way too many damn stairs leading to the door. It wasn't an easy trek the first time with Jensen. I mean, for fuck's sake, people coming up these steps are usually fresh out of detox. They barely have the energy to stand, let alone climb a staircase to redemption.

This place required him to be clean when he arrived, so after he came to me broken and desperate—at rock bottom—I sat with him for two weeks, helping him get through it. Detox, withdrawal, all of it. Megan helped out when I had to leave for the occasional meeting I couldn't afford to reschedule. He didn't leave mine or Megan's sight the entire time.

She wasn't happy about it. And she sure as hell didn't do it for Jensen. She did it for me and for Alley.

Megan's pissed at Jensen—empathy's never been her strongest quality. But I asked her to do it because I knew he wouldn't pull any shit with her. She can hold her own. Honestly? She's a little scary sometimes.

I finally reach the entrance and swing open the heavy glass door. I can't even pronounce the name engraved across it, something that roughly translates to wellness and refuge of Lucerne. It's the most expensive rehab in Europe, on every list when you Google top rehabs in the world. Their success rate is one of the highest. I didn't care where it was or how much it cost. Jensen's like a brother. I'd do anything for him. Period.

I check in at the front desk and take a seat in the lobby while I wait for a counselor to take me back. My mind wanders, and suddenly my palms go clammy and my stomach twists.

I'm glad Jensen came to me—that he trusted me to be his person here. But it feels like it should be Alley sitting here.

The counselor said they'd tell him she filed, but what's going to happen when that reality hits him? When I'm the one who has to tell him just how bad it really is? What if he relapses again?

I let out an exhale. *This whole situation is fucked.*

Alley came to see me before she left for Chicago—to tell me goodbye on her way out. She came back two weeks later to grab a few things from the apartment. I've never seen her look more defeated. She quit her job, packed her shit in a bag, and left. It killed me. It's *still* killing me.

And if I'm struggling to handle it, how the hell is Jensen supposed to?

My stomach twists tighter thinking about it. Having to break that news. To see his face. To knock him down when he's finally clawed his way out of the hell.

I sink deeper into the couch. He asked about Alley every time we talked. I avoided the question every time. Acted like I didn't know.

As much as I want them to work out, I'm not holding my breath. Alley's done. She's my friend, and I care about her. But she never asks about Jensen. I just hope he's not clinging to some false sense of what's waiting for him back home.

My phone vibrates in my back pocket, and I pull it out.

MEGAN

Do you have him yet? How is he?

A small smile tugs at my upper lip. She cares more than she lets on.

Not yet. I'm here now. Just waiting.

Moments later, I'm greeted by a middle-aged man named Tobias. He leads me down a quiet hallway to a small office with three chairs in front of a desk.

"Thanks for coming, Matt," he says, settling into his chair. "Jensen's made a lot of progress. I think you'll see that for yourself, but I wanted to give you a bit of a heads-up before he gets here and we go over everything."

I sit, nodding slowly. "I'm all ears."

He leans forward, elbows on his knees. "He's clear-headed. Engaged. He's worked the steps. Been brutally honest in therapy. Group work, individual sessions, developing good habits, working out... he's done it all. We're proud of how far he's come."

I swallow the lump rising in my throat. "That's good. That's really good."

"It is. But he's still holding on to the idea that he'll win Alley back."

Shit. There it is.

"He's not delusional," Tobias adds quickly. "He knows it won't be easy, but... he hasn't fully let go of that hope yet. And in recovery, sometimes that kind of hope is what keeps people grounded."

"So, he's doing well, but she's still his motivation?" I ask.

"Part of it, yes. The rest is genuine. You'll see."

Great. And I'm the one who gets to deliver the blow.

I glance toward the door, pulse picking up. "He knows she filed?"

Tobias nods. "I told him. A little over a month ago, after we talked it through with the team. It hit him hard, but it also pushed him deeper into the work. He had to grieve it. Process it. Imagine a future where she isn't waiting at the end of all this."

I nod slowly. "And now?"

"He's still scared of that future," Tobias says. "But he's facing it. Keep an eye on him, but let him breathe. He's got to stand on his own now. He's been open about his triggers, but that doesn't mean he won't run into new ones. Stress, rejection, shame—those are big ones. And transitions, like reentering normal life, can stir a lot of that up."

I shift in my seat, feeling like I should be taking notes or something. *Fuck, I'm not equipped for this shit.*

"If you notice him pulling away from people, skipping meetings, saying he's *'fine'* all the time when he's clearly not? Those are red flags. Big emotional swings are normal, but if they turn into avoidance— especially around difficult conversations—he might need a reset. He's learned to reach out, but if that stops... if he goes radio silent, that's when it's time to step in."

He leans back, folding his arms. "And if he starts rationalizing again, saying he's got it under control, that one drink won't hurt... that's a red alert."

I blow out a breath. "That's a lot of responsibility."

"Just remember, Jensen is responsible for Jensen. Your job is to be a good friend. Which you have been. He's talked about you a lot, and he's lucky to have you."

My eyes well up, and my voice cracks when I say, "It's me that's lucky to have him."

Tobias smiles, nodding. It's quiet for a moment before there's a knock on the door.

"You ready?" he asks, already standing.

I rise to my feet, bracing myself. "Yeah."

He opens the door, and Jensen walks in. The second he sees me, a grin stretches across his face.

"Hey, man!" I call out, walking toward him until we meet in a hug, clapping our hands on each other's backs.

"Hey, brother." Jensen's voice cracks, and goddammit, my throat swells, choked with emotion.

What a fucking ride these past two years have been.

"Thanks for coming," he says, pulling back. His eyes are misty, but they're clear. Clearer than they've been in a long time.

But mine aren't. *Jesus.* A few tears fall down my cheek, and I blink rapidly to hold them back. I didn't realize just how much I missed him.

"Damn, it's good to see you!" I exclaim, gripping his shoulder. "You look good! What are you, training for an Ironman or something? What the hell?"

Jensen's always been in decent shape with an athletic build, and his weight's fluctuated over the past few years, but I've never seen him like this. He's fit. And not just fit—the dude's yoked.

I knew this place focused on health—personal trainers, top chefs, whole-foods-only diet, life coaches, meditation—as well as top-ranked counselors and doctors. But I didn't expect him to come out this changed. It's like he's hit the gym every damn day.

Jensen chuckles through his tears. "Thanks, man. I've had a lot of gym time. How was your trip over?"

"It was good. Just worked on the plane. You ready to get the hell out of here and see Switzerland?"

We're spending the next week here exploring before heading back home.

"Hell yes," he says with a grin.

"I know you two have a lot to catch up on, so I'll try to make this quick," Tobias says, settling back into his chair.

We both take a seat opposite him as he launches into a summary of the past twelve weeks—Jensen's stay, his treatment, and his progress. Then he hands me a packet on how to support Jensen during the transition home.

"We've already gone over what this transition can look like with

Jensen thoroughly." Tobias looks to him. "He's ready," he adds with a nod.

He hands Jensen his discharge papers and walks him through each one as he signs. Then he passes me an acknowledgment form—something I need to sign to confirm I'm agreeing to support Jensen at home.

Tobias walks us out to the lobby, where a group of counselors and other patients are waiting to say their goodbyes to Jensen. He hugs them all, grinning through the tears, and it's clear how much they care. All I can think about is how I wish Alley could see this.

I want to be mad at her. I want to shake her and tell her he's not the same man she left. But I also saw her face that morning—when she walked out like she'd already buried him. And at the same time, there's this gnawing fear underneath it all. The kind that whispers, *What if this doesn't last?*

He looks like a new man. But I've seen new men fall apart fast. And I don't know if I could handle watching that happen to him again.

I take a few group photos for him with my phone as he says his final goodbyes.

The last hug comes from an older woman. She wraps him up tightly, holding on like she doesn't want to let go.

"I'm so proud of you," I hear her say, tears streaming down her cheeks. "Don't you give up on her."

He chuckles, wiping at his eyes. "Thanks, Judy." He gives her one last squeeze, then turns to me, grabs his luggage, and we walk out the door together.

Chapter Three

ALLEY

"I say we get one more round." Cooper tips back her martini, draining the rest in one smooth gulp.

"I really shouldn't. Benson's been keeping me up all night lately. I swear he's already teething." Vivian groans, slumping against the back of the booth.

"Why? You have to pump and dump anyway. Might as well make the most of your night out," Cooper says.

"Valid point." Vivian winces, pressing a hand to one of her boobs. "God, speaking of pumping... I don't know how much longer I can go before I start leaking all over the place."

"They're so big, Viv. Seriously... I can't stop staring at them. They look amazing. Every guy who's walked by has totally side-eyed your chest." Cooper turns to me. "Right, Al?"

"I'm sorry, what? I didn't hear you. I was too distracted by Viv's giant tits."

Cooper snorts, and we both dissolve into laughter. She holds up her hand, and I smack it in a sloppy high-five.

The three of us went out for appetizers and drinks at this boujee martini lounge. That's actually what it's called. The Martini Lounge. It's classy, with perfect mood lighting, big round booths that are ridiculously comfortable, and music that's loud enough to give the place energy, but not so loud you can't hear yourself think. There's billiards, darts, and a few other games scattered around the room. It's been fun —as fun as anything can be right now.

I turn to Cooper. "I'll have another," I say, because that's what I do now. I drink to have fun. To laugh. To forget. To numb.

Yeah, I'm well aware that's exactly the kind of thing I walked away from. And I feel guilty as hell about it. But I'm not an alcoholic. I'm not getting drunk and passing out. I'm just... definitely over my two-drink maximum, and it's not the first, or third, or even tenth time in the last four months. But it works. I laugh. I forget. I fake it.

Then I go home and cry.

I never used to get it—why people drank like this. But now I do. There's too much shit crowding the brain. It's hard to relax. Hard to stop thinking. Hard to let go. Well, that, and it's fun.

"Yes!" Cooper throws her arm in the air and flags down the cocktail waitress.

"Fine. Get me one too. I'll need it if Leo has any chance of getting laid tonight." Vivian sighs. "It's weird, after Isla was born, I was so horny. But since Benson... I don't know. I'm just so fucking tired, you guys."

"That's normal, Viv," I say, thinking back to all the conversations I've had with Megan and Amber. "Both my sisters-in-law—er, ex-sisters-in-law, said the same thing after baby number two. You're just exhausted."

"I know. But it still sucks."

"You're not exactly selling the whole kid thing," Cooper says. "The day I'm too tired to fuck Ryan—" She lets out a dramatic exhale. "—is the day I've died."

Cooper reminds me so much of Megan—crass, vulgar, horny. Honestly, they'd probably be best friends.

"Don't you dare not have kids," Vivian says. "They're great. They just sort of suck the life out of you and your libido... And your tits."

"Well, I could use a little life sucked out of these." Cooper laughs, pushing her boobs together. "I've always wished they were one size smaller."

I whip my head toward her. "It's a crime to wish for smaller boobs."

"Whatever. Your little B's are so perfect and perky. I'm jealous you never need a bra."

"I'd trade you in a heartbeat," I say. "Not that it matters. I've learned to love what I have. And Jensen always loved them."

God. Why do I do that? I hate bringing him up when I'm having a good time.

"And hey," I say to Vivian, shifting gears. "I bet you've had sex at least once in the last four months. That's more than I have." I laugh and take a sip of my drink while they both look at me with sad eyes. "Don't look at me like that. It's fine. *I'm fine.*"

I'm not, though. Not even close.

These girls are the only reason I've had even a few real laughs lately. They've basically saved me, made this bearable. I barely knew Vivian when I left Jensen. I was only supposed to crash with her and Leo for a few weeks while I looked for my own place. But they've been adamant about me staying.

Vivian had just had her second baby a few weeks earlier, and she was ecstatic to have the help and extra company to keep her sane. That's the trade-off: I help with the kids, let them sneak off for date nights, cook when I can. Of course, none of it's expected, but it's the least I can do.

They have their hands full. And honestly, I want to stay busy. *I have to.* Otherwise, I'll go crazy.

I love the kids, too. They're filling this hole in my chest I didn't even realize was there.

Vivian and I clicked instantly. Not long after, she introduced me to Cooper. Cooper's engaged to her fiancé, Ryan. She was in a real shitty relationship before him. Apparently the guy was a total dick—cheated on her for five years.

Ryan's great, though. I've met him a handful of times. They're cute and completely in love. Being around couples like them always makes me miss Jensen.

Who am I kidding? Everything makes me miss him.

Cooper's great. Loud. Fun as hell. The kind of person who makes you feel seen, even when you're nothing alike. She just gets me. There's never a dull moment when she's around.

We're interrupted by two guys. The taller one steps forward while his friend hangs back, trying not to look awkward.

"Sorry to interrupt, ladies," the tall one says with a smile. "Just... couldn't let the night end without saying you're all absolutely stunning." Then he looks directly at me—and thank God, it's at my face, because his friend's eyes are glued to Vivian's chest. "Mind if I borrow your friend for a drink?"

Vivian raises an eyebrow, and Cooper lets out a sharp laugh. "Seriously? I just watched you hit on some other girl five seconds ago."

I cringe.

Here it comes—Cooper going full mama bear. She always does this when someone tries to hit on me or Viv. I get it—she's got some trauma there. She assumes every guy in a bar is a cheating bastard, just like her ex.

"Totally fair," he says with a grin, holding up his hands, eyes now locked on Cooper. "That was a friend I ran into. But I've been trying to work up the nerve to come over here for the past twenty minutes. Figured I'd shoot my shot before the night's over." Then his gaze shifts to me again. "What do you say? Wanna grab a drink?"

A slow grin stretches across my lips. I'm impressed. And he's cute. Really cute. Or maybe I'm just really drunk.

Still... it feels good to be wanted. It gives me hope for the future. And I'll take any thread of hope I can get.

"I've gotta give you props for coming over, and for making it past this one first," I say, nudging Cooper with my elbow. "But I'm going through a divorce right now, and I'm just... not really in a place to have a drink. Or even flirt, honestly. I appreciate it, though. I really do." I press a hand to my chest. "I'm flattered. And if you ask me six months from now, I'm sure I'll say yes."

He tilts his head slightly, eyes narrowing as a slow, sexy smirk forms. "Well then, I'll be here in six months."

I roll my bottom lip between my teeth as he turns to walk away, his friend trailing behind.

"He was such a Brad," Cooper mutters, rolling her eyes.

I smack her arm. "No he wasn't. He reminded me of..." I stop myself, the emotion rising too fast. I'm afraid if I blink, a tear will fall.

"Of...?" Cooper prompts.

"No one. Never mind." I pick up my glass and take a long gulp. Was I really about to compare that guy to Jensen? I don't even know that guy. "He was cute," I say quickly, setting the glass back on the table. "How weird was his friend, though?"

"Oh my God. The friend alone was a red flag," Vivian says, laughing.

The two of them launch into a story about being hit on during a trip together, but I'm only half-listening. I swipe up on my phone and open Instagram, letting my thumb scroll on autopilot.

I do this a lot when I've been drinking—scroll through photos of my people in New York. Sometimes it makes me miss them less, and other times it makes me miss them more. I haven't figured it out yet.

I scroll past a picture of Zach and Joey at a concert and tap the heart. Scarlett's most recent post is of her and a few friends out to dinner. I like that one too.

I scroll further and freeze when Matt's post pops up.

It's Matt... and Jensen. In Switzerland.

I stare at the photo, like I'm trying to memorize every inch of it. They're bundled up in coats and beanies, the Matterhorn behind them. They've got their arms slung around each other in that casual, bro-ish way that doesn't look posed.

Matt's grinning like always.

And Jensen—

Jensen's smile looks exactly like it did the first time I saw him. Deep dimples. Straight white teeth. The kind of smile that could melt hearts. And right now, it's melting mine.

He looks good.

He looks really fucking good.

Tears prick my eyes, and I bite my bottom lip. *He's still in Switzerland? With Matt?*

I knew he was there, but still—Switzerland's always been on my list.

A million thoughts slam into my head at once. Is he clean? Did rehab work?

He looks clean. God, he looks so good.

I filed for divorce a few weeks after I left Jensen, but by the time the papers were ready to be served, he'd already left the country.

Matt's kept me in the loop. He told me Jensen really spiraled after I left—hit rock bottom, came to him for help. He left for Switzerland shortly after and checked into some high-end rehab.

Which is great. It really is. But it's delayed the divorce, and me trying to move on. And now he's out there vacationing with Matt like nothing ever happened, while I'm over here drinking just to laugh.

I press my thumb and forefinger to the screen, zooming in. I focus on Jensen—on his smile, his dimples, his eyes. They're clear as day. And he looks... happy.

A pang hits me right in the gut. It feels like envy, but that doesn't make any sense. Then I glance down at the fresh martini the waitress just dropped off. The one I'm drinking to forget how miserable I am. Or maybe just to forget *him*. Either way...

Jealousy creeps in, quiet and sharp, like a thief in the night.

I guess the martini's not doing its job, because here I am, still thinking about him.

And why?

He's clearly fine. In Switzerland. Having fun. Smiling. Clean. Happy.

That's what wrecks me. It's not that I don't want him to be clean, of course I do. It's that he waited until after I left. That he couldn't get clean for *me*.

That hurts like hell.

For two years, all I wanted was for him to get to this place, to be okay, to be sober.

And now that he is, it feels like a knife in the back.

I close out of the app and dab at the corner of my eye, catching the tear before it falls.

Suddenly, I'm no longer in the mood to be here, or to drink. I just want to go home. Be alone. Wallow.

Leo says that's not healthy.

"Hey." An elbow nudges my arm, pulling me out of the spiral. "You okay?" Cooper asks, her voice soft and full of concern as she studies me.

I take a deep breath, pull up the picture again, and slide my phone over to her.

"Look how good he looks," I say quietly.

"Let me see," Vivian says, and Cooper slides the phone across the table after taking a look.

They both fall silent as she studies it. Then, she offers a small smile and slides the phone back to me. "Ah, shit. He does look good, Al. I'm sorry. That's gotta be hard."

"Yeah. It is," I whisper.

"You know, it's okay to be sad about this," Vivian says gently. "You still love him. That's normal."

"I know. But why do I still love him? Why can't I move on? It's been four months." My eyes flick from Vivian to Cooper.

"Because you watched the person you loved more than anything disappear right in front of you," Vivian says softly. "It's like watching someone die. You loved him. You *still* love him. You don't just snap your fingers and make that go away."

She takes a deep breath, reaches for her martini, and takes a sip. "Trust me, you're going to feel this way for a long time. But it will get easier." She offers a small smile. "I promise. Eventually."

The mood has turned heavy, and I hate that I did that. If anyone here knows about loss, it's Vivian. She lost her husband and unborn child in a car accident.

And I'm over here bitching about my soon-to-be ex-husband because he's apparently doing great and looking better than ever.

Nothing like your widowed friend to give you perspective.

I muster a pathetic smile. "Thanks, Vivian."

Cooper drapes an arm around my shoulders. "I wish I could relate, but I actually hated my ex by the time I left him. My only fear now is running into him alone somewhere, unprepared... But I'm sorry you're going through this." She gives me a squeeze. "You still coming to hot yoga with me in the morning?"

My brow lifts. "The morning? After these?" I point to my drink.

She laughs. "Relax. There's a class at eleven. You know I'm not a morning person."

"And you know I'm not a hot yoga person. Can't we just do normal-temperature yoga? That last class made me want to throat-punch the girl teaching. You should really get into running, then you could run with me and Viv instead."

"Listen." She cups a boob. "These tits weren't made for running, okay?"

I laugh at that, and she keeps going. "Come on, I used to hate all yoga. I could never quiet my mind long enough to focus. But I promise this class will be better than the last one. It's flow style. You'll like it." She stirs her drink, then takes a long sip. "Plus, you'll be so busy plotting the murder of the dumb bitch kicking your ass for sixty minutes, you won't even have time to think about Jensen. Not for five seconds. It's fucking magic for forgetting an ex."

I try to hold in a laugh, but fail. "Fine. You talked me into it. I'll come strictly for that. Anything to keep my mind off him."

She lifts her glass, bringing it to the center of the table. "I'll drink to that," she says with a grin.

"To moving on to bigger and better things," Vivian adds, tapping her glass to Cooper's.

"To moving on," I echo, clinking mine against theirs before bringing it to my lips and swallowing down the sweet, potent liquid.

It's time to move on.

And then I think it again.

And again.

And again.

* * *

I STARE BLANKLY at the ceiling, blinking. This is one of the downsides of drinking. I always crash when I get home, but then I wake up in the middle of the night and can't fall back asleep.

I keep replaying the image of Jensen and Matt in my head, because apparently, I love to torture myself at night. My brain loves to play this game every time I lay down. It's called: *Let's think about Jensen and everything that makes me sad.*

Yeah. I really hate it.

I reach for my phone—because yes, I'm that stupid. Rolling onto my side, I pull up the photo of Jensen and Matt. My thumb brushes across the screen, like touching him could somehow take the pain away.

God, he used to make everything better just by being there. The way he'd pull me in, his arms tight around me—it was like nothing could touch me. He made me feel safe. Always.

I squeeze my eyes shut as a cry slips out.

"Dammit," I whisper.

I miss him. So damn much. And I hate it.

I hate that he hurt me. That it still hurts.

But more than anything, I hate that I still love him.

I swipe out of Instagram, a steady stream of tears now soaking my pillow, and open my texts. I search Jensen's name.

Dozens of messages come up. I only replied to one.

August 23—the day after I left.

JENSEN

Babe, where are you?

I'm done, Jensen. I can't do this anymore. I'm in Chicago, and I'm not coming back.

He called me after that. I answered. I owed him that much. It's not like I would end our marriage over text message. But I also didn't want to talk to him while he was high. It would have been pointless. He never remembered conversations we would have.

I told him what happened the night before. That he blew it, and that I was leaving and contacting a lawyer.

He begged me to come home. To give him one more chance. He cried—and somehow, I didn't.

That was the last time I spoke to him.

August 25.

JENSEN

I'm sorry, babe. I'm so sorry. Please come back.

There's a whole slew of messages after that which are similar, spanning the next two days. Then, they just... stopped.

Matt said they got in a fight and that Jensen went MIA.

Then came September 14, after I sent multiple calls straight to voicemail.

JENSEN

Al, I'm clean. I detoxed at Matt's. I'm going to a rehab in Switzerland. It's the best of the best. I leave in two days. I'd love to see you—please. Let me at least see you to apologize in person.

Please, babe. I love you. I'm going to get better. For real this time.

Babe. Give me another chance. I know I don't deserve it, but come on. I love you. We love each other. You're my best friend. God, please just text me back.

When I read that last one, a whole new wave of emotion crashes over me.

JENSEN

I can't imagine doing this and coming home to a world without you in it, Alley. You are my everything. Please wait for me. I love you.

I swipe back to the Instagram photo, my gaze locking on Jensen's face. "I love you too," I whisper.

I shudder, a quiet sob forcing its way out. I glance past the phone to the window. It's snowing, and the peaceful serenity outside does nothing to calm the silent storm inside me.

I picture him—laughing, teasing, watching football—memories flashing like snapshots. Our wedding. Honeymoon. Skiing. Joking. Kissing...

Fucking.

God, the fucking.

My eyes squeeze shut, desperate to remember what it used to feel like before everything fell apart. I picture Jensen hovering over me, breath warm against my skin. His mouth on mine. His hands sliding down my body, touching me like I was the only thing that ever mattered.

My chest tightens and my pussy aches, a steady thrum building between my thighs.

I let my hand slip beneath the sheets, drifting down to my underwear. I slide my fingers inside and press them against my clit, moving in slow, deliberate circles.

I'm wet—soaked, really. Four months of celibacy will do that to a woman. With Jensen's image burned into my mind, I sink deeper into the fantasy, working myself. My breathing grows heavier as I picture him sliding my underwear off, then unbuckling his belt. He undoes his pants, and I help pull them down. He's hard—so fucking hard for me. That image alone is enough to make me moan.

He settles between my thighs, lowering his mouth to my stomach.

Butterflies parachute through me, and I swear to God, I can feel his breath on my skin as he trails lower. I picture it—his mouth on me, tongue flicking—and I rub myself faster.

It feels so damn good.

Then he looks up at me.

No.

Goddamit, no.

It's not him. Not anymore.

The fantasy slips through my fingers like sand, and everything I've been trying to forget rushes back in. Jensen—high. The first night he took coke. The hollow look in his eyes. The dark circles. The lies.

"No," I whimper, circling faster, harder, determined to come. I need this.

Jesus. You're acting like I fucking hurt you.

No. Stop.

Come on. Talk to me, babe... What'd I do?

My hand stops, and I make a fist. Clenching my teeth, I squeeze my thighs together and groan.

Alley! Don't you walk away when I'm talking to you!
The sobs come hard now. Like they always do.
Please don't leave me with them.
More tears. More shaking. More sobbing.
Give me my fucking backpack!
Fuck you, Jensen!
That's the one. The worst one.
The one I always end on.
The one that plays on repeat in my mind.
Give me my fucking backpack!
Fuck you, Jensen!
I give up on the orgasm and pull up the photo again. I stare at Jensen through blurry eyes—my face puffy, nose running, pillow soaked.

"You chose your backpack," I whisper. "You chose your backpack over me."

Then I close my eyes and repeat the lie—
I don't love you anymore.
I don't love you anymore.
I don't love you anymore...
Until I finally fall asleep.

Chapter Four

JENSEN

THE RESTAURANT'S DIMLY LIT—candlelight and low music, the kind of place you take someone when you're hoping to get laid afterward. It's romantic as hell, and most of the tables are filled with couples. Definitely the kind of place Alley would love.

I'm here with Matt—and I am most definitely *not* getting laid tonight. But we couldn't come to Zermatt and not eat here. It's Michelin-starred, and Matt has a thing for hunting those down everywhere we go.

As we follow the hostess to our table, I nudge him. "Hey, I've been meaning to ask, would you mind reaching out to your tattoo guy? See if I can get a consult when we get back?"

He glances at me. "Really?"

"Yeah. I've been thinking about it for weeks."

"Alright, man. I'll message him now. How soon you talking?"

We slide into our seats as the hostess pours water into our glasses and tells us our server will be over shortly.

"As soon as possible."

"Could be a while. He's usually booked months in advance."

"Yeah, that's fine. Just whatever you can get."

"Okay." He pulls out his phone, grinning. "I can't believe you're serious. You always said you'd never get one. What are you wanting? Maybe he could squeeze you in if it's something simple."

"I want a full sleeve."

He looks up from his phone, staring at me like I've lost my mind. "No you fucking don't."

I nod, chuckling. "Yeah, I do. I want a reminder, a permanent commitment to staying clean. Something that I can see every day. I even had a friend in rehab who's an artist help me plan it out. He sketched a rough draft. But I know your guy's really good, so I'm sure he'll make it even better."

Matt's covered in tats—two full sleeves, a full leg, and pieces scattered across his chest, back, and side. He's been going to this guy for years.

"Shit. You're serious." He starts typing. "That might be harder to squeeze in, but I'm pumped about this. I'll see what I can do."

Matt's fingers move fast over his phone. When he says *see what I can do,* what he really means is *throw some money at it until it happens.* I could tell him not to bother, but it'd be pointless. He's going to do it anyway. That's just who he is.

"I know it'll probably take a few sessions so just whatever he has. Even if it's piece by piece."

Matt sets his phone down. "I bet he can do it all in three or four. You'll have to show me the sketch when we get back."

Our server walks up and introduces himself. "What can I get you two to drink?"

"I'll take a whiskey neat," Matt says.

"I'll just stick with water," I tell him.

Alcohol's no longer an option for me. My counselors told me to stay away from it for at least a couple years—give my brain time to rewire. I honestly can't remember the last time I went for a nice dinner and didn't order a drink.

Matt glances over. "Oh. Shit. Sorry, man." He looks back at the server. "I'll just have water."

"No, he'll keep the whiskey," I say, then turn to Matt. "You don't need to do that. What, are you never going to drink around me again? Come on, that's not realistic. I'm fine."

"You sure?"

"I'm sure. Someone might as well enjoy."

He did this last night too—started to order a drink at dinner, then changed his mind. It's fucking stupid. I don't need this to be a thing.

It's our third day here. After Matt picked me up, we spent a day exploring Lucerne before driving to Zermatt last night. It's killing me not to ski, but I can't risk it—my knee or my sobriety.

We've done a lot of talking and catching up. It's been good. I've actually had fun—something that almost feels foreign. I don't even know the last time I laughed like this. I mean, sure, there were laughs in rehab, but that's not the same as sitting around with your childhood best friend, shooting the shit and making dumb jokes.

The first few minutes of the drive were a little stiff—the usual *so, tell me about rehab* stuff—but after twenty minutes, we were laughing and reminiscing, just like old times. I've mostly talked about treatment, and he's filled me in on my family, new projects at work, and everything I missed while I was gone.

I haven't brought up Alley yet. I didn't want this whole trip to be about her, even if she's constantly on my mind. I wanted us to get back to our old rhythm before I mentioned her. And now feels like as good a time as any.

"Hey, on the bright side, Alley won't have to be the only sober one at parties anymore, right?" I take a sip of my water, casually feeling him out with the mention of her name.

A server drops off Matt's drink.

"Right." He picks up his whiskey and takes a slow sip. "You planning to see your mom before Christmas Eve?"

Seriously?

He's just going to sidestep that like I didn't just bring up the woman I love? My wife? He did this on our calls too. Every time I mentioned her, he'd skim past it—short answer, quick pivot, end of discussion.

It pisses me off. Not because I don't get it—I do. It's messy. It's awkward. And maybe he's still holding a grudge about how everything went down with Alley.

But Jesus. I'd rather he just say that than sit here dodging whatever bullshit he's trying to avoid.

Matt always gives it to me straight. He's solid. And he's never given up on me. I owe him everything. For being there. For showing up. For helping Alley when I couldn't. He's always been more than a friend. He's my brother.

But anytime I bring her up—

"Why won't you talk to me about her?" I ask.

He doesn't answer right away. Just picks up his glass and takes another sip, like the whiskey might soften whatever it is he doesn't want to say.

I let out a frustrated sigh. "I know I fucked up, man. I know what I did. And I know the chances of her taking me back are slim. But I've changed. I'm not going to relapse. It's different this time. I just... I need to see her. Talk to her. I need to show her."

"You really think it's that simple?" He sets his drink down. "You put her through hell." He sighs, rubbing his chin. "Look, I know you've done the work. I know you've changed, and I'm proud of you. I am. But she's gone, brother. She moved. She filed. And in four months... *four months*—she hasn't asked about you. Not once."

The words hit me like bricks to the face. I stare at him, stunned. *Fuck.* I thought I was ready for whatever he was about to say, but I wasn't ready for that. Nausea punches up my throat so fast it nearly chokes me. I force it back, swallowing hard.

"Not once?" My voice cracks. "Why didn't you tell me before?"

He shrugs. "What was I supposed to say? *Hey, your wife hasn't asked about you?* You were healing. You needed hope. I couldn't be the one to take it away." He shakes his head. "I've given her every chance to ask. She never has. And I've kept her in the loop, but only because she wanted to know why the papers hadn't been served."

He takes another sip, and I stare at his drink while gripping my water glass, rubbing my thumb against the condensation. *God, whiskey would be real fucking nice right now.*

"I'm not saying it's impossible, I'm just saying, don't go back thinking a speech is going to fix it. That ship might've sailed. She's in

Chicago now." His shoulders sag as he meets my gaze, sorrow deep in his eyes. "And I don't think she's coming back."

Words fail me. The shock spreads through me like a virus, poisoning every part of my body. *She hasn't asked about me once?*

All I've thought about for four fucking months is Alley. She's the first thing I think of when I wake up, the thing that carries me through the hardest parts of the day, and the last thing on my mind before I fall asleep. She's my number one. She's everything.

Jesus. I knew I'd messed up, but I don't know if I realized how bad things had gotten if she's that far gone.

I swallow the lump in my throat and take another sip of water, washing down my new reality. Nothing like fucking tap water to take the edge off.

My gaze lands on Matt's whiskey. "Yes," I say, answering the question he asked earlier. "I'm planning to see my mom before Christmas Eve."

I'm doing exactly what he's been doing for the past goddamn month—avoiding any more talk of Alley.

"Look. I'm really sorry, bud. Don't give up. I just don't want to give you false hope."

I nod, brushing it off. "I'm thinking I'll reach out to Megan first. She's hated me the longest, and if we don't talk, Christmas Eve's gonna be awkward for everyone."

Christmas is two weeks away. I've got mixed feelings about it. A week ago, I was excited—ready to come home, see everyone, make amends, get back to our normal life.

But I don't even know what normal is anymore. It sure as shit isn't the life I used to have. The one where I woke up next to Alley, drank coffee with her in the mornings, spent weekends at brunch or watching football...

That life's gone. And I don't know if I'll ever get it back.

"She doesn't hate you," Matt says, offering a weak smile. "I think things will go better than you think with her."

"Yeah? That's good, then."

The server comes by and we both order the same thing—the ribeye on a hot slab.

"My boss let me keep my job," I say, trying to steer things in a more positive direction.

"Really? That's great! When do you go back?"

"After the New Year. He told me to take some time to get settled back home. He was great about the whole thing."

My boss was one of the first people I was approved to call. I did it during a therapy session. I apologized, asked for forgiveness. I figured I'd hang up without a job. But that's not what happened. He told me his brother was an addict—that he understood. He said I'd have a job waiting for me. That he'd give me one more chance.

I'm grateful for that. More than I can say.

"How's Jordan?" I ask, mostly to keep myself talking. If I don't, I'll start thinking about how Alley never asked about me—how she probably doesn't even think about me. My pulse spikes. *What if she's over me? What if she's already seeing someone?*

My eyes flick to Matt's drink again. *God, just one would be nice. Just to relax. Slow the thoughts.*

Fuck.

No.

I force my gaze to Matt's face.

"She's good, I guess. Don't really know. I haven't talked to her in weeks... She's engaged, actually."

My brows shoot up. "Really? God, I'm sorry."

Matt shrugs. "Why? It's not like she was my girlfriend."

"Ah, come on. Cut the bullshit. I know you care more than you let on. It's *Jordan*. You two have been off and on since fucking kindergarten."

"Yeah, she's a good friend. Of course I care about her. I just hope she's not marrying him as a last resort, you know? I want her to be happy." He lifts his glass, but pulls it back before taking a sip. "It's just bullshit that we can't even be friends now. Like that's off the table because she's engaged. So yeah, that fucking sucks."

He's so in love with her. He just can't admit it. "So, Dr. Douchebag's still a douchebag?"

"Yeah. He's still a fucking douchebag." He takes a larger sip this time, sets the glass down, then looks at me. "I'm really sorry I didn't tell you about Alley until now. Let's talk about her."

Shit. Just hearing him say her name brings a rush of emotion to the surface.

"Thanks. But I'm good."

"Okay. I just thought..." He trails off, shaking his head.

"You just thought?"

"I don't know, man. I'm not trying to push. But they said I should try to get you to talk when something's bothering you—so you don't shut down and go looking for an escape. And this? Alley? Of course it's going to bother you. Fuck, it bothers me."

I let out a breathy chuckle. "Well, I don't exactly feel like diving into the fact that my wife hasn't asked about me in four months. Or that I'm going home to an empty apartment and a stack of divorce papers. I'm not spiraling. I don't want to use. Would I like a drink? Yeah. But I'm not going to. I just need to process it. I'm okay. Promise."

"Alright. I'm sorry I didn't say anything earlier. I didn't know how to tell you."

I attempt a smile. "It's alright. I get it. I'm still going to do everything I can to get her back, though. I love her too much to just let her go. Even if she doesn't love me anymore." My gaze flicks to the table, then back to Matt. "I just thought she'd at least wait, you know? Wait to see me clean. I never thought she'd file while I was in rehab." I pause, swallowing hard. "I need her to see me this way. To trust me again. I just want another chance—not to break her heart this time."

I pause, trying to keep myself together. "I'll respect her decision. I will. Eventually. But I'm not going down without a fight. I can't."

"I get that. And I respect it." He offers a small smile. "I miss her, too." Then he picks up his glass and drains the rest of his drink. "And I'm fucking rooting for you."

The corners of my mouth lift. That makes two of us.

If she asked me to walk away, I would. But only if I knew—really knew—that it's what she wanted.

But not before I burn the fucking world down for her.

This isn't just some girl I fell in love with—had a good ride while it lasted. This is *Alley*. My best friend. My other half.

My wife.

And I don't care what anyone says—therapist or not—it's not fucking normal to just accept it and move on.

You fight for the ones you love.

Alley did.

For me.

And dammit, you'd better believe I'll do the same for her.

Chapter Five

ALLEY

Sweat drips down my face as I reach for my towel. I blot hard, then chug half my water bottle in one go.

Holy shit. That felt good.

This is my third day in a row doing hot yoga with Cooper. We went Sunday afternoon after our night out and—she was right—I loved it. Hot flow is incredible. I've gone with her the last two nights after work, too. She takes a six-thirty class every Monday, Tuesday, and Thursday.

Tonight's instructor was my favorite. She kicked my ass, but somehow it was still relaxing—rejuvenating. And Cooper was right, I didn't think about Jensen. For a full hour, three days in a row now, I haven't thought about him.

I roll up my mat, welcoming the cooler air that's close to the ground. Sweat's still dripping down my forehead when I meet Cooper by the door.

"So, what'd you think of Rebecca?" she asks as we head to the dressing room for a shower.

"She was tough, but I really liked her. Her voice is so soothing. Like, my body is exhausted, but I feel like I just took a nap. How is that even possible?"

Cooper laughs. "Right? She's my favorite. And I knew you'd love it. This shit's my therapy. It heals the soul."

I hang my towel on the hook outside the showers and reach in, turning the knob to cold. No way in hell I want hot water right now. I peel my soaked leggings off, then drop them into a waterproof bag.

"Leo keeps trying to talk me into real therapy," I say. "He means well, and maybe he's right, but I'd rather just talk to him. Why go spill my guts to some rando when I can pick his brain for free?" I laugh as Cooper pulls her sports bra over her head, and I follow suit.

"No shit. I could never get into regular therapy either. It's just not for me. I always left feeling more pissed off than when I walked in—or mad at someone I wasn't mad at before. Then I found this girl who does hypnotherapy, and I loved it. That, hot yoga, and meditation? Total game changers."

"I totally get what you mean about therapy. I went when I was younger and I'd leave like, *Cool, so now I've unpacked my dad's alcoholism, but somehow I'm mad at Michael, who didn't even do anything this week.*"

We laugh as we step into our showers. The cold water hits my skin, and I stand there, letting it wash away more than just the sweat. I feel good. Like my soul was mended—just a little, but still...

I wish I could tell Jensen about it.

My brows furrow as I scrub my hair, my feel-good moment short-lived.

So much for not thinking about him.

* * *

I SETTLE into Cooper's car, pulling my phone out of my bag to turn the sound back on. My eyes drop to the screen as it lights up. I freeze.

Shit. I have a text.

From Jensen.

My pulse kicks up a notch. A thickness swells in my throat, and my fingers tremble as I stare at it.

Cooper must notice the shift in me because she asks, "What's wrong? Who is it?"

"Um..." I swallow, hard. "It's Jensen." I take a deep breath, trying to figure out what the hell my body is doing. Am I nervous? Scared? Sad? Excited? What is this?

"Shut the fuck up! What does it say?"

"I don't know." The words come out raspy. "What do I do?"

Her brows pull together. "Well, you've got to read it first to know what to do."

"Yeah. I guess you're right." But I don't open it. Not yet. "Why am I nervous to read it?" I let out a quiet laugh. "It's just a text. That's stupid, right? It's not even that big of a deal."

She turns onto my street. The yoga studio's only a few minutes from Leo and Vivian's. "What do you mean it's not a big deal? Of course it is. You haven't spoken to him in months—and he's your husband. He's out of rehab. You filed for divorce. It was only a matter of time before he reached out. He's going to try to get you back."

We pull into the parking garage and stop by the entrance of the condo. She throws the car into park, then turns toward me. "Do you want me to stay while you read it, or would you rather go in and be alone?"

"You think he's going to try and get me back?" I whisper.

"Without a doubt. Why wouldn't he? Look at you—you're a catch, Alley. And if he's clean now, he's not about to just let you go. He'd be an idiot if he did."

Her comment stirs something inside me. And I can't tell if it's fear, hope, or the sheer ache of missing someone who completely wrecked me. I knew he'd reach out eventually. But I didn't actually think about it. And now that it's here? I'm not ready. Not even close.

I served him papers months ago, and I expected hard conversations then. But now? After months of silence? After all this time spent trying to move on, trying to bury this—it's like I'm getting yanked back into something I've barely started to accept myself. I've been stuck, waiting for him to finish rehab. I feel like I've only just taken my first few steps forward.

One step forward, two steps back. That's what it feels like.

And it sucks.

What if it's everything I've wanted to hear? Or worse... what if it's not? *God, why is the one thing I want him to say the one thing he shouldn't?*

It's like I want him to want me—but only on my terms. Only if it comes with a safety net. A guarantee that he'll stay clean. That my heart won't break all over again.

But that's not how this works, and I know it. So—

"I want you to stay," I finally say.

My thumb hovers over the screen before I swipe up. My fingers tremble as I tap on the thread with Jensen's name.

I read it out loud.

JENSEN

Hey, Alley. I'm out of rehab. 105 days clean today. I know I'm probably the last person you want to hear from, and I can respect that. But I've spent every single day trying to become someone I can be proud of. Someone who deserves to be by your side. Deserves to be loved by you. I don't know where you stand anymore, but if you're open to it—even a little —I'd really like to see you when I'm home. I miss you. I love you. More than you'll ever know.

Cooper blows out a loud, slow breath. "God."

"Yeah."

A million thoughts and feelings hit me at once, but I can't seem to name a single one of them.

Maybe I do need therapy after all.

My eyes wander to Leo's parking spot. It's empty, of course. It's Tuesday—the one night he teaches at the university. He won't be home for two more hours.

I've become way too dependent on him.

"What are you thinking?" Cooper's voice pulls me from my spiraling thoughts.

"A little bit of everything, I guess. Part of me reads this and wants to cry—because I'm proud of him, because I'm happy for him, and because I won't be there when he gets home. Another part wants to wrap my arms around him, bury my face in his chest, and fall asleep to the sound of his voice while he tells me everything." I pause, blinking quickly. "And then there's the part of me that's simmering with anger. Like, how *dare* you think you can just text me like this and expect a response like everything's fine. That part of me wants to write back *fuck you.*"

A nervous laugh escapes me. "And then there's this small part that doesn't give a shit and wants to ignore it altogether. Am I crazy?"

A slow smile spreads across her lips. "No. Not at all. I remember feeling the same way when I was thinking of leaving my ex. It's different, of course. But it makes sense. I think it's totally normal to feel all of that. Which feeling's the strongest?"

I try to tap into it. The indifference is there—but the urge to hug him and punch him at the same time is louder.

"Probably the one that wants to hug him," I admit. "And that's the part that scares me most."

"That's because you're a good person, Al." Her gaze drops to her lap, then lifts back to me. "I'm probably not the best person to talk to about this stuff. You'll get better advice from Leo when he gets home." She laughs softly, gesturing toward his empty parking spot. "All I can tell you is what I've learned the hard way—surround yourself with people who love you, keep working on yourself, and the clarity will come. Just... don't do anything impulsive. That's never the right move."

"You're right." I smile faintly. "Thanks for being here."

"That's what friends are for. You want me to pick you up Thursday?"

"Yeah, that'd be great." I reach for the handle. "Thanks for the ride. Tell Ryan I said hi." I step outside, closing the door behind me.

I make my way up the stairs to the kitchen. The house is quiet. Vivian's probably upstairs putting the kids down.

I warm up some leftovers, settle onto a barstool at the counter, and open Instagram. I search Matt's name and pull up his account. His last post has a bunch of photos from Zermatt, most of them with Jensen.

I'm inwardly kicking myself for the self-torture, but hey, I'm only human.

Every picture of Jensen tells me the same thing.

I still love him.

More than I want to.

And I don't know what the hell to do with that.

* * *

I'm staring at the clock on the stove when I finally hear the door open. It's 9:46 p.m. A minute later, Leo steps into the kitchen.

"Hey, Al," he says in passing, heading straight for the sink. He pulls some Tupperware from his bag and rinses it before opening the dishwasher. Then he glances over at me with a grin. "Couldn't find anywhere more comfortable to sit?"

I smile softly, already having Jensen's text pulled up on my phone. I've been sitting here over an hour and a half waiting for him. Pathetic, I know.

I slide my phone toward him across the counter. "Jensen texted me, and I don't know what to do."

His brows pull together as he reaches for it, hesitating. He reads the message silently, then sets the phone back down. "It's a nice message. What are you thinking of saying?"

"So you think I should respond? Even if I have no clue what the hell I'd even say?"

Leo chuckles, rubbing his forehead. "You know, you really need to get yourself a therapist."

"Why? I have you," I joke.

He just folds his arms, eyes locking on mine, clearly amused.

"I don't know what to do," I whisper. "Do I ignore him? Respond? What do I say?"

His brows lift, but he stays quiet, waiting me out.

"I just don't want to mess anything up."

He smiles, gaze steady, eyes lighting up just slightly. "What exactly do you not want to mess up? Your marriage?"

Ah, shit. Classic Leo. Let me talk myself into a corner while he just sits there waiting for me to realize it.

"I don't know. My marriage, the divorce, trying to move on, him staying clean. Everything." I shrug. "Do you think I should respond?"

"You know I can't tell you what to do."

"I know. I just... value how you see things. You know me."

"Do I think you should respond?" He nods slowly. "Yeah. He's still your husband. You haven't talked in four months. He just got out of rehab. He's vulnerable as hell and probably scared shitless waiting to hear back. That text took a lot."

"I know, but—"

He holds up a hand. "I'm not going to tell you what to say. But if you're not ready, a simple *Hey, I got your message. I need some time to process, but I'm glad you're doing well. I'll get back to you soon*—that's enough."

I nod, swallowing the lump in my throat, eyes dropping to the counter. "Okay. You're right. Thank you."

"It's no problem. I'm always happy to talk it out with you," he says, resting his palms on the counter. "But you are capable of handling this on your own, despite what you tell yourself. You just have to ask yourself the right questions. Because it's going to be a confusing time now that he's out. He's going to keep reaching out, and you need to decide what it is you want."

He looks at me with that pointed calm of his, letting it land before adding, "Because if you're wavering, it's like being sixteen at a party."

I stare at him, not following.

"You didn't plan to drink. But everyone else is, and you're too afraid to say no, too unsure of where you stand. So you give in. Next thing you know, you're wasted and passed out on the floor, wondering how the hell you got there—when all you really wanted was to just hang out and feel like you belonged."

My lips curve at his analogy. "Speaking from experience?" I ask, raising an eyebrow.

He lets out a laugh. "Wouldn't you like to know." He pushes off the counter, making his way to me. He places a hand on my shoulder, gripping it firmly. "Any other questions?"

"No. I'm good." I meet his gaze. "Thank you."

"It's my pleasure. You've got this." He gives my shoulder a rub. "Good night, love."

"Night."

I don't move for a solid five minutes after Leo heads upstairs. The kitchen hums in the silence, and my head's spinning. God, I wish I could shut my thoughts off for two seconds.

Finally, I pull up my text with Jensen.

> Hi. I'm not sure what to say yet… but I wanted you to know I got your message. I'll think about it and get back to you soon.

My thumb hovers over the send button while my heart races. It's silly—I'm not even saying anything worth reading. Just letting him know I saw it. But I'm nervous.

I tap send, then drop my phone on the counter.

A second later, I snatch it back up and type again.

> Congratulations on your sobriety. I'm happy for you.

Send.

I want to tell him I miss him. That I love him so much it's killing me to be apart. That walking out of that apartment was the hardest thing I've ever done. And that I've wanted to ask Matt about him every day. Every. Damn. Day.

But I don't. Because I can't.

I have to remember why I left. My mom. My dad. My childhood. I won't repeat the cycle. I deserve better than what my mom had.

I blow out a breath, and the next inhale comes a little shakier—eyes burning, chest tense.

It's the truth. I *am* happy for him.

I blink, and a tear falls onto my hand.

I'm just sad for me.

Chapter Six

JENSEN

I slow the bike to an easy pace and pick up my phone from the cupholder. I have two missed texts. I turn my music down and open my messages.

The first one's from Matt.

MATT

> Hey man, Lucas said he'd come in Sunday for you and again in 3 weeks. Probably take 4-5 sessions to complete. Plan for a long day.

> That's great! Kinda shocked he had an opening that soon.

I know he didn't have an opening. Matt probably paid him a ridiculous amount to bump someone or come in on his day off.

MATT

> He didn't. But he owed me a favor.

I shake my head, grinning, and open the next message.

MEGAN

Made us reservations at that cute breakfast place a few blocks from your place. The one I like. Not the one that sucks down the street from it. It's for 9. I'll meet you there.

I'm meeting Megan for breakfast to talk. To apologize. To make amends—to grovel, basically. And I'm praying she doesn't stab me with a butter knife halfway through brunch.

Pressing on the brake knob, I come to a stop and reach for my towel. I wipe the sweat from my face, take a long swig from my water jug, and head for the elevators. I prefer running, but I'm being extra cautious with my knee. I can't risk anything right now. I'm finally pain-free.

Rehab sucked at first, but it wasn't all bad. The therapists and counselors were great. I made a few new friends, came out stronger, pain-free—and in the best shape of my life. They had me on an anti-inflammatory diet—low carb, gluten- and sugar-free. It was rough in the beginning, but I'm used to it now. It's not for everyone, but it worked for me, and I feel great, so I've just stuck with it. Besides, keeping the same structure helps keep me grounded.

They assigned me a personal trainer, and working out was part of the deal. It wasn't optional. Waking up early to hit the gym just became routine. Every day in there was about healing, confronting your past, building better habits, and staying clear-headed when the urges hit.

Turns out, sweating your ass off can help you think straight.

I text Megan back while I wait for the elevator.

See you at nine.

* * *

I'M HALFWAY down the hall for a shower, protein shake in hand, when the doorbell rings. Muttering a curse, I turn back toward the door. When I open it, there's a middle-aged woman standing in jeans and a coat zipped halfway.

"Are you Jensen Adams?"

My eyes drop to the manila envelope in her hands and it guts me. "Yeah," I reply, hesitant.

She hands it over. "Mr. Adams, you've been served."

She's already walking away before I've even wrapped my fingers around it.

I stand there, frozen, watching her disappear down the hall. A wave of failure and fear hits me all at once as the elevator doors slide open. She steps inside, taking whatever hope I had left for my marriage with her.

"Fuck." I rake a hand through my hair and swing the door shut behind me.

I toss the envelope onto the counter without opening it and head straight to the shower. Peeling off my sweaty gym clothes, I step inside and turn on the water. I let the cold stream hit my back while I wait for it to warm.

Once the water's hot, I turn toward it, spitting it out as it runs down my face. I slick my hair back with my palm, then pump shampoo into my hand. I scrub it in, and the scent hits me—Alley. The steam carries it, flooding the shower, flooding me.

"Goddammit," I mutter. The suds run down my chest, disappearing down the drain. I look around, and a weight presses heavy on my lungs. Her shampoo. Her conditioner. Her body wash. All the scents that used to cling to me after we fucked—when I held her in bed.

It's all still here.

I press my palm to the tile, eyes clenched shut, the water beating down like it might wash away the ache clawing at my chest. I let out a sharp breath, trying like hell to hold it together.

Maybe I've been blind the past three days—trying too damn hard to stay positive. I walked around this place, looked at old photos, thought about her. But now—

She's everywhere.

I smell her. I see her.

Fuck. I can practically feel her.

In my head, she's right there on the other side of the glass, pushing her panties down to her ankles, lips curving as she steps in beside me, bare skin pressing against mine.

My dick twitches, and I let out a growl. My eyes snap open, and I slam the water off.

"Fuck this." I shove a hand through my hair, then drag both down my face, squeegeeing the water from my skin. I wrap a towel around my waist and step out, leaving a trail of water across the floor.

Storming into the kitchen, I tear open the envelope and pull the papers out. A weight presses down on me instantly—like something heavy just dropped on my shoulders. My next breath is thick. Labored.

There it is.

Petition for Dissolution of Marriage.

My chest rises and falls, slow and strained. It feels like I just lost a fight I never even got to show up for.

I skim the first few paragraphs, the legal jargon blurring together.

Division of property.

No minor children.

No shared debt.

So fucking formal. Like it wasn't a life we built—just a contract to terminate.

I guess she didn't need to text. Didn't need to call. Her answer's right here.

She could've told her lawyer to hold off. But she didn't.

I scan the next few sentences and pause when I come across reason for divorce.

Petitioner asserts that the marriage has suffered an irretrievable breakdown.

"Irretrievable." The word tastes bitter in my mouth. I scoff. "Fuck."

I toss the papers down like they're on fire. Planting both palms on the counter, I brace myself as my heart hammers in my ears.

I squeeze my eyes shut. *Just breathe.* In and out. That's all. One breath at a time.

My eyelids flutter as I sniff, holding back the pressure building in my chest. I won't let this wreck me.

I count to five. Then again.

Inhale. Exhale. Again.

Eventually, my heart rate starts to slow. I open my eyes and glance at the clock on the stove. *Dammit.* I'm supposed to meet Megan in twenty minutes.

I can't do it. Not right now. I'm too close to breaking. Too fucking fragile.

I push away from the counter, head to the bathroom to grab my phone and text her.

> I'm really sorry, but I need to reschedule. I can do later today or tomorrow.

I drop the towel and throw on boxer briefs, sweats, and a T-shirt. Phone in hand, I turn toward the kitchen, a sudden craving for a drink hitting me, fast and strong.

My phone dings.

MEGAN

> Figures.

Shit. She doesn't believe I've changed. Probably thinks I've relapsed—that I'm using again. It hurts more than I expected. The disbelief. The lack of faith.

Fuck that.

I text her back, shaking my head.

> The fact that you have so little faith in me hurts in ways I can't even explain. I'm not using. Something came up.

MEGAN

> The fact that you can't show up to a breakfast that was planned twenty-four hours ago to mend a relationship speaks volumes. I have a babysitter at my house and I'm already on my way. Fuck whatever came up. If this was important to you, you'd make it happen.

I slam the phone down, swing open the liquor cabinet, and stare up at all the liquid courage glaring back at me—Jameson, Maker's Mark, Grey Goose, Casamigos Blanco, Patrón Silver, Hendrick's. Bottles of wine too—Pinot, Cab, Malbec, Sauvignon.

Christ. I had a problem long before the addiction.

It's a goddamn liquor store in here. I built this arsenal one bottle at a time—celebration, stress, sleep, sex. There was always a reason. This was always the answer.

I grab the Jameson—closest to me—and twist the cap off. Then I walk to the sink, turn on the tap, and tip the bottle over. The brown liquid spills down the drain in a steady stream, and I watch it disappear.

One down.

Then I do the same with the rest. The tequila. The vodka. The bourbon. The wine. One by one, I pour every single bottle down the drain, until it's all gone.

I rinse my hands and dry them on a towel. Gripping the counter, I stare at the empty bottles, feeling equal parts defeat and satisfaction. They almost had power over me. *Almost.* But they didn't. They don't. Not anymore.

I pick up my phone. I can't be alone right now. I'm too raw. Too tempted. My body's yearning for an escape. I think about texting Matt, but the need to make things right with Megan is stronger.

Get fucking comfortable being uncomfortable.

> I'm sorry, Meg. I was just served with divorce papers. I'm emotional—and honestly, I could use the company. It's hard, and I'm tempted. Would you mind coming over instead?

Her reply is instant.

MEGAN

Already in the elevator.

Asshole ;-)

A breath escapes me—shaky, but laced with relief. A small smile tugs at my lips. She still loves me. She still gives a shit.

A minute later, there's a knock on the door.

I haven't seen Megan since I detoxed five months ago, and I'm not going to lie, our last encounters weren't pretty. She was scary. Mean. A bitch.

We've been close our entire adult lives, and she and Alley were practically sisters. But things have been strained for over a year now.

I open the door, and there she is. Megan. My sister. Here to save me from myself.

She gives me a weak smile. "Hey Jackass." Then, without hesitation, she pulls me into a hug—arms looped around my waist, ear pressed to my chest. I go still, letting the calm settle over me, then fold my arms around her. It's the first real step toward something better since I got home.

"Are you okay?" she asks, her voice tight.

"Not really," I admit. "But I will be... eventually."

She pulls back, blinking fast. "I'm sorry you're going through this. And I'm really sorry you've had to do it alone." Her voice catches. "Dammit," she mutters. She takes a deep breath, steadying herself. "I'm sorry I haven't been here for you."

"You don't owe me an apology. You were there for Alley when I wasn't. I couldn't be more grateful for that." I step aside to let her in, then head for the kitchen. "You want something to drink?"

She follows me in but stops short when she sees the empty bottles lined up on the counter.

"Don't worry," I say quickly. "I didn't drink them. Dumped everything down the sink." I half-laugh, trying to lighten the mood. "So what I should be asking is, Want some water?"

She huffs out a laugh. "You could've at least saved the wine for me." She makes her way to the Nespresso machine. "I'll just make a coffee, if that's cool."

"Yeah, of course."

She helps herself, opening the cupboard and grabbing a mug. "You want one?"

"Nah. I'm good. Had one this morning." I take a seat at the counter, rubbing my palms on my pants. They're damp. My hands won't stop sweating.

I've just got to rip the damn Band-Aid off.

"Meg." She looks up, mug in hand. "I'm sorry," I say softly. "For everything. For what you had to see." My eyes flick to the divorce papers still sitting on the counter. "For losing her." I squeeze my eyes shut, trying to keep it together with each shaky breath. This isn't about me. It's about her—what I put her through. How my choices hurt *her*.

When I open my eyes, Megan's are red and misty, and a steady stream of tears is running down her cheeks.

"I know," she says, voice trembling. "And I'm so fucking mad at you for it."

I nod, letting it land. Letting her be mad. "You don't have to forgive me. I don't deserve it. I know that." I pause, my voice low. "But I'd really like us to be friends again. If you can stand being around a fuckup little brother like me."

She sniffs and wipes at her nose, collecting herself. "Stop. You know I love you. You're my baby brother." She takes a breath and blows it out slowly. "I guess there's only up from here, right?" A laugh slips out. "Can't really get much worse."

I let a smile stretch across my lips. "Well, it could actually get a lot worse."

We both laugh, and it lightens the air around us.

"I'm glad you're back," she says, looking down at her mug. Then her eyes meet mine. "And I swear to God, if you relapse, I'll kick your ass."

I chuckle. "Noted."

My eyes drift to the divorce papers on the counter, and my chest tightens.

"I'm gonna get her back," I say, my voice breaking the stillness.

"What?"

"I'm gonna get her back," I repeat, this time with more conviction.

"You think?"

"Yeah." I nod, reassuring myself. "I just need to see her. Remind her of what we have, you know?"

Her brows pull together. "I don't know, Jensen." Her voice is soft but pointed. "I've talked to her... and it doesn't seem like she's interested in trying to make things work. Maybe it's time to start thinking about what's next. Let her go—move on."

Let her go? Move on?

"No." My voice is steady, firm. "I don't think it is."

I know I sound delusional, like I'm clinging to denial. After everything Matt's said, and now Megan? I told myself I was ready for this moment. For these papers. But now that they're here, I'm more determined than ever not to give up. Not to *let her go.*

Now is the time to dig my heels in, finish this war I started—the one I put in the middle of my goddamn marriage.

She hasn't even seen me yet. And when she does, I know she'll feel it. We've been through hell and back, dragged through every kind of wreckage—but this whole time, we've been fighting for the same damn thing. *Us.*

She just doesn't see it yet. But she will.

They say believing is half the battle.

Well, I fucking believe in us.

Megan lifts a brow, lips twitching. "Well, selfishly, I hope you're right. For both our sakes."

* * *

MEGAN ENDED up staying for a couple of hours. We talked, then watched a movie. She left about twenty minutes ago.

I wander into the kitchen, looking for something to eat, but stop when I pass the papers again.

I take a photo of them. Might as well let Alley know I got them. The sooner I talk to her, the sooner I can start earning back her trust.

We've got a long road ahead—and I'm determined to put all this shit behind us.

> Got these today. I knew it was coming, but... yeah.
> Hit harder than I expected. When can I see you?

I attach the photo and hit send.
I debated adding that I love her. But she knows I love her.
And if she doesn't...
She's about to.

Chapter Seven

ALLEY

There's this rule of three I remember from a lecture in college—humans can only survive three minutes without air, three days without water, and three weeks without food. That's it. That's all we need to stay alive.

I have those things, and I'm grateful for them. I truly am. Every day that air fills my lungs is a gift denied to many. I know that.

The list for happiness is a little more complicated. There's the basics: connection, purpose, security, identity. And then there's the bigger stuff, things that bring each person joy.

If I had to make a list of those things, I could fill a page, easily. Vacations. Sun. Coffee. Friends.

But the first thing on that list?

Jensen.

And that's the problem. Jensen doesn't just top the list—he makes everything on it better. What's a vacation without him there to share it? How do I enjoy a warm, sunny day without him? Coffee and quiet chats on Saturday mornings? Gone. And hanging out with friends, like I am now?

It's not the same. Not as meaningful as it used to be. I can't go home and tell him about it. I can't share the laughter or the little moments. Every joy feels half-formed now, like a joke, but no one's there to laugh with.

I look down at my drink—the one I've been nursing all night. It's my second, and it's nearly gone. I'm really trying not to go over my two-drink max again. I'm not my father. I'm not Jensen. I don't need alcohol to have a good time.

But somewhere along the way, the line started to blur.

For so long, I had to be strong—for me and for Jensen, trying to help him while not falling apart myself. When I finally left, it was like everything I'd been carrying for two years came crashing down, and I just completely lost who I was. The rule that used to be concrete, non-negotiable, suddenly felt flexible.

Maybe it's the looming divorce. Or the things I've seen that I can't unsee. Maybe it's the cold side of the bed. Or the hollow ache that comes from missing the only person who ever really saw me—the one person I care about more than anyone else.

I glance around the lounge at Tapped Out, a members-only club Leo co-owns with Matt. It's classy—dim lighting, moody atmosphere, strict dress code. I've been to Matt's club a few times in New York, but this is my first time here. It's newer. Bigger. Impressive.

Leo and Vivian leave Monday to visit her family for the holidays, so tonight they're hosting a small holiday get-together with close friends.

Usually, the drinks make me fun. I laugh, loosen up, have a decent time. My friends are great, and the buzz feels good. But tonight, it's not working. Not after the text Jensen sent yesterday.

I let it get to me. What was the point of that message? To make me feel guilty? Like I'm the bad guy in all this?

It's not like I don't already feel those things.

I tip back the rest of my drink, letting it burn down the thoughts, and set the glass down harder than I mean to.

I cross my legs, bare thighs brushing together. I'm wearing a short black romper I bought last minute with sheer balloon sleeves and an open back. It's wintery and flattering. My hair's long now, curled in loose waves. I look good. And thanks to the two mojitos, I feel sexy.

There are good-looking men everywhere. And part of me wishes I could find one to take me home, get my mind off Jensen.

I lock eyes with a guy a few tables over, and a shiver runs down my spine. He's tall, handsome, flashing a smile like he knows exactly what I'm thinking.

He has no idea.

My eyes narrow as I try to picture it—him and me, somewhere private. His lips on mine, his hands on my body. But every time I blink, all I see is Jensen.

I scoff quietly to myself. If only it were that easy—for someone to fuck him right out of my mind.

Yeah... right.

It's a war between my heart and my head. I know I should move on. I filed for divorce. I made that final call. But my heart still belongs to him. And even if I didn't see Jensen in every stranger's face, it's pointless. I'm still married.

So here I am. Thinking about how this night should be fun. Picking at the cheese board. Drinking mojitos. Waiting for something to change.

Alone.

Okay—not *alone*. But everyone else is paired up. Michael and Stella. Leo and Vivian. Cooper and Ryan. Me, my sad thoughts, and my now-empty drink.

"*Die Hard* is not a Christmas movie!" Stella insists for the third time, as Michael and Ryan try to argue their case.

"If it's not a Christmas movie, then why do we watch it every December?" Michael counters.

"Because you make me," Stella shoots back.

We all laugh—well, sort of. I'm trying.

"*Home Alone* is hands down the best. Don't even argue," Cooper says.

Vivian grins. "It's good, but I love Jim Carrey. *The Grinch* will always be my favorite."

Leo points at Cooper. "No, she's right. *Home Alone* takes the win. And Stella, I'm sorry, but I'm with the guys. *Die Hard* counts."

"What about you, Al?" Vivian asks.

"Oh, um... *Home Alone*, for sure. But I love the second one. I'm a sucker for New York." A smile tugs at my lips, and for a second, I let myself enjoy the moment.

That's when Adam shows up. And hey, at least I'm not the only single one anymore.

"Hey!" everyone chimes in at once.

"Hey guys. Sorry I'm late, got held up at the office."

Leo stands to greet him, slapping his back. "No worries, mate. Glad you made it."

"Here, why don't you sit next to Alley," Vivian offers, sliding out of the booth.

Adam scoots in beside me.

"Hey, Al."

"Hey," I reply, trying to sound upbeat.

The cocktail waitress swings by, and Adam orders a drink while Cooper, Leo, and Michael ask for refills.

Adam's cute. He always has been. But when I glance at the side of his face, I feel... nothing.

Damn. If my childhood crush can't even get me excited about being single, I'm screwed.

The truth is, I'm terrified of being divorced. You'd think I'd be used to the idea by now. I've had four months to prepare. And what's worse is, I don't know if it's the idea of being single that scares me—dating, putting myself out there, being vulnerable, being lonely—or if it's knowing no one will ever measure up to the Jensen I loved when things were good. When he was mine. When he was still *him*.

No one else will ever be that great. Ever.

Shit. Am I being too brash? Do I give him another chance? I clearly *want* to.

But all I have to do is remember our last night together. And the one before that. And the week before that.

The night he chose his backpack over me.

Laughter pulls me back to the present. Leo catches my gaze from across the table and gives me a wink. On the end, Ryan pulls Cooper in for a heated kiss. It makes me envious as hell, and at the same time, it makes me want to cry.

I grab my phone from my purse. I still need to text Jensen. I can't live in this nothing space any longer.

Pulling up our text thread, I reread his last message. Then the one I sent a few days ago.

And then I read them again.

I don't know why this is so hard. The decision's been made. We're getting a divorce. Seeing him would only confuse things. Hurt us both.

My fingers move before I can talk myself out of it.

> Hey… I've had some time to think about it, and I really think it's best if we let our lawyers handle everything. I don't want to question my decision. I don't trust myself to see you. But I'm really happy you're doing well. Thanks for reaching out.

Thanks for reaching out? I stare at the words. They feel cold. Robotic. Final. But maybe that's what they need to be.

I hit send.

There. One step forward.

Now—on to getting over him.

My eyes drift back to Adam.

Feel something, dammit. Come on, he's hot. He's backup material.

Nope. Still nothing. Not even buzzed.

He turns to me suddenly, one eyebrow cocked. "Why are you shaking your head?"

Shit. "What?" I grab my empty glass and take a sip of air.

"You were shaking your head. And your drink's empty."

"I know," I grumble. "There was still a drop at the bottom."

"Oh my God." Adam laughs. "You're drunk."

"I am not." I run a hand through my hair before giving him a playful shove, eyes locked on his. "I have a very healthy buzz, and that's all."

"What was that—are you flirting with me? You're definitely drunk." He lifts a finger and waves it in front of me. "Here—follow this."

"You're such a jackass." I roll my eyes and follow it anyway.

He laughs again. "Okay, okay. You're not drunk. But you did look lost in your own thoughts. Care to share?"

"Care to share?" I snort. "Is that the new Care Bear slogan?"

"What the hell is a Care Bear?"

"Stop it. You're older than me. How do you not know what a Care Bear is?"

He shrugs. "No sisters, I guess."

I squint at him, a smile tugging at my lips. "I can't tell if you're joking."

His lips twitch, then break into a grin. "I'm just pulling your leg. Big fan of Grumpy Bear. And whatever the fucking lion's name was. He was cool."

I laugh, and damn, it feels good. First time all day I haven't thought about Jensen.

Adam's gaze meets mine. "So? What were you thinking about when you should have been having a good time?"

I cross my arms, caught off guard by how easily he sees through me.

Before I can answer, Cooper calls out across the table. "Hey, Al— we're going to the bar. You coming?"

"Maybe later," I say, forcing a smile.

Michael and Ryan stay behind as the others slide out of the booth.

Adam raises his eyebrows, still waiting.

I glance at him, then exhale. "Honestly?"

He nods.

"I was sitting here trying to imagine being single again. Trying to figure out how I'm supposed to move on when there's not a single guy in here who even sparks my interest. No offense." I glance at him. "Present company included."

"Ouch," he says with a laugh.

"Hey, you asked." I shrug and keep digging my own grave. "I was thinking, maybe if I could just go home with someone—*anyone*—they could make me forget about him. Just for one damn night, you know? Have some meaningless fun. Feel good... That'd be nice."

His expression's unreadable, and he doesn't say anything.

So I keep talking. Because why stop now? "And then you showed up," I say, forcing a half-smile. "And I thought, *maybe Adam could be the backup plan.* You know, if we're both still single in five years." I glance at him as I reach for my water, sipping through the straw, anything to lighten the weight of what I just admitted. "And that's when I shook my head."

He lets out a long breath. "Whoa. Okay. First of all, a backup? That's brutal. Come on. I deserve better than that," he teases. "Second, we tried that once. Didn't go well, remember? I seem to recall a very drunk, very sad Adam at Michael's birthday party who made out with his best friend's little sister after five tequila shots."

He grimaces, and I can't help but laugh.

"And third—now this one's important, so listen up." He points a finger at me. "All the guys in here—the idea of going home with one of them? That's not you. You're just lonely. You're hurting. But you don't actually want any of them." He grins, nudging my shoulder. "Or me, for that matter."

He takes a sip of his drink. "Trust me. I've been there. Cue the birthday party make-out session."

I laugh softly and glance down, fingers fidgeting with the edge of my napkin.

"It's supposed to hurt, you know." His voice drops, almost a whisper. "That's how you know it was real. If it wasn't, it wouldn't be this hard. Wouldn't hurt. Wouldn't mean anything."

Then he meets my eyes. "You don't want someone to make you forget, Alley. You just want the guy who broke your heart to fix it."

His words knock the air from my lungs. "God," I whisper, shaking my head, the tears falling too fast to stop. "I feel like such an idiot."

"You're not," he says gently. "You're just sad."

"I just... miss him so much." I press a hand to my chest. "It hurts."

"Yeah," he murmurs. "I'm sure it does." He pulls me in for a side hug—steady, quiet, grounding.

I dab at the tears with a napkin, trying to gain composure. The last thing I want is to break down here with all my friends.

"I think I'm going to go," I say quietly. "Would you mind telling Leo and Vivian?"

He hesitates, clearly wanting to say something, maybe talk me into staying, but then he just nods. "Sure. I can do that. Let me get you an Uber. I'll walk you out."

I give a tight-lipped smile. "Thanks."

We make our way to coat check, and a comfortable silence settles between us. My thoughts spin, circling the mess I made of tonight. *He probably thinks I'm crazy.*

"I'm sorry," I say finally, breaking the quiet. "I don't know what that was all about."

"I do," he says, voice soft.

"Yeah. I guess I do too."

"You don't need to be sorry, Al." He pauses, then grins. "Well, maybe for the whole backup plan thing. That was pretty rude."

I give him a shove, laughing. "Shut up. It was a worst-case scenario."

"Stop. You're making it worse. Now I'm a worst-case scenario?"

"No." I press a hand to my forehead, which is now pounding from the mojitos and the crying. "Shit. This isn't coming out right. Damn those mojitos."

"Oh, sure. Blame the mojitos." He chuckles, then tips his head. "Alright, fine. I'll make you a deal. In ten years, if we're both still single, we can be each other's worst-case scenarios. How's that?"

Grinning, I tip my head back. "Oh my God. You're the worst."

My smile fades a little when I meet his eyes.

He gently grips my shoulders. "Hey, you're grieving, you're lonely, and you still love him."

I nod, my voice barely a whisper. "I do."

"You're going to be okay." He smiles, then he nods toward the curb. "Come on. Your Uber's here." He opens the door, and I slide into the backseat. "Text me when you get home."

He shuts the door, and I lean back, letting my head rest against the seat.

I toy with my wedding ring, thoughts spinning and blurring. Tonight was... a lot.

Shit. I remember the text I sent, and panic flutters in my chest. *Did I act too quickly? Do I really mean it?*

Are we... over?

I take a deep breath, a quiet surrender. I made a decision. I texted him. It's done.

It's like Leo said, I don't want to be the sixteen-year-old drunk at the party. And I sure as hell don't want to be the thirty-two-year-old still acting like her.

I want more than this. I want to move on. And I can't if I keep hovering in the space between before and after. It's not good—for anyone.

I glance down at my hand, remembering the moment Jensen slid this ring onto my finger and how happy I was.

A fresh wave of tears blurs my vision.

The proposal.

The football game.

His love for me.

Mine for him.

I twist the ring slowly, hesitating—not because I still believe in us, but because it feels like the last piece of me that belonged to him. The final thread.

I slide it off, the metal cold in my palm, heavy with everything we were. Everything we lost.

I close my fingers around it. And through the blur of tears, I whisper to myself, "I love you."

Goodbye, Jensen.

Chapter Eight

JENSEN

I throw my arms up in frustration and glance over at Matt.

"You've gotta be kidding me," he mutters, gripping his hair with one hand. "How did he miss that pass?"

"Who fucking knows. He can't catch a ball tonight to save his life."

It's Monday Night Football—something Matt and I have done for as long as I can remember. It's one of my favorite pastimes.

Matt stands. "I'm grabbing a beer. You want another one of those?" he asks, gesturing to my sparkling water like I'm dying to have another one.

"Nah, I'm good."

We're at his place, where the fridge is always stocked with beer and the liquor cabinet makes what I had look like child's play. But I'm fine. Surprisingly fine. It's been easier than I expected, just shooting the shit and watching football, completely sober. It almost feels like old times. Only now, it's not quite the same. We're missing someone— a beautiful blonde in my jersey, curled up and cheering beside me.

I reach for my water, wincing as my inner arm brushes the side of my ribs. It's still tender—heat trapped beneath the wrap, reminding me of the slow drag of the needle. The dull burn. The permanence of what I chose to mark into my skin.

The tattoo looks damn good so far. We got most of the outline done, and even started shading a few parts of the forearm. It was a long session, seven hours straight before we both tapped out.

He told me I could take some Tylenol for the pain, but I'm not going down that rabbit hole again. It's just Tylenol, I know. But that's how this whole thing started. No drugs. Not even pain relievers. Not for a couple of years, at least.

Matt plops down on the couch a few cushions over. "When do you talk to your parents?"

"Tomorrow. I want to get it over with before Christmas Eve. My mom's already losing her mind over not seeing me yet." I chuckle. "She's gonna lose her shit when she sees this tat."

Matt grins. "Yeah. Remember when I got my first one? She's not even my mom, and she flipped." He takes a swig of his beer. "But hey, maybe I've softened the blow."

"Yeah, right," I snort. "She took it personally when Megan got that tiny one on her foot. Didn't talk to her for weeks. This?" I glance down at my arm. "This'll push her over the edge."

"Your dad will think it's cool."

"Yeah. Dad's always been more open minded when it comes to this sort of thing."

"How does Alley feel about them?" Then, almost instantly, he grimaces. "Shit. Sorry. That just came out."

I shrug. "It's fine. Honestly? I'm not sure. We never really talked about it, but she's never said anything about not liking them."

He shifts in his seat. "Have you heard from her at all since... you know..." He makes a vague gesture with his beer. "The papers?"

"Yeah. She texted me back." I pause. "Middle of the night on Saturday."

Matt raises an eyebrow. "And?"

I exhale, the words catching like barbed wire in my throat. "She said no. That the lawyers can handle it." My gaze drops down to my wedding ring. I twist it, the familiar metal smooth against my skin. "Like it's no big deal. Just sign the papers and move on." I lean forward and grab my phone from the coffee table. "But she also said something I can't stop thinking about." I pull up the message and hand it to him. "Here. Read it."

His brows scrunch together as he reads. "She doesn't trust herself to see you? That's basically her saying she knows she'd end up in your bed."

"Right?"

He scrolls down, snorting. "Thanks for reaching out? What the f—" He trails off, eyes still scanning. "And then you responded with, '*I understand. I'll respect whatever you need. Just know I meant every word—and nothing you say or don't say will change how I feel about you.*'" He looks up. "What the hell is that? Sounds like something you'd send your grandmother."

He tosses the phone back. I catch it and reread the message, already second-guessing myself. "Shit. I don't know, man. I'm trying to be respectful. I just want her to know that no matter what she says, I'll stay clean. I'll keep loving her. No pressure. No drama. Just... patience." I drag my hands down my face with a groan. "It's just so fucking hard to do from here."

"Yeah, and while you're at it, maybe send her a cardigan and a prayer candle." He leans forward. "Come on. Make her *want* you. Remind her what she's missing. Hit her with something that says, *I still get hard just thinking about you.*"

I stare at him. "That's what you'd text someone in the middle of a divorce?"

"Okay, maybe not *exactly* that," he says, shrugging. "But something that makes her *feel* it. Women want to be respected—but they also want to feel wanted. Give her both. She hasn't had sex in months either—get her panties wet. Make her remember how good it was. How good *you* were.

I shake my head, a half-smile tugging at my lips. "So what do you think I should say?"

He takes a sip of his beer, eyes narrowing like he's crafting the perfect speech. "You say something like, '*Alley, I miss you more than you could ever know. I think about you every second of the day. When I'm watching TV. When I'm at the gym—*'" He glances up briefly. "Gotta remind her you still look good. '*Or when my hand's wrapped around my cock, picturing your pretty lips—*'" He pauses, then shakes his head. "No, better make it about her. '*When my face is buried in—*'"

"Jesus," I cut in. "I can't say that."

"Why not? She's your wife. Remind her."

"Because you don't just text that after getting served divorce papers. That reads like Stockholm syndrome. I'm not trying to fuck some random chick. I'm trying to get my wife back." I shake my head again, letting out a breath. "Christ... Is this why you're single?"

He chuckles. "Hey, I do a lot of sexting. Don't knock my methods." He leans forward, grabbing a chip, then shoots me a look. "Hate to break it to you, but you're about to be single too if you don't let her know just how bad you still want her."

Shit. I *am* about to be single. The thought alone makes me nauseous. And I hate to admit it, but... he's not wrong. What do I even have to lose at this point? What's the worst thing she could say? *Let's get divorced?* Newsflash, Jensen. Already happening.

"Okay," I say slowly. "Maybe you're right. I'll send her another message." I glance at him. "Something thoughtful. Not sexual."

The Bears score a touchdown, tying up the game. Two of my fantasy players are in, and I'm barely paying attention. My focus is completely on Alley now.

The room goes quiet when the game cuts to commercial. I look over at Matt—he's sprawled on the couch, beer in one hand, the other draped along the back cushion.

His life looks so simple from the outside. No one to let down. No expectations. Just work, friends, and the occasional hookup. I used to envy that—how easy it seemed. But knowing what it feels like to be loved by Alley, to wake up next to her, to be the one making her laugh. Losing her might break me. But not loving her at all would've been worse.

"I spoke to my lawyer the other day," I say casually.

Matt mutes the TV, sitting up a little. "And?"

"He said I've got thirty days to respond. If I don't agree with the terms, I can file a response and request mediation. Then I'd at least get the chance to see her." I toss a hand in the air. "You know, without showing up on her doorstep uninvited."

Part of me wants to just get on a damn plane and go to Chicago. But what would that prove? That I can't respect her boundaries? I don't know what the right move is. I just know I don't want to lose her.

"So are you going to?" He takes another sip of his beer. "Push for mediation?"

I nod. "Yeah. It's already in motion."

"What reason did you give?"

I scoff, shaking my head. "You should see the terms of the divorce. She only asked for twenty-five percent of everything." I still can't believe it. "It's so Alley—never taking more than she needs. She made twenty-five percent of the income, so I guess she thinks that's all she's entitled to from our life together."

My stomach knots thinking about it. Cutting everything in half. Cutting *us* in half. "And she only listed a few things from the apartment, mostly stuff that was hers to begin with."

I press the glass bottle of water to my lips and take a swallow. Everything tastes bitter—the words, the thoughts, the water, reality. Bitter and fucking rancid.

"Guess she doesn't want anything that reminds her of me." I rake a hand through my hair. "Of us."

He's shaking his head. The game's back on, but he doesn't unmute the TV. "Don't say that. She's just hurt. You've both been through a lot." He gives me a half-smile. "So, what's the plan then?"

I run my tongue along my teeth, thinking. "I thought about sending her something." My brows pull together. "Something small but meaningful. Maybe bagels?"

"Bagels?"

A short laugh puffs out of me. "Yeah. I know it sounds lame, but… it's kind of an inside joke." I toy with my ring again, the memory of our wedding day slipping in—her sliding it onto my finger. She laced our hands together and brought them to her lips, smiling like I was the only thing in the world that mattered. "I don't know. Maybe it'll just piss her off."

I let out a sigh. "I don't want to make things harder for her. But if she thinks I'm just gonna walk away and not fight for her—then she's out of her mind." I lean back, head falling against the cushion, gaze fixed on the ceiling. My hands fold behind my head. "Nope. I'm not signing those papers until I see her. Until she tells me to my face she doesn't love me anymore. That this is really what she wants."

"Damn. Well, if you need anything, let me know. You know I've got connections in Chicago."

"She's at Leo's?" I ask.

He nods.

"I need you to get his address."

"No problem," Matt replies. "So what's Keith say about all this? Bet he thinks you're crazy."

Keith's one of the best family attorneys in the city. He's Dad's friend from law school and doesn't take on small cases anymore, but he agreed to help me. He's a shark. The kind of guy who can spot bullshit from a mile away and tear it apart in ten seconds flat. I'm obviously not using him like that. I just want him to drag this out and buy me time. Time to see Alley. To make things right. To show her I've changed. To remind her of what we had and that it's still there.

"He said if we counter by offering her more than she asked for, her lawyer's obligated to respond. It forces a back-and-forth. Cleanest way to push for mediation and get us in a room together without making it ugly. She'll have to sit across from me. Listen. Talk. Even if it's just for an hour." A grin tugs at my lips. "We're countering with seventy-five percent of everything."

Matt lets out a low whistle. "Damn. You're gambling with high stakes. What if she agrees?"

"I'm more than happy to give her everything. She deserves it. But she won't. She never would. It's just not who she is. She wouldn't agree to it even if she hated me."

Matt watches me for a second. "That's what's different about you now."

I turn toward him, and see his expression shifting into something more serious.

"You're not fighting to keep her. You're fighting to be the guy she deserved before she left."

I almost smile. "Even if it's mostly just to get us in the same room?"

He chuckles softly. "Yeah. The underlying goal is genuine. You love her. Even she won't be able to deny that."

I don't say anything. But the weight of that truth hits harder than any defensive lineman tonight.

My arm throbs under the wrap, but I don't reach for anything. I let it burn.

I didn't get the tattoo for her—not exactly. But she's a part of it. In the art, the meaning. A reminder of who I was when I lost her, who I am now, and who I want to be.

This pain? I earned it.

This time, I stay with it.

I'd live in the discomfort every day if it meant proving to Alley that she's worth it.

* * *

I PULL my shirt over my head and toss it in the hamper with my pants. Grabbing the balm for my tattoo, I dip my finger in, gather a gob, and rub it in. My gaze lands on the stack of letters I wrote in rehab.

Every Sunday in group therapy, we wrote a letter. It could be to anyone. Send it or don't—didn't matter. Just write.

There's a lot of healing in writing. Nina always encouraged us to pick someone new each week, even ourselves.

I never did.

I wrote twelve letters.

All to Alley.

I didn't send a single one. It never felt right.

I pick them up, flipping through until I find the one from November second. The hardest one I ever wrote. It was the Sunday after they told me she'd filed for divorce. I'll never forget that day. The dust had started to settle. I was beginning to understand what I'd done —where I'd been. Where I still had to go. There was finally light at the end of the tunnel. Then they sat me down on October thirtieth and told me she filed.

The realization that no matter what I did from that moment on, it still might not be enough. I could lose it all anyway.

I set the letters back down with a sigh and comb a hand through my hair.

I want her to read them, someday. I want to tell her everything. About rehab. Therapy. The process and how she helped me through it. God, every day, she helped me push through. Still does.

I slide into bed, phone in hand, and catch up on work emails. Then I open my messages and go to the thread with Alley.

The message I sent her earlier after Matt left stares back at me.

> I want to respect your wishes. I won't show up at your door. I won't push. But I need you to know, I miss you so goddamn much it physically hurts. I miss hanging out with you. Doing nothing. Laughing our asses off. Holding your hand. Spooning. The way you make me feel—how you make me want to be a better man. I miss your voice. Your laugh. Your smile. The way your dimple makes me feel like it's the first time seeing you, every damn time. I miss watching football with you. I miss you, Alley. Every part of you. You say you don't trust yourself to see me? Baby, I don't trust a single inch of me not to show you how sorry I am. I love you. I'm not asking you to say it back. I'm only asking for the chance to prove it.

She left it on read.

My throat swells, eyes blinking fast.

I'm trying to stay positive. But damn, it's getting harder. Every day feels like I'm drifting farther from the end goal.

I plug in my phone, turn off the lamp, and roll to my side—the hardest part of my day staring back at me.

Darkness.

Nighttime.

Sleep.

It never comes easy.

The battle between my thoughts, my past, and the future crashes into itself the second I close my eyes.

I take deep, slow breaths. Count. Repeat. Meditate.

Just like they taught me in rehab.

Chapter Nine

JENSEN

I've always had this ability to get what I want. Whether it was charming teachers for better grades, making every sports team I tried out for, or getting the popular girl to go out with me. I had to work for it, sure, but I always found a way.

Take Sabrina Mendenhall, for example—the most popular girl in high school. She lost her virginity to me. I made her laugh, reeled her in with personality, then sealed the deal with confidence and good looks.

Same with Alley. Same with everything.

Until I fucked it all up.

Life was easier back then. If something didn't go the way I planned, I'd just pivot—pick a new path and keep moving. But it's not that simple when you're thirty-five and married, still cleaning up the wreckage of an addiction that took hold before you even saw it coming. There's no easy out. No quick fix.

Rehab wasn't easy, nothing about getting clean was. I think part of me thought I'd show up and magically get better. I didn't. Rehab was the worst and best thing that ever happened to me. The hardest thing I've ever had to try at. That alone was frustrating—that I couldn't charm my way to sobriety.

I learned a lot about myself there. Addiction's complicated as hell.

There's no single cause. It's layered. In therapy, I dug deep and started to understand some of the things that made me more susceptible.

Addicts don't look like me. Or so I thought. I was too strong, too disciplined, too in control. But it wasn't control. It was arrogance. Blind spots dressed up as confidence. And the worst part? I was never taught how to lose—because I never had to.

Horns blare around me as traffic halts on the bridge. "Fuck," I mutter. I should've stayed at my parents' a couple more hours. With tomorrow being Christmas Eve, and rush hour traffic, it's a graveyard of glowing red taillights.

I just saw my parents for the first time since I've been back. We talked, and it actually went better than I expected. I was nervous, and it wasn't easy. I had a lot of shit to work through with my mom. Stuff that came up a lot in rehab.

Not that it's her fault. I take full responsibility for my actions. But she's always babied me—treated me different than my siblings, like I was fucking special. I never knew why, and no kid's ever gonna complain about that. Hell, I loved it growing up.

I love my mom, and we've always been close. But my whole life, she's been more of a friend to me than a parent. She never taught me consequences or how to deal with shit, not like she did with Jeff and Megan. She made my life easy. I was never held accountable. Life was a fucking walk in the park—until pain meds became my crutch.

There's never been confusion with my dad about his role. He was the parent. There were moments when I was younger that he would have beaten me black and blue if my mom had let him.

Even still, he never hid his anger. He wanted to punish me, and sometimes he did, behind her back. I thought he was being a dick for it then. Now? I kind of wish he'd done it more.

That's the thing. I *wanted* my mom to be mad at me.

All these other people on my list—the ones I need to talk to, make things right with, apologize to—they're all pissed at me. Or at least they were. But my mom? She never was.

How the hell was I supposed to know what's real? What I'm actually worthy of? Fuck, did I even earn the things I thought I did, growing up? Or was she behind the scenes the whole time, pulling strings, opening doors before I even reached for the handle? Manipulating opportunities I thought I worked for. Jesus. No wonder I can't tell the difference between confidence and control. My whole perception of life's been warped in the worst possible way.

We talked about some heavy shit tonight—stuff from when I was little. My mom cried. A lot. I've seen her cry plenty of times, but never like that. Never that emotional, that vulnerable. And now I finally get it. Why she was so scared. Why she never wanted to be the one to punish me, even when I fucking deserved it.

"You have a new message from Megan. Do you want me to read it?" Siri blares through the speakers, interrupting my thoughts.

"Read the message," I say aloud.

"Talked to Amber and Matt. They can do the Berkshires the third week in February. So plan on that. See you tomorrow."

The Berkshires. Shit. That's only seven weeks away.

Seven weeks to prove I'm worth another chance—because I don't even want to think about going without Alley. I don't know if I could. It might be too triggering.

Fuck, just being at my parents' house was triggering. Sitting on that same couch where I detoxed... remembering the fallout between my mom and Alley. Where everything started to fall apart.

I'm already bracing myself for tomorrow night. Christmas Eve. It's always been my favorite day of the whole year. Charades. The food. The way my family packs into the living room like it's a sporting event.

That first year with Alley was by far my favorite. We hadn't even been dating that long, but that night? That's when I knew I was falling in love with her. The last girl I'd ever bring home. The first woman I'd ever say *I love you* to. My last first date. My last first kiss. My last time sleeping with someone new.

She'd won the Best Guesser award. Her cheeks were red with embarrassment, and her dimple popped from all the laughter. Our eyes locked mid-speech from my mom, and things had never been more clear. It was like Cupid shot me straight through the goddamn heart. She was it. The one.

The only one.

Hard to believe that was five years ago. Tomorrow night's going to be tough without her.

A memory barrels in—a fucking nightmare buried so deep it feels like a missile to the chest, making it hard to breathe. Christmas Eve. Last year. Alley. My family.

Holy shit. I was on Oxy, and that night, I locked myself in the bathroom at my parents' to do a line of coke. Alley was outside the door, begging me to come out, to finish charades. I'd gotten up right in the middle of it. When I finally opened the door, she was crying. Screaming. And I left. I fucking left her there. On Christmas Eve.

I took the car and—God, I don't even know where I went. Can't remember. But I know I didn't go back.

Guilt and remorse hit all at once, and my eyes sting. I swallow hard and grip the steering wheel. *I'm such a fucking asshole.*

No wonder she left me.

These memories come in at random—half-remembered flashes I'd do anything to make untrue. Every time one hits, it knocks the wind out of me. I've been out here apologizing, asking for forgiveness like I left a damn dish in the sink. But the truth is, I stood at the center of everyone's lives with a bomb I didn't even know I was holding—then lit the match.

In therapy, we talked a lot about forgiveness. Problem is, with addiction, the person I need to forgive the most is me. And that's a hell of a lot harder when the memories keep popping in like a fucking Pez dispenser loaded with shame.

Mom's constant softness taught me I'd always be forgiven. It's like I never developed the muscle to cope with failure, loss, or rejection. This whole thing—the addiction, losing Alley—it's the first real consequence that's ever stuck. And I failed it. Fuck, I failed it worse than I ever imagined.

Traffic picks up, and I let my foot press heavier on the gas.

I can't spiral right now. I've come a long way. Accomplished a lot. I went to rehab. Got clean. I didn't talk my way into sobriety—I pushed through. Did the work. Changed my diet, my habits, my mindset, my entire lifestyle. I worked with therapists and counselors. I cried. I journaled. I did shit I never thought I'd do.

And now, there's only one thing left to do.

Get my wife back.

My phone rings, and I glance at the holder on the dash. It's Keith.

I hit accept and pray he has news from Alley's attorney.

* * *

MY EYES POP OPEN. It's still dark, but the glow from the nightstand hits my eyes. I reach for my phone, a new text lighting up the screen.

It's from Alley. It's 2:11 a.m.

I take a shaky breath, pulse already picking up. I open the message.

ALLEY

> Hi. I don't really know what to say, or why I'm texting you right now. I couldn't sleep. But thank you for saying all of that. I think about you too. I'm not sure why I'm telling you that… I guess I don't want you to think that I don't. Tonight's… hard.

A wave of relief rolls through me. Not explosive. Just strong and steady. It's the first real sign of hope—something to fuel the fire I've been barely keeping alive.

I let out a breathy laugh. "She still loves me."

That's all I needed.

A little vulnerability.

Proof that she misses me. That she cares. That she still loves me— even if she won't say it yet.

I lie back down, a calm settling in. My resolve stronger than ever.

I don't text back. Not yet.

A grin spreads wide.

She still fucking loves me.

Chapter Ten

ALLEY

THE SMELL of wassail fills the air, grounding me in familiarity—in tradition. My hands wrap around the warm mug, a smile pulling at my lips as I watch the complete and utter chaos of excitement unfold before me.

I've spent a lot of Christmas Eves with Michael, but this is the first at his house with Stella and the kids. My dad's here too. I haven't spent Christmas with him in fifteen years. Watching the kids unwrap their gifts from me and Grandpa masks the ache in my chest, the feeling that something's missing.

The wassail is the only thing that feels the same. Christmas Eve was always spent at Jensen's parents' house—playing games and laughing until it hurt. Last year, though, the laughter was minimal. There was tension with his mom, and unspoken awkwardness. No one really knew how to act around him. He was there... until he wasn't. But Matt, Megan, and the rest of the family did their best to make up for it.

I'm trying hard not to think about it—that Jensen's there right now, playing charades, having fun, living life.

And then he goes and sends my favorite bagels and coffee to the house this morning with a note that said, *Thanks for the text. Hope the bagels aren't stale.*

It was sweet. It even made me smile, then cry. But it doesn't erase anything. I've had to crawl through the fire to get where I am—scarred, bruised.

Bagels can't undo the damage that's been done. Even when your heart's breaking. Even when someone still loves you. Even when you still love him.

Life just goes on.

There's something both peaceful and terrifying about that—knowing everyone has their own lives. Their own grief and joy. Their own challenges. We all live at the center of our own universe, with people and moments spinning in and out of orbit.

People come and go. Jobs change. Tragedies happen. All the while, you're just sitting in the middle of it, realizing maybe you don't matter as much as you thought you did.

Sometimes you stay in someone's orbit for years. Sometimes it's just a season. But eventually, everyone leaves, and they move on—whether you're there or not.

Savannah, Michael's oldest, who's seven, screams with joy as she opens her gift from me—a gymnastics set with a matching leotard from the American Girl store. She recently got into American Girl dolls and just made the competitive gymnastics team.

She runs over and throws her arms around my neck. "Thank you, Alley."

I squeeze her, the simple act nearly bringing me to tears. I needed that.

"Ah, you're welcome, sweet girl."

I had the best time shopping for it. The American Girl store in Chicago is huge. Being there brought back so many nostalgic memories—me and my mom shopping for my Samantha doll, then having tea together for my birthday.

Savannah disappears into her room and comes back with a doll, immediately stripping it down to put on the new leotard. I watch her, awestruck. The weight of sadness begins to lift, and I let out a laugh. A real laugh. No alcohol. No pretending. Just joy.

My dad's hand falls to my knee with purpose, giving it a squeeze. He grins at me, and I can't help but smile as I look around the room, my heart suddenly overwhelmed with gratitude for the love and support surrounding me.

And for the first time in a long time, I think I'm going to be okay.

I can do this.

* * *

I FINISH up the last of the dishes just as my dad walks down the stairs after saying goodnight to the grandkids. Michael and Stella are tag-teaming bedtime duty, so I've been cleaning up the mess left behind in the kitchen.

Michael cooked an incredible dinner, as usual—prime rib with butternut squash and a salad that tasted like it came straight from a Michelin-starred restaurant.

My dad pulls out a barstool and slides into it, settling opposite me at the sink. I grab a pot and towel it dry, watching him.

"What?" I ask, giving him a sly smile.

"Hmm?"

"What's on your mind? I can tell you want to say something."

"Oh..." He sighs, folding his hands. "Just thinking about how lucky we are."

I pause mid-dry, raising an eyebrow. "Dad. Come on. Spit it out."

He's quiet for a moment, his eyes turning misty. He swallows. "I'm just..." His gaze finds mine. "I'm really proud of you."

Damn. A fresh sting burns behind my eyes.

Setting the pan down, I grip the counter and take a deep breath through my now runny nose. The tears fall freely as I choke out, "Thanks, Dad."

He offers a small smile. "It's hard. What you're doing. It takes a lot of strength to walk away from someone you care about. Someone you love." His voice is steady, strong, even as the emotion lingers in his expression.

My next breath is shaky, my chest and shoulders trembling. I nod, too overwhelmed to respond.

His gaze drops to his hands. "You know, you remind me so much of her," he says quietly. He blinks rapidly, his eyes locking on mine. "Your mother."

With that, everything spills out—messy and free. The past fifteen years of missing my mom. The twelve I wasted hiding from my dad. The ache of the last four months missing Jensen. The guilt—for leaving him, for giving up. The overwhelming sadness that sits in my chest every single day when I think about everything I've lost. Everything I let go of.

It's not just my marriage.

It's losing my best friend. My person. The job I left, the friends I never see, the future I thought was mine. The kids we'll never have. The names I'd picked out, and what they might've looked like.

God, it's so heavy.

"But she was stronger than I was," I whisper. "She stayed when things got hard. When you went off on your benders. She stayed."

He lets out a sound—part laugh, part something else. "Oh, Alley girl... I think that made her weaker." He shakes his head slowly. "She should have left. Long before she got sick. You all would've been better off if she had."

My brows pull together, scowling. "That's not true."

But deep down, I wonder if he's right. "Maybe it would've been better for us then." A small smile tugs at my lips as I blink through the tears. "But where would I be without you now?" I whisper. "And where would you be if she had left?"

"Nah. You'd be fine without me. You've always been strong. Independent."

"But what about you?" I ask again.

"The truth?"

"Of course," I say without hesitation.

He lets out a long breath, eyes distant. "No telling where I'd be. Probably lost at the bottom of a bottle. Barely breathing. That's the truth of it."

His words hit me like a freight train. I immediately think of Jensen —how Matt said he spiraled worse than ever after I left. How that still feels like my fault, even though I know it's not.

My dad interrupts my thoughts. "Or maybe I would've gotten

sober and stayed that way." He smiles softly. "Hard to know what losing your family might do to a man. I'm sure I'd have gotten worse before I got better, that's for certain. But I like to think, eventually, I'd have ended up right here. Sober. Happy. With my family again."

He clears his throat. "I was a lost cause for a long time. Whether you were there or not, I had to hit rock bottom on my own. I had to lose everything, then claw my way out of the hell I'd created to find the light again."

He lets out a heavy exhale. "Either way, I'm right where I'm supposed to be. And you are too. Doesn't matter which road we take. One might be rougher—more lessons, more bruises—but you come out smarter, stronger. I think we end up where we're meant to. Fate always finds you."

I smile as his words settle in.

We had a scare with Dad a few months ago, the same night I left Jensen. He ended up in the hospital with liver issues—his ammonia levels were high, and his liver enzymes were through the roof. The doctors said they caught it early, but he's still at risk for complications.

Ever since, he's been different. More open. Nostalgic. Sentimental.

"I guess I've never really thought of it that way," I say somberly. "I used to believe everything happened for a reason... until Mom died." I pick up another pan to dry, needing the distraction. "I can't find a reason for that. And now Jensen?" I shake my head. "I can't find a purpose for that either. Except maybe the universe just really hates me."

He nods slowly, fingers laced in front of him. "I used to think that too, that pain had to have a purpose." His voice drops, low and thoughtful. "Not everything happens for a reason. But everything that happens can become one, if we let it. We don't choose the cards we're dealt—just how we play them."

He swallows. "You've been dealt some bad hands in life." He frowns, nodding slowly, then meets my gaze. "But you've always been good at poker." His lips curve, pride shining in his eyes. "You've always known how to play a losing hand better than most, Alley girl.

Look around you. You're winning. Every day, you're winning. And I couldn't be more proud of you."

With that, he pushes away from the counter and walks toward me. His words—*God, his words*—crack me open in the best possible way. I melt into his arms, wrap mine around him tight, and let myself break. Let myself just be, present, aware, and okay with where I am.

I've never been more grateful to Jensen for helping me reconnect with my dad.

A small smile tugs at my lips, the taste of salt lingering from my tears.

Maybe fate found me after all.

* * *

I FLIP off the light at the top of the stairs. The tree glows in the corner, lighting up the living room in soft gold. The rest of the house is quiet and dark. Leo and Vivian are gone this week for Christmas, and I never stopped to think about what that meant for me—for my Christmas morning.

I drop my bag of gifts by the stairs and walk to the couch. Sinking into the cushions, I take in the holiday decor—the tree, the nativity on the mantel, the stockings over the fireplace. Vivian insisted on hanging one for me. It was a sweet gesture. But looking at it now, I realize there's no one here to fill it. No one to have coffee with by the fire. No one to watch open gifts.

A pang of sadness squeezes my chest. It hits all at once, how empty it feels. How alone I really am. Maybe I should've stayed at Michael's. I'm going back over in the morning anyway. I shift to the side, pull my feet up onto the couch, and drape a blanket over my lap, eyes fixed on the tree.

My phone buzzes from inside my purse. My brows knit—it's past midnight, and Michael and Stella were headed to bed when I left. I dig it out, and my breath catches when I see the name on the screen.

Jensen.

I press the side button automatically, a natural reaction to stop the vibration. My grip tightens around it, heart racing as I stare at the name. I debate what to do with the few seconds I have left to decide. *Why is he calling?*

I know I should send it to voicemail, but I don't want to. I want to hear his voice. Want to hear my name on his lips. Want to not feel so alone.

I tell myself something could be wrong, that it might be important. Why else would he call? And before I can talk myself out of it, my thumb slides across the screen.

I bring the phone to my ear, breath shaky. "Hi." It's barely audible, barely a voice at all.

"Hey, Al."

Silence. Just the ache. Just the hurt. Tension, somehow felt through this tiny device.

"I'm surprised you picked up. Glad you did, but... surprised."

My eyes close, letting the sound of his voice wrap around me like the hug I so desperately need. *Oh my God, I miss him so much.*

I don't know what to say. I could spill everything, talk to him, let him make it better like he always has. But instead, because I feel my resolve weakening, I hear myself say, "Why are you calling, Jensen?"

"I don't know, I just..." He goes quiet for a moment. "Wanted to hear the sound of your voice. I thought you'd send me to voicemail." He lets out a soft, broken chuckle. "Figured I'd hear your message telling me you'd call me back, and try to believe it."

My lips quiver, the emotion creeping in so fast my next breath shudders—loud enough to notice.

"And I wanted to apologize." His voice cracks. "For last year. When I left you at my parents'. I didn't realize—didn't even know I did that until yesterday. God..." The words strain, his composure slipping.

He doesn't say anything else, and I know it's because he can't. He's too emotional. We both sit there, miles apart, listening to the sound of our pain in every breath.

He finally sniffs, then says quietly, "Anyway, I just needed you to know that. You deserved better."

"I did," I choke out. "And I still do."

"I'm not that man anymore, Alley. Please. Give me a chance."

A chance. Like he hasn't had dozens of them.

I need to end this call—because if I don't, I'll slip. I'll give in. I feel it, the pull in my heart and my mind that wants to run to him. That wants to say, *It's okay. I still love you.*

I've come too far and cried too many tears for it all to be for nothing.

"I have to go," I say quickly. "Thank you for the apology. And for the bagels and coffee."

"Alley—"

"Merry Christmas, Jensen." I hang up, dropping the phone in my lap. I sink deeper into the couch, letting the cracks of my pain bleed. Letting the tears soak my cheeks. I stare at my initial on the stocking above the fireplace, the lights flickering in the distance, and let the silence haunt me.

Numb me.

Until I fall asleep.

Chapter Eleven

ALLEY

My hands shake as I reach for the overpriced glass water bottle. I take a sip, my throat parched, pulse unsteady. My palm slides against the condensation, slick and cold. The large, oval table sits in a modern Midtown office on the thirteenth floor.

The chair is fine. Not comfortable, but not awful either.

God. Why am I thinking about chairs?

Because if I don't, I might throw up.

It's been three weeks since Christmas. Two since my lawyer called to say Jensen rejected the divorce terms. I had a choice—drag it out with a fight, or agree to mediation.

He countered by asking for only twenty-five percent.

It's generous. Too generous. But that's Jensen—thoughtful, intentional. He knows exactly what to say and how to show up. And somehow, it doesn't feel manipulative. Because I also know that if I'd signed, he would've followed through without question.

I know what most people would say—that he's trying to do the right thing. Maybe even trying to make up for what happened.

I'm sure that's part of it, but he wants to see me. He knew I wouldn't sign, and that this was the only way I'd sit in front of him.

So here I am.

I told myself I wouldn't cave. That I'd stay strong. I've ignored every text and call since Christmas Eve.

I know it's harsh. Bitchy, even. But I don't trust myself.

After that call from him, it was all I could do not to get on a plane and come running back. So I ignore him. Pretend he doesn't send me coffee, or lunch, or flowers. That I don't read every thoughtful text, or see the pictures he sends from our past. That they don't wreck me. That it doesn't feel like the kind of hurt that's almost beautiful—because he can't not remember. Just like me.

I just keep praying it stops.

But it doesn't.

And right now? I'm scared.

It's been almost five months since I last saw him, and I've spent every one of them trying to unlove him. To untangle myself from the want. To not look at the photos of him on Matt's Instagram, or the video of him doing a polar plunge in Switzerland—where he strips down to his underwear and dives into a freezing lake. How I zoom in on the new abs he's sporting. As if memorizing him might quiet the ache that never seems to leave.

God, I've tried everything. Breathwork. Long walks. Hot yoga with Cooper. Midnight venting with Leo. Girl talk with Vivian.

Little by little, I've been getting better. It's been getting easier. But now I'm sitting here, palms sweaty, stomach in knots, terrified that one look at him will unravel all of it.

I don't want that.

I glance at the clock above the door. He's late. The meeting was supposed to start three minutes ago.

The mediator sits quietly as our lawyers chat like they're old buddies, papers out in front of them.

His lawyer's familiar. I think he's one of Jensen's dad's friends— maybe he was at our wedding. I'm not sure; doesn't matter. What I do know is he'll be the best damn lawyer there is. Between Jensen's dad being a lawyer and all the high-powered people Matt knows, I'd expect nothing less.

My lawyer's good too. He's younger, one of Scarlett's friends. But he had a great resume and was reasonably affordable. As affordable as a lawyer can be in New York.

I clear my throat, suddenly aware of how dry it is, and reach for the water again. My eyes flick to the door when I hear voices, my pulse picking up speed, body going tense. I fix my gaze on the condensation sliding down the glass bottle in front of me as the door opens.

I don't look up. I can't. A shaky breath fills my lungs, my eyes betraying me as they drift to the movement across from me.

To Jensen.

Holy shit. He looks good. Fitted navy chinos, a camel-colored belt, crisp white button-up—and goddamn confidence he wears better than cologne.

He flashes me a grin as he slides into his seat. "Hi, Al." His dimples set deep, eyes locked on mine. They're clear, bright, familiar— that deep ocean blue making it hard to look away. Making it hard to breathe.

My throat somehow gets even drier. I can hardly swallow. It's like a desert in my mouth.

I am so screwed. Or, in Jensen's words—I'm fucked.

His arms flex as he pulls himself up to the table, folding them in front of him, eyes still on me.

Oh my God. I knew he'd gotten in better shape—the polar plunge video—but I didn't realize he'd gotten so much buffer.

Is buffer even a word?

I swallow, or attempt to. My heart's fluttering so hard it feels like there's a bird trapped in my chest.

"Hi," I breathe out, eyes locked on his biceps, the fabric of his shirt pulling taut. *Yep. Definitely buffer.*

"It's good to see you." His voice is low, smooth, genuine. "You look beautiful."

And you look hot as hell.

I reach for my water... again, my hand shaky, the glass cool against my palm. "Thank you," I say, forcing my eyes away from him and to the mediator.

Cool. I can't even act normal around my own husband.

Both lawyers greet Jensen, and he stands to shake each of their hands.

My attention derails the second I notice ink on one of his forearms.

What the hell? He got a tattoo?

His sleeves are rolled a few inches, and sure enough—definitely a tattoo.

My mind spins. *What is it? How big? Are there more? What else is he hiding under that shirt, aside from the six pack?*

I use this minute of polite pleasantries to study him, letting my eyes roam. Taking him in like it's the first time. Like he did when we met, coming out of anesthesia, unable to keep his eyes off me.

My gaze lands on his face. Sharp jawline. Clear skin. Scruff. His hair's longer now, messier.

My eyes drop to his mouth.

Dammit. Don't look at his mouth. Don't look at his mouth.

What is wrong with me? Is this what five months without sex does to a person? Or is this just... me missing him?

I've been so worried about seeing him. Bracing myself for this day. Replaying every possible scenario. Reminding myself why I left, why I have to follow through.

It was going to be hard enough, sitting across from the man I love to sign divorce papers.

But this? Tattoos. Muscles. That mouth.

Clean.

Clear eyes. Steady voice. That Jensen confidence I haven't seen in so long—the same confidence that stole my heart five years ago.

Jensen 2.0 showed up. And I'm supposed to stay strong? Pretend like this is what I want—to be divorced? To sign the papers while he's looking at me like I'm the only person in the room. Like I'm still his.

Like he loves me.

Shit.

Chapter Twelve

JENSEN

Her lawyer's voice is calm and steady. "As you're aware, Ms. Adams originally proposed a 25/75 split in favor of Mr. Adams. In light of his recent rebuttal, Ms. Adams is now open to a 50/50 division of marital assets."

I sit back, hands clasped in front of me, eyes on her profile. She won't look at me—not when I'm watching. But I've caught her glancing over, her gaze flicking my way, lingering. I'm no expert at reading people, but I know Alley.

I know her better than anyone.

I know the scar on her ankle and the one on her knee from a scooter crash when she was twelve. I know the birthmark on her ass—it's small, looks like a mole, and it's cute as hell. I know how to make her laugh until she cries.

And I know this is killing her. The act. The pretending she doesn't care.

I study her, not caring that I've been staring for most of the meeting, or that she's caught me more than once. I'm not trying to hide it. She's my wife. I want her to see me looking at her, admiring her. If this is the only way I can show her how much I love her, then I'll keep staring.

She looks gorgeous, but that's no surprise. One of my favorite versions of Alley is in the mornings—half-asleep, hair kinked, fresh face, oversized T-shirt and no pants. There's something vulnerable about it. The way she hides her face, thinking she looks like shit. How she's self-conscious about morning breath, and I couldn't care less. When I see her like that, I just want to wrap myself around her and kiss her until she believes she's the most beautiful woman in the world.

Her hair's longer, the longest it's ever been. Her black sleeveless dress hugs her perfectly, teasing every bit of what's underneath.

Her eyes shift from the lawyer's to mine. She narrows them slightly, brow furrowed as she takes a deep breath, then flicks her gaze to the table.

Shit. If that wasn't lust written all over my face...

But it was all over hers too.

I should know better than to read too much into a look. But the few times I've caught her gaze... it doesn't feel like hate. Doesn't feel like someone who wants to get a divorce. If anything, it feels like the opposite of that.

Like someone who wouldn't mind getting fucked in a utility closet instead of sitting here in this stuffy office.

A smirk tugs at the corner of my mouth. *She doesn't really want this.*

I cling to that thought, because it's the only thing giving me enough confidence to get through this meeting still a married man.

I didn't know what to expect today. I've been scared shitless, telling myself for months that Alley still loves me. That if I could just see her, talk to her, things would be different.

I know it's not that simple. Especially after weeks of being ignored, texts left on read, calls sent to voicemail. It's been fucking brutal. And now, seeing her like this? Avoidant. Standoffish.

I've got my work cut out for me. That's for damn sure.

I've fucked up more than anyone ever should. I know I don't deserve Alley—not after everything I've done, everything I've put her through. But I also know I can make her happy. When things are good between us, they're really good. We can get back there. I know we can.

This is my last chance to show her who I've become. I don't need to win her over today. I just need to delay the signing. Plant seeds.

Remind her of what we were. Show her who I am now. Prove I'm still someone worth loving.

"We appreciate the revised offer," Keith says. "As you know, Mr. Adams has always maintained that he wants a fair resolution. Given the reasons behind the divorce, he still believes you deserve more than fifty percent. But he's prepared to accept these terms, assuming we can clarify the division of the primary assets, specifically the furniture and joint investment accounts."

"I don't want any of the furniture," she says.

"Al," I say gently. "Come on. You picked it out. It's just as much yours as it is mine."

She finally meets my gaze. Her voice is soft, but steady. "*We* picked it out. And I don't want it."

"I'll pay to have it moved. You'll have enough to hire movers either way."

"It's not about that, Jensen."

I nod. "Then what's it about?"

She swallows, eyes locked on mine. She doesn't answer right away.

"I don't want reminders," she says at last, her voice barely above a whisper. "Of us." Her gaze drops to the table. "It's too hard."

My throat locks, but I hold it together. "Well then... at least sell it. Don't short—"

"Jensen." She looks up, eyes brimming with unshed tears. "Just keep it, okay? Please."

"Okay." It's all I can manage, not because I agree, but because I'll lose it if I try to say anything else.

"Well, it sounds like we've come to an agreement," the mediator says, glancing between us like it's just business. "Let's review the listed assets to ensure we're all on the same page before proceeding."

Her lawyer slides a printed packet across the table. "We've itemized everything—bank accounts, home furnishings, vehicle equity, retirement and investment accounts."

"We've cross-referenced with our own copy," Keith replies. "I believe we're aligned on most of the valuations."

I nod along as they start going through the accounts—the stocks, the retirement breakdown. But something about hearing it out loud makes my stomach turn. It's like watching someone list off the contents of your life at an estate sale—only I'm still alive.

Panic sets in, a cold sweat rushing through me. *Fuck.* They're not just talking about dividing furniture. They're dividing us. This is happening.

I told Keith to do whatever it takes to avoid signing today. I don't know what he has up his sleeve, but this very much feels like we're headed straight for pen and paper. The nausea crawling up my throat is anything but calming.

I swallow hard, my hands tightening in my lap. It takes everything in me not to walk around this table and remind her—*beg her*—to come home with me. Watch football with me. Just hang out. *Talk to me.*

"Could we—" I interrupt, glancing at our lawyers, then back to Alley. "Could we have a few minutes alone?" I ask them, but I'm only looking at her. "Just you and me. Please." My voice cracks on the last word, and it's pathetic.

"Jensen," she says softly.

"That's up to Ms. Adams," her lawyer says.

"Please, babe. Please." I hold her gaze with the desperation of a man heading off to war.

She holds it, her eyes glistening.

Her attention suddenly shifts to her watch, brows pinching. Then she's digging through her purse. "I'm so sorry," she says, pulling out her phone. "I need to take this call. It's important." She stands, already heading for the door as she answers. "Hey. What's going on?"

The door closes behind her, leaving me in the thick, awkward silence of my insufferable desperation.

"This is going reasonably well," the mediator says, his voice slicing through the tension.

No, actually. It's not going well. At least not for me. *Jesus.*

Alley's lawyer shuffles some papers, and Keith turns toward me. "How you holding up? You okay?"

I let out a slow breath. "What does that word even mean right now?" I rub my hands over my face, pressing my fingers into my forehead. "This is happening, isn't it? I'm going to walk out of here divorced."

He takes a beat before answering. "That's a very probable outcome." Then he leans in, lowering his voice. "Don't panic. I said I'd stall." He leans back again, giving me a firm nod—subtle, steady, like he's still got this under control.

The door opens, and Alley steps back in, moving quickly toward her purse.

"I'm sorry. I have a family emergency. I have to go."

Her eyes are wet, and she wipes at her cheek like she doesn't want anyone to see.

I stand. "Al. What is it?"

She looks at me, and for a second, it feels like she might actually come to me. Fall apart in my arms and tell me everything. Like before.

But her gaze shifts to her lawyer instead. "We'll have to reschedule. I'm flexible."

"Is everything okay, Ms. Adams?" her lawyer asks gently, concern pulling at his features.

"I'm not really sure."

My chest swells. My fists clench at my sides. She's falling apart—and I can't do a damn thing about it.

She glances at me one last time before turning back to him. "Let's just try to get this over with as soon as possible. I'm sorry for wasting everyone's time."

She doesn't wait for a response. She's already pulling the door open.

I'm across the room before I can think. "Alley," I call after her as she rushes down the hall.

She glances over her shoulder. "Jensen, please. We can talk later."

"Alley, wait—"

She reaches the elevators and stabs the down button.

"Please," I say, softer now as I catch up. "Just tell me what's going on."

Her lips part, then close again. She shakes her head. "It's my dad."

The elevator chimes, and the doors slide open. She steps inside, turning back toward me. "We'll reschedule," she says, voice strained, then meets my gaze as I take a step forward. "Jensen, please... don't follow me."

I stop cold, chest aching to be there for her. I nod, forcing myself to stay rooted in place.

"Wait," I say again, as I throw my arm out to stop the doors from closing.

I reach into my back pocket and pull out the folded envelope. The last letter I wrote to her. "I wanted to give this to you." I hold it out. "I wrote it in rehab."

Her eyes flick down to the envelope, then back up to mine.

"You don't have to read it. But it's yours. Just... take it."

She hesitates, then steps forward and takes it from my hand. Doesn't say a word. Just clutches it, eyes glossy.

The door closes.

And she's gone.

My wife's fucking gone again.

My eyes close. "Shit." I back up, hands laced behind my head as I suck in a shaky breath.

God, I wanted to prove I'd changed. Instead, I just proved I could still lose her.

My arms fall to my sides, and I turn in defeat. *How many times can you lose something before it's no longer yours to lose?*

I make my way back to the office, shoulders sagging. I pull out my phone and text Matt.

> Hey man. I was in mediation with Alley. She had to rush out—some kind of emergency with her dad. Can you find out what's going on?

MATT

> Sure thing. I'll reach out to Leo so I'm not bothering her if it's serious.

I let out a sigh of relief.

> Thanks.

Chapter Thirteen

ALLEY

I STARE BLANKLY at the hospital bed in front of me, the steady beeping of the medicine pump driving me absolutely insane. *Where the hell is the nurse?*

It's been going off for five minutes. One of the IVs is empty and needs to be swapped. There's a button to silence the alarm. I could call someone. I could even do it myself. But I don't have the energy to get up, let alone do someone else's job. I'm mentally and physically wrecked.

It's been over forty-eight hours since I arrived in Chicago, and I've hardly slept.

After Michael called about Dad, I stopped by the hotel in New York to grab my suitcase and headed straight to the airport. I cried the entire drive, just sat in the back of the Uber and fell apart. It's just been one thing after the other. Between seeing Jensen and now this with my dad, I can't seem to catch a break. I caught the soonest flight I could and came straight here. I haven't left since.

Michael and Stella were here earlier with the kids. Only two visitors are allowed at a time in the ICU—and no kids. I sat out in the waiting room with them while Michael and Stella were with Dad.

He's sleeping now. He hasn't been awake much today. His skin's jaundiced, and his belly's still bloated. He's hooked up to everything—

oxygen, IVs, a catheter, blood pressure monitors, meds... even an NG tube.

It reminds me too much of when Mom was here.

I suck in a sharp breath. *Don't go there.*

I've tried to sleep, but I can't. I'm too worried. And now I'm so far past exhausted I've crossed into crazy. Every time I close my eyes, colors flash behind my lids, and they twitch like they've forgotten how to stay shut.

The machine keeps beeping.

Goddammit.

I push up and walk over to silence it. My eyes drift to Dad—his yellowed skin, the furrow in his brow. Even asleep, he looks like he's in pain.

I plop back onto the sofa bench by the window. I'd almost forgotten what it's like to be the one visiting. The one sitting with a loved one. Sleeping on this godforsaken *"couch"*.

It still surprises me that I became a nurse. I hate hospitals. I spent so much time in them when my mom was sick. And in the end, I hardly ever left her side. I just sat there and watched—as she slowly died.

But I still remember the nurses from that time. The way they made us feel seen and cared for. The ones who connected with my mom and made her laugh. They were a small light in the middle of the darkest time in my life. And something about that stayed with me. I wanted to be that person, the one someone remembers when the worst is happening, because I helped it suck a little less.

That's what made me want to be a nurse. Problem is, I don't know how people work in the ICU. It's suffocating in here. Depressing. I tried different units—ICU, emergency, extended stay—but none of them were right. Those shifts felt like carrying a brick on my chest. I'd come home and cry, completely drained. Emotionally. Mentally.

That's why I ended up in PACU. There are harder days, sure, but I've only had a handful of scary or heavy moments.

My new job's been great. I'm working for a plastic surgeon group in downtown Chicago. I get everything I loved about PACU, but with better hours. I still miss it, though. It's where I fell in love with nursing. Where I met Zach.

Where I met Jensen.

Which is another reason I can't sleep.

I can't stop thinking about him.

Mediation was intense. The way he looked. How he looked at me —the way it made me feel.

I don't know what that means for me.

In a way, I'm grateful I was called away—not for the reason why, but for having a reason to leave. I would have signed. I was ready. I'd been mentally preparing for that day for months. I walked in determined to leave that room divorced.

But now?

I'm not so sure.

Jensen's the reason I'm even here with my dad. He encouraged me to make peace, drove me to see him, waited outside while we talked. He was a constant, steady strength for me. He's also the only one who really gets it—the guilt I carry when it comes to my dad.

I wrote him off for ten years. Abandoned him when he needed me most. He was hurting, and I just... left. I ignored his calls, let his texts go unanswered. I didn't visit when I stayed in Chicago. I acted like he didn't even exist.

God, that's exactly what I'm doing with Jensen. Ignoring him. Shutting him out. Pretending it's easier not to feel anything. But it's not easier. It's eating me alive.

The realization hits so hard I gasp, a sharp breath that startles me.

But I don't cry. I hold it in. Swallow it down. I let it all out before my flight, and I've been holding it together ever since.

I exhale—slow and steady. Then take another breath, this one even deeper.

Oh my God. I'm an avoider. When things get hard... I run.

I hide.

I bring my hand to my lips and chew on my thumbnail, my fingers shaky and cold.

I knew I did this with my dad, but apparently, it's a pattern.

I try to make sense of it, but my brain's operating at five percent, max.

I *did* try. I *did* stay—for a long time.

I squeeze my eyes shut and press my fingers to my temples. My head is throbbing. *Did I try hard enough? Am I supposed to give him another chance?*

I could at least respond to his texts. He's still technically my husband, and I've been treating him like some guy I dated once and don't know how to get rid of.

Shit. I've been so caught up in how hard it would be for *me* to see *him*, I haven't thought about how difficult all this might be for him.

He texted a few weeks ago about working the steps. Said he just wanted to talk. Make things right. Apologize. And I just... ignored him.

Like an asshole.

The bare minimum would be giving him the decency of closure.

I know he wants more, but that doesn't mean I have to.

The worst part is, I *want* to talk to him. Now, more than ever. I want to fall into his arms and cry. Tell him everything.

Honestly? I wish he were here.

My gaze shifts back to my dad, a sudden wave of new emotion flooding in. This. Right here. It's what matters.

The people in your life. The ones you love. The ones who love you.

And *God,* does Jensen love me.

I dig in my purse for ChapStick but come up empty. With a sigh, I pull the whole thing onto my lap, rummaging through the chaos. My hand brushes against the folded envelope Jensen gave me.

I pull it out and smooth it flat. My name is written across the front in his handwriting. My fingers tremble, and my heart pounds so loud it drowns out the machines.

I want to tear it open, but I'm frozen. Terrified of what's inside. I'm not even sure what I'm afraid of. That he'll tell me he still loves me? Beg me to come back?

I already expect all of that.

No, what scares me is that I'll read whatever's inside and forget everything I've seen. That I'll let it be okay.

That I'll go back.

I've pulled it out at least a dozen times in the past two days. Each time, I get so damn close. And then I chicken out.

I keep replaying mediation—how he couldn't stop looking at me. I wanted to stare back, to take him in. But every time I glanced over, he was already watching me, just smiling, unapologetically. His eyes were full of something I didn't know how to handle.

He looked so damn good. And I hated how much I wanted to touch him. To be near him again. Just for a second.

I won't lie to myself. I wanted more than that. And when he pleaded with me at the end—right before the call came in—that look in his eyes almost broke me.

If we'd been alone...

If I'd let him talk...

I think I would've caved.

I close my eyes, take a steadying breath, and slide my thumb beneath the seal—

A soft knock hits the door just before it creaks open.

"Hey, Al... can I come in?" Matt steps inside, casually dressed but somehow still managing to make it look expensive. I shove the letter back into my purse and rise to my feet.

"Matt!" I'm already moving before I even register it. The door clicks shut behind him as I throw my arms around his back. His arms open, and I lean into him, the hug familiar and grounding.

"What are you doing here? How did you even know...?"

But I already know. Jensen.

He told Matt. Then Matt asked Leo. And now... here he is.

"I texted Leo," he says, casually. "He told me about your dad. How you holding up?"

I pull back and shrug.

That's it. There's nothing else to say.

Matt's brows crease. "I want to hear about your dad, but I need to tell you... Megan's here."

A smile breaks across my face.

"And Jensen."

My heart skips a beat. Then slams into overdrive. *Jensen's here?*

"He is?" I ask, too fast. The words are out before I even realize I said he instead of they.

Matt's lips twitch as he studies me. "They're out in the waiting room. If you want to say hi."

I nod before I can stop myself.

"Only if you want to," he says gently. "No pressure."

"Um... yeah, okay. We can go say hi." I draw in a shaky breath and immediately start rubbing under my eyes. "Oh my God," I mumble, patting my cheeks and combing my fingers through my hair. "I look like hell."

Matt's grin widens, like he knows exactly why I care.

He opens the door, and we head down the hall together. My heart's racing, and I keep fussing with my hair, trying to pull myself together.

"Hey, Al," Matt says softly, placing a hand on my back.

"Yeah?"

"You look great." He flashes a half-grin, then presses the button that opens the double doors to the waiting room.

I hear Megan before I see her. "Shut up, you did not!" she laughs, elbowing Jensen just as I spot her.

They both stand, and Megan practically runs to me, throwing her arms around my shoulders. I do the same, swallowing the lump rising in my throat. I'm too happy to see her to cry.

"Oh my God." She squeezes tighter. "I've missed you so much."

"I've missed you too."

She pulls back, and my eyes shift—drawn to Jensen standing just behind her.

His gaze finds mine. Quiet. Patient. Loving.

Something tightens in my chest, hot and aching, impossible to ignore. I don't think. I just move. One step toward him, then another.

"Hey, Al," he says softly, arms parting—just enough to welcome me, but not too much. Like he's giving me room to choose.

I don't hesitate. I walk straight into him and collapse, my hands twisting in the front of his shirt. Every tear I've swallowed over the last forty-eight hours breaks free as I fall apart in his arms. I melt into him, releasing everything while his arms wrap tightly around me—like he's been waiting to catch me all along.

For weeks I've avoided him, but now, without saying a word, he's given me exactly what I needed.

I feel his lips press to the top of my head as he whispers, "Hey, baby... I've got you."

He feels safe.

He feels *good*.

He feels...

Like home.

Chapter Fourteen

JENSEN

I PULL HER IN CLOSER, resisting the urge to bury my face in her hair. Emotion surges through me, hard and fast, but I swallow it. This is all I've wanted for five months—hell, for a long time. To be here for Alley. Really be here. Clean. Sober. Her safe person again.

A sob wrenches out of her as she trembles in my arms.

"Hey, baby... I've got you." The words tumble out. It's what I'd say. It's what I've always said.

I glance up, catching Megan's and Matt's eyes. I almost forgot they were there. Megan's eyes are misty, and Matt just looks proud.

Alley slowly stills against me, and a part of me wishes this moment would never end. Because I don't know what it means or if I'll get another chance to comfort her. But God, I hope it's not the last.

Her sobs quiet, her hands loosening their grip on my shirt. She presses her palms to my chest, and I ease my hold, letting her pull back.

She wipes at her cheeks. "Sorry," she mumbles.

"Don't be sorry," I whisper back.

Her hands trail down to my abdomen, fingers lingering like she's trying to remember me. Then she slides them to my sides and around my back, wrapping her arms around me. She presses her ear to my chest and exhales.

I take an even deeper breath, afraid to move—to ruin this. For months, I've put in the work. Every day. To grow. To be the best version of me I can be. And I *have* grown. I *am* better. But no amount of push-ups, cycling, clean eating, or staying sober can fill this hole in my chest the way Alley just did.

It's like I've been staring at the same damn puzzle for months. I've put every piece in its place except one. The full picture's right in front of me. But no matter how hard I try, I can't finish it—because the piece that makes it matter has been missing.

Her.

She's the missing piece.

I'll never be complete without her.

And right now—her arms around me, her face buried in my chest—I start to believe we might actually survive this.

That maybe... she'll come back home.

She finally pulls away, and Megan steps in, quick to fill the silence. "Matt and I are gonna grab a bite to eat. Why don't you two head down to the cafeteria, grab some food and talk."

Alley's eyes flick to mine, and she offers a small smile. "Okay."

Just one word—but it hits like a drum in my chest.

She agreed to have dinner with me.

In a hospital cafeteria, sure, but still...

She wants to talk.

* * *

Twenty minutes later, I'm sitting in a booth across from my favorite person.

The walk down was mostly quiet. A *thanks for coming* from her. A *you're welcome* and *I want to be here for you* from me. A few side glances from her in the hallway. And I couldn't take my eyes off her in the elevator.

I haven't heard from her since she rushed out of mediation, which makes me think she probably hasn't read the letter. At least—fuck, I hope that's why. Because if she has, and still didn't reach out... I don't know if anything I do will ever be enough.

I didn't even plan on giving it to her. I shoved it in my pocket that morning as a last resort. If it came down to signing the papers—if I felt desperate enough, like there was nothing else I could do or say—then maybe I'd hand it over.

But I panicked. Gave it to her without thinking. It's the one from my last week in rehab. The final letter I ever wrote.

Is it desperate? Yeah. But I'd been clean and clear-headed for fourteen weeks. It's honest.

I glance down at the roasted chicken on my tray, guaranteed to be dry. They offered a side of gravy, but I held it.

Across from me, Alley stares at her food. She looks exhausted. Still the most beautiful girl I've ever laid eyes on, but there's something hollow in her cheeks, something fragile about the way she moves. Like she hasn't eaten or slept in days. She's lost weight, too. Not in a purposeful way, but in the way stress wears you down, like she's had so much on her mind she forgot to take care of herself.

She looks up, eyes roaming over me, lingering. Her gaze drops to my hands, then to her own as she reaches for her spoon.

No ring.

Shit. My stomach knots, but I stay focused on her face.

"Tell me about your dad," I say gently. "What's going on?"

She picks up her spoon, poking at her mashed potatoes. "He has cirrhosis of the liver." She pauses. "You know... from all the drinking."

I don't know much about that, only that it's not good. I expect her to say more, but she doesn't.

"Shit. I'm sorry. Can you explain it to me? Not like a nurse, just... for a regular person. Is he going to be okay?"

"His liver's not working like it should," she says quietly. "It's not processing toxins, so they've got him on fluids and meds to help clear the ammonia out of his system. He's jaundiced, his stomach's swollen..." Her voice trails off as she sets the spoon down, still full of potato.

"Yesterday he was confused. He didn't know where he was or why." She finally meets my eyes. "That means the toxins reached the brain." She takes a deep breath. "He'll probably be here a couple weeks, maybe longer. It depends how he responds to treatment. It's one of those things where only time will tell." Her voice drops even quieter. "He could stabilize and be okay for a while. It could flare up again. This could go on for years... Or he could be gone tomorrow."

She swallows hard."He most likely wouldn't qualify for a transplant if he gets worse. Not after all the drinking. And even if he did—it's a long list." I just..." Her voice breaks. "I can't lose another person I love."

She closes her eyes, shoulders sagging as a tear slips down her cheek. It takes everything in me not to rush to her side, pull her into my arms, and kiss every trace of hurt away.

"You haven't lost me," I say, voice low and steady.

She squeezes her eyes tighter as she shakes her head. "Jensen—"

"I'm right here, Alley."

She doesn't answer. Just swipes at her cheek, trying to hold it together.

When she finally opens her eyes, she avoids mine, letting my last words hang in the tension between us.

I take my first bite of chicken and chew—but not for long. A second later, I'm pounding my fist against my chest, coughing. "Holy shit," I choke out, grabbing my glass of water and downing half of it to force the bite down. "That's so dry it's a choking hazard."

Her lips curve—barely—but it's the closest thing to a smile I've seen from her in months.

"What'd you expect? It's hospital chicken. You've gotta drown that shit in gravy." She finally brings the mashed potatoes to her mouth, then pauses. "What are you, worried you're gonna get fat?" She smirks, then flips the spoon upside down and pulls it out slow, her tongue catching every last bit like it's the best thing she's tasted in weeks.

Somehow, my mouth gets even fucking drier. My dick twitches in my pants, and I let out a sharp breath of a laugh. "Would you judge me if I said yes?"

And there it is...

A smile.

The most beautiful smile stretches across her face, complete with that one dimple that puts me on my knees every goddamn time.

I'd fucking kill for that smile.

Heat flashes through my veins as I try to steady whatever the fuck's happening in my body.

"Yes." A small laugh escapes her lips as she shakes her head. "So, holding the gravy—is that your recipe for all the new muscles?"

A smirk tugs at my mouth, and I lean in a little, cocking a brow. "So, you noticed, huh?"

"Hard not to." Her eyes roam over me, slicing heat into every inch of skin as they drag across me. They land on my forearm, where I've got my sleeves pushed up just a few inches.

"And the tattoo... That's new."

I chuckle, low and deep. "Yep. A lot of things are new."

"It's like I don't even know you anymore," she says, spooning up more potatoes.

That one hits harder than I want to admit. Because in some ways, she's right. And in others, I've never felt more like myself.

"I'm the same where it counts."

My gaze follows her spoon as she brings it to her lips. She takes another bite, pulling the spoon from her mouth slow—slower than before. My eyes stay locked on her lips, and my brain short-circuits. *Jesus.*

I shift in my seat. "Alley..." I clear my throat, trying to play it cool. "If you keep sucking on that spoon like that..." I let out another low chuckle. "Fuck." My voice drops. "You trying to kill me?"

She pauses, eyes lifting to mine, brows arched. The corner of her mouth quirks. "Didn't know walking zombies turned you on."

I laugh—hard.

She grins, a little sheepish, but there's a sparkle in her eyes. "Come on. I look like hell, Jensen."

"You could never look like hell," I say, still smiling. "You look tired as shit, yeah, but still the hottest zombie I've ever seen."

"You're such a dumbass," she says, laughing.

Fuck, I'll take it. That laugh? I've missed that laugh.

"And yet..." I nudge her foot under the table. "You knew exactly what you were doing with that spoon."

"No!" She points the spoon at me, eyes wide. "I didn't realize I was doing that. I swear. I'm just really hungry."

"Sure," I murmur, "let's go with that."

She rolls her eyes, but that dimple's still there. And for a second, it feels like old times. Catches me right in the goddamn heart.

I steady my breath—her closeness, her laughter—it feels so fucking good.

Not to mention, I'm painfully turned on. It's been more than six months since I've had sex. The longest I've gone since I lost my virginity, and I can't stop picturing my wife's beautiful lips around my cock.

But it's not even about that.

I just want to take her out to a real dinner. Go for a walk. Cuddle during a movie. I want to stay up all night talking to her. I miss her.

I want to hang out with my best friend.

I let myself stare, taking her in, soaking up every second.

God, it feels like I'm standing on the edge of everything. I'm *this fucking close* to getting it all back... or losing it for good.

Chapter Fifteen

ALLEY

WHAT THE HELL am I doing?

He makes one joke about the way I was eating my potatoes, and suddenly I'm smiling like it didn't take everything in me to walk away from him five months ago. Like he didn't make our lives a living hell for two straight years. And let's not even talk about the fact that my dad's in a hospital bed fighting for his life.

I'm in a cafeteria flirting with my soon-to-be ex-husband like I'm on a dinner shift at work.

That is so messed up.

But it's also the best feeling in the world.

To be laughing with Jensen.

To feel his gaze on me.

To be turning him on.

I'd take this moment over silence any day. Over grief. Over the ache of pretending I don't care.

My heart squeezes tight in my chest. I didn't realize how much I *needed* this. *Shit. Does that mean I need him?* I can't let myself go there. I'm finally—*finally*—in a place where I can see the light again. Jensen walks back into my life for five minutes and flips the damn switch, like nothing ever happened.

The light's so bright, it's blinding me. Fooling me.

I *cannot* be this easy.

That is absolutely pathetic.

"Do you remember our ice cream fight?" Jensen asks, smirking.

That smirk—I've seen it hundreds of times, and it's still just as sexy as the first.

"Of course I remember." I scoop up another bite of potatoes, this time putting on a show. I close my eyes, wrap my lips around the spoon, and drag it out slow—soft, sinful, completely over the top. I moan, just barely, trying not to laugh.

He folds his arms across his chest, one brow raised. "So you remember what happened when you did that with the ice cream?"

"Yep," I say, lifting another spoonful to my mouth. This time, I don't bite. I lick it. Slow. Deliberate. Eyes locked on his. My tongue flicks along the back of the spoon, teasing and playful. "I don't think you're going to tackle me in the cafeteria."

His jaw flexes. His eyes drop to my mouth. And just like that, it's like all the air's been sucked out of the room.

For a split second, he looks at me like he used to, right before we'd... well, you know.

Like he wants me.

More than just this.

Like nothing else exists.

Like it hurts to look at me.

Then he blinks, clears his throat, and looks away.

The tension fizzles fast, reality pouring cold water over the moment. God, I hate how quickly I miss what was just there.

I set the spoon down, suddenly needing to ground myself in something solid. Something safe.

What was that?

It's like muscle memory kicked in.

This is *me* and *Jensen*.

It felt so natural—*so normal*—I didn't even think about what it might do to him.

Or to me.

"Sorry," I murmur, eyes dropping. "Got carried away."

"It's fine, Al."

"So…" I force my gaze back to his. "Tell me about Switzerland." I offer a small smile, a peace offering, and he takes it.

"Switzerland was great. Cold as shit, but really beautiful. Great food. Clean air. Matt made me do a fucking polar plunge in the Alps." He chuckles, shaking his head. "Thought I'd never see my balls again."

My smile's back. It's that easy with him. "Oh my God, that's insane. I could never."

What I don't say is that I've already watched that video a hundred times… along with other things I probably shouldn't admit to.

He keeps talking—about the mountains, the hikes, the long talks with Matt.

"I loved it. And I'm really glad I got to spend that time with Matt. It was good for us, but—" He pauses, eyes catching mine. "I kept thinking about you. Wishing you were there."

He shrugs. "I don't know. You've always wanted to go. It just… didn't feel right without you."

My eyes sting. My throat tightens. *Goddammit.* We were feeling the same thing, thousands of miles apart. I do want to go to Switzerland. Badly. And even now, after everything, I still want to go with *him*.

"It sounds like you had a great time either way," I say softly. "I'm happy you got to experience that."

I shift the conversation, asking more questions about his family, his job…

But I don't ask about rehab.

Part of me doesn't want to hear about it. I *can't* hear about it.

Not after everything I've done to forget. Every day, I fight to erase certain memories from my mind, haunting images of Jensen. Of our home. Of the shit I had to see.

I don't want to talk about anything that takes me back there.

So I sit here with him because this feels like old Jensen. Like old times—if old times had a giant crack running through the middle. But mostly, it just feels good.

And I need all the feel-goods I can get.

It doesn't mean I'm seeing him tomorrow. Or next week. Or that I'm not signing the divorce papers.

It just means I'm still human.

And for now, I'm letting myself feel something other than pain. Even if it's just for tonight.

Even if it breaks me again tomorrow.

* * *

I ADJUST the pillow beneath my head, the plastic lining crinkling in my ear. I'm on the couch, curled on my side, facing Jensen. He's angled toward me, elbow propped on the back, head resting in his hand.

My dad's asleep, he has been for over an hour. It was a busy day with visitors and tests. He was moved out of the ICU earlier today, after the doctor made his final rounds. All things considered, he's doing well.

Now that he's more stable, the visiting rules are a little more relaxed. I even have a bigger recliner now. Plus this couch. I'm praying I actually get some decent sleep tonight.

Megan and Matt flew home yesterday after spending the morning here. But Jensen's still here. He's been with me the past three days.

He's crashing at Matt's condo while he's in town. He went back there after they left to take a few meetings he couldn't miss. He's leaving tomorrow night—needs to be back in the office Monday morning.

There's been a comfort to having him here.

I've been carrying this ache in my heart for years. It started small, just a crack. But with every lie, every tear, every slammed door—every time I begged him to stop—it grew. Until it felt like a wrecking ball had torn straight through it.

It finally feels like that hole might be patching up.

Even though Jensen's the one helping mend it, I'm not letting myself forget that he's also the one who put it there.

It's been nice, though—hanging out, talking, laughing, like before.

He stands and I watch, wide-eyed, with a grin plastered to my face, as he turns toward me and pounds his chest like a gorilla. Then he bends both elbows, brings his fists together, and flexes, letting out a whispered roar.

I laugh as quietly as I can. "That Yankees fan was more entertaining than the game. But he unbuttoned his shirt first, remember?"

Jensen chuckles. "Is that my cue to take off my shirt?"

I shake my head, rolling my eyes and smothering a laugh. But also —*yes please. Take it off.*

"I'm joking," he says with a grin. "How could I forget? He had a giant NY tattooed on his chest."

"Oh my God, yes. He was a die-hard fan."

We'd gone to Boston for a quick weekend getaway to see a Red Sox–Yankees game. There was a wild Yankees fan in front of us.

He wasn't just a fan. He lived, breathed, and slept Yankees. Full on uniform. His Brooklyn accent carried through the entire section.

When the Yankees hit a home run, he stood, turned to face us, ripped open his shirt, and roared like a gorilla.

It was hilarious.

"How many beers do you think he had?" I ask.

Jensen sits back down, facing me. "God, who knows? At least seven. But it felt like he pre-gamed hard. He was loud before the anthem even played."

"He was a lot, for sure." My cheeks ache from smiling. We've had a lot of laughs down memory lane tonight. "That trip was fun."

"Yeah. It was... We've had a lot of great trips."

"We have."

His eyes burn into mine, and it's so comfortable, so familiar, but it sparks a buzz under my skin. I look away, letting my gaze wander around the room until it lands on a plant one of Dad's neighbors dropped off. I laugh quietly to myself. Like Dad could ever keep a plant alive.

I turn back to Jensen. "How's Phyllis?"

"Random subject change," he says with a grin, "but alive and thriving. I know how important she is to you."

My brows pull together. "But you were gone for three months. Who watered her?"

"I told Matt when I left that if I came home and Phyllis was dead..." He puffs out a laugh. "I'd have no shot at getting you back."

That makes me laugh. "Are you serious?"

"Dead."

"Thank you."

He leans in just a little, his voice softer. "All I ever want is to make you happy, babe."

Babe.

He keeps calling me that, like old times—like we've fallen back into the roles of husband and wife.

I don't stop him.

His expression shifts, serious now, as his eyes roam over my face with something I can only describe as longing. Butterflies stir low in my stomach, an almost foreign feeling.

I forgot.

Forgot what it feels like—

To have Jensen Adams look at me like that.

"You should come see her." He scoots a little closer, his hand reaching for mine. He takes it gently, rests it on the couch between us, and starts tracing my palm with his finger.

His touch glides across my skin, mapping the lines and patterns like he's memorizing them.

Holy shit, I can't breathe.

A current shoots straight to my core, igniting something that's been buried for too long.

Desire. Fear. Need.

It all collides inside me, swirling until I can't tell one from the other.

He smooths his palm flat against mine. "Al," he says softly, his voice low.

"Don't," I whisper, my vision blurring. "Please, don't."

I don't know what's happening.

And I don't know what to do.

His eyes flutter shut, and he takes a deep breath. He doesn't speak, just squeezes my hand, then lets go.

"I should go," he says quietly, pushing up from the couch.

Panic shoots through my chest, and I sit up straighter. "No, wait."

He pauses.

"Stay." My voice is barely a breath. "Please."

His shoulders drop slightly, like the weight of those words hits somewhere deep. He hesitates, then nods once, silently, and sinks back down beside me.

Good Lord, I don't even know if I want him to come or go. To push him away or pull him close. I've never been more confused in my life. All I know is, I don't want him to leave. I want to be near him.

None of it makes sense anymore.

I shift closer, placing my pillow near his leg, and lie down, my hands resting near my face. His fingers find mine again, tugging one hand into his lap—no tracing this time. Just holding. Just the quiet comfort of skin on skin and my husband's familiar presence.

I stare at my dad, exhaustion pressing heavy on my chest. *We can't control the cards we're dealt, only how we play the hand.*

That's what he said on Christmas Eve. And right now, I feel like I've just been dealt one card short of a royal flush.

Do I throw it and risk everything—pray for the one I need to win?

Or fold before I lose it all, again?

The odds aren't great.

Thirty percent.

That's how many like Jensen make it past the first year and stay clean. On a good day.

Maybe I don't have to decide yet. Maybe I just let this be what it is —time with Jensen. Not a choice. Not a fork in the road.

Just... this.

His fingers drift into my hair, combing gently.

It's not clarity. It's not a decision. But it feels good. And for now, that's enough.

I close my eyes, letting the calm flood in, soft and steady. Jensen's touch grounds me like a live wire finally cut.

The thoughts slow.

The buzz of exhaustion begins to fade.

And for the first time in days, I sleep.

* * *

I STIR at the sound of hushed voices in the distance. I crack an eye open, just enough to see that it's still mostly dark, with a faint glow coming from the other side of the room. Must be the nurses taking Dad's vitals and distributing meds. I snuggle back into my pillow, relief sweeping through me when I realize how well I slept.

Jensen's voice cuts through the quiet, and suddenly I'm wide awake. I strain to hear, opening my eyes like that might help.

Jensen's standing near the bed. It's inclined just enough for my dad to take a drink. The dim light above him is on, and my dad looks more alive than he has since I arrived.

"Can I get you anything else?" Jensen asks, placing the water jug back on the tray.

My heart lurches—Jensen's only met my dad a couple of times. He doesn't know him. They don't have a relationship. Yet, he's up early, helping him like he would his own dad.

"No, I think that's all for now. Thank you. I'll let you get back to sleep."

"Actually," Jensen says, "I'd love to talk, if you're up for it."

My dad's brows furrow. "Yeah, sure."

Jensen turns, and I quickly shut my eyes. When I peek again, he's pulled a chair close to the bed and is sitting—bent forward, elbows on his knees.

"Listen, Craig, I know I'm probably the last person you want to see or talk to. You don't even know me. But I've got a list. People I need to talk to. You're on it." He clears his throat. "I'm working through the steps. One of them is making amends with the people I've hurt."

"I'm very aware of the steps, son. And I appreciate what you're doing. But I hardly know you. You don't owe me anything."

Jensen's head falls. I watch his shoulders rise and fall. He rubs a hand over his mouth. Then he lifts his gaze again and meets my dad's eyes. "Yes, I do. I hurt your daughter. And no words will ever make up for what I've done. Nothing I do can erase the hell I put her through." His voice cracks. "But I want you to know I'll spend the rest of my life trying. If she'll let me. There's nothing I want more than to show her how much she means to me. How much I've changed."

He leans back in the chair. "Anyway... I don't expect forgiveness. Not from you. Not even from her. But I needed to say that. To let you know how sorry I am. And I hope I can have your blessing—to at least earn the chance to be in her life again."

My dad's face is somber and serious. He's listening, and every line etched into his skin shows it. The corners of his mouth twitch briefly before settling again. "I know how sorry you are. And I know you never meant to hurt her. I also know you love her."

He presses the button on the side of the bed, sitting up a little straighter. "I've been in your shoes. And because of that, I can't knowingly give you my blessing."

Jensen's shoulders sag.

"But I also won't discourage it." His tone softens. "You're your own man. A good one, at that. You come with your demons and your battles, but I understand it's your duty to love her. Protect her. Make her happy."

He draws in a shaky breath. "You made promises. And you broke them. You hurt her." His lips tremble, and his voice cracks. I struggle to keep my own eyes dry. "God knows you hurt her." He cries now. The tears fall freely, his voice choking. "Goddamn, you put her through the same thing I put her mother through. And I hate you for it. I really do."

Yeah, there's no point trying to hold back tears. Not with my dad crying. Not when every word he says cuts like it's for me, too.

I can't see Jensen's face from here, but I catch a hand lifting to it—maybe gripping his jaw, or covering his mouth. I'm not sure.

My dad swipes at his cheek, and it's so raw—so beautiful in its own way, seeing him like this. Being a father in a way I didn't know he was capable of until recently. Defending me. Loving me. *God, it kills me.*

My dad exhales shakily, voice quieter now. "But my hell, does that girl love you." His eyes stay locked on Jensen's. "Alley's her own woman. A smart one. She's always had a good head on her shoulders, and I trust her to find her own happiness. I'm not going to tell you what you can or can't do. You do what you need to do as a man. As a husband. She'll make her own choice. Whether that's you or someone else."

The room falls silent. For a long time.

I don't know if Jensen doesn't have the words, or if he's too choked up to say them.

Finally, his voice breaks through the stillness. "Thank you, sir. For saying that. Because, what kind of man would I be if I didn't fight for her?"

"The kind that realizes what's best for Alley might not be what's best for you." My dad says quietly. "And if you really love her, you'll be brave enough to let her decide."

I press a hand to my chest, trying to steady the ache.

God, Dad.

He always knows exactly what to say. I close my eyes, the weight of his words settling in the room.

Jensen wanted permission.

But Dad gave me the power.

Chapter Sixteen

JENSEN

"IT'S NOT YOU, Jensen. This CFO's riding my ass like he gets off on it —calls, emails, budget reviews at seven a.m. He's fucking relentless about cutting costs. I can't afford you anymore."

Priya takes a long sip of her negroni, still holding the glass as she adds, "It's either cut ties with you or start firing people. Something's gotta give."

My eyes follow the glass as she sets it down. It doesn't bother me that she has a drink and I don't. It's getting easier, and a flicker of pride pulses through me.

"Look, Priya, you know I don't hand out freebies like candy. But I cleared it with my team. You renew, and we'll knock fifteen percent off if you sign before the end of the month." I pause, letting that land as I reach for my water. "I'll also upgrade your package to include predictive insights and assign you direct support from our Chicago hub. That alone saves your ops team hours every week."

She's baited me, and even though I knew she would, I came prepared to walk right into her trap.

Priya Anand is ruthless. Blunt, brilliant, and easily one of my favorite people to work with. I closed my first six-figure contract with her eight years ago, and every renewal since has come with a drink, a smile, a pricey steak, and a list of fresh demands.

She wouldn't lie to me. I've built a deeply trusted relationship with her. When she says the new CFO is a tight-ass and she's found a cheaper service, I believe her. We're not the cheapest. But I also know she won't get what she gets with me anywhere else—the best experience.

Her lips press tight together. "Fuck me."

She's also crude as hell—mid-forties, single, and capable of taking even the toughest New Yorkers by the balls.

I lean back in my chair, folding my arms. "Nah. You know I have a wife, Priya. Besides, it wouldn't be good for business—you know, long term."

She lets out a soft laugh. "See? That's what I like about you. You're loyal." She pauses, takes a breath, and lets it out slow. "You always did know how to go for the kill."

Shaking her head, she picks up her glass and brings it to her lips, a wry smile peeking through the rim. "Fine." She sips her drink and sets it down. "I'll think about it. Let me run some numbers when I get back to the office. I'll get back to you by Monday."

Yes. She doesn't have to think about it. That's just the game she plays. It's a done deal.

"As always, you have my appreciation," I reply.

"I didn't say it was a sure thing."

I take a bite of my steak. "I know." But I say it with such arrogance, she just shakes her head, amusement flashing in her eyes.

She glances at her watch. "Shit. I gotta run. We good?"

I nod. "We're good."

She stands, pushing in her chair. "I'll get back to you Monday. Let you know my decision."

"Looking forward to another great year."

"We'll see." She smirks as she turns and walks away, leaving half her steak untouched, but her drink demolished.

As soon as she's out of sight, I lean back in my chair and blow out a breath. That's a weight off my shoulders.

I pull out my phone. I've got a dozen messages and emails from work—but all I care about is the text from Alley.

ALLEY

Thank you for lunch. That was sweet. How'd your meeting with Priya go?

A grin stretches across my face. It feels like things are falling back into place—slowly, but surely.

You're welcome. I just wish I could've eaten with you. Fed Priya right from my palm. She said she'd get back to me Monday, but she's in.

I DoorDashed lunch to Alley at the hospital. Her dad's been there ten days now. He's stable, but she still barely leaves. Hopefully, he'll get to go home sometime next week.

After I close my tab, I'm calling my sponsor, heading to an AA meeting, and then to the airport. It's Friday, and I'm planning to spend the weekend at Matt's place in Chicago again. I'm hoping Alley might let me take her out, maybe even get her to sleep in a real bed. It doesn't have to be mine, though that'd be fucking great.

But I'm not pushing. I know she needs time, and I'm letting her take the lead.

The server drops the check at the table. I sign, leave a fat tip, and silently pray no one at work takes a second look at this receipt.

I slip into my coat and head outside. I step onto the sidewalk and raise my hand for a cab, then freeze. My gaze locks on the bar across the street. *Whiskey's.*

My lips twitch into a half-smile.

I pull my phone from my back pocket, snap a picture, and send it to Alley.

Remember our first date?

She texts back before I can even put my phone away.

ALLEY

Of course I do. That was the best first date I'd ever had.

I grin like an idiot.

> I remember how determined I was to get you to fall for me. To be the one who made you smile. To hear your laugh again… To bring you home. I knew I wouldn't sleep again until you were my girlfriend.

I pause, press send, then add—

> It's the same determination I feel now.

I don't wait for a response. I might not get one after that. At least not right away.

I hail a cab and slide into the backseat, then turn toward the window, staring out as the city blurs past.

I just want the next eight hours to fly by.

I can't fucking wait to see her.

* * *

"COME ON, Michael and Stella will be here soon. You need to get out of here. Let's go do something," I say, practically begging.

I'd be fine doing nothing, as long as I'm with her. But she needs this—fresh air, a change of scenery—something that doesn't involve antiseptics and shitty hospital food.

I also don't want to be here when her brother shows up. I'm not quite ready for that encounter.

I've faced her dad, was even here when Leo and Adam stopped by, but big brother? I expect Michael to be the least forgiving of all.

No thank you.

Not yet.

She looks up from her Kindle—some smutty romance, I'm sure. It's what she's always reading.

Craig chimes in. "He's right. You need a break. You've hardly left my side this whole time. Now go on. Do something for you."

She feigns offense. "Rude." Her eyes flick between her dad and

125

me. With a resigned sigh, she finally gives in. "Fine. I'll go." She stands, pointing a finger at her dad. "But only because Michael's on his way."

"Good. Get out of here," her dad says with a chuckle.

She bends down and kisses her dad's cheek. "Call the nurses if you need anything before he gets here."

"Jesus," he mutters. "I'm a grown man. I can take care of myself."

She shoots him a look as she turns to me, her brows raised. I meet her gaze with a grin.

I'm beyond excited to get her out of this damn hospital. Even if it's just for a few hours.

"Alright. Let's go," she says, grabbing her coat.

I open the door and follow her to the elevator.

"Where are we going?" she asks as the doors slide open. "We already ate dinner and it's zero degrees outside."

"Don't you worry about it."

She raises an eyebrow, amused, but doesn't press it. She knows I won't tell her anyway. I've always loved planning things for her, letting her find out as the night unfolds.

It's not like I have some elaborate plan. I talked to Matt at the airport. He gave me a few ideas. Places we could go just to talk. I figured we'd grab a coffee and drive. Maybe find a park with a view. Hell, I'll even take her to the art museum. She loves that stuff. It's not for me, but it's warm, quiet, and good for conversation. Maybe even hold her hand... if she'll let me.

"Oh, you've got big plans for us, huh?" A hint of a smile tugs at her lips, and I fight every urge to kiss them. It's like fighting gravity—a natural reaction. Meant to be. Fucking science. No matter how far we've fallen, sooner or later we're bound to land. Together.

I force my gaze elsewhere as the elevator doors open. I'm a patient man. I waited a month before sleeping with Alley. Two years of being engaged. Five months clean. Those lips will touch mine again. She's a magnet. And we've always been opposites.

I just have to hold out a little longer.

"I wouldn't say big plans," I say, turning right instead of left toward the exit. "This way."

"Are we going to the cafeteria again?" Her brows pull together in a scowl, like she's genuinely disappointed.

"No. Just grabbing coffee from the café for the drive."

"Oh. Okay." I glance over, catching her expression as it softens.

Alley loves warm drinks—coffee, hot chocolate, wassail. Especially on cold winter nights. It's why we got the Nespresso. She wanted to be able to make lattes anytime. Curl up on the couch with a blanket and stare out the window.

We grab our drinks and head to her car.

"Keys," I say once we're in the parking garage.

I always drive when we're together, and she doesn't hesitate, just hands them over. Like nothing's changed.

I open her door and she slides in, then circle around to the driver's side. It's cold as hell out, our breath visible in the air.

"Hurry," she says through chattering teeth.

I slide in, turn the ignition, and crank the heat, silently praying it warms up fast.

She hugs her drink to her chest like it's her own personal space heater, and I tap one of the locations Matt sent me, heading north toward Montrose Harbor.

Alley notices and lets out a soft laugh. I barely catch it over the blast of the heater. Then she goes quiet for a second—long enough for me to wonder why. "Montrose Harbor?" she finally says, glancing sideways. "You trying to get laid?"

I chuckle, glancing at her as I pull out of the parking space. "Nah. Why would I want that? You're just my hot wife I've been dying to kiss for months."

She glances over, lips pressed tight together, dimple popping. I've seen that look before, holding back a smile, teasing... happy. She's softening. And fuck, I want to throw the car in park and pull her onto my lap. I grip the steering wheel tighter. *Soon—I hope.*

She waits a few seconds before answering, her eyes locked on the side of my face. "It's not happening. Just so you know."

"You sound disappointed," I tease. "Don't worry, if you're lucky, you might get a kiss goodnight. But..." I stop at a red light and turn to meet her gaze. "Only if you're a good girl." I cock a brow, smirking. I've peeked inside those books of hers. I've even read a few of them.

You better believe I'm going to flirt with my wife. I'll be respectful, but I'm not afraid to turn up the heat. Someone's got to remind her of the way things used to be.

She feels it. I know she does. The tension. The longing. Our chemistry has always been on another level. Last weekend, when she asked me to stay after I got up to leave? It was like she pushed me away only to pull me back.

Her eyes search mine, steady and unflinching. But that suppressed smile is still there, brows raised. "Been reading my books?" she asks, shaking her head with a soft laugh. "Then what's the plan once we get to the harbor?"

"To talk. To be with you. Just us. Without the weight of everything else. Of all the other shit."

"Hmm. I guess that would be nice."

"Unless, of course, you *want* to make out," I say, as casual as possible. "Then I'll happily rearrange the itinerary. We can save the talking for later. But only if you really *really* want to." Her grin spreads wide, and for a second, I catch a glimpse of the girl I fell for. "And hey, if you can't, I get it. But I'm sure Lola misses me. Clark reminds me ten times a day how much he misses you."

"Ten times a day, huh?" Her gaze lingers on the side of my face. "That's a lot of boners in a day. Even for Clark."

"Well, you've always been my kryptonite." I flash her a smirk. "When it comes to boners."

"I'm your kryptonite?"

I glance over, and before I can talk myself out of it, I reach for her hand, threading my fingers between hers. She lets me, but she's tense. Like she's not sure if she should pull away or relax into it.

"You've always been Clark's kryptonite," I say, giving her a sideways grin. "But me?" I shake my head, thumb brushing across her knuckles. "You're not my weakness, Alley. You're my fucking rock. My anchor."

She goes quiet. Her eyes flick to our hands, then back to the windshield. I let the silence hang, and her fingers soften around mine.

Relief floods through me, tangled with desire, as I chub up. Jesus, what am I, fourteen? I'm just holding her hand. But even that, the skin on skin, the fact that she's letting me touch her—it wakes up the part of me that misses our deeper connection. The part that *feels* her. All of her.

And sure, it involves sex, but it's more than that. Do I want to rip her pants off and bury my face in her pussy? Yeah. Of course I fucking do. But more than anything, I want to show her how much I love her. I want to worship her—in every way. Make her feel seen. Desired. Safe.

Make her feel *loved*.

Alley won't sleep with me until she trusts me again. She doesn't just give that part of herself away. No—I'll have to earn it. Just like I did the first time.

I give her hand a squeeze. "You took your ring off." My pulse kicks up a notch as I say it. I've been holding that in for over a week.

She looks down at our hands, then back up at me. "Yeah, I did. About a month ago."

She doesn't expand, and I don't press. I just dig my heels into the sand and dive in headfirst. "What can I do to get that back on your finger?"

Her lips tug upward, but fall just as fast. "I don't know. I don't know yet if it's going back on."

Jesus, she isn't going to make this easy, not even a little. This is a goddamn marathon—uphill, a thunderstorm brewing ahead, and nothing but rough, muddy terrain to trudge through.

I turn into the harbor and follow the map to the exact location Matt sent me. "Are you at least open to dating me again? Letting me take you out, earn your trust back?" I throw the car into park and look at her. "Because here's the thing, babe. Eight billion people in this world—and I only want you."

She leans back into her seat, head falling to the side to meet my gaze. Her chest rises and falls with a deep breath. She doesn't say anything, just looks at me like she's trying to decide if she can trust me or if I'm full of shit.

"All on your terms, of course," I add, because the silence is killing me. "You say jump, I say *how high*. You say kiss me..." I throw a smile her way. "I'll fucking kiss you. Tell me to go to hell…" I exhale, jaw tightening. "That one's gonna be tough, but if that's what you want"— my gaze drifts forward, nodding slowly before I look back at her— "then I'll fuck right off."

A sad smile pulls at her mouth. "I don't know what I want, Jensen." She shakes her head. "I don't know what I'm doing."

Pressure builds in my chest, but I nod anyway. "That's okay, babe." I lift her hand to my mouth, pressing my lips to her skin. "I do."

Chapter Seventeen

ALLEY

"THAT'S OKAY, BABE." He lifts my hand to his mouth, pressing his lips to my skin. "I do."

My pulse skips a beat. It shouldn't turn me on the way it does—him taking control, not afraid to go for what he wants...

But when the thing he wants is me? *God, that's hot.*

I take a shaky breath, holding his gaze as his thumb moves slowly over my skin. Goosebumps ripple up my arms, anticipation swirling low in my stomach. My heart thunders in my chest—confusing the absolute shit out of me. I'm scared. Every instinct says to run.

But I want to run straight into Jensen's arms.

I want to climb into his lap and lose myself in him. I want him to throw me into the backseat and do all the things I know he's thinking about. The things he's so damn good at.

I *wish* I could forget the last six months ever happened and just *feel* him again. But even when I try to forget, I can't. *What the hell am I supposed to do with all that?*

"Let's go back to that thing you said about a kiss," I say softly.

His lips pull into a smirk—the one that's owned me from day one. His confidence and charm? They're *my* kryptonite.

And tonight? He showed up fully charged with both.

"Yeah? What about it?"

I don't answer—afraid my lips will betray me again. A Fleetwood Mac song plays in the background and it's the only thing keeping me grounded. The silence stretches as he waits for me to answer. My lips part, but no words come. Just this ache, this want, this terrifying hope.

He leans in, tucking my hair behind my ear, and my breath catches.

Oh my God, I'm so nervous.

His lips hover near my ear as he whispers, "You want me to kiss you?"

I nod slowly, even though a part of me is screaming *no*—the scared part. The part that's hurt. The part that still remembers everything.

He pulls back just enough to meet my eyes. "I need to hear you say it, baby."

My entire body feels like a live wire as I search his face—so open, so steady. Trusting. The piercing blue of his eyes somehow striking, even in the dark. "Yeah," I whisper. "I want you to kiss me."

I want it so badly it almost hurts.

His lips curve into the sexiest grin as he cups the back of my head, his thumb brushing across my cheek. Then—with zero hesitation—he crushes his mouth to mine.

He doesn't kiss me gently.

Oh my God.

It's like he's starving.

My lips part on instinct, welcoming the warmth—the taste of mint and Jensen and memory. I melt into him, the storm inside me quieting. No thoughts. No fears. Only this. Only him.

His tongue coaxes mine, and I open further, letting him in.

It's good.

It's really, really good.

Too much and not enough, all at the same time.

I moan into his mouth. I don't mean to. Can't stop it.

"Fuck, Alley." He kisses me again, deeper this time. Rougher. Hotter. Like he needs me. Like a man who's been shipwrecked and I'm dry land.

My fingers curl in his jacket, and a steady pulse builds between my thighs. Heat spreads through me like liquid lightning.

Holy shit. I want more.

He pulls back, resting his forehead against mine. His bottom lip catches between his teeth like it's taking everything in him not to devour me.

"Jesus," he mutters, breath ragged. "I can't keep kissing you or I'm going to fuck you right here in the backseat of this car. That's where I'm at, Al. So if you're not ready—don't ask me to kiss you again unless you want the whole damn thing."

God. Is there a woman alive who wouldn't want to hear those words?

"I can wait." He chuckles—low, rough, addictive. "I've gotten good at resisting things that test my willpower. But damn, babe. You test it like nothing else ever has."

My heart pounds in my ears. My breath's caught somewhere between my chest and throat.

"Okay," I whisper, barely audible. "Let's stop, then. I'm not sure I want that."

Lies. Of course I want that. My body's begging for it.

"Yet," he says.

My brows pull together.

"You're not sure you want that *yet*," he repeats, his voice smug.

I let out a shaky laugh. "God, you're so cocky."

He grins, shaking his head. "Confident. There's a difference." Then he lifts my hand again and presses a kiss to my knuckles like he's some old-school movie star—a modern-day Jimmy Stewart. "And you love that about me. You always have."

"I guess I did miss your ego... a little."

He chuckles. "Careful, babe. You keep talking like that, you'll fall back in love with me."

His eyes find mine—and hold.

"Love was never the problem, Jensen."

He swallows hard, like that hit deeper than expected. And I'm not sure if he hears it as a blessing or a warning.

After a moment, he nods. "Guess that's a good thing, then."

I shake my head, still staring at his mouth. "Is it?" My voice is soft.

Raw. "Because it's confusing as hell for me. Wanting you—but not trusting that it'll last. Being too scared to just give in."

His thumb drags across my hand. "I get it, babe. I really do. But it's a fucking relief to hear you say love's not the problem."

"I wish I felt the same way."

His gaze moves slowly over my face, pausing at my lips before meeting my eyes again. My stomach flutters. My pulse refuses to calm.

"So when you ask me if I'll date you again... it's not that simple for me. Nothing about this is simple." I take a breath. "It's not a yes, but it's not a no either."

He takes a deep breath, then lets it out slowly. "That's good enough for me. I'll take anything in between, Alley. As long as there's still a chance."

A comfortable silence settles between us, even without a clear answer. At least everything's out in the open.

My eyes drop to Jensen's lap—briefly, but long enough to notice his erection straining against his joggers.

I can't help but smile, a soft laugh slipping out. "Good to know I still give you boners."

He groans, tipping his head back against the headrest. "God, don't start," he says, chuckling under his breath.

"What?" I tease, biting back another grin. "It's nice to know some things never change. That boner brought us together."

"I told you, you're Clark's kryptonite."

His gaze meets mine and the tension is palpable—the kind you can't joke away.

We both feel it.

And if we sit here much longer, I'm going to give in.

"Hey," he says softly. "Will you promise me something?"

"What is it?"

"Promise me, if you're really going to go through with the divorce, don't drag me along. Just tell me. Rip the damn Band-Aid off." He pauses, brows furrowing. "I'd rather hear there's no chance now than have you give me hope just to take it away later."

"I can't give you an answer right now," I admit, my voice catching. "That's the truth. I don't know if this won't still end in divorce." I pause, taking a stabilizing breath. "I want this. I really do." My eyes close, fighting the sting. "I want you."

When I look at him again, I'm not sure how I'm even holding it together. "It's all I've ever wanted. You. And for so long, that was enough." I glance down, trying to steady my breath. "But it's not anymore." I shake my head slowly. "It's not just about you. It's the addiction—I don't trust it. I don't trust that it won't show up again. In three months. Three years. Ten." I meet his eyes, voice barely holding steady. "That scares the shit out of me, Jensen."

His eyes close, lips pressing tight, like he's trying not to break.

"I want to trust that everything will be okay. That this will all work out," I say softly. "But that's where I am."

"Sucks to hear," he says. "But I can handle that."

The guilt creeps in and crashes over me all at once. I blink through the burn of fresh tears. "I'm sorry I didn't respond to your texts. That I didn't call. I've just... I've been so hurt."

I press my head into the back of the seat, trying to get a grip. "I've been struggling. I'm so fucking sad. I'm a mess. And I knew—" My voice cracks. "I knew that if I talked to you..." I glance his way. "If I saw you... I'd forgive you. I'd fall back in."

I shake my head, my throat tightening. "And it shouldn't be that easy. You put me through hell. You did some really fucked-up things."

He leans in, wrapping his arms around me the best he can over the console.

"Shit," he breathes, pulling me closer. "Fuck, babe. I know. I know."

Then he cups my cheeks—his hands trembling—and presses his lips to mine. It's firm. Desperate. Like he thinks he can kiss away the pain. The memories. The ghosts that still haunt me.

And God, I want him to.

I wish it were that easy.

But it's not.

I kiss him back—frantic. Like if I stop, I'll lose him again. For good.

His hands slide into my hair, his body shifting closer.

It feels like we're free-falling—both of us. Trusting the parachute.

Will it save us?

Or take us down together?

He pulls back, breathless, sinking into his seat. "Seriously, babe." His voice is low, gravelly. "We can't keep kissing like this if you're unsure of where you stand."

My lips tingle, and I'm practically gasping for air, stunned by his restraint.

He lets out a shaky breath, turning his head toward me. "I don't want you doing anything you'll regret. I'd rather wait until you're sure."

Then a smile spreads across his lips. "Clark can't handle emotional rejection."

A smile tugs at my mouth. I can't help but appreciate the shift. He's been vulnerable, and so have I. We both know he means *he* can't handle it. "Well, I wouldn't want to do anything to hurt Clark."

He reaches for my hand, and I weave my fingers through his.

I flash him a grin. "You know how I got caught by a cop making out in a car, shirt off and all?"

He nods. "Your first boyfriend?"

"Yeah," I say, laughing as the memory resurfaces. "It was here. In this parking lot."

His grin stretches wide. "No wonder you asked if I was trying to get laid."

"This is where everyone goes to make out—or do more—in a car. How'd you know about it?"

He huffs out a laugh. "Matt."

I laugh harder. "Why am I not surprised? Wow. He's not even from here and still knows all of Chicago's secrets to getting lucky."

We laugh together, and as it fades, the air shifts into something lighter. Something familiar. Comfortable.

We're parked beside a row of yachts, swaying gently in the breeze. I glance out over Lake Michigan, the skyline shimmering in the water below. It's beautiful here. Quiet. Secluded. The kind of place people come to escape—or hook up.

Or maybe to try again.

I've always loved this city at night.

I turn to him. "How's Matt?" I pause, drawing in a breath, and ask the question I've been avoiding—just one of many. "How are *you*?"

His eyes meet mine, and there's something soft in them. "Tonight?" He exhales. "I'm good. I'm more than good."

It's the first time I've asked about *him*.

It's a step.

I'm not sure if it's in the right direction, but it's forward.

Maybe that's what tonight's all about.

Not a reset. Not a promise.

Just... a beginning.

* * *

BY THE TIME I get back to the hospital it's late—almost 1 a.m. That's almost 2 a.m. in New York. But I need to talk to Scarlett. It's the weekend, she might be up. And if she's asleep, I know she turns her phone on silent, so I won't wake her.

I take a seat in the waiting room and call her. It rings a few times and then goes to voicemail.

I end the call right as a text comes through.

> Goodnight, babe. I love you. Looking forward to our next make-out in the backseat at Montrose harbor… Maybe we can get to second base?

I laugh softly, shaking my head.

ALLEY

> Don't hold your breath.

For two years it's been so heavy. I feel like I've been swimming with a weighted vest, holding on to Jensen—barely keeping us afloat. Trying to save us both. It's been a lot. *Too much.*

Tonight, I feel like the vest was taken off. At least a few pounds were unloaded. And that feels incredible. I'm scared shitless, but my lungs fill with air a little bit easier.

My phone vibrates in my hand. It's Scarlett.

"Hey," I say quietly. "I hope I didn't wake you."

"No, you didn't. I was just finishing something."

"Something? Or someone?"

She just laughs. "I don't have to answer that."

"Yeah, okay. So how was he?"

"Meh. I've had better."

I laugh this time.

"What's up?" she asks.

It's silent for a minute before I blurt, "I kissed Jensen—er, I let him kiss me. No, I definitely kissed him. Asked for it, even."

God, I'm a mess.

I wince as I wait for judgment, my lips pressed tight, eyes squeezed shut.

"Okaaaay," she finally says slowly, like she's still trying to wrap her head around it. Then, "Shit, Alley. I love you, but what the fuck are you doing? Did you forget how bad it got? You cried on my couch for weeks. You barely ate. Barely slept. You said you were done."

"I know." It's all I can say. I feel stupid, because she's right. Of course she's right.

She exhales loudly. "I'll support you. Always. So if this is what you want, I'm here for it. But, I need to know this is truly what you want and not just what feels good right now. That you're not getting caught up in the moment. I need to know you're thinking clearly."

"Of course I haven't forgotten. Trust me, I know how this looks. But it feels different this time. I never felt that before. I *hoped* for it. I wanted it... but I never really felt it like I do now. I mean, he's been clean for six months. *Six months.* That's half a year. A hundred and eighty days. That's a *miracle* compared to where we were. That's got to count for something. And what if, Scarlett? What if he stays clean forever? Do I want to throw away that chance? If he stays clean, there's no one else I'd rather be with."

"I know that's how you feel *right now.* You still love him. But that will fade with time. You're still young. You're beautiful. You have your whole life ahead of you. You'll find someone else. Someone who won't break your heart."

Dammit. It's harsh. But that's what I love about her. She will never sugar coat the truth. Doesn't bullshit anything. We have the kind of relationship where we give each other grace because that's what friends are supposed to do.

Even still, it stirs a bitterness deep within. Scarlett was the least forgiving and understanding of all my friends. She told me to leave from the first time I told her. And when I mentioned that he had come to visit me in the hospital, she told me to be careful. She knows me better than anyone—second only to Jensen.

"I don't want to find someone else," I mumble into the phone, holding back tears.

"But you will."

"Is that why you're still single?" *Shit.* That just slipped out. I didn't mean it like that.

"That's different," she says, no offense taken, thank God. "I'm happy with the way things are. Sure, if someone came along that checked all my boxes, I'd be happy about it. But I'm perfectly content being single. At least for now. Plus, I'm way harder to get along with than you." She pauses. "But that's beside the point. Okay. I've said my piece. Spoke my truth as best friend. And now, also because I'm your best friend, I want to know all about this kiss. *Don't* leave out any details."

A grin spreads across my face. She checks all *my* boxes when it comes to best friend. Honest *and* supportive.

I divulge the evening in full detail, leaving nothing out, and she listens, making a point to ask questions and react appropriately.

By the time I say goodbye I don't have any more clarity than before. If anything, I feel more conflicted. Scarlett's words linger, challenging my thoughts. Talking me out of the way that I feel.

I let the war between my heart and mind continue as I drift off to sleep. Giving all the fresh ammunition I can to my heart—

Because that's who I want to win.

Chapter Eighteen

ALLEY

"Mmm. Oh my God. This whipped goat cheese with the fig jam is to die for," I say, grabbing one more and popping it into my mouth.

"Ew. Goat cheese tastes like what I imagine a foot would taste like." Cooper makes a face and points to the next tray. "I like the caprese skewer things. What do you think, babe?"

She looks at Ryan, who sits next to her. He finishes off a sample of red wine and lifts a brow. "The tomato things? Not my favorite. But not a no if you love them." He reaches for the bottle and pours himself another sample. The plastic tasting cups are just slightly larger than a shot glass.

Across from me, Vivian lets out a noise that can only be described as sexual. "Oh my God. I'm with Alley. This is divine," she says, tossing the rest of her goat cheese bite into her mouth.

We're menu tasting for Ryan and Cooper's wedding this spring. Cooper said Ryan's too agreeable, so she brought us as backup to help make the tough decisions.

"So the goat cheese is out?" Sandy, the event manager, asks, pen poised above her clipboard.

"No, not yet. If everyone else likes it, I'll keep it as an option." Cooper glances at Ryan. "Babe? Can you try the goat cheese thing and tell me your thoughts?"

He picks one up and pops it into his mouth, chewing thoughtfully. "I like it."

She stares at him. "And?"

"Babe. I like all the food." He shrugs. "You know I'm just here for moral support. You brought Alley and Viv to help you decide. If you actually trusted my opinion, you wouldn't have brought them." He shoots a look at Sandy, already reaching for the wine bottle again. "I just want to make sure we're serving this wine."

Cooper shakes her head, grinning. "It's a good thing you're hot."

"I'm going to go check on the entrees," Sandy says, pushing up from her chair. "Excuse me for a few minutes." She disappears around a wall of greenery.

The wedding venue is at Lakefront Conservatory—a glass-enclosed rooftop garden that overlooks Lake Michigan. It's gorgeous and intimate, the perfect setting for a small wedding like theirs.

"Wait, have any of you tried this other cheese thing yet?" Vivian asks, biting into one of the manchego tartlets. She dabs at her lip with a napkin. "It's really good."

"No. I picked one up, but it smelled like pussy, so I put it back," Cooper says, laughing.

Ryan perks up. "Wait—which one smells like pussy?" He reaches for the manchego appetizer. "I'll be the judge of that. This one, Viv?" he asks, grabbing one.

"Watch. This'll be his favorite," Cooper mutters, rolling her eyes.

Ryan brings it to his nose and inhales dramatically. "Ah, the sweet smell of pussy," he says with a smirk, making all of us burst out laughing.

He takes a bite, washes it down with a sip of wine, then turns to Cooper. "This one's the winner." A wide grin spreads across his face as Cooper smacks his arm.

"You're absolutely useless here, you know that?"

"Yeah, but I'm useful when it matters." He pulls her in for a kiss. "Tastes and smells like cheese, babe. It's good. You'd like it."

She goes in for another kiss, and soon they're whispering to each other while Vivian shoots me a side glance.

They're cute, and their easy affection pulls a smile from me. Jensen and I used to be like that.

I was never very affectionate with any of my exes—especially not in public, but then Jensen came along and flipped my whole world upside down. He brought out a side of me I didn't know existed. A side that felt sexy and confident. I'd always been reserved with other men—almost self-conscious, constantly worried about how I came across. I never felt that with Jensen.

"Okay, I'm back," Sandy announces. "The entrees are almost ready, so if you can pick your top three, we'll clear the appetizers and move on."

Cooper turns to Vivian and me. "What are your favorites?"

"I like the goat cheese, caprese skewer, and the beef tenderloin crostini," I say.

"Goat cheese. Crab cake. Caprese," Vivian adds.

Cooper and Ryan start rattling off their picks to Sandy just as my watch buzzes with a new message. I pull out my phone.

It's from Jensen.

JENSEN

Hey, babe. Can't stop thinking about last night—about you. When will you be back? Wanna grab dinner tonight? NOT at the cafeteria.

A grin creeps onto my face as I roll my bottom lip between my teeth, heart fluttering. I fell asleep thinking about him—about our kiss, my talk with Scarlett, and the mess of confusion that is my life right now.

I'd already planned this tasting with Cooper before I knew he would be in town. He said he had work to keep him busy, but clearly, he's anxious to see me.

I'm not sure. At least another hour. We've only made it through the appetizers. You should see Ryan. He only cares about the drink menu. Lol.

JENSEN

> I remember feeling the same way when we did our tasting. Remember how many hot toddies I had? You had to drive us home. And I already know you remember that drive. 😏

The memory flashes—vivid and hot. Me driving Jensen's car, his arm stretched across the console, hand in my pants.

He fingered me until I came on Park Avenue.

I squirm in my seat. *Jesus.* Just thinking about it gives me full-body tingles, and it makes me both nervous and excited to see him again tonight.

If he wants to tease, I can tease right back.

I glance around the table. My stomach flips in that guilty, don't-want-to-get-caught kind of way. My thumbs move quickly as I type back.

> Of course I remember. The term "coming home" took on a whole new meaning. And thank you for the reminder while I'm surrounded by friends. My panties are soaked now, thanks to you.

The message turns to read, and a text bubble pops up.

He's typing.

And I hate to admit it, but I'm giddy waiting for it.

"Yo, Alley." Coopers voice cuts through the air.

My head snaps up, a grin still plastered to my face. *Shit.* I've been completely checked out, and I have no idea for how long.

Sandy's gone again. Vivian and Ryan are deep in conversation. Cooper stands up with a look that tells me I'm not as sly as I think I am. "Come with me for a sec," she says, already walking past me.

I push up from my chair and follow her around the corner behind a water feature. She turns to face me, tucking a piece of hair behind her ear.

A slow smile spreads across her lips. "Something happened. You've been different all day. You seem... happy."

My brows scrunch as I feign offense. "Wow. Should I be insulted that you think something must've happened just because I'm happy?" I ask, laughing.

She taps my elbow. "No! This is a good thing. I haven't seen you this genuinely happy... like, ever, to be honest. You've got a whole different vibe about you." She crosses her arms, waiting, then gasps as her jaw drops. "Oh my God. You had sex, didn't you?"

I haven't told Cooper or Vivian, or really anyone, much about Jensen being in town. Just that he's here for me, supporting me. Leo and Adam dropped by the hospital one night while Jensen was there, and since I've kind of turned Leo into my unofficial therapist, he knows a little. But even that's been limited.

"No! I didn't have sex." *I wish.* God, I'm so touch-starved it's pathetic. I practically came from Jensen's text, just thinking about that day in the car.

Her brow arches higher. "Then what is it? Something's different."

I could lie. But I don't want to. If there's one thing I know about Cooper, it's that she doesn't judge.

I hesitate—then finally cave. "Fine. I kissed Jensen."

Her eyes go wide, but before she can say anything, I rush on—because I'm not sure I want to hear her reaction yet. "And it was so good, Coop. Like, *really* good. But I don't know what it means. I don't know if I'm ready to give him another chance. All I know is... I loved kissing him. And I've loved spending time with him." My smile fades. Moisture gathers behind my eyes as I cross my arms and bite my thumbnail. "And I'm scared." I exhale sharply, shaking my head. "I can't just forget all the shit he put me through, you know? I want to trust him, but I don't. And it's not fair. To either of us."

She lifts a finger. "Okay, we'll circle back to the kiss because—*fuck* yes, I am here for it—but first, let's talk about this ball of anxiety you've become."

I huff out a breath, half-laughing, half-defeated. *Ball of anxiety.* That's exactly what I am.

"Look," she says gently, "I'm not a therapist. But I've had to do a lot of work these last couple of years. Yoga, meditation, Buddhist teachings—the spiritual shit I used to roll my eyes at. I had to go inward. Make it about *me*. *My* healing. *My* journey. Because, while Brad made my life a living hell, it was never really about him."

She takes a deep breath, like she's bracing to give me a whole speech. "And here's the thing—most of the time, it's not really about the other person. Sure, other people can fuck with our lives. That's no joke. But it's about us. Where we were. What we chose. Why we stayed." Her expression softens as she adds, "What we can learn."

I shift my weight, arms crossed tight—like that might somehow shield me from whatever she's about to say.

"You're trying to make sense of something that broke you."

Her lips press into a tight line, thinking, before she continues. "But maybe it's not about sense—it's about power. You know when I stopped hating Brad? When I realized I wasn't even mad at him anymore. I was mad at *myself*—for staying. And the second I stopped seeing myself as the victim in my own story... I wasn't one anymore."

I blink rapidly, gaze dropping to the floor. *God, I hate how much truth there is in her words.* They sit in my stomach like a rock. I've always said I'd rather be in my shoes than Jensen's. No one wants to be the addict. That's a shit hand.

But that doesn't mean I haven't been throwing myself a pity party for months now.

She goes on. "You love him. He loves you. But more importantly? He treats you well. He's showing up for you. He's good—down to his bones." She shakes her head. "I'm not saying stay or go. I'm saying choose. Because the second you stop living in limbo? That's when you'll feel peace again. And you'll know, once you make a decision, if it's the right path for you. I truly believe that. Energy shifts, and the universe works for us, if we allow it. If we trust it. Girl, forgive your-self. Move forward—in any direction. Just pick one. You deserve to be happy."

I swallow hard, the truth of her words settling in my throat. It's not what anyone *wants* to hear—that I'm stuck because of me. Because I haven't been brave enough to let go or move on.

It freaking sucks.

I dab at the corner of my eye, catching the tear about to fall.

But it's also empowering. The things she said. Making it about me.

What I want. What I can learn. Owning my life. I've never looked at it that way. It makes sense. Even if I still don't know what I want to do about Jensen.

What I do know? I don't want to feel this way anymore. I don't want to be the victim in my story. I was the heroine when I left. But somewhere along the way, I let fear take the reins again. I lost the power I gave myself all those months ago.

"God, that was a lot. Come here." Cooper pulls me into a hug, holding me tight. "I hope I didn't say anything that upset you. I meant every word with love. I just want to see you happy. And today? You seem happy."

I wrap my arms around her, resting my chin on her shoulder. "Thank you," I manage, my voice tight. "I really needed to hear that."

She gives me a pat before pulling back, her eyes locking with mine. "Okay, can we go back to the kiss now?"

"Coop!" Ryan's voice carries over the trickle of the water feature as he rounds the corner. "Oh, hey. There you are." He glances between us, catching the weight of whatever he's walked into. "Uh, Sandy's back with the entrees." He flashes a smile. "We need the decision makers."

"Give us two minutes. We're coming."

Ryan nods, turns, and disappears, and Cooper gives me one last squeeze. "You've got this, okay? Stop doubting yourself and just do what makes you happy."

"Thanks, Coop."

We head back to the table and I slide into my seat, then tap my phone screen, and a new message from Jensen pops up.

I swipe into it.

JENSEN

Jesus. Don't fucking tease me like that, babe. You know all you have to do is say the word—I'll have you dripping down your thighs before dessert.

Heat flashes through me, and I grip my phone, biting back the biggest grin.

Oh. My. God.

* * *

Vivian pulls the G-Wagon into her designated parking space and we step out, making our way to their townhome.

The rest of the tasting went smoothly—full of laughter and easy conversation.

Viv and I talked on the drive back. I told her about kissing Jensen. She just smiled and said, "If it felt right in the moment, that's great. I'm happy for you." No pressure. No judgment. Just support. Her and Cooper have both been through so much, and they look at life through completely different lenses. They're both wise in their own ways, and I feel lucky to have them as friends.

Leo's voice carries down the hallway as we head upstairs, along with another voice I'd recognize from a mile away.

Scarlett.

I step into the living room with a grin, locking eyes with her. She's sitting adjacent to Leo, while Isla sits cross-legged on the floor with a book.

Scarlett practically launches off the couch and barrels into me. We collide in a hug, laughing as we sway side to side like we're fifteen again.

"Oh my God!" I squeal. "This is the best surprise!"

She laughs in my ear. "I've missed you so much!" Then she turns to Vivian. "Hi, I'm Scarlett." She pulls her into a warm hug too. "Your husband is a gem, by the way," she adds, gesturing toward Leo, who's now striding over.

"We were just getting acquainted," Leo says, leaning in to kiss Vivian, "and talking about having everyone over tonight for poker and drinks. It's short notice, and I know Michael's working, but if Stella can get a sitter, I think everyone else is in."

Oh, shit... Jensen.

My gaze shifts to Leo. "Jensen's still here," I say, glancing at my watch. "I'm actually supposed to get him in an hour. We were going to visit my dad, and then grab dinner."

The tension in the room tightens, just slightly. I swallow against the cottony lump forming in my throat.

147

I know Leo and Vivian don't care. But Scarlett's different—she'll be harder to get on board, slower to warm back up to Jensen. She's protective, and she witnessed a lot of it. And she's not quick to forgive. Even though she said she'd support me, the other things she said still echo in my mind, twenty-four seven.

I flick my eyes between Scarlett, Leo, and Vivian. "Do any of you mind if he comes?"

"Not at all. He's more than welcome," Leo says.

"I'm excited to meet him," Vivian adds at the same time.

I turn to Scarlett.

Her eyes drop for half a second with a flicker of disappointment flashing before she smooths it over with a neutral smile. It guts me. I know exactly what that look means.

She sighs. "Of course I don't care. Not that it's up to me. And you know I love Jensen. I just love you more."

"Thank you," I whisper, pulling her into another hug.

She squeezes me, then leans back. "You should go get him. Visit your dad, grab dinner. I've got a friend downtown I can kill a few hours with. I'll just meet you back here after."

I arch a brow. "You sure?"

"Yes. I'm here until Tuesday. We'll have plenty of time."

My lips curve into a grin. "You're the best."

Chapter Nineteen

JENSEN

It's been almost twenty-four hours since we kissed in the car. Since her lips met mine after she asked me to kiss her. Since I had to resist the temptation that is my wife.

Being an addict and being around the thing that used to fill the craving is hard. Detoxing, rehab, getting clean... it nearly breaks a person. The physical pain. The mental unraveling. It's excruciating in so many ways.

But the thing with addiction now that I'm clean is—I rarely think about it. Yeah, I've wanted to drink a handful of times. I've wanted to take a painkiller—but I haven't wanted Oxy. I haven't wanted coke. Not since rehab.

But Alley? Jesus. She makes everything else feel easier. I might not be in physical pain without her, but the ache? It's worse. Relentless. Never stops. Not getting another taste of those perfect fucking lips would haunt me for months. The hunger I feel for her would never end. My heart would never stop bleeding. Being without her could rip my fucking soul in two.

I can't stop thinking about it all. The kiss. The way she looked at me afterward. The part where it looked like it killed her to stop as much as it did me. The way she had to catch her breath after I pulled back, but then said she wasn't ready—like she remembered she wasn't supposed to want that.

"What else do you need before we go?"

Alley's voice pulls me from my thoughts. She shuffles around the hospital bed, handing Craig his water with one hand, a pile of trash from his tray in the other. She tosses it in the garbage by the door, then turns back just as her dad's sitting up to set the jug back on the tray.

"Here, let me get that," she says.

"Jesus Christ," he mumbles. "I'm perfectly capable of putting my water back."

"I know you are."

I watch her with quiet awe. The way she moves—efficient, patient, gentle. She doesn't even flinch at his tone. Just keeps taking care of him. That's who she is. Always putting others first, even when they don't make it easy. It's one of the many things I love about her.

She's going to be an incredible mother one day. I just hope I'm the one who gets to see it.

A sting burns in the back of my throat. We were trying to get pregnant a few years ago, right after we got married. Before I went and fucked everything up. Before I became someone she couldn't trust.

We started using condoms after that, not that we were having much sex. My libido was shot to shit, and I was gone all the time—physically and emotionally.

God, I was such a dick.

Out of nowhere, a half-memory tumbles in. It scratches at the surface, faint.

Did she push me off her?

I think we were in the middle of doing it one night and she got mad.

Fuck. I can't be sure. It's blurry. Like my mind won't let me go back there.

"Dad, stop. Just let me get it. You're supposed to take it easy."

Craig scowls. "How is me getting up for my book not taking it easy? I walk around these halls every damn day. I can get it myself. It'd be good for me."

He's stubborn, and I get it. Wanting to do things yourself. Needing to prove you're capable.

"I'm sorry. You're right. I can't help myself. I don't know how to be here and not work. To not *do* something."

She carries so much guilt when it comes to her dad. Has for years. Even back when we first met, she pretended to be sure of her decision to shut him out, but I knew better. She's always felt the weight of it.

I drop my gaze to the floor, trying to get a grip. *Christ.* These past few years have broken me open in ways I never expected. I used to be able to count on one hand the number of times I'd cried as an adult.

Now?

I've lost track.

"Well then, get out of here." His face softens. "You've done enough, Alley girl. You've been here almost as much as I have. Go on. Enjoy your night."

He may be stubborn, but he's got a heart of gold and a soft spot for Alley.

"Alright, I'm leaving."

My mind wanders back to the memory. *Did she push me off? Did I do something?*

It's almost there. So close...

"Hey." Her voice breaks through. "You ready?"

"Yep," I say, catching a smile before she turns and makes her way to the couch. My eyes zero in on her ass as she bends to grab her coat and purse.

She's wearing leggings. My favorite ones too. Her ass looks incredible in them.

Normally I'd make a dirty comment about how she's gonna get it wearing those in front of me.

But tonight, I bite my tongue. Because she's obviously not going to get it. And I don't know when she will...

If she will.

She turns back around, and I clear my throat, shoving the desire down. Last thing I need is to get hard in front of her dad.

We say our goodbyes to Craig, and I open the door for her,

following close behind. I reach for her hand as we make our way down the main hall.

She takes it in hers, lacing her fingers between mine.

Like before.

Her hands are cold, and all I can think about is warming them up —warming *her* up. Getting her hot.

Sweaty.

Jesus, what's wrong with me? We barely left the room and now three seconds of contact and I'm thinking about sex again?

She gives my hand a squeeze. "Thanks for coming with me to visit Dad. Means a lot."

I glance toward her. Dark brown eyes stare back at me, shining with gratitude and...

Is that hope? Desire?

Fuck. Does she want me right now, too?

Fucking.

Stop.

Dumbass.

"Of course. I like coming to visit your dad." I nudge her shoulder gently. "Doesn't hurt that I get to hang out with you."

Her lips curl into a smile as we round the corner, approaching the meditation room—a room that's dimly lit and quiet. No one ever goes in there.

No one ever goes in there.

My pulse picks up. I haven't stopped thinking about our little make-out last night for one second. Had to rub one out when I got home—partly to avoid blue balls, but mostly because I wanted to.

The sudden urge to be alone with Alley spreads through me like wildfire. Anticipation climbs up my neck—impossible to ignore.

I glance at her, realizing she just said something and I have no idea what it was. She's looking at me, eyes bright, smiling wide, that dimple peeking through.

I swallow the lump of nerves building in my throat, an unfamiliar feeling when it comes to anything sexual.

Fuck it.

I open the door to the meditation room and pull her in. It's empty. *Thank God.*

"Jensen, what are you—"

The door clicks shut behind us, and I press her back against the wall. My lips are on hers before she can even finish the sentence.

Her mouth opens for me—hot, ready.

Fucking needy.

Jesus Christ. This woman.

Last night's kiss was careful. This? This is desperate—for both of us. Like neither of us could wait another minute to finish what we started.

My hand cups the back of her neck, thumb trailing along her jaw. The other grips her hip, pulling her taut against my already hardening cock.

Her hands travel up my torso, across my chest, then around my neck. She gasps as my hand moves, sliding up to her tits. I swipe across one—testing the waters, waiting to see if she stops me.

She doesn't.

Instead, she groans into my mouth and tugs at my neck, scraping her teeth along my bottom lip before sucking it in. A gentle reminder of what that mouth can do to my cock.

Holy shit. She's pulling all her best moves here when it comes to making out.

She rolls her hips into my firm length and I let out a brazen, "Fuck."

I palm her breast, then skim my thumb across her pointed nipple.

"Fuck, baby. No bra?"

Alley has little boobs, and I fucking love them. But I didn't expect to find her braless. My dick immediately approves, pressing harder against my jeans.

She laughs softly in my ear as I press my mouth to her neck, sucking at her skin. My thumb and forefinger pinch at her nipple through her shirt, making it stiffen even more.

Her fingers dig into my shoulders. "Oh my God, Jensen." Her voice is breathy, hot against my face.

My lips crush back into hers. I'm not thinking anymore. The craving I have for her consumes everything else.

But I can't *not think* when it comes to Alley. I can't push her into something she's not ready for.

And what? Are we really going to fuck right here in the meditation room?

I don't know where the plan went sideways. I just meant to steal a kiss. Remind her what we had last night—what we've always had. But now my cock is aching for her more than ever, and fuck, I've never wanted to rip her clothes off and thrust into her more than I do right now.

I bring both hands to her face, cupping her cheeks gently, and pour all that pent-up tension into a kiss.

Then, I force myself to slow down. To breathe. To stay in control.

Be the man she needs.

The man she deserves.

Her hands roam down my body, slipping toward the hem of my shirt.

I break the kiss and wrap my hands around hers, bringing them to my chest. I chuckle softly, low and deep. "I want to say I'm sorry," I murmur, pressing a kiss to her pinkies, "but I'm not."

She presses her lips together, trying to hide a smile, but her dimple gives her away. Her cheeks flush pink. I love when Alley blushes.

It's cute as hell—and a total turn-on.

"You've always had a way of getting me to do things I'd normally never do."

"You used to trust me." I tilt her chin up, locking my eyes on hers. "I like to think there's still a small part of you that does."

Her gaze searches mine, and I freeze. Not sure why the hell I said that.

She most definitely doesn't trust me anymore. I wouldn't be here trying to earn it back if she did. We'd be in New York. She'd still have her job at the hospital. Shit, we might even have a kid.

I force the thoughts away. No point dwelling on what we don't have when she's standing right here.

"And for the record?" I add, brushing a kiss against the corner of her mouth, "that's not even a sliver of what I dream about getting you to do." I smirk, then soften my voice. "But I can wait. There's no pressure. I want you to be ready. And more importantly, I want you to trust me."

She just half-smiles, still catching her breath. That's all.

No *I'm getting there.*

No *I do trust you.*

Just a half-smile.

And I guess if that's all I get...

It's all I get.

I release her hands and turn for the door, opening it and stepping into the hall.

She follows, then reaches for my hand, gripping it tight.

She reached for *my* hand. Maybe I get a little more than a half-smile. Maybe this is her way of telling me she's trying to trust me again.

It's not a promise. But it's effort. And after everything I put her through? Effort means everything.

I'll fucking take it.

* * *

WELL, this is officially the most uncomfortable I've been since rehab... or maybe ever. I'm not awkward in social situations, even when they're new. I've always been an extrovert. Good with people. Confident.

We're all seated around Leo's poker table on the first floor of his townhome. The place has four or five levels, I'm not quite sure, but it's big. All I know is I'm on the lowest one with Leo, Alley, Cooper, Ryan, Adam—and Scarlett, who no doubt hates me.

This is so unlike me. To feel out of place. Intimidated. I'm Jensen Fucking Adams. I walk into rooms and command them. But here?

Here, I feel stupid as shit. Like I've got something to prove. And Scarlett's glares sure as hell aren't helping.

Leo tosses his cards onto the pile. "Fuck all, again. That's four hands in a row." He drains the last of his whiskey with a dramatic sigh. "I need another drink and a bloody miracle."

"It's a good thing you're not poor," Ryan quips, and he and Adam both crack up.

Leo leans back, lights a cigar, and takes a long drag. "I'm going to be if you keep taking all my money." He passes the cigars around, and Ryan, Adam, and Cooper each grab one.

"I've got jack shit again too," I say, throwing my cards down.

I used to love this. Drink in one hand, cigar in the other, chips stacked high, my girl laughing beside me. Nights like this used to be my favorite. Now I'm sipping sparkling water like a fucking child.

It's hard tonight. I want a drink. I want to loosen up, laugh, feel included.

But it's fine.

I'm fine.

Adam gathers the cards and starts to shuffle, and Leo stands to refill his drink.

I've always liked Leo, and everyone else here has been great. But it's not like Leo doesn't know all my darkest shit. He's a therapist, for Christ's sake, and Alley lives here. I know she talks to him. She always has.

I don't know what the rest of them know or don't know. But they know she moved here because of me. That she was going to divorce me. That she's been sad—because of me.

Laughter buzzes around the table. Even Alley's laughing, tucked between me and Adam, and it pulls a smile from me.

Vivian's not playing. She was upstairs earlier, putting the kids to bed. Now she's curled up on the couch with a glass of wine, just taking it all in. She chimes in occasionally, but it looks like she's thoroughly enjoying the break and relaxation.

Cooper stands, pushing her chips to Ryan. "Here, babe. I'm all pokered out."

"Me too," Scarlett says, nudging Adam—who she's been flirting with all night. "Do you want my chips?"

It irritates me.

Look, I've always liked Scarlett. She's always been part of my life with Alley. She's Alley's best friend—so, by default, she's my friend. But right after Alley first told her about my addiction, she told Alley to leave. *Leave him.* Like I was some expired item. *Toss him aside and move on.* Like I wasn't her best friend's husband. Or the guy who helped her move when no one else could. Or the guy who let her crash on our couch after her breakup with that one asshole.

Jesus. I watched her throw herself at Matt for five fucking years, and now she's doing the same thing with Adam?

Okay, that's petty as hell. I know. But I'm wound so tight tonight I can barely think straight. And it's getting to me...

Because she's acting like she fucking hates me.

I just wish she gave a shit that I'm trying to make it right.

Cooper strides to the bar along the back wall and opens the fridge. "Who wants another drink?"

"Beer me, babe!" Ryan calls out.

She pulls one out and sets it on the bar.

"Hey, Al," Cooper calls over her shoulder. "There's a few stouts in here. You want one?"

"No, I'm good. Thanks though."

"Really?" Cooper turns, brow raised. "You love a stout."

"I'm not drinking tonight," Alley says coolly.

My eyes shift to her. "Babe, if you're not drinking because of me... you don't have to do that. Seriously. Have a beer. I'm good."

"No, babe." *She called me babe.* She hasn't called me that in months. "If you're not drinking..." She shrugs. "Why would I?"

I shit you not—I think I just fell in love with my wife all over again.

I catch Scarlett rolling her eyes. "I'll take one," she says, throwing me a look as she stands and joins Cooper at the bar.

I take a deep breath, biting my tongue. If we were in New York, I'd say something. Have a come-to-Jesus moment with her. But I can't do that here.

Cooper brings Ryan's beer over and starts collecting empty bottles and glasses. "Jesus, babe. How drunk are you?"

"Pretty fucking drunk, babe. But whatever I'm doing—it's working." He nods at his mountain of chips, and she laughs, leaning down to meet his lips with a kiss.

Adam tosses his cards into the pile. "I'm out." He stands and stretches. "Hey, Coop, I'll take one of those beers."

"And I will raise..." Alley says, counting her chips. "Seven. Because that's all I have left." She laughs, and Leo, Ryan, and I all match the bet before flipping our cards.

Ryan wins. Again.

"That was the last of my bloody chips," Leo mutters, taking a long sip of his freshly poured whiskey.

"Damn. Me too." Alley tosses her cards into the pile but stays put along with Leo.

"Don't look now," she whispers, nudging me, "but Scarlett may have found her next victim."

I glance across the room. Adam's on a stool, legs spread wide. Scarlett's standing between them, her hand sliding along his bicep.

That's Scarlett—being Scarlett.

My leg bounces under the table, anxiety pouring out of every limb.

"I don't know why I never thought about them. God, they'd actually be so great together." Alley's grin stretches wide as her hand drops to my thigh, steadying it—steadying me. Like she knows what a mess I am inside.

I glance down at her, then smile. She always sees the best in people. She's not noticing the fact that Scarlett's practically auditioning to fuck Adam, or that she seems to loathe me tonight. She just sees her friend, trying to find someone who makes her happy.

And she sees me. Nervous. Out of my element.

Trying.

I wrap my arm around her shoulder, give it a squeeze, and pull her close. I kiss her temple. "I love you," I murmur, before I can stop myself. It just slipped out. But it's what I feel. And I'm tired of holding it in. I love her too much not to say it.

She doesn't say it back, but she smiles and laces her fingers through mine. My thumb strokes hers as Ryan deals the next hand. I'm almost out of chips, but I couldn't care less. All that matters is that my wife is holding my hand. That she invited me here to be with her friends. She's giving me a second chance...

Or fiftieth.

Four hands later, Ryan's swept the table and I'm out. Everyone's buzzed or drunk by now—except Alley and me. Early 2000s hip-hop plays over the speakers, and Vivian's passed the video baby monitor off to Leo and is pouring herself another glass of wine.

The group's scattered between the bar and the couches. I'm standing at the bar—with my fucking water—across from Ryan.

Tonight's the first time I've met him, and he's cool. He's in tech, I'm in SaaS, and there's a decent amount of overlap. Conversation's been easy. He's asked a lot of questions about me, what I do, even how things are going with Alley. He's taken an interest, and I appreciate it more than I'd like to admit.

Alley brushes past me, opening the fridge and bending down for another sparkling water. My eyes drift to her ass, still listening as Ryan talks about working with Cooper. She straightens, and my gaze shifts back to him.

He and Cooper have a wild story.

A moment later, I feel a hand low on my back as Alley scoots in beside me.

She waits for a pause in the conversation before cutting in. "Ryan, did you tell Jensen about the first time you met Matt?"

Ryan throws his head back with a laugh. "No. Forgot you two are tight."

"Oh, they're not just tight," Alley says, turning to me with a grin. "They're like brothers."

"What happened?" I ask, already bracing myself for a Matt story.

"We were at Tapped Out, the club Matt owns with Leo. They'd been making rounds all night, and Cooper was at the bar. Matt hadn't met anyone in our group yet. He hit on her, and she told him she was engaged, so he backed off and moved on."

He pauses to take a sip of his beer. "About an hour later, Leo brings him over to meet everyone. Matt looks at Coop, then me, and goes, *Shit. I'm sorry, man. I totally hit on your fiancée. Good for you though—she's hot.*"

Ryan chuckles. "He just fucking owned it. Didn't even try to play it off. I thought that was pretty cool of him." He laughs again. "We gave him shit all night, and he took it like a champ. Cooper even threw in some jabs, like—*Hey, Matt, I'm heading to the ladies' room. If you're gonna watch me walk away, just be sly about it."*

We all laugh now, and Alley shifts, positioning herself in front of me. She leans back, then takes my arms and wraps them around her.

What the hell? Ten minutes ago, I felt completely out of place. Now I'm standing here, holding Alley in front of everyone, and it's the closest I've felt to normal in weeks. Her making the move? Her choosing this? It's more than I could've hoped for tonight.

I pull her in tighter, resting my chin on her head. Something inside me settles, easing all the discomfort from earlier. It feels right, like all the pieces are starting to fall back into place.

I soften into her.

Well... not all of me.

One part stiffens, pressed right up against the curve of her ass.

Our laughter fades, and Cooper comes over, stealing Ryan's attention. But not before he says, "It's great to have you here, man."

"Thanks. Good to be here."

Alley turns, her arms sliding around my back, chin tilted up toward me. "You were really great tonight," she whispers. "Thanks for being here."

"I just want to be wherever you are, babe." I press a quick kiss to her lips.

She lays her ear against my chest and tightens her grip around me. I close my eyes and breathe her in. The scent of her shampoo fills my nostrils—coconut, vanilla, and the beach in Hawaii.

It smells like our shower. Her pillow. Memories.

It smells like her. And *God,* I don't ever want to stop smelling that smell.

Reminds me of our first date—the hug goodnight after I kissed her for the first time. The first night she slept over. The first shower I took after she moved in.

Fuck, I love that smell.

But I love it most when it's on her.

Chapter Twenty

JENSEN

"Matt, will you hand me the salad?" Megan asks, slathering butter on a thick slice of sourdough. He passes it over, and then her eyes land on me. "So, what's new with Alley? Are you guys getting back together? Is she coming to the Berkshires? And—because we're all dying to know—have you, you know..." She glances toward my niece and nephew at the counter, then lowers her voice. "Slept together?"

Megan texted Matt and me earlier asking if we wanted to come over for Sunday dinner. I'd just landed from Chicago a couple hours ago—barely had time to go home and shower before Matt showed up at my door ready to go.

Alley was with Scarlett all day, so I moved my flight up. Figured if I wasn't seeing her, I might as well get back early.

I finish chewing my roast and wash it down with a swig of water. "I don't know if we're getting back together. I haven't asked her about the Berkshires. And not that it's any of your business"—I stab my fork into a potato—"but no. We haven't." I pop a carrot into my mouth and chew. "I'm hopeful, though. Soon."

Megan frowns, letting out a sigh. "Dammit. I thought you guys were spending all this time together?"

"We are."

"So, what—you've just been talking?"

"That's kind of how it works, Meg."

Matt chuckles, lifting his glass of Cabernet to his lips.

Megan shoots him a glare. "I *know* how it works," she says defensively. "I'm just surprised that's *all* that's happened. I was hoping you'd be a little farther along in this whole *win-her-back* journey." She sets her fork down. "I really want her to come to the Berkshires. Are you asking her soon? Amber and I are booking spa appointments. I need to know if it's for two or three."

"Jesus, do you hear yourself?" Matt says, thank God. "Do you realize how selfish that sounds right now?"

Megan scowls. I'm used to her being this way. Blunt. Selfish. But for fuck's sake, read the room.

"Hey," Kevin cuts in. "Not cool, man." He glances at Matt, then turns to me. "She just misses her."

Only Matt really knows what's been going on. He's the only one I've told about the kiss Friday night, and I texted him this morning about the whole meditation room situation. And Leo's.

"It's fine," I say, mostly to Matt, then turn to Megan. "I'm sorry I can't give you a clear answer on the Berkshires. I'd say just book it, and if she doesn't go, you can cancel. I'll pay the deposit to hold the appointment. But I don't know..." I shake my head, frustration creeping in. "I don't know where she's at with any of it."

Matt shifts in his seat. "Wait, I thought yesterday..." He trails off, hesitant. "I thought things were going well?"

Megan's eyes narrow. "What do you mean *yesterday*? What happened yesterday?"

I shoot Matt a look before answering. "Nothing, Meg. It's not a big deal." I exhale, then proceed to tell her anyway. "She kissed me. Invited me to Leo's. Introduced me to her friends. But..." I stare down at my empty plate and rub the back of my neck. *God, I don't even know how to explain it.* "She hasn't asked me anything. Not about rehab. Not about my tattoo. She hasn't told me she's mad. Hasn't brought up the past at all. She acts like nothing happened, but she doesn't trust me. I don't know what she wants... and I don't think she does either."

I pause, running my hands over my face with a groan. "It's fucking weird."

They all gape at me.

"She hasn't asked you about rehab?" Megan shakes her head. "That doesn't sound like her. That's, like, such a big deal. Such a huge thing in your life." She picks up her wine glass, then sets it down hard. "So you're not having sex, and you're not even talking about the shit that actually matters?"

My face burns. Maybe I shouldn't have told them that. This weekend was a huge win. I've been trying to shove all my fears aside, act like everything's going according to plan. Been hyping myself up for weeks. But fuck, I'm tired of pretending this isn't messing with my head.

Because it is.

My biggest fear is that she'll suddenly pull away after all these steps forward. That she'll never open up—never ask about rehab, or my rock bottom, or even tell me how she feels. I want her to know— about all of it. I want her to care.

I'm trying to trust the process. To be patient. But it's hard not to let the doubt creep in.

I nod slowly. "Seriously." My brows furrow. "I don't know what it means. If she just isn't ready... or doesn't want to know. But we can't move forward if she won't talk to me."

"Have you asked her?" Megan presses.

"No," I admit. "I haven't wanted to push. I've brought stuff up, hoping she'd ask or say something, but she doesn't. She changes the subject." I shrug. "Guess we'll have to see. This weekend was good. We really connected. She reached for my hand a few times." A low chuckle slips out. "Even called me babe."

"Well, that's great." Megan offers a small smile. "Sounds like progress is being made." She takes a sip of her wine. "So when do you think you'll ask her about the Berkshires?"

"Fuck, Megan," Matt says, laughing. "Give him a minute."

"Just book the appointment, babe," Kevin says gently. "He'll let you know when he talks to her."

"Fine. I will." Megan presses her lips together "Sorry, little brother. I hope it works out. And not just for the Berkshires... For you."

"Thanks, Meg. Appreciate that. And thanks for dinner."

* * *

I STARE at the stack of letters in my hand. I'm in my closet, and it's well past one in the morning. I can't sleep.

Tonight got to me. I'm not exactly sure why—Megan's poking, my own insecurities—either way, my head's a mess.

On the surface, it's all wins—she reached for my hand, called me babe, invited me to hang with her friends. Even kissed me goodnight on Saturday.

But underneath it all, I feel the weight of the mountain I still have to climb. Earning Alley's trust again. Her refusal to talk about the past. The fact that she lives in Chicago now. She has a job, a life, friends. She's not just visiting. And last night? She looked happy. She's settling in. Making Chicago her home.

I should be feeling better. Hopeful, even. But the more I think about my time with Alley, the more confused I am. Does she think we'll just go back to normal with a massive fucking elephant in the room? We don't need to unpack every detail of our history, but to never talk about it? Ever?

I shuffle through the letters. I have no idea what half of them say. I was in such a raw, vulnerable place when I wrote them—every emotion imaginable flooding through me.

I'm not sure which version of me ended up on the page.

I get to the last one. Week eleven. That's another thing—she still hasn't read my letter. Week twelve is missing. I'd hoped she would've read it by now. That it might give her a push toward me.

Maybe she did and didn't say anything. Maybe that's why she's been more open.

Or maybe she still doesn't know what she wants, and I'll be back in that damn lawyer's office in a few weeks.

Shit. I press my fingers to my forehead, rubbing hard. I'm going to drive myself crazy.

I pull week six from the stack—November second. Two days after I found out she filed.

I grip the letter, swallowing back the nausea rising. I can't go back to that headspace. To how I felt when I wrote this.

I've hit some lows in my life. Done some shit. Felt the worst of it. But that day? That day gutted me in a way nothing else ever has.

I would've rather been detoxing.

I let out a heavy breath. *That's not going to happen. I'm not the guy who wrote this.*

To prove myself right, I slide my finger under the seal of the envelope and pull the letter out. My hands shake. I have no idea why. Maybe part of me's afraid to confront my past.

Just like Alley.

I unfold the paper and read.

Alley,

Yesterday was the first time I've been clean and thought, I'd rather be dead.

That thought came right after Tobias and Nina told me you'd filed for divorce.

Don't worry. I'm not planning to give you this letter.

Ever.

Because I'm too fucking angry.

I'm angry at everyone today. At Tobias. At Nina. At whoever the fuck is in charge up there, the universe, God, fate. I don't know. And I don't care. I hate them all.

I've spent the past month doing everything they've asked of me. Surrendering. Trusting. Writing my inventory. Owning my shit. Digging into the ways I've hurt people. Clinging to the idea that something greater could help me find peace.

Yeah. Fuck that.

Just when I started to believe in something again... you gave up on me.

It feels like I was halfway up the fucking mountain, finally breathing, and you shoved me off the edge.

I'm mad at you, Alley. God, I'm so fucking mad at you.

I've never been mad at you before.

Not when you yelled at me. Not when you flushed my pills. Not even when you'd tell Matt shit I'd done. I wasn't mad. I deserved all of that.

But today?

This broke me.

You walked away.

You filed.

We were the one thing I always believed in.

I know I hurt you. I know I fucked up. And I'll probably never fully understand how deep that pain goes, especially from your side.

But Jesus... you're just going to walk away?

After everything we've been through? After knowing how goddamn good we are together? How good we could be again?

I need you to hear me right now. Really fucking hear me.

You are the ONLY one for me.

Since the moment I saw you, since I woke up after surgery and saw your face, I haven't thought about anyone else. Not once. Not in passing. Not in private. Not even in here, when I've been more alone than ever.

Not when I was spiraling. Not when I was using. Not now.

I've never wanted anyone else.

And I never will.

I'll never want to kiss another woman.

Couldn't sit across from someone else at dinner without wishing it was you.

No one else will ever be good enough.

The thought of you not being in my life is unbearable.
But worse than that?
I hate myself for putting you in this position.
This is on me.
All of it.
I know that.
I take full responsibility. But God, please give me another chance. If there's even a small part of you that remembers the good...
Please.
Don't let this be the end.
I love you more than this life. More than fucking air.
More than myself.
Love,
Jensen

My hand drops to my side, and a burning stings the back of my throat. I blink, and a goddamn tear falls down my cheek.

I stare blankly at the empty hangers in front of me.

Her hangers.

I crumple the paper in my hand. I never planned to give her this one anyway.

"Fuck," I mutter, voice rough.

Grief crashes over me like a wave—the kind that knocks you down and drags you under. I clench my fists and hurl the ball of crinkled, useless words at the wall.

I rake a hand through my hair, pacing. I need something to help me sleep.

Something to shut my fucking brain off. Something to help me forget.

I bolt into the kitchen, rifling through the medicine cabinet like a madman. I'm not looking for Oxy. I'm not.

Just... something to help me sleep.

Benadryl. Ambien. I don't care if it's fucking chamomile tea.

There's nothing.

A memory pops in, and I pivot, beelining back to the bedroom. I reach under the mattress and pull out the small tin of edibles I stashed after Alley left. When I completely lost control and spiraled. I forgot I had them.

I used to take these all the time to help me sleep.

I sit on the edge of the bed, heart pounding, and set the edibles on the nightstand.

I stare at them.

They're just edibles.

They're practically harmless. People take them every day. Medically. Recreationally. To relax. To sleep. To laugh.

But I can't fucking take these.

I grab my phone and call Matt.

It rings, then goes to voicemail.

I text instead.

SOS. Hey, man. I need you.

I should call my sponsor. But I don't want to wake him.

Fuck, I hate this. I hate that this is who I am.

I haven't felt like this since that first weekend back—when Alley served me the papers and I went looking for alcohol.

Since then I've been fine. It's actually been easier than I expected.

So maybe this is okay. I'm just having a moment of weakness. It's fine, as long as I don't give in.

Did anything even happen? Or did I just create a whole story in my head? I'm assuming Alley feels a certain way—I've spun myself into a panic, possibly over nothing.

Taking a deep breath, I swipe up on my phone, and tap the first name in my favorites.

It rings.

Rings again.

Rings three times.

"Hey, what's up?" Her voice is groggy. Soft. Full of sleep.

"Al..." I say, my voice choking. I pinch the bridge of my nose, eyes squeezing shut. *Shit. Why did I call the one person I don't want to see me like this?*

"What's wrong?" she asks, more alert now. I hear the sound of movement, but I don't say anything. My regret hangs in the air. "Jensen... What's going on? Are you okay?"

I let out a slow breath. "Yeah. I'm okay. Sorry to wake you. I couldn't sleep." I think about keeping the edibles to myself—but I don't want to lie. I don't want her to see me as weak either. I'm supposed to be the protector. The strong one. Not the man who almost unraveled at one in the morning over a fucking gummy.

She already spent two years cleaning up my mess. What if telling her pushes her away? What if it undoes everything we've worked toward the past few weeks?

But I can't rebuild trust without giving her mine.

"I found some old edibles. Thought about taking one to help me sleep. I didn't. But I wanted to. I tried calling Matt, but he didn't answer so..." I trail off, voice rough. "I called you."

That's it, you fucking idiot—keep talking. Hey, babe, wanna sign up for this shit for the foreseeable future?

Jesus Christ.

She's quiet for a second. "Okay." Her voice is soft, patient. "What do you need?"

"I don't know. Just talk to me?"

"Alright... how was your flight?"

"It was good." I exhale, tension fading slightly. "How was your day? What did you and Scarlett do?"

"We went to a hot yoga class with Cooper, then grabbed lunch with her and Vivian at The Purple Pig." She yawns, and guilt tugs at my chest. "Then we visited my dad and went to Michael and Stella's for dinner. Ended the day with lattes in the hot tub on the rooftop patio. It was a good day. What'd you do when you got home?"

"Not much. Just went to dinner at Kev and Meg's with Matt." And then, without thinking—and because I'm desperate as shit with anxiety—I blurt it all out. "I need to know where you stand, Al. I need to know if I'm going to be back in that lawyer's office next month. I need to know why you won't talk to me about any of it. Why you're not angry. Why you haven't asked about rehab." *Jesus, I'm falling apart.* "I need to know where your head's at, babe. I'm driving myself crazy. And if you're really going to follow through on this divorce... I need you to tell me now, because I'm just—" I swallow hard, my voice catching. "Every time I'm with you, I fall in love with you all over again."

Fuck me.

The sound of my breathing fills the silence. My heartbeat pulses in my ear, and it feels like a goddamn eternity before she finally speaks.

"I don't know where my head's at, Jensen. I'm trying to just be okay with that. I'm trying to enjoy my time with you while I figure it out. And I haven't asked about rehab because..." She pauses, her voice cracking. "Because I don't want to talk about it. I don't *want* to remember all the things I've tried so hard to forget while I'm trying to let myself love you again. Trying to trust you again."

She breathes in shakily. "And I definitely don't want to know about the things that helped you get better while my dad is lying in a hospital bed—possibly dying—from a disease I'm still trying to forgive you for."

She sniffs, and it feels like a knife to the stomach. To be the one making her sad. And not just tonight, but for so damn long.

That realization sits heavy, and I feel like a fucking moron for not connecting the dots sooner. For not realizing that her silence was tied to her pain.

For thinking I could just remind her of us and kiss it all away.

I rub my forehead. "Jesus. I'm so sorry. That was really selfish of me. I just... sort of spiraled and got in my head. I'm not used to feeling that way."

"Yeah, well, welcome to being human and second-guessing your-self." She lets out a soft, sad laugh. "It's about time."

I shift the conversation. "How's your dad?"

"He's good. He had a great day. I think he gets to go home Tuesday or Wednesday." She pauses. "And then I just pray he gets better... before he gets worse."

"He will," I say, quiet but certain.

She yawns again, and I take the hint. "Well... I'm sorry for waking you. I'm really glad about your dad. And I'm excited to see you this weekend. I'll let you get back to sleep."

"Are you going to be okay? I can stay on the phone while you fall asleep, if you want."

"You mean while *you* fall asleep?" I let out a quiet laugh.

"Hey, it's the thought that counts."

"Get your sleep. Night, babe."

"Goodnight."

The line goes silent. I set my phone down and glance at the edibles. They don't hold the same appeal anymore.

Nothing is worth losing Alley over.

Or losing myself.

Chapter Twenty-One

ALLEY

The keypad to Matt's condo in Chicago clicks open, and Jensen pulls the door wide with a smirk.

"You sure you wanna come in?" His voice drops low, teasing. "I've pictured you naked on at least three different surfaces in here."

I roll my eyes and brush past him, stifling a laugh. "Do you say that to all the women you bring here?"

He chuckles behind me. Jensen's been joking all night about us being on a first date. *What if we were on a first date and I did this?* (Cue Jensen holding my hand.) Then, *What if we were on a first date and I did this?* (Cue his hand falling to my ass.) He's done this forever, and it's always made me laugh. It helps lighten the tension, because let's be real, this is weird—to be "dating" again.

Not the kind of dating married couples do to keep things fresh. Actual dating. Starting over. Rebuilding trust. Letting him kiss me again... and maybe more.

God, I'm getting really excited about it.

"Nah," he says, stepping close behind me, his voice warm at my ear. "I usually don't like the others enough to get past dinner."

His hand brushes my waist as the door clicks shut. Then his mouth finds mine. Soft. Sure. Daring me to stop him.

I don't.

Those Jensen butterflies ripple through my core, sending a wave of heat down my body. *Dammit.* Why does he have to be so sexy? So funny? So loving?

He's the definition of irresistible...

If only he wasn't an addict. If we didn't have a history of lies and heartbreak.

His hands comb into my hair, and I gasp for air as the kiss grows hotter—charged with pure need. I swear I could get off just by rubbing against him. When it's been this long, it doesn't take much.

God, he feels so good. Every time he kisses me, it's like that first kiss all over again.

Cooper's words loop through my mind nearly every day. *Just choose. Make a decision.*

But Jensen's call the other night froze me. I know there are going to be spirals. Temptations. Hard days. But the what-ifs...

What if he hadn't called?

What if he'd taken the gummy? Drank the alcohol? Or worse...

I can't even let my mind go there. If it did, I'd run again.

I'm proud of him for calling. I am. And I'm trying, *really trying*, to be okay with where he is in his journey. Because this man holding me in his arms?

I love him more than life.

So much it hurts.

But... *what if?*

I know too well: *once an addict, always an addict.*

I'm still here, though. Still wanting him. Still wondering. Toeing the line between insanity, love, and lust.

I break the kiss, catching my breath. "We could have sex, you know," I whisper. "Just for tonight." Forcing my gaze to his, I try to calm my racing heart. "But I'm still unsure about what I want long term. And honestly, I don't think I'm in the best headspace to make big decisions right now. Not with my dad just getting home. But..."

I press my hand to his stomach, fingers slipping beneath the hem of his shirt. "It'd be fun." I brush my lips over his.

His forehead drops to mine. "Fuck, babe. Don't tell me that." His shaky breaths mingle with mine, and I take a moment to explore the firmness of his abs beneath my fingertips. *Good Lord, it turns me on.*

The meditation room kiss last weekend? *Wow.* I could've dropped to my knees right then and there. I was ready to tear his clothes off. Completely forgot where we were. It caught me off guard.

I *want* him to say it's fine. To take me right here in the kitchen. I *want* to rip his shirt off and study every inch of his skin. Of his tattoo. I *want* to feel him inside me again.

But I need him to hold back. To respect the space of uncertainty I'm still in. To prove that he's still the same patient man—the kind with a willpower only God could give. The one who never rushed me. Not even when he was starving for more.

Because that's the old Jensen. He could ruin you in the best way... but only once he has permission.

I'm giving it.

... Sort of.

He pushes away from me with a restraint I haven't seen since we first started dating. "I'll go get the package for Leo."

Dammit. But also, I needed that. To see him resist.

He turns, walking toward what I assume is the master bedroom. Matt had something shipped here for Leo and asked if I could take it to him.

His place here is nice, an upscale condo in downtown Chicago, but it's *normal* nice. Not like the ritzy, oversized penthouse he owns in New York.

Everything about tonight has felt normal, in the best way. Jensen took me to dinner. Then a comedy show, where we laughed our asses off for two straight hours. It's been fun. Maybe the most fun I've had since I moved here.

Jensen's always been a good time, though. It's one of the many reasons I fell for him in the first place.

He appears again, carrying a medium-sized box in his arms. "C'mon. I'll walk you down to your car."

My heart sinks a little. *Why did I suddenly want him to set the box down and say screw it?*

I reluctantly open the door and trail after him down the hall like a sad, love-sick puppy.

"Is it heavy?" I ask. "I can take it so you don't have to come all the way down."

"No. But I'm not letting you go to the parking garage this late by yourself."

A smile tugs at my lips as we walk. We reach the elevator and he presses the down button. He's always been the perfect gentleman.

Except in the bedroom.

My mind betrays me, flashing to him spreading my legs, a wicked grin on his mouth as he lowers his head.

Good Lord. Stop.

"You picturing me naked?" Jensen asks with a smirk.

"No!" I reply way too quickly. "Why would you think that?"

He cocks a brow, like he knows I'm full of shit. "Because that's the same smile you use in the bedroom, babe."

"Psh." I roll my eyes. "This is a normal smile." *Good lie, Alley.*

He smothers a grin, pressing his lips tight. "Whatever you say."

"Don't do that."

"Do what?" he asks, innocently.

"You know exactly what." I glance at him, trying—and failing—to hold back a smile. "I was just thinking about how fun tonight was."

"It was fun."

The doors slide open and we step inside. Jensen presses the button for parking and sets the box down.

He folds his arms across his chest. "So, if this was a first date, would I get another? Would you go home and call Scarlett and tell her all about me?"

I scoff-laugh. "Yeah. I'd say, *This guy I just went out with took me back to his place. Totally thought he was gonna get laid. But I put him in his place.*" My smile shifts into a teasing grin.

He chuckles, low, dark and wicked, as he steps in close, backing me into the elevator wall. "Oh yeah?" he murmurs. "Is that what happened?" His hands press against the metal on either side of me, eyes locked on my mouth. "Seems to me like you wanted it." A corner of his mouth twitches. "You were even picturing me naked. Don't deny it."

Holy shit. My breath catches in my throat as I stare up at him, heart pounding.

We jerk slightly as the elevator hits the ground floor.

"You're lucky these doors are about to open, or I'd be the one putting you in your place." A cocky half-grin tugs at one corner of his mouth as he backs away, picking up the box and stepping into the parking garage while my stomach does literal flips.

I take a steadying breath and follow, staying a few steps behind him to keep some distance. The broad muscles of his back flex with every step. I've never pinned myself as a back girl, but *Jesus, his back.* Everything about him tonight is turning me on.

He did just have me pinned against the elevator wall, though. I plead the fifth.

I pull the key fob from my purse as we approach the Lexus, and the lights flash as I unlock it. Jensen opens the back door and sets the package on the seat. Then he turns to me, cups the back of my head, and his mouth is on mine in an instant. And just as quickly, it's gone, disappointment sinking low in my gut.

He opens my door. "Night, Alley. Can I call you?" He smothers a grin, still playing the first-date card.

I shrug, cool and casual. "You can call me." I slide into the seat. "But I don't know if I'll answer."

He laughs. "Text me when you get home, alright?"

"I will."

He shuts the door, and I start the engine, taking deep breaths to let my heart settle. He stands there, waiting for me to leave. I know he won't go back upstairs until I'm out of sight.

I shift into reverse and back down the narrow lane, cars stacked on both sides. As soon as I'm out of sight, I find the nearest spot, pull in, and shift into park.

Leaning back against the headrest, I inhale deeply through my nose and let out a shaky breath. My heart races as I replay the evening —every joke, every glance, every kiss. But more than anything, what stands out is the way I feel—a lovely little cocktail of hope, love, lust and confusion.

Meanwhile, Cooper's words play on loop in my head. *You'll know once you make a decision, if it's the right path for you.*

But will I?

There's so much going on. Dad went home on Wednesday. I got him settled, went grocery shopping, made sure he had everything he needed. I've stopped by each day after work to check on him, spend a little time together. Michael and I even set up a meal delivery service for the next week so dinners are taken care of.

It's been an emotional few weeks. Cirrhosis is unpredictable, and even now, with Dad doing well... You never know when he just won't be again.

Jensen has made it all bearable. That has to mean something. Doesn't it?

I shake my head against the headrest and close my eyes. I need some kind of sign. Something that will give me clarity.

I start from the beginning.

Seeing him in mediation. The phone call, me leaving in a hurry. Him following.

The look of worry in his eyes.

The letter he handed me.

The letter.

Oh my God. How did I forget about that?

I pull my oversized purse onto my lap, fingers diving into the chaos. It has to still be in here. I unzip the inside pocket, and sure enough, there it is.

I pull it out, toss my purse onto the passenger seat, and break the seal.

Slowly, I slide the letter from the envelope. *Why have I waited this long to read it? And why am I so flipping scared to do so?*

Just do it. Read it.

I exhale, unfold it, and grip both sides, my hands trembling. I bring it closer.

Dear Alley,

It's my last week here in rehab. Pathetic that I had to end up here in the first place, I know...

But I did it.

Detox was the most physically brutal thing I've ever endured. Therapy was emotionally and mentally exhausting. But the hardest part of all of this has been being away from you. And if that wasn't hard enough, knowing you might not be there when I get back... that's a kind of pain I don't even have words for.

Because you are my life.

My entire world.

I dab at my eyes, already brimming with tears.

Shit.

I keep reading.

I can't imagine breathing air that doesn't have you in it. Waking up to an empty bed in the morning. Not seeing your smile. Not hearing your laugh.

You make my life better, Alley. Every part of it.

If this is the last letter I ever get to write you, then thank you.

For loving me. Even when I didn't deserve it.

For showing me what true happiness is.

For teaching me what really matters.

For helping me get clean.

For making me a better man.

A tear drops to the page, and an audible cry escapes.

The weight of everything sits heavy on my chest, making it impossible to breathe easy.

Everything before you feels small now. Petty. Unimportant.

I don't want this letter to be about me. But I need you to know... I've grown. I've faced parts of myself I never would've looked at if I hadn't crash-landed here.

I'd take this all back in a heartbeat if I could. Of course I would.

But not for me.

For you.

Because I've come out of this stronger. Better.

And maybe you'd say the same thing, that walking away from me made you stronger.

But you were already strong, Alley.

You're the strongest woman I know.

And I truly believe that together, we can become the best versions of ourselves.

I set the letter down, my vision too blurred to read. *Oh my God.* I lift the hem of my shirt and dab at my eyes, catching the tears pooling in them.

I know I've apologized in every letter up to now.

I'm not going to do that today.

Today, I just want to remind you of what we have. Of the friendship we built. Of the love I still feel for you every single day.

I love you, Alley.

I will never love anyone the way I love you.

And I don't want to.

I fell in love with you way too fast. God, it was fast.

And I've fallen in love with you all over again, every day since.

And I'll keep falling, every day, for the rest of my life.

If there's even the smallest part of you that still loves me... that still wonders...

Baby, I'll be here.

I'll catch you this time. I swear.

I'm not going anywhere. And neither is the love I have for you.

Love,

Jensen

I set the letter down and let my lungs fill with a giant breath of air. Then I pull it back, reading the line again.

If there's even the smallest part of you that still loves me... that still wonders...

Baby, I'll be here.

I'll catch you this time. I swear.

I sit there, crying. Staring. Wanting to run into his arms and let him hold me. To fix this. Fix all the parts of us that are broken.

All these months I've been wondering why I haven't been able to move on. And it's because of this.

Because I'm married to Jensen Adams. I'm married to a man who would hang the moon for me. Who loves me so hard, it nearly killed him trying to get better for me. The kind of man who would put me first, no matter what.

But only when he's clean.

That's the part that stops me.

Every. Time.

I get close, and then the fear of relapse whispers in my ear.

But when has loving someone ever been about certainty? When has taking the leap of falling in love, or getting married, ever guaranteed anything? God, tomorrow isn't even a guarantee. Each day, we all walk around like we have forever, when in reality, we could be gone tomorrow.

And there it is.

My answer.

I don't want a today if there's no Jensen in my tomorrow.

I've already had six months of them, and it's been miserable.

The sound of my own tears pulls me back to the present. An acute awareness settles, and a calm washes over me. I shift into reverse, ease the car out, and head for the exit.

As I approach, I turn the wheel and circle back to the spot I was in before. The one closer to the elevator.

Just make a choice, Cooper said. *You won't find peace until you do. You'll know if it's right.*

Maybe that's why I haven't felt at peace.

Because leaving Jensen was the wrong choice. Because no matter how far I run, I'll never stop wanting him. Never stop wondering what would've happened if I'd stayed.

What do I even have to lose at this point? Jensen? Time?

I was already losing him. God, I already did.

And when I did, all I wanted was to find him again. To get him back.

And what's time anyway, if I don't get to spend it with the one person I want to?

Shit. Here goes nothing.

I throw the car into park and shove the door open, practically tumbling out. I don't think. Don't stop to grab my purse.

I just run to the elevator.

I stab at the up button at least a dozen times until the doors finally slide open.

The ride up takes an eternity, and my heart thunders in my chest. I swear you can see it through my shirt. My whole body trembles as I make my way down the hall, walking as fast as I can without running.

I reach the door. My knuckles rap against it, fast and frantic, just like my heart.

I wait for what feels like forever, then knock again. Harder this time. I'm practically vibrating with nerves.

Come on. Open the door.

Finally, it swings open.

I bring my gaze to his, trying not to hold my breath as he takes me in.

His brow lifts. "Hey, babe. What's wr—"

"I read your letter," I say, my voice breaking.

I don't wait for him to answer.

I just step forward and crash my mouth against his.

Chapter Twenty-Two

JENSEN

Her lips are on mine before I can respond—warm, all-consuming—and I meet them with the same intensity. It's everything I've hoped for. Everything I've needed.

She came to me. She read the letter.

She's here.

Alley pulls back, her hands fisting in my shirt. "Dammit, Jensen. Why didn't you just sign the papers?" Her voice cracks. "Why the hell are you still here trying to make this work?"

Is she serious?

We'd be here all fucking night if I listed the reasons I'm still here.

I take a slow step forward, backing her up against the wall. "Jesus, Alley. I'm here because I *want* us to work. I'm not trying to make this harder for you." I search her eyes. They're red, wet from crying. "How could I not fight for the best thing that's ever happened to me? Huh? You really expect me to just let you walk away and be fine with it?"

She doesn't move. Doesn't breathe.

"Because that's fucking crazy, if you think that." My voice drops. "You're it for me, Al. There's nothing I wouldn't do for you. Nothing I wouldn't give up." I squeeze my eyes shut, almost pleading before I open them. "I just wanna be the guy who gets to wake up next to you. Tell you about my shitty days after work. The good ones too."

I cage her in, pressing both hands flat against the wall above her head, exhaling slow. My eyes lock on hers, begging her to see it—how much I mean this. "God, babe," I whisper. "I love you. I wanna start a family with you."

I swallow, nostrils flaring. *Ah, fuck.* I refuse to get emotional right now.

"Don't you think I want that?" she snaps, her voice cracking. "I always wanted that." She wipes at her nose, eyes shimmering. "But you went and ruined everything."

"I know I did." My voice breaks.

She just stands there, eyes searching mine, chest rising and falling —sharing air, sharing this mess I made.

She lets out a shaky breath. "Sometimes I just wish you were an asshole."

My brow furrows. "What?"

"Then I'd feel good about leaving you." Her laugh is small and broken. "I could just walk away, you know?"

I scoff, jaw tightening. "Is that really what you want?"

"No." Her chin trembles. "But I don't know if I can do this."

"You don't have to, babe. I'll carry it. All of it." I kiss her forehead. "I'll stay clean, Al. I swear on everything."

Gripping her chin gently, I tilt her face to mine. "I'll respect what-ever you want. If you leave, if that's what you choose, I'll be okay. Eventually. But I'll love you either way. Long after you're gone. Because, *God,* I'll never stop loving you."

A tear slides down her cheek, and she wipes it with her sleeve.

Then she kisses me again, slow and tentative at first. But when she skates her tongue across my lips, it becomes something more. Grows urgent. Like she needs me to breathe. Like this kiss is the only thing keeping her alive. Her hands slide up my chest and wrap around my neck.

Swear to God, it puts life back in my soul. I feel whole. Complete. For the first time in months.

Because Alley? She's my other half. I'm not even a quarter of the man I'm meant to be without her by my side.

My hand cups the back of her neck, and our tongues tangle in a heady mix of longing, apologies, and everything in between.

I let her take the lead. I don't know what she's thinking, or what she wants, and a small part of me worries she hasn't thought this through.

But it doesn't change how I feel.

I know what I want. It's never changed. It never will.

I want her.

All of her.

Now.

Always.

Forever.

She moans into my mouth, and just like that, I'm done pretending I can take this slow. I kiss her hard. Desperate. Turning up the heat in an instant.

Her hands grip the back of my neck as she kisses me like she's trying to erase the past, and I slide my hands down her waist, anchoring her against the wall. Our mouths collide, hot, deep, demanding.

Her fingers bunch in my shirt, yanking me closer. Her thighs brush mine, hips shifting, and it's fucking chaos, in the best possible way.

She pulls away again, breathless. "I'm still mad at you." Her eyes glisten, lips swollen from our kiss.

I nod, swallowing the lump in my throat. "I know, baby."

Her mouth finds mine again, and I kiss her back.

"I want to hate you," she breathes against my lips.

"I know."

She's trembling now.

I kiss the corner of her mouth. Her cheek. Brush away the tears with my thumb.

"But you don't," I murmur.

Her eyes close, and I rest my forehead against hers.

"No," she whispers. "I don't."

She leans in again, lips brushing mine, searching—like all the answers are hidden in my mouth.

So I let her look for them.

This time, when I kiss her, it's not about sex or heat or desperation. It's about love. About survival. About fucking fate.

I keep it slow, pouring everything I have into it. Everything I've ever felt for her. Everything I've missed these past two and a half years. I want to kiss it all away. Make her feel good. And more than anything, I want to be the one who gets to make her happy.

I bring my hands to her face, thumb sweeping over her cheek, and suck her bottom lip into my mouth, tugging gently. She whimpers, and I let my lips trail sideways. I press kisses along her cheek and jaw, until I reach her ear. I flick my tongue against her earlobe, then murmur, "I can't imagine a life where you're not in it. Please don't make me find out what kind of hell that would be."

She doesn't say anything. Just shakes her head.

Her breath leaves her, sharp and shaky, and when I make my way back to her mouth, it crashes into mine. Nothing soft about it this time. Her tongue slides against mine, and the sound she makes nearly undoes me.

She's moving, pushing me through the kitchen until my back hits the opposite wall. Her fingers comb through my hair, and she's kissing me like I'm oxygen and she's been suffocating without me.

My hands roam greedily, over her tits, down her back, gripping her hips like I can tether her here with me. She rolls them once, and I groan, burying my face in her neck. My cock's never been so fucking lonely.

"I need you, baby," I rasp, dragging my lips along her jaw.

She tugs at my shirt, breathless. "Off. Take this off."

I help her yank it over my head and drop it to the floor, then grip the hem of hers and lift. She undoes the clasp of her bra, letting it slide down her arms.

Our chests collide, bare skin to bare skin. It feels so fucking good. It's fire and lightning and that deep kind of ache that only she can touch.

She pushes back, a spark in her eyes as her hands skim down my chest. My abs flex under her touch as her nails drag lower. Her gaze roams over my body, hungry and slow. "You have no idea how badly I've wanted to see all this."

Jesus, she's killing me. I suck in a breath, body already reacting. Then I grip her thighs and lift her off the ground without warning. She gasps, legs wrapping around me instantly, grinding against me, and fuck, if it doesn't make me harder.

I spin, pressing her back to the wall again, trailing my mouth down her neck, biting, sucking, tasting. Her breath hitches when I drag my teeth across her collarbone and kiss the curve of her breast.

"Tell me to stop," I growl, one hand braced under her ass, the other sliding between us.

She shakes her head, hard. "Don't you fucking dare."

My fingers work to open her jeans as I kiss her again. It's wild and hot, all tongue and teeth and breathless moans. Every time our skin brushes, she makes this soft little whimper that shoots straight to my cock.

"You're shaking," I murmur against her lips.

"So are you."

"Yeah," I whisper, kissing her again. "Because I've never wanted anything this bad in my life."

I trail my hand down the front of her open jeans, fingers pressing against the thin fabric of her panties. I groan when I feel how wet she is for me. "Fuck, baby. You're soaked."

"I've wanted this just as much as you," she breathes. "You think I don't dream about this? That I don't get off to you?"

"Christ. Don't tell me that."

She grinds down on my hand as I rub slow, deliberate circles over her clit, and I'm seconds from losing it.

"Jensen," she pants. "Take me to the bedroom."

Reluctantly, I pull my hand away. I grip her ass firmly and walk us both to the master bedroom.

I toss her onto the bed, and she laughs as my fingers wrap around her jeans and tug, peeling them off in one swift motion. I toss them aside, then slide my hands slowly up her thighs, savoring every perfect inch. Her chest rises and falls in shallow bursts, her eyes sultry and dark. She looks sexy as hell.

"You're unreal," I murmur, kissing the inside of her knee, then dragging my mouth higher. "The hottest fucking woman I've ever seen."

She reaches for me, but I grip her hips and pull her to the edge of the bed, locking eyes with her as I hook my fingers around the sides of her panties.

"Jensen—"

I yank them down and toss them aside without breaking eye contact. Then I spread her thighs and settle between them, my hands locking her in place.

Time to make her feel good.

I don't give her time to think. I dive in, tongue flicking over her clit, slow and deliberate. She gasps, back arching off the bed.

"Oh my God," she whimpers, her fingers fisting in my hair, thighs trembling around me.

I grip her hips tighter. "You're so fucking wet," I murmur, kissing her inner thigh before diving back in. "You taste unreal."

I groan against her, devouring her like it's been years—because it fucking feels like it. I've been starving for her.

She cries out, grinding against my mouth, her whole body shaking. "Don't stop."

Never.

Not when she's like this. Naked. Breathless. Fuck... begging.

I flatten my tongue and lick her slow, thorough, then suck her clit into my mouth while sliding two fingers inside her. She lets out a guttural moan, nails scraping into my scalp.

"I—oh my God—I'm gonna—"

"Come for me, baby," I rasp, thrusting my fingers deeper. "Let me feel it."

She does... hard. Six months of ache pouring out all at once.

Her thighs clamp around my head as she cries out, body spasming, a string of half-broken moans falling from her lips. I don't stop. Not until she's losing her goddamn mind for me.

"Jensen," she gasps, breathless. "It's too much."

Jesus. No shit.

If I stay down here, I'm gonna come in my pants.

It's been too damn long.

I kiss the top of her pussy and pull away. "One more, baby." I trail kisses up her stomach, over her tits, and back to her mouth. My hands follow, fingers grazing her soft skin. "Give me another."

I kiss her mouth like she's mine.

Like she never left.

Her hands roam over me, nails scraping, fingers greedy. She grips my hips, presses her thumbs into that hard V of muscle, and I groan. Then she's unzipping my pants with trembling hands, pushing them down. I shove them off, boxer briefs too, kicking them away—releasing my hard cock, and letting her see exactly what she does to me.

Her eyes go wide. "Jesus, Jensen. You look so good."

I chuckle as she wraps a hand around my length, stroking slow, causing me to hiss.

I brace myself above her. "You still mad at me?" I rasp.

She laughs softly, dragging her thumb over my tip. "Yes."

I lower myself, nudging between her legs. "Good."

Then I slide into her in one slow, devastating thrust. "Because I plan on fucking you until you're not mad anymore," I grunt, hips rolling deep.

She gasps—tight, hot, perfect—and I groan, "God," as I pull back and thrust again. "And I don't care if it takes tonight, a week... six months..." Another thrust. "Five fucking years."

Her nails dig into my back, her body arching under mine.

"I'll love you until you're mine again," I whisper against her mouth. "And I'll keep loving you... till the day I fucking die."

God, I've missed her like this.

Her eyes close, and she lets out the sexiest sound I've ever heard. I move my hips—

And this. Is. Everything.

Our bodies collide in perfect rhythm. Like they were made for this. Husband and wife. Kissing. Making up. Fucking through all the hard shit. Coming together in a way that's rough and raw and healing.

Her head tips back. "Jensen, I'm gonna come."

Good.

I thrust harder, faster, burying deeper with every stroke until she's gasping for air and then—

She falls apart again, her body jolting as she comes around me.

I wait until she finishes, then pull out, sensitive as fuck.

"What are you—"

I grab her hips, flipping us, dropping to my back. "Get on top. Ride me."

She bites her lip through a smile, then sinks down on my cock. She moves slow, hips rocking in a cadence that blurs my vision.

"Oh my God, it feels so good," she pants.

I take her hands in mine, guiding them to my chest so I can watch her. *Feel* her.

She grinds down, her pace picking up, breath going ragged. My hands slide up her sides, thumbs brushing over her nipples, and she shudders. I wrap my arms around her, pulling her flush against me, and thrust up hard and fast. Our slick bodies slide together as we both start to unravel.

And then we come...

Together.

I close my eyes, voice gruff as I groan, "Fuck."

Her body shudders around me, and mine follows with a rough, strangled moan. I bury my face in her neck, trembling, clinging to her.

She collapses on top of me, and we lie there. Breathless. Stunned. Fucking satisfied.

Sex has always been great with Alley. More than great. But this? This was like nothing before.

Sure, maybe it's because it's been so long... for both of us. But it was more than that. It was like all the good and the broken shit from our past came crashing together in one big clusterfuck of grief, guilt, and longing—colliding in the best possible way.

It was incredible. Explosive. Intense.

We *needed* this.

Her arms tighten around me, and she nuzzles her nose into my neck. I press a kiss to her temple, tightening my hold too. "I love you."

She's quiet. But it's not uncomfortable, even though I want more than anything for her to say it back.

It's okay if she doesn't.

After a long pause, I feel her take a shaky breath, and a strangled cry bursts out of her.

Shit.

Shit. Shit. Shit.

She gasps, her whole body jerking. "God, I'm sorry," she chokes out, barely getting the words past the sob.

Did I read this wrong? "Shit, babe," I whisper, rubbing my hand across her back as she breaks in my arms.

I'm torn. I don't know what to say. I don't know if she's crying because she's happy or—

God, I hope it's not regret. Because that meant everything to me.

Her sobs grow louder. *Shit.*

It tears at my chest, pulling my heart in every direction. I thought I'd reached the top of the mountain I'd been climbing. I'm over here saying I love you, thinking everything's fine now. That *we're* fine. Like having sex could somehow erase the past.

Fuck. Who was I kidding? We've barely even started chipping away at the mess I made.

But if Alley's going to cry, I want it to be in my arms. I want to be the one she feels safe with. The one who gets to hold her. Comfort her.

I shift to my side and gently roll her onto her back. Her hands spring to her face, covering it in embarrassment.

"Hey." My voice drops low, almost a whisper. I thread my fingers into her hair. "Come on, babe. It's dark. I've seen you cry before... You're beautiful. Let me see you."

I lower my lips to her clavicle, pressing soft kisses to her skin. Again. And again.

"I'm right here, baby," I murmur.

My hand drifts across her stomach, soft, explorative, comforting. My lips and fingers graze over every inch of skin as I worship her, trying to make up for everything I've done. Because the truth is: she's crying because of me. Because of what I put her through.

And that stings. I feel it deep—bones aching, nerves burning—like I'm bleeding from every pore. Her pain is my pain.

I kiss my way back up her body. Her sobs begin to quiet, and after a moment, she lowers her hands, wiping beneath her eyes and across her cheeks. I can feel her gaze on me as I taste my way to her lips. When I meet them, I kiss her with fervor. They're soft, swollen, and they come to life beneath mine. Her fingers dig into my shoulders, and when I finally pull away, her eyes find mine.

I brush my thumb along her jaw. "Talk to me. What's going on? What are you feeling?"

Her lips tremble, and she swallows. "I'm scared," she whispers. "I'm so scared."

I close my eyes, letting it sink in.

She's scared. Of course she is. Scared she can't trust me. Scared I'll hurt her. Scared I'll fuck up again.

My jaw clenches. My chest tightens. I feel it everywhere. Like pressure building behind my ribs.

I open my eyes and press a kiss to her forehead. "I get it," I murmur. "You have every reason to be scared. I gave you every reason." I pause, fingers grazing her hairline. "But I know I can make you happy." I stroke her cheek, voice low. "I know you. I know how to make you laugh. How you take your coffee. Every song that reminds you of your mom. The guilt you carry with your dad... I know every part of you."

She doesn't move. Just lies there, tears silently slipping down her cheeks. It *kills* me.

"You do," she says softly. "But you're also the person who broke my heart."

Fuck.

That guts me.

Feels like the air was sucked out of the room. Like I was hit in the sternum. Clean. Precise.

And deserved.

"I know," I whisper. "And I'll spend every day making sure I never do it again."

Her eyes search mine, then squeeze shut. "I'm sorry."

When she opens them, I hold her gaze. "Don't apologize. Not for this. Not to me. I understand why you're scared. And it's me who should be sorry. That you can't trust me. That I'm not your safe place, when that's exactly what I should have been. I'm sorry I wasn't there when you needed me most. Sorry that I'm the reason you needed someone in the first place."

I swallow down the regret rising in my throat, my eyes dropping to the pillow. It hurts less, looking away, avoiding the pain in her eyes. But I force myself back to her. "You'll never know how sorry I am. The guilt I carry—it's constant. Knowing the things I did that hurt you. And for causing pain I don't even know about."

I blink fast, breathing deep, trying to keep it together. "I hurt a lot of people. But nothing's heavier than knowing I pushed you away."

Her chest rises with a deep inhale. "And you'll never know what it was like to witness it. Up close. Watching as everything I knew to be safe and real became the thing I couldn't trust. The thing that terrified me. I had to stand by and watch the person I love burn everything that mattered most."

Tears stream down her cheeks, and I nod, taking it in the best I can.

And God, it's the worst. But in the best way. Just hearing her speak her truth. It means she trusts me, at least a little. Trusts me enough to let it out. To hand me the weight so I can carry it.

I don't say anything. There's nothing I could say to make it better. Listening is the best thing I can do right now. I learned that in therapy.

And in this moment? I hear her. I see her. And I'm owning my shit.

I fall to my back, eyes on the ceiling. She scoots closer, resting her head in the crook of my arm, her leg tangling with mine.

I stroke her shoulder, wrapping my arms around her, breathing her in. Just soaking in the moment.

She drags her palm across my abs, then up to my chest, feeling every inch. When she reaches my shoulder, her fingers lift and trace a slow line down my right arm, the one that's tattooed. Then she reverses the motion. Starts over: torso, chest, shoulder, arm.

Repeat.

My breathing slows. I focus on the rhythm of her touch, silently thanking the universe. For her. For this feeling. Time slows, and I close my eyes. Happy to fall asleep like this.

Right here with my wife.

I don't know what happens tomorrow...

But she's touching me.

She's feeling me.

She's here.

With me.

Chapter Twenty-Three

ALLEY

Don't ask me how I ended up naked, lying on Jensen's chest, tracing his muscles and tattoo like he's an Etch A Sketch, but here we are.

Was it a moment of weakness?

Maybe. I don't know.

But I don't regret it.

The sex was phenomenal. But it was more than that. I felt connected to him in a way I haven't in so long.

Even last spring, when he was clean, things were okay, but I was still holding back. I still am, I guess. Only now... it feels different. Maybe it's because we've been spending so much time focusing on the thing that really matters: our friendship.

Could also be the fact that neither of us has had sex in six months.

Either way... I felt the difference in him.

That's the thing, though. Right now? I trust him. This man beneath my fingertips, he's steady and strong. I trust him to hold me. To keep me safe. To love me. To put me first.

But I don't trust addiction.

I don't trust alcoholism.

I don't trust the disease.

Because it comes back like cancer, quiet and lethal, biting you in the ass when you least expect it.

I won't be a casualty again.

Jensen's fingers brush against my shoulder, my arm, my side, warm and comforting. I love his hands. They've always done something for me. He's so damn good with them. The way he's rough but gentle, making me feel desired and fragile all at the same time.

And his tongue—*holy shit, his tongue.*

I roll my bottom lip between my teeth, rocking into him without thinking. He trails a finger along the side of my breast, and between the sensitive sensation and the memory of what that man can do with his mouth, a flutter pulses deep in my core.

It was all so overwhelming, his hands, his mouth, the way he looks at me. I was feeling so much. Like everything I've been holding in came rushing to the surface all at once. The fears. The memories. The heartache.

One big, messy—but incredible—release.

No wonder I broke down. I know it's only Jensen, but still, crying after sex? It's mortifying.

He was great about it. Handled it perfectly. I couldn't have asked for a better response.

My hands press against his muscles.

Goddamn.

Jensen has always looked good. Seriously. He has. But this? I practically melted in his arms like molten lava the second he took his clothes off.

And the tattoo? Yeah. I'm a sucker. I bit.

It's hot. It's really, really hot.

Combine that with the body? There was no stopping it.

But that's all just extra. It's not what matters. What matters is *him,* and how he's made me *feel.* How we've laughed all night and fallen into this rhythm that almost feels like it did before.

Flirtation. Friendship. Comfort.

And mind-blowing sex.

I lift my fingers to his bicep, the arm draped across his stomach and teasing the crap out of me. I trace the lines of his tattoo, and he stills beneath my touch.

I haven't really gotten a good look at it. Even now, it's dark.

There's only a faint glow from the hallway and city lights slipping through the windows. Just enough to make out the larger images. There's a lion. An owl. But I can't make out the rest. It's too shadowed to tell.

I haven't asked Jensen much. Not about the tattoo, or rehab—or anything deep, really, unless it involves my dad.

I keep thinking I'll bring it up, but the fear of what he might say lodges in my throat every time I get close.

So instead, I go for something easier. Something safer. Something that won't dig up old scars I'm not ready to face.

I draw in a steadying breath, heart pounding a little harder. "Tell me about your tattoo," I say softly, lifting my head to look at him.

His lips curve into a smile, and I instinctively kiss them. His fingers find my hair and pull me in closer, deepening the kiss. He scrapes his teeth along my bottom lip in that dominating, almost possessive kind of way.

The kind that makes me feel like the sexiest woman alive.

"I've been waiting for you to ask about it." His voice is low, husky. Shivers prickle down my spine.

He reaches behind him and flips a switch, turning on soft lights that illuminate the headboard, like the kind you find in a hotel. Leave it to Matt to have every bell and whistle, even when it comes to lighting.

He sits up, forcing me to as well, and suddenly, I feel very naked... because I am.

It's not a big deal. He's my husband. He's seen me naked a thousand times. But I still feel self-conscious. Exposed. Vulnerable. Flawed.

"Can I wear one of your T-shirts?"

He hesitates, eyes dragging over me like he's engraving every inch into memory.

"You can," he murmurs. "But let me look at you a little longer first."

Heat flashes through me, my cheeks burning, a slow pulse building between my thighs.

Jesus. I'm turned on by him just looking at me?

He gets his fill, then walks to his suitcase and grabs a shirt. When he slides back into bed beside me, he hands it over.

I toss the shirt over my head and snuggle up beside him, his arm wrapping around me.

"In rehab, there was a lot of therapy. Working the twelve steps. Taking accountability. Finding something to believe in."

My pulse ticks faster. I'm not ready to hear about rehab, but I don't want to stop him.

"We also had a lot of reading and writing time." He clears his throat, abs flexing—I can't help but notice. "They had a lot of books on stoicism. It's something that's always piqued my interest, but I guess I never really took the time to understand it. I started reading about it my second week there."

He pauses, and I turn to look at him. His jaw is set tight, eyes narrowed.

"I don't really know how to explain it, but... it changed me. You know I've never been a faith guy. I've never needed things to make sense. But I needed something to believe in there. Something to make it all make sense. Like if I could just understand why. Why this happened. Why to me. Why I lost you. Why I needed rehab..." He trails off, his eyes closing. His chest rises and falls, and I feel the warmth of his exhale kiss my forehead.

"One of the main principles is accepting what's beyond our control. What happened had already happened. I couldn't change it. But what I could do was accept it. Realize that everything from here on out was up to me. My thoughts. My emotions. My actions. Sometimes we can't control the situation, but we can always control how we choose to react to it. And if we align ourselves with the universe, keep learning and growing, shifting when we do, trusting the process, we set ourselves up for a lifetime of happiness."

He gives my shoulder a soft squeeze. "And then there are four fundamentals of stoicism: wisdom, temperance, courage, and justice. That's what the lion, owl, and lotus represent." He gestures to the images on his forearm. "And this scale? That's for justice." He lifts his arm, showing me the back of his bicep.

"The whole sleeve is for everything that's made me who I am

today. What's made me stronger, better, and what reminds me of the man I want to be."

"And what about the anchor?" I ask, brushing my fingers over his bicep. No sooner are the words out than I realize my initials are etched at the core of it.

The corner of his mouth lifts. "That's you, babe. I told you the other day, you're my anchor. The day you came into my life was the day I found where I was going. You ground me. Make me stronger. You make me want to be the best version of myself."

My throat swells, and I try not to blink as moisture fills my eyes. "What if we get divorced?"

He just shrugs. "Doesn't make it any less true."

I stare at him, stunned. Speechless.

He tattooed my initials on his arm knowing I'd filed for divorce.

It's so incredibly stupid. And yet, somehow, it means more to me than words could ever explain.

His fingers find mine, and I turn toward him, eyes glistening. "What are the dates on the anchor?" There's one on each side.

"This one's the day I got clean," he says, pointing to the first. "The day I chose to change my future." His eyes burn into mine. "That's not changing. Ever."

I nod slowly. "And this one?" I ask, pointing to the second. It's a random date, five and a half years ago.

He smiles, a soft chuckle following. "That's the day I met you. The day of my surgery." He squeezes my hand. "Nothing on this arm has made me a better man more than you."

I pull his arm toward me, running my fingers along the ink, taking it all in. It's done really well. The lion is stunning, fierce and detailed, and the only color on the entire sleeve is in its eyes. A piercing, vibrant blue.

"These eyes look like yours."

"That's what they're supposed to be," he says. "The lion represents courage. It's kind of a mirror for me, learning to live with my fears and anxieties, instead of running from them. Choosing the right thing even when I'm staring down my own weaknesses."

"That's cool," I murmur. "It's really beautiful."

"Thank you. Matt's guy did it. It's still not finished. There's more shading and detail to fill in."

My fingers drift higher, tracing the anchor on his bicep. I pause when I reach the current year, printed just to the side of my initials, slightly off-center.

My brow furrows. "Why is this just the year?"

His head tips back, eyes peering down at mine. A smirk curves across his lips, and it takes everything in me not to lean in and melt into it.

"That's not done yet," he says, nodding toward the empty space. "I'm waiting for the full date."

"What do you mean?"

He lets out a deep, low laugh. "That'll be the day I get you back. The day you move back in with me."

I shake my head in disbelief, pressing my lips together to keep from smiling. God, that's so Jensen. That confidence. That cocky charm that somehow never crosses into arrogance—it does something to me. It's swoony and heartwarming. But more than anything, it makes me believe in him.

Gives me hope that maybe this version of Jensen is here to stay.

I'm crawling into his lap before I can think, straddling him. My palms press against his solid abs as I slide my hands up to his chest, eyes never leaving his. "What if I never move back in?" I whisper.

"Then I guess I've got a random year tattooed on my arm until I can add the rest. If anything, it'll be a reminder of what I lost. And to do better."

His hands find my thighs, slowly sliding up. Anticipation, mixed with a need to show him how much I love him, burns low in my core, and a slow ache builds between my legs.

"But I'm not going anywhere, baby," he says. "Even if it stays incomplete for months or years. Even if it takes—"

My mouth cuts him off, and he meets my kiss with the same quiet devotion.

I've never wanted something to be more true than this: Jensen. Changed.

Better. Stronger. Here...

Waiting for me.

Loving me.

Being the husband I know he can be.

He was the best boyfriend. The best fiancé.

And then he lit our marriage on fire.

His hand slips under my shirt, cupping my breast, thumb grazing my nipple. I moan, grinding down onto him, his length pressing firm against me in all the right ways.

He deepens the kiss, arms wrapping around me, pulling me close, skin against skin. The warmth reminding me that tonight, I'm not alone.

I'm still scared. Still angry.

But not at him.

At me.

His grip tightens, and he lifts his hips, giving me the friction I'm desperate for. I gasp, and it draws a low groan from his throat.

He rolls me to my back, his elbows framing my face. "I love you so much, Alley."

For so long, I made everything about Jensen. About the addiction. About life being unfair. About my dad, and *his* disease.

I let myself drown in all of it. And somewhere along the way, I lost *me*.

"I promise, if you let me, I'll spend every day becoming the man you need. The man you deserve."

But this isn't about Jensen anymore. He's his own person. He'll make his own choices.

This right here, right now...

This is about me.

My healing. *My* journey. What *I* want.

Jensen's done the work. He's changed.

Have I?

He messed up. Badly. He broke my trust in him.

And I let it break me.

All this time, I've been mad at him. At life. Drinking, wallowing, trying to make sense of it all. When really, I should've been doing what Jensen was doing.

Becoming better.

His hand glides down my stomach, slow and deliberate, gaze locked on the trail he's leaving behind. Sparks fire through me, the ache turning sharp. He pauses at my pubic bone, veers to the side, and grips my hip, fingers digging in just enough to make me shiver. Then his eyes drag back to mine.

Like he's asking.

Waiting.

Letting *me* decide.

My chest tightens, breath shallow under the weight of his stare, those blue eyes burning into me, full of restraint and hope and want.

And God, I want this.

I want him.

I want to trust him again. To stop running. To let him love me.

To believe we still have a chance at happy.

He presses a kiss to my forehead, then his gaze meets mine.

"Okay," I whisper. "I want to try. I want to make this work. You and me."

I nod slowly, grounding myself in it. "I'm all in."

Chapter Twenty-Four

JENSEN

I STEP out of the shower and tie a towel around my waist. My workout ran over, and between thinking about last night, Alley still naked in my bed, and where the hell we go from here, I lost track of time at the gym. Now I'm running late for the 7 a.m. AA meeting.

I walk swiftly into the bedroom, where my suitcase is sprawled open, and quietly sift through it for clothes.

"Come back to bed," Alley murmurs across the room, startling me.

I turn toward her, hand gripping the towel at my waist, and do a quick once-over of her body beneath the white sheet. It's pulled up over her tits, but just barely. She stretches with a yawn, arms overhead, and the sheet slips down just enough for a nipple to peek out.

Shiiit. I'd love nothing more than to climb back into bed and have her for breakfast.

"Can't," I say, turning back to the suitcase. I grab what I need and drop the towel.

"You're not gonna turn around? Let me say good morning to Clark?"

I chuckle and turn around, giving her a full view of my cock before stepping into my boxer briefs.

A gorgeous smile spreads across her lips. "There he is. God, I missed him." Her brows furrow. "Are you leaving? It's Saturday."

"Yeah. I'm headed to an AA meeting. There's one at seven that I've been going to the past few weeks. Then I've got a call with my sponsor at nine."

"I'll come with, if you want?"

"This one's not an open meeting. But I appreciate that." I walk over to the bed and lean down, brushing a kiss across her lips.

"Oh my God," she says, laughing. "How'd that morning breath taste?"

"Just like I remember." I flash her a grin, and for a second, I forget we're at Matt's place. Forget we're not in New York. Or in our own home. That we just slept together for the first time in over six months. It just feels like a normal Saturday morning.

A calm settles in my chest. It's steady and grounding. *Maybe we're gonna be okay.* "You can stay and sleep. Wait for me... I'd love to take you to breakfast when I'm done."

She sits up, bringing the sheet with her, and I try not to look disappointed. *Damn.* I wanted to see her tits.

"No, no," she says quickly. "I'll get up and out of your hair." She pulls the sheet up tighter. "I don't want to mess with your routine."

Fuck. She's uncomfortable.

I know Alley. *Really well.*

I don't think she regrets last night, but... I can't quite read where her head's at right now. Normally, she'd flash me her tits and crack a joke about needing her vibrator since I'm leaving.

Maybe she just doesn't know where we go from here or how to act. Or maybe I'm overthinking it and everything's fine.

"You know I'm a creature of habit," I say. "But you're not in the way. I like you being here. I like knowing you're here waiting for me."

She smiles. "I don't have any of my things. I'll go home and get ready for breakfast while you're gone."

Home. The word lands like a punch to the kidneys.

She means Leo and Vivian's place.

Her real home is in New York.

I move quickly, stepping into my pants and tugging a shirt over my head. Her eyes follow me as I cross the room, grabbing my watch and phone.

I check the time. *Shit.* If I don't leave in two minutes, I'll be late.

I glance back at her, sheets still pulled up over her like she's a one-night stand or something.

And I fucking hate it.

Yeah. That's not happening.

I catch her gaze and grin. Tossing my phone aside, I take a few strides toward the bed and tackle her, wrapping myself around her as she falls back. The sheet slips from her hands.

"Jensen," she laughs, and I crash my mouth into hers, letting her know she's still the most beautiful fucking woman in the world. That she's desirable and turns me on, morning breath and all.

"Mmm. You taste good, baby." I trail kisses down her jaw to her neck, one hand cradling her head, the other cupping her cheek.

"Stop!" she groans. "This is so unfair. You've brushed your teeth and showered and look all hot, and I'm gross and grog—"

I cut her off, tongue slipping in, teasing and toying with hers. She softens beneath me, slowly giving up her insecurities. Her arms wrap around my neck.

I break the kiss. "How many times have I told you not to talk about my wife like that?"

Before she can answer, I'm kissing her again. Her fingers skim my neckline as she pulls me closer.

I draw back, eyes fixed on her smile, that damn dimple making me want to forget every obligation I have for the rest of the year. "I have to go."

"Okay."

I don't move. Can't. Her smile has me frozen in place. I press my mouth to her neck, then drag my tongue down to her collarbone.

She arches into me. *God, I love knowing she still wants me.*

"You make it so hard to leave," I murmur low against her skin, my hand palming her breast. She rolls her hips against mine and *fuck,* now I'm hard as a rock.

It takes every ounce of willpower, but I finally tear myself from her.

Choosing an AA meeting over fucking your wife? If that's not commitment to sobriety, I don't know what is.

"I'll pick you up from Leo's at 9:30," I say, standing. "And then we're having a serious discussion about your *home*."

* * *

I STEP out of my AA meeting and onto the streets of Chicago. It's cold as shit, but the sun's out, which makes it bearable. I've got some time to kill before my weekly check-in with Rob, my sponsor.

I wander into a coffee shop on the corner, order a drip, and slide into a seat by the window. The place smells like fresh beans and burnt toast, and it's filled with quiet conversations.

I pop my AirPods in and call Matt. The phone rings three times before he answers.

"Hey, man. What's up?" His voice is thick with sleep, and I glance at my watch. It's 8:30 a.m., which means 9:30 in New York. Not exactly early, but not late either.

"Shit. Did I wake you?"

I hear a woman's voice in the background, muffled. Matt mumbles something back to her.

"Yeah, but it's all good. Needed to get up anyway."

"Late night?" I ask.

He chuckles. "You could say that. Hold on."

Here we go. He's walking away from whoever he was with so he can tell me all about his wild night.

I hear a door slide open, then shut. *The patio? It's freezing.*

"Just a sec... Turning on the heaters... Alright. You there?"

"Yeah."

"Talk to me, Goose. How'd it go with Alley last night?"

"Wait. You're not gonna tell me about your wild night first?"

"Not a big deal. Just a threesome. Ran into a girl I know. Her friend was hot too, so..."

Jesus. I can practically see him shrug through the phone. *Had a threesome*, like it's nothing.

"Anyway, one thing led to another, and we were up pretty late."

"Holy shit, dude. What is your life?"

"I don't know. It's not important. Tell me about Alley."

I grin like a dumbass, watching people pass by on the sidewalk, still thinking about waking up to her naked. "It was great. Took her to a comedy club. We laughed, had fun. Then we went up to your place to grab that package for Leo, and we started making out." I take a sip of my coffee. "Long story short. We slept together."

Matt lets out a whoop and laughs. "Hell yeah, man!"

"I know. It was great. And not just the sex, the whole night. Everything felt right."

"That's great." He chuckles again. "Megan's gonna lose her shit. So is she coming to the Berkshires, then?"

"I haven't asked her yet. I will this morning. I'm picking her up in an hour for breakfast."

"So, what else happened? What now?"

I fill him in on the rest of the night, what we said after, how it felt. All the shit I've been thinking about since I woke up.

Then he basically gives me a play-by-play of his night—in great detail—and my brain practically explodes.

He finally wraps up the story and says, "I ran into Jordan and her fiancé last night."

Well, that explains everything.

He scoffs. "She acted like she barely knew who I was. Can you believe that? We've known each other since fucking kindergarten. She was my first girlfriend. First kiss. First fu—well, no, not the first, but the first one I actually remember. And it was awkward as hell."

"This the doctor guy?"

"Yeah. Dr. Richard Fucking Douchebag. She's so bad at dating."

I let out a loud laugh. Yep. This is so Matt. He's not a stranger to threesomes, but they only happen when he's too drunk to think straight. And he always gets too drunk when something happens with Jordan.

"Ah, man. I'm sorry. You've really got to let her go, though. I know you've been friends forever, but she's getting married. Just... be happy for her."

"Cut the shit, bro. Do you hear yourself? Could you imagine if I said that to you about Alley after she left you? Just be happy for her? What the fuck?"

"Not the same. One, she's my wife. Two, you claim not to love Jordan, even though we all know you're full of shit. You either do, or you don't. You can't have it both ways."

He goes quiet, then exhales loudly. "That's enough introspection for a month. I'm going back inside. Gonna have some morning sex. I'm really happy for you, brother. Tell Al I said hi. And you better get her to commit to the Berkshires or I wouldn't want to be you when Megan finds out she's not coming."

"I'm on it. And hey, don't tell Megan about me and Alley. You know how she gets. I'll tell her when I'm ready."

"You know I wouldn't do that. That's your shit to tell."

"Alright. Later, man."

"Later."

I end the call. Perfect timing. Ten minutes until I'm supposed to check in with Rob.

I send Alley a text while I wait, a smirk forming as I type.

> Had to sit through an entire AA meeting thinking about you naked in my bed. Rude. Also… pretty sure everyone saw my boner. You owe me.

She responds immediately.

ALLEY

> Wasn't me who had to leave.

> Also, not like me to put out on a first date.

I chuckle to myself. She's always loved playing into the scenarios I come up with.

> Glad you were willing to drop your standards for the night. I love when a girl puts out on the first date. You were hot. Pretty great in the sack too.

ALLEY

> I'm sorry, pretty great? wtf.

> Guess I need a refresher. You free in 30? Go for round two.

> I'll make it worth your time.

ALLEY

> Ha. Idk... deciding if round one was good enough to go for round two.

Oh, shit.

She's gonna play dirty. That's my favorite. I'm grinning like a complete fool, sitting here, alone.

> Don't kid yourself, babe. They probably heard you come all the way back in New York.

ALLEY

> That's bold talk for a guy I gave a pity lay to.

> Cute. But we both know you loved when I pinned your hips to the bed and spread your legs like the good girl you are. Then licked your pussy until you came all over my tongue. My fingers were dripping, baby. It was more than good for you.

ALLEY

> You think that's cute? Babe... I'm not even wearing panties right now. Might touch myself a little. You know, just to see if round one holds up in memory.

Fuck. My cock jerks and I shift, readjusting myself as discreetly as possible. I start to text her back, but notice the time. It's 8:59.

> Shit, babe. Just got me hard in the coffee shop. I have to call my sponsor. To be continued... and I will ruin you.

Chapter Twenty-Five

ALLEY

Back at Leo and Viv's, I take the stairs two at a time up both flights. Jensen will be here soon, and even though I told him I was leaving to get ready, I ended up staying in bed for another hour and a half.

One, I was ridiculously comfortable. Matt did not skimp on the mattress or pillows. And two, my mind wouldn't stop racing.

I felt weird this morning. That's the only way to describe it. Jensen's seen me naked and disheveled a thousand times, but for some reason, I felt self-conscious.

Waking up to him already having gone to the gym and getting ready for an AA meeting that early on a Saturday... it shook me.

Don't get me wrong. It was a good surprise. I just... couldn't help how it made me feel. Like suddenly, I wanted to be the kind of person who got up early to work out. Not the kind who sleeps in, then wakes up looking like they just spent a month on the show, *Naked And Afraid*.

I should be doing things to better myself, too. Why should he be the only one doing the work?

Well, technically, he *is* the one who screwed it all up.

So, maybe it's fair.

But damn, whatever the reason, I felt insecure. Like I wasn't good enough for him.

I used to get those thoughts in the beginning, back when we first started dating. I mean, he was a rich Upper East Sider who turned every head in the room, and his best friend was a billionaire. It was intimidating. But Jensen was all in. He shut those insecurities down fast.

It was only toward the end, when the drugs took over, that something shifted. And for the first time, he wasn't good enough for me.

Not the real him, of course. The addict version. The one who stopped showing up. But now, seeing him show up again, every day... It's amazing. Just... feels like it's too good to be true. Like it might not last. I remember feeling like things were too good to be true before, and look how that turned out.

It could just be nerves, though. Or maybe it's something deeper I haven't let myself unpack yet.

I shake the thoughts away, telling myself to pull it together. I throw my hair on top of my head and take a quick shower.

After brushing my teeth, I pull off a half-assed version of getting ready: messy bun, mascara, lip gloss. Then I throw on some leggings, a long sleeve shirt, and a thick pullover. It won't fit under a coat, and it's definitely not warm enough for February, but I'll only be outside a few minutes.

I enter the kitchen and practically run into Leo. "Shit. Sorry." I brush past him to fill up my water bottle.

"Hey, Al." He pauses what he's doing and turns to me. "Noticed you didn't come home last night."

I glance over as I set my bottle under the filtration spigot. He's leaning against the counter, arms crossed, brow raised, lip twitching with that all-knowing look.

A grin stretches across my face before I can hide it. I laugh softly. "Yeah, I'm not talking about this with you."

"Why not? You talk to me about everything else. What, now you only share when you need something? But when it's the fun stuff, your lips are sealed?"

I press my mouth shut, fighting a smile. "Yep. You're like a brother. And you're married to my friend. No sex talk with you. Sorry."

He chuckles. "Fair enough. And you just confirmed all I needed to know. I'll get the full Vivian version later, after you've had your girl talk. You seem extra chipper this morning. I take it you're happy?"

"You're prying."

He lifts his hands in mock innocence. "Therapist. Guilty. Where you headed in such a hurry?"

"Jensen's taking me to breakfast."

"Where to?"

"Not sure, but you know I love Wildberry. Vivian got me hooked on it."

He takes a sip of his cappuccino. "She never gets sick of it."

Vivian walks into the kitchen with Isla. "Morning."

"Morning," I say as Leo adds, "Speak of the devil," greeting her with a kiss and taking Isla from her arms. "Where's Benson?"

"He's still asleep if you can believe it. But he woke up at four to eat, so I'm not complaining." She turns to me, grinning. "Did you not come home last night?"

Leo raises his brows at me, and my stupid smile gives everything away.

"Oh my God," Vivian gasps. "You spent the night with Jensen?" She heads for the espresso machine. "Tell me everything."

I glance at my phone. It's 9:07, and Jensen hasn't texted me yet, so I slide onto a barstool. Leo grins with satisfaction.

"You can leave," I joke.

"Oh, I'm not going anywhere. Besides, Isla needs breakfast." He sets her down and starts bustling around the kitchen while Vivian makes her coffee. She brings it over, takes a sip, and leans against the counter across from me.

"Okay. Ready." She waves her hand. "Tell me everything."

"I don't have a lot of time, so here's the condensed version. We went out last night, had a lot of fun. I went up to the condo with him to grab a package for Leo." I glance his way. "Which is still in my car, by the way." Then I turn back to Vivian. "Anyway, when I left, I was all conflicted. I wanted to stay but I was scared. And then I remembered the letter he gave me."

"You still hadn't read that?"

I shake my head. "So I did." I pause, my voice going softer. "And then... I don't know. Something shifted. It was like I could actually feel what he was feeling. How broken he'd been. And then how he just... wasn't anymore."

My eyes sting, but I keep going. "He's really put in the work, you know? Changed. He's like this even better version of who he was before. And, *God*, he just loves me so much. For a moment, I just saw everything clearly. I didn't want one more minute wasted without him."

I let out a breath, glancing between them. "Maybe that's dumb. Because I know it could all be taken away at any moment. But that's the only way I can explain it."

"That's not dumb at all," Vivian says gently. "I get that."

Yeah. I guess she would.

I let out a small laugh. "After that, I went back upstairs and basically jumped him."

Leo chuckles with his back to us. "Sorry. I'm not listening. Carry on."

"*Anyway,*" I say, narrowing my eyes at his back. "We did it. And it was maybe the best sex of my life." My head tips back. "*God, it was so good.* Though, to be fair, it's been a *very* long time."

A grin spreads across Vivian's face. "I'm so happy for you, Al. And it's not the same, but... I remember when we"—she nods at Leo—"sort of took a break from each other."

"Sort of?" Leo snorts. "You ran away for a whole month." He looks at me. "Seems to be a theme with you women."

"We just know how to make a man work for us, that's all," I tease. "Sometimes they need a good kick in the ass."

His eyes sparkle with amusement, and it makes me want to throw a pillow at his face and laugh at the same time.

Vivian lifts a brow at Leo. "Did it work?"

He nods, crossing the kitchen. "It worked." He stops in front of her, pressing a kiss to her lips. "Men are stupid creatures who need a woman to put us in our place. Thank God I have you."

"I sense sarcasm."

"Only a little." He grins. "Without you, us men would probably be beating the shit out of each other and having a wank every five minutes."

Vivian laughs. "Damn straight. Now go feed your daughter so I can drink my coffee in peace, otherwise a wank's all you'll be having later."

We all crack up as Leo mutters something to Isla about not making Mommy mad.

Vivian turns back to me. "Anyway... when he finally came after me? Best sex ever."

My phone dings with a text.

"Oh, just a minute. It's him."

JENSEN

Hey, babe. Almost there. Meet you in the parking garage?

A smile pulls at my lips as I type a quick reply.

Cumming.

That'll make him laugh. It'll also help make up for the weirdness of this morning—bring us back to who we've always been.

I drop my phone in my purse and stand. "I've gotta go. We'll talk later."

I give Vivian a quick hug.

"Don't overthink things," she says. "Just have fun."

"Thank you." She just gets me. "Bye Leo. Bye Isla."

"Bye, Al."

With that, I head down the stairs to the parking garage, keys in hand.

* * *

"Where do you want to go?" I ask as we pull out of the parking garage.

Guns N' Roses fills the car, and a wave of nostalgia washes over me, equal parts my dad and the early days with Jensen.

They both love eighties rock. My dad played it nonstop growing up, and it became such a trigger after I moved to New York. One night, a little over a month into dating, Jensen had me over for dinner. I remember it was right after we'd slept together for the first time because all we wanted to do was stay in and have sex. We ordered takeout, and he turned on a playlist filled with the classics: Guns N' Roses, Aerosmith, Black Sabbath.

Buried heartache came knocking, and I tried to ignore it. But when R.E.M.'s "Losing My Religion" came on? I almost lost it.

I'd shoved it all down for so long, I didn't expect the emotion to hit so hard. It came out of nowhere. I asked him to change the playlist, and when he asked why, I told him about my dad for the first time.

He was so great about it. Didn't judge me for not speaking to him, didn't tell me I was wrong, didn't try to fix it. He just listened and held me, made me feel seen in a way no one ever had.

Then we had incredible sex, of course.

That night was the first time I ever had that feeling—where you wonder if you might love someone. When your heart whispers to the deepest parts of your soul that he might be the one.

I look over at him, no longer triggered by the music but comforted by it instead. And that's because of him. Because he encouraged me to talk to my dad after all those years. I stare at the side of his face, overwhelmed with gratitude. For everything he's ever done for me. For all the ways he's loved me.

And for the first time in a long while, the good memories outweigh the bad.

He glances at me. "You open to a change of plans?"

"Yeah. What'd you have in mind?"

He nods toward the backseat, and I twist around to look. A few grocery bags sit on the floor behind him.

"I thought we could head back to Matt's. I'll make you breakfast. We can hang out. Talk."

I raise a brow. "You wanna talk, huh?" He totally wants to get naked. *Subtle, Jensen. Real subtle.*

"I do want to talk," he says, holding my gaze. Then the corner of his mouth pulls into that cocky smirk. "But if talking turns into something else... I won't complain."

A laugh slips out of me. "I'm sure you won't." *I wouldn't either...* but I'm not telling him that.

I wouldn't be mad if he drove out to Montrose Harbor again and pulled me into that backseat.

In fact, the more I think about everything he's done these past few months...

The more I realize just how badly I want to get back to Matt's.

* * *

"Holy crap, did you buy enough berries?" I joke, pulling out the fourth container. He got them all: strawberries, blueberries, blackberries, raspberries. I set the raspberries next to the bananas, then pull the eggs out of the sack and fold the reusable bag, placing it on the pantry shelf.

"Do you want me to start the bacon?" I ask, reaching into the next bag and pulling it out.

As I move to grab more of the groceries, my hands are met with resistance. Jensen's close over mine, gently pulling me toward him. His hands slide up my arms. "I haven't stopped counting the minutes until I get to do this again."

He cups my face and kisses me. No tongue. Just warm lips brushing over mine, slow, soft, sensual. He holds back just enough to have me melting into him, aching for more in a way I didn't know I could. I part my mouth slightly, inviting him in, but he doesn't take the bait. He takes his time, teasing me with slow flicks of his tongue before burying a fist in my hair. He tugs gently, tipping my chin up to gain full access to my neck.

His mouth skims along my jaw, then lower, his breath warm against my skin. The tip of his tongue traces a path to my clavicle, and a flash of heat races down my spine, settling in my core as desire pools between my thighs.

Dammit, Jensen. I've made it way too easy for him. I don't know how. But the way he so easily turns me on—the way he loves me so hard—I'd do anything to feel him like this.

"Are you hungry?" His deep voice sends a shiver up my neck.

"Yes," I whisper.

He chuckles, low and wicked in my ear. "You want me to start the bacon?"

"No."

"Then what do you want?"

"You," I breathe, my mind scrambling to form words.

His breath ghosts along my jaw, voice dropping even lower. "Good. Because I want to devour every inch of you."

The soft and slow is gone in an instant as he kisses me hungrily, sucking my bottom lip into his mouth. A moan forces its way up my throat as he deepens the kiss, his tongue teasing mine.

His hands move down my body, slow—taking his time, fingertips grazing every curve, until he reaches my waist. He grips it firmly and tugs me closer, pressing his hard length against me.

Jesus. My mind blanks.

Just... *Jesus.*

My arms instinctively fold around his neck, and I can't think, can't lead. I'm in response mode only. Submissively his. I arch into him as he backs me against the island. His hands explore my ass, then wrap around my thighs as he lifts me. I open my legs and he steps between them, setting me onto the counter.

His palms glide up my sides, guiding my arms above my head before breaking our kiss. His eyes stay locked on mine as he swallows, his Adam's apple bobbing. The tension sizzles. Then his fingers curl under the hem of my shirt, tugging it up and over my head.

A cocky smirk tugs at one side of his lip, and God, it's the sexiest thing. Like he's got me right where he wants me, and there isn't a damn thing I can do about it. I love that smirk. It makes me feel like I'm the most desired woman in the world. Like he'd pick me. Every. Time.

Over and over.

And he does. He keeps choosing me.

Even when I shut him out.

Even when I ignore him.

Even when he knows I don't trust him. Not completely.

Even when he tells me he loves me, and I don't say it back.

He keeps coming back. He keeps showing up. He keeps loving me. And it's that kind of love that makes me believe we can make it. That we'll come out the other side stronger than ever.

It wraps around my heart like armor, filling every crack, shielding it from the pain I once thought would break me.

He lowers my bra and runs his tongue along my nipple. *This obviously doesn't help my case.* My head falls back, and I gasp. He closes his mouth around it and sucks, his tongue flicking in slow circles that send a buzz straight through me. *Holy shit. I feel like I'm two beers deep.*

I lean back on one hand, the other cradling the back of his head, pressing him closer.

He growls against my skin. "Fuck, Alley." His teeth scrape gently, drawing a breathy, "Jesus," from me.

His hands snake around to my back, fingers fumbling with the clasp of my bra. Both my hands thread into his hair now as he licks and sucks and kisses across my breasts.

I scoot closer to the edge, desperate for pressure as the pulsing builds, loud in my ears, impossible to separate from the ache deep inside me.

His mouth makes its way back to mine, and I kiss him with so much force it feels like I'm back in high school—caught up in every new sensation, pouring everything I'm feeling into one hot, desperate make-out.

He pulls away suddenly, dragging a hand through his hair. "Dammit, babe. I'm never going to get anything done again."

I laugh softly against his neck as he lifts me off the counter and sets me down. But the second my feet hit the floor, his mouth is on mine again, possessive and carnal.

"I want to quit my job and be with you all fucking day. Every day."

I wouldn't hate that.

We stumble backward down the hall, his hands already sliding into my leggings.

I grin against his lips as my fingers dip beneath his waistband. I'm still not sure what I'm doing. Still don't trust this fully, but I'm trying. Trying to be present. To just let myself feel what I'm feeling and go with it.

God, this feels so good.

I unbutton his pants in a rush, tugging the zipper down. My fingers brush his firm cock and he groans. "Jesus Christ. Do you know how many times I've thought about this the past few months?"

We hit the bed and fall back together, his hands roaming greedily over me. "How many times I've fucked you in my mind?"

I wrap my hand around him and give a slow, deliberate stroke. "Probably the same amount as me."

Right now? All I feel is Jensen: his hard cock in my hand, his hungry lips on mine, his possessive hands claiming me.

And in this moment, it makes me feel so many things. Nervous. Excited. Wanted.

More importantly, it reminds me what it's like when two people are working toward the same goal. What can happen when they both give more than they take. When they show up for each other.

When they trust each other.

And I want to trust him. I want to believe this is what forever could be—because it feels so damn good to be loved by him.

He yanks my leggings and underwear down, and before I can catch my breath, a moan pours from my lips as his finger glides along my wet, sensitive center.

"God, I missed your pussy."

I squeeze my legs together, desperate for friction, for more. And *damn*, the dirty talk? I've missed that. It's always been such a turn-on, and I know I just soaked his fingers.

He drops to his knees without a word, spreading me open, his breath hot against my slick skin before his tongue makes the first slow, devastating pass. My head tips back, a sharp gasp tearing from my throat—

Yeah... breakfast can definitely wait.

Chapter Twenty-Six

ALLEY

I TAKE a bite of bacon and chew, giving Jensen a once-over, or maybe a twice-over. Honestly, I've lost count of how many times my eyes have wandered over his bare chest while we've been eating.

He's across from me at Matt's small kitchen table, wearing nothing but a pair of joggers. I'm in one of his T-shirts and the thong I was wearing when I came over.

We'd just had sex. Then took a shower where I gave him a blow job. And still, I couldn't stop staring while he stood at the stove making bacon. His pants sat low on his hips, and that stupid, perfect V makes my mouth water. And then there's the faint trail of hair leading down to—

I swallow the bite, washing it down with a sip from the latte I made on Matt's Nespresso machine.

Jensen finishes chewing, then says, "So, I have something to ask you. And before I do, you should know, if you don't say yes, Megan might actually kill me. Just a little FYI."

"Wow, no pressure or anything." I pop a berry into my mouth, smiling.

"What are you doing in three weeks? Thursday to Sunday?"

"I'd be working Thursday, but Friday to Sunday? Probably doing you. Why?"

His bacon crunches as he takes a bite. He leans forward, elbows on the table, chewing while his tongue swipes the corner of his lip before it curves into a smirk. "What makes you think I don't have plans with someone else?"

"Hmm." I narrow my eyes, pretending to think. "The fact that you just came down my throat three minutes after I took your cock in my mouth."

He chuckles. "Alright, you win. But how about you do me in the Berkshires? We leave Thursday the twentieth. You know it's expected I go. But it's a hard pass if you're not coming, because I'm not giving up blow jobs for skiing. And you know how much I love skiing." He flashes that grin that's impossible to refuse. "I'm hoping you'll let me have both."

"I work Thursdays. I'd have to see if someone can cover for me. It's too late to request the time off, and I already took a lot of days while my dad was in the hospital."

I'm not sure how I feel about this. Part of me wants to go. I love the Berkshires, but I'm not sure I'm ready for something like that. Not ready to dive back into family stuff so soon. Not ready to get attached again. Because what if this goes south and I lose them all over again? It was hard enough the first time.

I love Jensen's family. I miss them.

Well, most of them. I'm dreading the day I have to face his mom again. I'd avoid her forever if I could, partly because I know I need to let go of the grudge I've been carrying for way too long. And because I know we'll have to talk, really talk, if we're ever going to get past it. And that won't be a fun conversation.

Jensen's doing it, though—having all the hard conversations. Making amends. Apologizing. Righting his wrongs. It's humbling, removing the ego and admitting your faults. It's hard.

And it sucks.

Christy wasn't the only one in the wrong. I was too. Not for my blow-up, I think that was understandable. Justified, even. But for everything since. Every time she's tried to make amends, I've shut her out. I haven't been forgiving. I won't let it go.

And that's wrong of me. We all made mistakes. We all have

regrets. We were all just trying to stay afloat, doing what we thought was best for Jensen and for ourselves in that moment. Each of us with our own reality. Our own perception.

There's no manual for addiction. Sure, there are tools—Al-Anon, group therapy, the dos and don'ts.

Do give tough love.

Don't enable.

Do let them fall so they can choose to get back up.

Don't pick them up every time.

The problem is, most of us don't follow the rules. Especially when it's someone we love. We give second chances wrapped in hope. We call it love. We call it grace. But really? It's fear. The fear of losing them. The fear of letting go.

His gaze is on me, hopeful, waiting patiently for me to answer. This means so much to him. I know it does. He's trying so damn hard, making every effort to make up for the past. He's been practically perfect. Everything I could ever want, and everything I've hoped for.

I let out a small sigh. *I did tell him I wanted to try. That I was all in.* "Let me ask around about Thursday. But either way, I'll come Friday to Sunday. Maybe fly in Thursday night."

He exhales, lips curving into that sexy grin that always gets me. Warmth shoots through me, the kind that swells in your chest when you stumble across an old photo you forgot you had. I love seeing him happy. Love giving him this win.

"Thanks, babe. Means a lot to me. And it's a relief. Megan's been on my ass. You know how she gets."

I laugh. "I can only imagine."

"You have no idea," he murmurs, shaking his head.

We eat in comfortable silence for the next few minutes, until Jensen looks up again. "I have another question."

"Shoot."

"Will you come to New York next weekend? It's Super Bowl. I'll get your plane ticket. Actually..." He pauses, eyes steady on mine. "I really want you to just start using the joint account again."

He sets down his fork. "Let me take care of you, babe. Come back home."

Shit. My heart flutters, picking up speed, nerves rising in my throat. *Why is my body reacting like this?*

Memories flash—our apartment. Jensen. Me. Panic. Fear. Loss.

"I'm not sure I'm ready for that," I say slowly, feeling the resistance in my chest.

He nods, disappointment flickering before he forces a small smile. "That's okay. Thought it was worth asking."

Dammit. As good as it felt to make him happy moments ago, it feels just as awful to be the one taking it away.

He loves the Super Bowl. It's a whole thing every year with Matt, sometimes the rest of his family, too. We could watch it in Chicago, and I know he'd do that for me. But I don't want him to sacrifice more than he already is. Maybe I can find a way to make it work.

"What if I stayed at a hotel? Or I could maybe even fly in for the day, arrive in the morning, leave that night? It's not a long flight."

His brows pull together. "You don't want to be in our home?"

The way he says it—*God*, I can't even describe what it does to me. I watch the moment he connects the apartment to my fears, and it breaks me open. My heart actually *hurts*.

"Um..." He shakes his head, like he can will away the truth, then forces another smile. "I'll take whatever I can get. We'll figure it out. Whatever's best for you."

"The doctor who does surgeries on Mondays has tickets to the game, so I actually have that day off. We can look at flights today," I offer.

His whole face changes, satisfaction replacing the defeat. It eases the tightness in my chest a little. "Let's book both flights. God, Megan's gonna be stoked. Want me to add you to the group chat?"

"Sure." I do miss an Adams sibling group chat. They've always had two: one with Amber and me, and one with the guys and Megan. And I'm either all in or I'm not. I can't half-ass this. Even if I'm not entirely ready, I have to keep moving forward. Face my fears.

We finish eating and cleaning the kitchen... and somehow end up exhausted and naked on the couch again.

Jensen never put a shirt on. And he wouldn't stop touching me while I did the dishes. He stood behind me, kissing my neck and shoulders, his hands trailing everywhere. I almost turned around and let him have me right there, but I hate leaving a mess. So instead, I pressed my ass back into him, moaning softly when his hands slipped into my underwear. Let him tease and work me into absolute oblivion while whispering sweet and dirty things in my ear. It took twice as long to get through the dishes, and I even sprayed him a few times with the water just so I could focus.

He's distracting. So damn distracting.

And now here we are, cuddling on the couch. *Matt's couch. Yikes.* I didn't think about that... and now I can't help but wonder how many other naked girls have been here. I shove the thought away. *Gross.*

Jensen's fingers trace lazy circles along my stomach, his arms wrapped snugly around me. I sink back into him, letting my arms fold over his. God. Twice in one day and it's not even lunchtime. Add in the second round of late-night shenanigans that went well into the early morning, and... yeah.

This could definitely become a problem.

* * *

I sit up carefully, not wanting to wake Jensen. We crashed on the couch, and when I grab my phone, I see we've been out for—an hour and a half? *Holy shit.* I rarely nap, and when I do, they're usually short.

A text from Leo pops up.

LEO

I'm taking Viv out tonight. Don't know your plans, but wanted you to know we hired a sitter. Just in case you were planning to be here.

Ok, thanks for the heads up. I'll probably stay at Matt's with Jensen. Glad you guys get a night out! Also... I need a therapy session.

LEO

That's great. Are you going to call my friend I referred you to and make an appt?

Lol. No. I just mean I need you to carve out some time for me to chat. Ha.

LEO

WHEN are you going to get yourself a therapist?! I should refuse to talk to you. Force your hand.

Blah, blah. But you're the best therapist I've ever had. Why would I go anywhere else?

LEO

I'm not your bloody therapist. I'm your friend.

More like a brother… therefore, better than a therapist because you love me and won't let me make stupid decisions.

With that in mind… Jensen invited me out to New York next weekend and it gave me so much anxiety thinking about going home—back to our apartment. Why did it do that? Should I go? I was thinking maybe I'd get a hotel…

LEO

Christ, Alley. Seriously. Make a damn appt.

It makes sense, though. That's where most of the trauma was, yeah? All your worst memories. Even if you have good ones there too. The trauma can overpower the good unless you process it and work through it. Which is why you NEED to get yourself a BLOODY THERAPIST.

I laugh softly. I love pushing his buttons.

LEO

Not to mention couples therapy. You could use someone helping both of you while you navigate this.

I frown, mulling it over. He's probably right. I know I need my own too. I'm just not there yet.

> Fine. You're probably right with that one. Got any recs for a couples therapist?

He shoots over a contact, and I save it in my phone before searching for Zach's name.

I snap a selfie of sleeping Jensen and me, careful not to expose any body parts, and send it to him. He and Joey have been in Jamaica for the past two weeks, and he made me promise him updates. He's been way easier to share this stuff with than Scarlett. Probably because Joey has a pretty colorful past, and hearing his stories makes him more open to believing people can change.

> Pretty sure I haven't gotten anything done this weekend... well, except for Jensen. Lol.

I stand, step into my underwear, and pull Jensen's tee back over my head before heading into the kitchen for a drink. I grab a glass from the cupboard and fill it with filtered osmosis water.

My phone buzzes.

ZACH

HELL YES, BOO! GET IT!!!

Balloons float up my screen and pop, and my grin stretches a mile wide.

Chapter Twenty-Seven

JENSEN

I PACE MATT'S KITCHEN, palms sweaty, nerves buzzing. Alley's on her way over, and I'm a fucking mess. Not because I'm nervous to see her—we spent most of yesterday together. I picked her up from the airport in the morning, took her to breakfast, then grabbed coffees to go and bundled up for a walk around Central Park. We had lunch, couples massages, and stopped at a new cozy bookstore where I let her wander (for what felt like forever) and choose whatever she wanted. We sat at a table with another coffee for over an hour, laughing as I read dirty scenes from some of the books she was deciding on. It was fun and easy and exactly what we needed.

She had dinner with Scarlett and stayed at her place last night. She plans to go back there after the game tonight.

I'm nervous because she's coming *here*. To our building. Where our home sits a few floors below. Matt said she's only been back once, a few weeks after she moved out, to grab some things.

I just want everything to be perfect. For her to feel comfortable. For her to miss this, and miss being here with me.

Who am I kidding? I want her to stay the night with me. Tonight. In our home.

Megan and Kevin are coming...

Oh, and Scarlett too—so, that'll be fun.

Like I said, I'm a mess.

I blow out a breath, raking a hand through my hair. Then check the fridge for the third time, making sure the sparkling waters are cold.

"Jesus, dude. Calm down." Matt's voice carries from the foyer as he comes down the winding staircase with two cases of beer in his arms.

"It's not like you're trying to impress some new girl or get laid for the first time," he says, setting the beer on the counter and slapping my back. "This is *Alley*. Your *wife*. I know you're nervous, but you don't need to put on some show. That's just gonna make it fucking weird." He waves a hand in front of me. "Whatever this is? Not normal. The last time I saw you this nervous was when you took Ashley Bengal to junior prom. Relax."

I stop pacing and plant both hands on the countertop, smirking. "And do you remember what happened that night?"

Matt laughs. "Touché."

I had sex with Ashley Bengal that night. I still remember the sweet smell of her Vera Wang perfume. I'd bought it for her birthday a few days earlier.

He cracks open the beer cases and starts stocking the fridge. I join in, pulling bottles from the cardboard and handing them to him.

"Don't question my methods," I say. "They've never failed me."

"Except for that one time you got hooked on Oxy." He pops open a beer, takes a swig, and eyes me over the neck of the bottle. "Too soon?"

I chuckle. "Only if you want a black eye to go with that beer."

He howls, swaps the beer for a can of Liquid Death water, and hands it to me. "Got you some of these. I know it's not exciting, but I didn't want you to feel left out."

"Thanks, man. I appreciate it." I really do. I take the can from him and pop it open. The cold condensation seeps into my palm, and it's crazy how just holding a can or bottle can quiet the craving to blend in. Means a lot that he thought about me.

The elevator doors slide open, and Alley and Scarlett step into the foyer. *God, she's beautiful.* I grin, and my pulse kicks up a notch as my eyes roam over her. She's wearing one of my jerseys. She must've taken it when she packed, and that alone punches me right in the fucking feels. It brings back memories of Sunday nights on the couch with her curled up in it.

"Hey, Al. Hey, Scarlett," Matt calls out as I'm already moving toward her.

We meet halfway, and I don't slow down. I crash into her, mouth first, tasting her. My hand slides into her hair, the silky strands combing through my fingers as she makes this soft *mmm* that shoots straight to the tip of my dick.

I finally break the kiss, still grinning like a stupid-happy fool. She gives me a slow, sexy smile, catching her bottom lip between her teeth. My gaze drops. *Jesus Christ.* She's wearing biker shorts. My jersey's big. I'm six-two, and on her? It looks like she's wearing nothing underneath.

She knows I lose my mind when she wears those shorts.

It's hot—*she's* hot. I'm getting hard, and it's a fucking problem.

"Damn, baby," I murmur. "You look hot."

"Thank you." She plants another kiss on my lips before turning to hug Matt, who's hovering a step behind me.

Scarlett's already hugged him and is now unpacking items from the paper bag she brought in.

"Hey, Scarlett," I call out.

"Hey." She doesn't even look up.

Christ. This should be fun.

* * *

"Super Bowl in the Berkshires was so much fun two years ago. We should've done that again," Megan says as the game cuts to commercial. There's only three minutes of playtime left before halftime.

"Yeah, but Jeff and Amber couldn't go this weekend, remember? Hence, why they aren't here," Matt says as he stands. "I gotta pee."

He disappears down the hall. I turn my head, finding Alley in the kitchen with Scarlett, manning the appetizers. She's mixing a dip and chatting with Scarlett, who's perched on a stool across from her. Megan gets up and joins them.

Seeing Alley and Megan together again here in New York was one for the books. I don't know who cried more, but it gave me hope. Hope that even if it takes Alley a while to trust me, maybe she'll stick around for the others. *God, that's pathetic.* I don't know if she'll ever fully come back to me. But if flirty Super Bowls and separate hotel rooms is all I get? I'll fucking take it.

"How long is Alley in town?" Kevin asks.

I grab the remote and turn the volume down. Between the girls in the kitchen, and the TV, it's loud. Matt's ceilings are high and everything carries in here. "She leaves tomorrow."

He nods. "How's having her back home?"

"It's been great, but she hasn't come home yet. She's staying with Scarlett."

"Oh, damn. You okay with that?"

"Not much I can really do about it," I say with a shrug. "But I'll be in Chicago again next weekend. And then we have the Berkshires. I'm just taking it a day at a time. She'll get there."

He gives me a half-smile that says *I'd hate to be you*, and shifts the conversation to work.

Matt sits back down and asks Kevin a question, and Alley's laugh pulls my attention. I look over my shoulder, catching her watching me. She doesn't look away, just holds my gaze, a faint grin tugging at her mouth before she finally looks down at her phone.

Seconds later, mine buzzes.

ALLEY

Do you have a boner?

I chuckle to myself. She's so damn cute.

Why? You wanna sit on it?

ALLEY

Depends...

On???

ALLEY

On whether you can be sneaky.

A grin spreads wide across my face.

Babe—sneaky's my middle name.

ALLEY

Wanna meet me in the back room?

Depends…

ALLEY

On???

I feel Matt's eyes on me, but I don't look up. I'm too focused on the next text. Gotta get it just right if I want her all hot and bothered.

Whether you can be quiet when I drag my tongue up the center of your pussy. I don't want anyone to hear when you cum. That's for me. Only me.

I look up. Matt's smirking, glancing between Alley and me, eyebrow raised. It's hella fucking obvious.

Don't care.

I catch her reading my text. Her eyes go wide, and she bites her lip, failing to hide the smile that's creeping in as she types.

ALLEY

Hope you brought a gag.

My blood's already rushing south before she even drops her phone on the counter, says something to the girls, and walks out of the kitchen. Down the hall. Toward the back room.

I stretch my arms over my head, then stand. "Gotta pee."

Matt chuckles. "Sure you do," he mutters. Then, louder, "I know how you always love the halftime show."

He's not wrong. Alley and I have a reputation for disappearing during halftime. I can't even remember the last one I watched since meeting her.

Oh well.

If you'd told me six months ago we'd be back to sneaking off during halftime, I don't know if I'd have believed it. But here she is, flirting with me like I'm hers again.

I head down the hall and make a right just as Alley slips into the back room. My pace quickens. My cock's throbbing, and with every step closer to her, I get harder.

God, I've missed this.

I step into the room, and Alley's lips are on mine before the door closes behind me.

"Lock the door," she whispers against my mouth.

Don't mind if I do. My hand's already reaching for it.

* * *

Kevin and Matt clink their shot glasses of whiskey together and tip them back in one smooth motion. Envy hits me right in the gut. That nagging ache to be included, to just feel normal.

But only a little.

Megan's voice pulls my attention. "Al, I can't even tell you how happy I am that you're coming to the Berkshires. I screamed when I read Jensen's text that you were in." She grins, and it warms my chest. Seeing Megan and Alley talking and laughing like the good old days? It's pretty fucking special.

"I can confirm she did, in fact, scream," Kevin says, eyes glazed from all the shots.

We're all spread around the kitchen counter, some standing, some sitting.

Alley's grinning, her eyes shining with a happiness I haven't seen in so long. I can't seem to keep my eyes off her. I don't want to miss a second of that joy, and I can't stop thinking about the halftime show in the back bedroom. Rough. Bossy. Wild. We kept laughing, trying to stay quiet, and then just as quickly, we stopped caring if everyone heard. It's one I'll never forget.

Her eyes shift to Megan. "I'm excited to go. Excited to see Amber and Jeff too."

"So how does it feel being back in New York? Has it been weird settling back in at home?"

Shit. I grimace, tightening the grip on my drink. I can't believe I didn't mention Alley wasn't staying with me. That she wasn't coming *home.* But then, why would that come up? And why wouldn't Megan assume she was staying with me? She's just making conversation—but it's a loaded question and it's too soon. *Way too damn soon.* Matt mutters a low *Jesus* beside me, and it's exactly what I'm thinking.

I keep my gaze on Alley, watching, waiting, trying to read her reaction. *Where the hell are you in all of this?* One minute she's jumping me in the back room and the next...

Her arms fold across her chest. *Protection. Discomfort.* "It's been good." She glances at me. "Jensen and I had a lot of fun yesterday hanging out around the city."

She doesn't say anything else. Just lets Megan think what she wants. Fine by me.

Across the counter, Scarlett shifts her weight, eyes flicking from Alley to Megan and back again. There's a beat of hesitation before she blurts, "Alley's not staying at home. She's staying with me."

Alley shoots her a look. Scarlett shrugs, mouthing a quick *sorry.*

Matt plants a hand to his face. Kevin shifts in his seat. And my stomach is tying itself in knots.

Megan frowns. "Why?" She looks between me and Alley. "I mean... you two seem fine. We all heard you during halftime. So..."

"Meg," I cut in, shaking my head.

She exhales, turns to Alley, and waits for an explanation.

Alley stares at the counter, tension thick in the air.

"She's not ready yet," Scarlett cuts in before Alley can speak. "She literally has nightmares about the shit that went on in their apartment." She looks around. "I don't even think you all know the half of it."

"Scarlett," Alley says softly.

My eyes stay locked on her. *I'm here. I'm right fucking here. I'm not going anywhere.* If she'd only look at me...

"No. I'm sorry," Scarlett says, turning to Alley. "I saw it, okay? I sat there and listened to you cry. I heard every horrible story. I watched you fall apart." She points at Matt. "And you did too. Honestly, I don't know how you let this go so easily."

Jesus. This parachute's a knapsack.

Matt straightens beside me. "I did," he admits. "But I know Jensen. And I know what he's done to fix this. I've seen it." He pushes off the counter. "I need some air," he mutters, heading for the balcony. The sliding door opens, then closes, awkward silence following.

Alley blinks fast, her chest rising and falling. *Dammit. She's trying not to cry.*

"Scarlett," I say, "I know you're angry with me. You have every right to be. But stop shoving me under the bus. Alley's her own person. She gets to choose what she does with her life."

"Yeah. And she also gets to choose where she wants to sleep, Jensen. And she doesn't want to go back to that apartment."

"No shit!" My voice jumps, sharp enough to surprise me. "Jesus, Scarlett." I drag a hand down my face. "Let's hash this out right now. Whatever you've got to say, say it, so we can move on."

It doesn't help that everyone here but Alley and me is drunk.

Scarlett's eyes well up, lips pressed together. She takes a shaky breath, and then it all comes out in a sob. "God! I'm so angry with you! You don't even know how she was." Her voice cracks, hands shaking as she wipes her cheeks. "You don't even know. You hurt her so much. Made her cry every fucking day."

Alley loses the fight to keep it in. *Shit.* Her breath hitches, shoulders trembling, and there's this small, broken sound that guts me. I move swiftly, wrapping my arms around her. She falls into me, and my chest aches so hard I feel it everywhere. My eyes burn. My throat swells. The tension in here makes poker night feel like a fucking vacation.

"I know," I tell Scarlett, my voice low but steady. "And I'm sorry. I was selfish. I was fucked up. And if I could take it back, I would. Every single bit of it."

Megan watches from the corner, arms crossed tight, her expression heavy. Kevin looks like he's wishing he could be anywhere but here.

Scarlett scoffs, folding her arms with a glare sharp enough to cut glass.

"We all saw it, Scarlett," Megan says, voice soft but edged with grit. "And we all love Alley. It broke all of us. But we also love Jensen.

We watched *him* break, too." Her voice wavers, the defense blind-siding me in the best way. She blinks back tears, but they spill regardless. "Trust me, I know how pissed you are. But look at them." She gestures to Alley and me. "God, they were the perfect couple. What they had was beautiful. Doesn't this..." She points again. "Doesn't seeing them like this make you want it to work?"

Dammit, Meg. Her words hit me square in the chest. My throat burns as I fight to keep my emotions in check.

Scarlett shakes her head hard. "No. I'm sorry. It doesn't." She grabs both her purse and Alley's. "I'm leaving. Come on, Al. Let's go."

Alley doesn't move. Her arms just cinch tighter around my waist.

I press a kiss to the top of her head before loosening my hold. "Scarlett, please. Just... talk to me."

"I don't want to talk to you."

"Jesus. What more can I do?" My voice cracks. "You were *my* friend once, too. I'm doing everything I can to make things better. Why can't you see I'm trying?"

"Trying doesn't erase what you did." Her voice is choked. Raw. "You can't undo the damage. Yes, you were my friend, but I'll always be Alley's friend first. And she deserved better than what you gave her. I don't care how it started, your true colors showed in the end. That erased all the good."

My jaw tightens. "Is that all?" I bite out. "Don't hold back."

Her eyes narrow. "Fine. You better not fucking hurt her again." She takes a step closer, heat practically rolling off her. "Do you even remember the last night before she left? Or the night she dressed up for you in lingerie and you never came home? Or how about that double date, when you lost your damn mind?" She shakes her head, disgust flashing in her eyes. "Didn't think so."

I rake a hand through my hair, a groan tearing out of me. "Fuck." My gaze locks on hers. "You think I don't know what I did? What I lost? You think I don't hate myself for it? I wake up every day praying she doesn't run. I go to sleep begging she'll still be there when I open my eyes."

I step forward, my voice shaking. "Don't think for a second I don't know I failed her. That she deserved better. That I'll never be good enough."

I force a breath, willing myself to calm down. "I hurt her. I hurt all of you. Maybe that erases all the good for now. But I'll still show up for her. Every damn day. Because I love her."

I hold Scarlett's gaze, palms damp, heart pounding. "I know I messed up, but I'm here now. I'm not walking away, and I don't expect you to forgive me." I glance at Alley, then back to her, my voice softer now. "You matter to her, which means you matter to me. All I'm asking is that you give me a chance. I swear you won't regret it. I'll be the man she deserves. Better than I was before."

The silence hangs between us like a bomb, ready to blow. Scarlett's face is blotchy from crying, her eyes bloodshot and glassy. She looks between me and Alley, torn. There's nothing left to say. I've stripped myself bare and begged for mercy. If she can't take me as I am now, she never will.

In rehab we talked a lot about redemption and making amends. But nothing prepares you for this: standing in front of someone you hurt, armor gone, praying they'll see the man you're trying to be.

Scarlett takes a long breath, pressing her fingers under her eyes to wipe away the last of her tears. Her shoulders sag. Then she looks at me and sighs. "Fine."

My head snaps in her direction, brows furrowing. *What?*

"I'll give you a chance. I'll try." She looks at Alley. "For Alley."

Relief rips through me, and I'm moving, pulling her into a hug before I can even think. "Thank you."

She hesitates, stiff at first, then slowly wraps her arms around me, cautious, like she's still unsure.

When she lets go, Alley's already there, arms open. They cling to each other, voices thick with emotion. "Thank you," Alley says softly. "I love you."

"I love you too. I just want you to be happy," Scarlett says back.

"I know," Alley whispers. "I know."

They step apart, and Alley turns to me, eyes steady. "I'm going to come home tonight."

My brain short-circuits. For a second, I think I misheard her, but she holds my gaze, unflinching.

"Really?" My voice comes out low and rough, almost disbelieving.

She nods once.

God, this is everything. My chest tightens, air threatening to escape all at once.

I pull her in, arms locking around her, praying she doesn't change her mind.

She's finally coming home.

Chapter Twenty-Eight

ALLEY

THE BOTTLES CLINK TOGETHER as I toss them into the glass recycle bin. That's the last of them. I move on to gathering garbage from Matt's living room and kitchen, scooping up paper plates and half-empty cups.

The patio door slides open.

"Al, you don't need to clean up. Maggie's coming tomorrow morning," Matt says as he walks toward me.

"It's fine. You know I can't leave a mess."

"But you don't live here. You don't even have to look at it. You can just... leave."

"I know." I don't look up. I just keep moving. I'm afraid the night will catch up to me if I stop.

Matt doesn't press. He passes me, grabs a Voss water from the fridge, and disappears back outside.

Everyone's gone now, except for Jensen and me, but the tension left behind still hovers like a thick fog. Even after Scarlett hugged Jensen and I told him I'd stay with him tonight, the awkwardness that followed was suffocating. No one knew where to look. Kevin cleared his throat, muttered something, and went to the patio. Scarlett slipped out without saying another word. Megan trailed after Kevin.

Now it's just us.

Jensen held me, whispering the sweetest things, though I couldn't tell you what they were. It's like I blacked out in his arms, letting them hold me up while the silence rang in my ears and the haze blurred my vision.

Eventually, he loosened his hold, and I slipped away, going straight into cleaning mode. Picking up empty plates and wiping countertops. Moving like a robot.

I told him I'd stay with him.

I want to. I really do. But I'm nowhere near ready, and now I'm nervous. Nervous to walk down the same hallway that seemed never-ending the morning I left. To step into the elevator that carried me out when it felt like bricks were crushing my chest. To walk into the place I used to call home. The place that holds some of my best memories of Jensen. Of us. Where I fell in love with him.

But it's also where all the pain is. Where I sat for hours, staring at the walls while they stared back at me, watching me cry. Where promises and vows were broken by lies and locked doors.

So I keep cleaning.

I was proud of him tonight. For being so vulnerable with Scarlett. The way he stood up for himself. Owned his shit. Tried to fix it with her, for me. In front of everyone.

It felt like every answer I'd been searching for came crashing into me at once. *Here they are. Here he is. The old Jensen. The man you fell in love with.*

He's still here.

He's. Right. Here.

All I had to do was reach out and tell him that I wanted him too. Tell him I'd go home with him. So I did. At the time, it felt like the obvious choice. How can we work on our relationship when we only see each other a few days a week? It seemed like the right thing to do. A simple decision.

Except... it's not. Nothing about this is simple.

My fingers tremble as I pull open the drawer to the trash, tossing in another handful of garbage. I grab a rag and start wiping down the counters. I'm a clean freak on a normal day, but when I'm stressed? I go into overdrive.

Once I started cleaning, Jensen went out on the balcony with Matt.

The patio door slides open again. This time, it's Jensen's voice that pulls my attention. "Hey, babe. You ready to go?"

* * *

WE STEP OFF THE ELEVATOR, my grip tightening around Jensen's hand. My heart beats faster with every step down the hallway. *This isn't a big deal,* I tell myself. *It's fine. You're fine.*

Nerves crawl up my spine as Jensen punches in the code. Zero. Four. One. Three.

"Babe?"

I look up.

"You okay?"

No. I nod anyway. "Yeah. Of course." I smile but it's forced and stiff.

He pushes the door and we both step inside, and I feel... okay. *I'm okay.*

My gaze sweeps across the kitchen and the living room, and I let out a sigh of relief. Warmth rushes through me, spreading into every limb, bringing the kind of comfort I can only call *home.* Not Vivian and Leo's place. Not Matt's. *Ours.*

I set my purse on the stool and take a slow, steady breath. A smile curves my lips as Jensen heads for the fridge, grabbing two waters.

I make my way into the living room, letting the feeling of being here soak in. My fingers trail along the back of the couch, my gaze catching on Phyllis, my elephant ear plant, in the corner by the window.

She's *thriving.*

The backs of my eyes sting as a sudden wave of emotion slams into me. I press my lips together and sniff. *He took care of Phyllis.*

I'd pictured her hanging on by a leaf or two, half-dead—not like this. She's taller, fuller, stronger than ever.

I can feel Jensen watching me, patient and quiet, letting me take it all in.

"You took care of Phyllis," I say, turning toward him.

His head dips in a small nod. "Told you I did."

I brush a finger under my eye, overwhelmed by how much this stupid, simple thing matters.

"How you feeling?" he asks, crossing the room, waters in hand. "You wanna watch a movie? Go to bed? Talk?"

He knows. He knows me so well that he understands exactly where I am right now, even if he doesn't fully get it. Even if he's unaware of the full weight of his choices and their consequences, their effect on me. Even if he doesn't remember. He's still aware.

He's not making jokes. Not making a move, though I wouldn't say no, especially after that halftime show. *Good Lord.* But he knows it's not the time. And that alone tells me—this is the Jensen I fell in love with.

The man who waited a month before we slept together. The man who memorized my coffee order after a single run-in at the coffee shop, before he even knew if he'd see me again. The man who showered me with affection and attention. Who always knew what I needed, in every moment of every day.

I slide my arms around his back and tilt my chin up. "I just want to be with you. Talk. Snuggle. We can get ready for bed and then... will you just hold me?"

His lips twitch, one corner curving into that trademark smirk that always makes me feel more at ease.

"I'd love that, babe." He rubs my shoulders, presses a kiss to my forehead, then threads his fingers through mine and leads me toward the bedroom. Down the hall.

My eyes flick to the office door, and a spark of panic taps against the edge of my peace.

As we near it, he slows, opens the door, and pushes it all the way until it's flush against the wall.

A calm pours over me, my pulse steadying. *Oh my God.* He can't possibly know how much that means to me. How much I needed it.

His hands come up to cup my face, his eyes meeting mine. "Office door stays open. Always." He leans in, brushing his lips over mine—

soft, tentative—then kisses me again, firmer this time but no tongue. Just quiet devotion.

"Let's get ready for bed," he says with a smile. Then, he smacks my ass with a low grunt, his bottom lip catching between his teeth.

I laugh, the sound coming easily, and it feels so damn good. It's so natural. Images flash in my mind, ones of us laughing, teasing, and having fun. Ones I'd buried, because the bad always took over.

But not tonight.

Tonight's about new beginnings. About moving forward and leaving the past where it belongs.

* * *

It's dark.

Jensen's fingers trace slowly back and forth, skimming the top of my breast. I'm turned on, but more than that, it just feels good—being wrapped in his arms, spooning. It's my favorite way to cuddle: his chest pressed to my back, my head half on the pillow, half on his bicep. Every space between us sealed tight. His bottom arm draped over mine, my top arm holding his.

It's intimate, warm, and the way we usually fall asleep after sex.

But we haven't had sex.

"Is it worse to have me here and *not* have sex than to have me at Scarlett's?" I murmur.

"Nothing's worse than not having you here." His voice is low and gravelly, and it sends a slow vibration down my spine.

I tighten my hold on him. "I love this. Being held by you. It's one of my favorite things."

"I love holding you."

I told him earlier I didn't want to have sex tonight. Not because I don't want to—*God, I do*—but because I needed to be here. Really be here. I wanted to feel our home. Feel Jensen. Feel everything without sex soothing my anxiety or giving me a false sense of security.

It's worked. Everything about being here feels right. And damn, it feels good to be back in my own bed. Leo and Vivian's is comfortable, but it's not mine.

We've been reminiscing again. We talked about tonight, too, about Scarlett and Megan, and about Matt standing up for Jensen. That meant everything. Jensen asked if I was mad at him. Or at Scarlett.

I told him I wasn't.

I'm not. Mad isn't the right word. Frustrated, maybe? It was awkward and uncomfortable—very non-self-aware of Scarlett and Megan, but I get it. I just wish I hadn't been in the middle of it all. The questions from Megan. Stuck between Jensen and Scarlett. I don't blame any of them for their feelings, especially Scarlett.

I didn't tell her much for a long time, and even after I did, it took me a while to open up fully. But in that last month before I left, when Jensen relapsed again and everything fell apart, she was one of my go-tos. I spent the night at her place more than once. Cried for hours on her couch. Told her things Jensen had done that I've never told anyone else. Not even Matt. And Matt knows more than anyone about what went on with Jensen.

Scarlett's the person I called at Leo and Vivian's when I had a rough day, which, in the beginning, was almost every day until I started getting closer to Cooper and Vivian.

She saw the pain. She heard the shit. She felt it too.

Jensen's thumb grazes the pointed peak of my nipple. I'm in my pajamas, a silk cami set that barely covers my boobs, with cheeky shorts to match.

I feel his cock jerk. He's been hard this whole time, and it makes me feel a little guilty. But he's assured me it's fine, that this is what he wants. To just be here with me.

His thumb brushes past again, and a flutter stirs deep in my stomach. Then his hand slides over mine, weaving our fingers together before softly curling them closed.

I give his hand a squeeze. *God, he's given me so much.*

He's sacrificed his entire life for me these past few weeks, not to mention the five months before. He's been showing up every single day, doing the work to be the best version of himself, while I drowned my feelings at the bottom of a glass, just like my dad.

Jensen was in rehab. In therapy. In the gym. Getting stronger in every way, and I was avoiding all of it. Venting to Leo and calling it therapy. Confiding in friends and asking them what to do instead of figuring out my own shit. He's been doing everything in his control to make all this possible, and all I've done is show up.

I know it's because I've got my own demons to face—and that I've been avoiding them while trying to rekindle what I have with Jensen. It feels counterproductive to dig into the hurt while I'm trying to hold space for love and forgiveness. I need therapy. I know I do. I'm just... not ready yet.

I'm not going to berate myself for it. I've learned to give myself grace. I am where I am, and I can live with that because I can't change the past. I can only change right now, going forward. The future. But I owe him something. I can give more.

I shift slightly in his arms, my voice barely above a whisper. "Can I ask you something?"

He doesn't move. Just smooths his thumb over mine. "Yeah, babe. Anything."

I close my eyes briefly, the question heavy on my tongue. I just have to be brave enough to let it out...

"Will you tell me something about rehab?"

He stills. Even his breathing stops, and for a second, I wonder if I've upset him. If maybe he doesn't want to talk about it. But then I remember, he asked me why I never ask about anything, that night he called about the edibles.

Finally, he takes a deep breath, his exhale warm against my head. "What do you want to know?"

"I don't know... Will you tell me about your first day there?"

It's quiet for a moment before he lets out a low hum. "The first day? I hardly remember it. Matt was there with me. Dropped me off. I was clean. I had to be for at least ten days before checking in. Matt and Megan helped me detox." He pauses. "Sorry, that's not what you asked."

His hand slips from mine, sliding low across my stomach. "First day felt really clinical. Check-in's a blur. I had to give them my phone and my watch. I still didn't feel great, even after two weeks clean. I was jet-lagged, still lacking nutrients... everything that makes you feel alive, you know? You were gone, I wasn't eating much. Lost a ton of weight. I was weak."

His fingers draw together and spread again, brushing softly over my skin. Heat seeps into my thighs, my attention splitting, half on his words, half on the way his touch makes it hard to breathe.

But I'm listening.

"We had lunch, then they showed me my room. It was really nice and had a large bathroom. But no TV, no lock on the doors. Every room had at least one big window. Mine had two since it sat on the corner. Then they ran a bunch of tests and labs. Honestly, I felt a little like a lab rat.

He shifts behind me, adjusting himself, his hand brushing over my hip.

"I met my counselors, my therapist. Got my daily schedule. Had a psychiatric evaluation. It was really rigorous. After dinner, they gave us downtime. I'd planned to go back to my room and be alone, but Max sat down across from me. He became my first friend there. He was from LA, youngest child in a wealthy family, mom who babied him. We clicked instantly. Even though we were both only half-alive at that point," he chuckles, "we just got each other."

His hand moves back to my arm, sliding over it until he finds my fingers. He weaves them with his, tugging me closer before continuing. "He had a fiancée and a baby. She walked out on him, took the baby, and he spiraled... Worse than I did. Woke up on the street one morning, tried to see his kid, and she wouldn't let him in. Then she filed a restraining order. That was his wake-up call."

He falls quiet, and I can feel it, *sense it,* how close he is to breaking. I lean back, straining my neck to see him, then roll all the way over to face him. His arm slips around my waist as I shift, and my hand smooths up his chest, resting against his cheek.

"Hey... you okay?"

He swallows and nods, but his eyes shut and a tear falls.

"Fuck. Sorry." He swipes it away, his lips trembling. "He relapsed. A few weeks ago. Ended up in the ER. Almost died."

His voice cracks, and the sound splinters through me. The ache that hits isn't just for his friend. It's for him. For the possibility of loss.

But then panic slams into my chest, making it hard to breathe. *This could be him.* At any time. *God.* The what-if wraps around my throat, squeezing tight until it's suffocating.

I force myself to form words. "Don't be sorry," I whisper.

He shakes it off. "I hadn't heard from him in a few weeks, so I wondered if he'd fallen off, but then he texted me last week to say he was okay. That he was headed back to rehab."

He exhales, swiping at his cheek. "Everything's just so fragile. Life. People..." His voice is trembles. "Me."

Shit. That hits me, hard. Scares me to death. But at the same time, all I want is to be here for him. To soothe his fears. I've carried so much anxiety for what feels like forever—most of it because of him—but these past few weeks, he's been the one easing it. He's been masking his own anxiety, putting on a strong front for me. And I've needed that.

But now I'm realizing... he's not as cool and collected as he lets on. He's stressed, too. Maybe even a little scared.

I'm not used to seeing him this way. Even when we were dating, Jensen always carried himself like nothing could touch him. Never showing weakness. Not to me. Not to anyone.

Now, he's unraveling in front of me. Not in a chaotic way. Not in an addiction spiral. In a quiet, honest way.

It terrifies me, knowing he's scared of failing, of relapsing, of losing me. But it's this vulnerability that anchors me to him now. Because this humility is exactly what was missing before. It's the absence of ego. He's being real. Human. Fragile. Somehow, that makes me feel safer than I ever did when he was bulletproof. It lets me hold on. It lets me believe.

He's not being perfect. He's being brave.

I meet his gaze, and it feels like the first time I'm truly seeing him since rehab, deep, down to his core. The man I know, but don't. The man he's becoming.

I see the hurt. The pain. The fear of losing his friend, his sobriety... Me.

His eyes search mine, the deep blue in them calming me in a way words never could. They're filled with sorrow, remorse, and the endless love he has for me.

I shift onto my elbow and lean down, grazing my lips over his. "Hey," I say softly.

I want to tell him it's going to be okay, but I don't know if it will. I want to promise his friend will get better. Promise we'll work out. But I can't.

So I kiss him instead.

I let my feelings take over, because it's the only way I know how to tell him what I feel without actually saying it. My hand slides through his hair as I press my lips firmer against his. They part, and he dives his tongue into my mouth. His arms wrap around me, inhaling like I just poured air into his lungs.

He pulls me even closer, possessing my mouth, running his hands along my body. Holding me like I'm his tether. His lifeline. And I want to be, because he feels like mine, too.

God, he has me coming undone.

I told him no sex tonight. I meant it. But now his hands are on my hips, his tongue's in my mouth, and I can't remember why I ever said that. I want him more than ever. I want his hands on me. His mouth consuming mine. And I want his cock buried deep inside me.

Right here. In our home. In our bed.

I want all of him.

He rolls me onto my back, mouth hovering over mine. He licks his lips. "You said you didn't want this tonight."

My gaze roams over his eyes, his face, his mouth. I nod, my voice barely a whisper. "I changed my mind."

"You sure?" His hand skims over my stomach, fingers slipping just beneath the waistband of my shorts. The tease makes my body arch into his, and I gasp against his mouth.

Yes, I'm pretty damn sure.

I nod again, biting my bottom lip as my hand drifts over his abs and down to the firm length of him, rubbing firmly over his pants.

A low chuckle rumbles in his chest as his hand slides farther, knuckles grazing my underwear. His fingers stroke lightly over the thin fabric, teasing, fueling the craving that's already consuming me.

He arches an eyebrow, a slow smirk forming as he pushes my underwear aside, his fingers gliding over the wet surface. He circles them against my clit, and I gasp, hips rolling into his hand.

His gaze locks on mine—somber, dark, but aching.

He's never broken like this before. Never failed. Never doubted his worth. And now he's struggling to believe he deserves love and happiness, maybe even me... I need him to know that he does.

I'm too scared to say it out loud. But I can show him. In the way I kiss him. In the way I melt into his touch. The way I give myself over to him, chasing the high only he can give me. The way I let him in.

That's how I tell him I love him.

Chapter Twenty-Nine

ALLEY

I crack my eyes open, blinking until they adjust to the brightness. *Dang, I slept in.* Either we forgot to close the shades or Jensen opened them, because sunlight pours into the room.

I roll over, reaching for him, only to find cold sheets.

Oh, yeah. The gym. Dammit.

I'm still adjusting to him being gone every morning. He takes one rest day a week, and even then, he's up by six. Sometimes he'll come back and slide in next to me—wake me with his mouth and his hands. Those mornings are my favorite. I love morning sex, even if I've never been a morning person. I don't need to sleep until noon, but 7 a.m. still feels like a dreaded chore.

I'm in New York again. Jensen was supposed to come to Chicago this weekend, but with the Berkshires trip in two weeks, we decided I'd come here now and he'll go to Chicago next weekend.

I grab my phone from the nightstand. *Shit. It's 9:30?* I definitely slept in.

I have a text from Scarlett waiting on the screen.

SCARLETT

Hi. You still wanna grab lunch today?

Things are still a little awkward after last weekend with Jensen and Scarlett, but we've talked since. She apologized, and promised she'd try harder. I'm hopeful it'll start to feel natural soon, that she won't have to *try* to be okay with him being around.

> Yes! I just woke up. Can we do a later lunch? Maybe 2:00?

SCARLETT

> That works for me.

I set my phone down and sit up, rubbing the sleep from my eyes.

After hitting the restroom and brushing my teeth, I make my way to the kitchen, expecting to find Jensen.

He's not here.

My brows pull together. *Is he still at the gym?* Maybe he slept in, too. I head back into the bedroom. His gym bag is on the floor.

I grab my phone and text him.

> Morning, babe. Where are you?

Jensen's phone dings, snapping my head up. My eyes land on his nightstand, where it's plugged into the charger.

A chill slides down my spine, panic stirring low in my stomach. *Where would he be on a Saturday morning without his phone?*

The only place he'd go is the gym. *Maybe he went to grab coffee or food.* No, he'd wait for me. Or at least tell me. *Why doesn't he have his phone?*

Jensen never goes anywhere without it.

Maybe he went with Matt to grab coffee.

I tap into my messages, typing Matt's name.

> Hey, are you with Jensen?

I stare at the screen for two minutes. It stays on "delivered."

Shit. The panic starts to rise, crawling up my throat. I rake my fingers through my hair, forcing myself to breathe. *It's fine. Everything's fine.*

Walking to the bathroom, I tell myself over and over that this is nothing. He'll be home soon. *There's no need to worry. He forgot his phone. He just went... I don't know where. But wherever he is, it all makes sense. Everything is okay.*

I strip my shorts off to take a shower, but images from the past slam into me. Jensen—high, teeth clenched, talking way too fast. Nodding off in the middle of the day. Pinpoint pupils. Sweating. The godforsaken office door, locked. Drugs. Lies.

'I turn on my heel, beelining for the office. The door's wide open. Jensen promised to keep it that way. It hasn't been closed once since I've been here.

I start yanking drawers open and slamming them shut, feeling underneath for a hidden stash—like before.

There's nothing.

Next, I head to the closet, pulling open anything that will open, dumping shit all over the floor. I'm making a mess, acting completely nuts. And the worst part is, I feel crazy. My heart's erratic, pounding volatile in my chest. My fingers shake, but so does the rest of me. It's like I've been over-caffeinated, and a steady buzz of insanity thrums through my veins. My hair's a mess from sleeping, I'm pantless. God, I'm a wreck. My brain's running a million miles a minute, what-ifs ricocheting through me, colliding with every memory. *Did he relapse? Did he go meet Seth? Are there drugs hidden here?*

My breaths turn rapid and shallow. Sweat beads at my hairline. Moisture stings behind my eyes, hot and burning with fear.

I fumble through Jensen's gym shorts drawer until my fingers hit something solid. My pulse spikes as I dig through the fabric and pull out a leather-bound pouch, zipped and tucked—no, *hidden*—inside one of his pairs of shorts.

Shit. My hands tremble as I pull it free. Tears fall down my cheeks. I bite my knuckles, holding back the sob caught in my throat. *Why is this hidden?*

"Shit." I stare at it. Too scared to open it. Too scared of what I'll find. Too scared to be hurt again. To not trust him. Again.

"Shit," I whisper again, lips quivering, voice shaking.

My thumb and forefinger grip the zipper. I tug it open a half inch before it catches. I yank harder, frantic, but it won't budge. I try again, dropping it in the process, yelling a sharp, "God! Fuck!"

I snatch it back up, sniffing hard as snot drips from my nose. My brain's white static. Pure chaos. I can't think straight.

A faint noise barely registers as I fight with the mangled fabric stuck in the zipper.

"Goddammit!" I cry.

"Babe?"

My head jerks up. Jensen stands in the doorway, brows drawn tight, worry etched across his face as he takes me in.

"What's in here?" My voice is raw, wild, unrecognizable. I'm panting like I've run a marathon, gasping for air. "Why was this hidden in your drawer?"

His eyes drop to the pouch, then back to me. "Al..." He takes a slow step forward.

"Don't! Just—" I flinch and pull harder at the zipper, desperation leaking from every pore. "FUCK!" It won't budge.

His eyes go wide.

I fling it at him. "Open it. Right fucking now." My voice cracks. I'm hysterical. "I can't." *Sob.* "I can't do this again." I suck in a breath, pressing my palm to my chest, like I can hold myself together from the outside.

He nods. Slow. Quiet. "Okay, babe. I'll open it."

His steady fingers work at the zipper while I practically hyperventilate. After a beat, it slides open with maddening ease, and he holds it out to me.

I snatch it and dump the contents onto the floor. Chips and photos scatter across the floor, some face up, some face down.

I crouch, picking one up. It's a sobriety chip. They're all sobriety chips. Seven days. Two weeks. One month. Ninety days. My gaze drops to a photo of us in the Berkshires.

There's nothing else.

No pills.

No coke.

No lies.

Just pieces of him and proof he's still clean.

My legs give out, the closet spinning, and I drop to the floor. Relief whips through me so hard I almost black out, sobs tearing out of me louder than before.

Jensen crouches in front of me. "Babe," he says softly. His eyes are red, nostrils flaring, fighting not to break. His fingers weave into my hair, his face pressing into it. "God, babe," he chokes, pulling back to cup my face. "Look at me."

My eyes dart everywhere, too rattled to land on his.

"Al. I'm right here. Eyes on me, babe. Remember? Eyes on me."

My eyelids flutter shut.

He remembers.

It's what he said to me the night before our wedding. I was so nervous about walking down the aisle, knowing all those people would be there. He took my hands in his, looked me dead in the eyes, and said, *Eyes on me, babe. The whole time. Just... eyes on me.*

When I open my eyes, they finally land on his. A blanket of calm wraps around me, the jitteriness melting from my limbs.

"Just breathe, alright? I've got you."

I suck in a sharp breath, letting it out slow.

"That's it, babe. Deep, slow breaths."

His forehead rests against mine, and the grounding is instant. My breathing evens, each exhale puffing out my cheeks. His thumb swipes away the tears streaking my face.

I loop my arms around his neck, cupping the back of his head, and suddenly, the person who sent me spinning is the one steadying me.

Just like it used to be. Before our trust shattered.

Jensen was always the one who could take my burdens and make them his. The one who helped shoulder the weight. Who could turn my tears into laughter.

He's here.

He didn't betray my trust. He didn't lie.

When I needed him, he caught me.

Finally.

God, finally.

Chapter Thirty

JENSEN

Fuck.

Alley's sobs slow, each one coming softer than before.

"That's it, babe. Nice, slow breaths. You've got this. I'm right here."

Fuck.

I'd gone to the gym this morning, came back, showered. She was still out of it. I dinked around for a bit, then decided to grab us coffee and bagels from one of our favorite roasting companies. Completely forgot my phone. By the time I realized, I was already halfway around the block.

She's rocking now, small whimpers slipping out between shaky breaths, and my stomach knots so tight it's hard to breathe. It guts me, watching my wife break down because of the shit I've put her through. It's a different kind of pain. One that cuts deeper than any withdrawal ever could.

And it's the fucking worst.

I don't know what else to do—just stay here and hold her? Try to get her up, get some food in her, maybe coffee? *No. Stay.* Definitely stay.

I start to lower myself beside her, but her hands clutch at my neck.

"I'm not leaving, babe. Just sitting right here next to you."

She loosens her grip, and I ease down, pressing a kiss to her temple. I smooth my hand over the back of her head, down to her shoulder, gently nudging her to my lap.

Her head lands in the crook of my thigh and hip. I rake my fingers through her hair, palm stroking her back. She's shaking—not convulsing, but trembling from the inside out. Like aftershocks. Deep, rolling waves coming from her core.

God, I just want to hold her. Carry her to bed. Wrap myself around her, put some weight on her, ground her. But I know better than to move her right now.

I've only had one of these. It was the third day in rehab. Everything hit me at once—the failure, the fear, the fact I couldn't talk to anyone but Matt for twelve weeks. The reality that Alley was gone, and I had no way to reach her. I got sick that day too. I was fully detoxed, over two weeks clean, but my body was so stripped and starved of nutrients. It hadn't had any real care for so long, it's like it didn't know what to do with the sudden influx of attention.

I'd ended up on the floor in my room when I was supposed to be in a group session. Couldn't talk. Couldn't move. The world was spinning, everything and everyone was feeling farther away than ever, and all I could do was lie there and panic. My body had finally had enough. I'd been playing dangerously for years, daring something to happen to me. Daring the universe to fuck with me. And it did. Struck me like a bolt of lightning. That's what it felt like.

I close my eyes now and focus on my breathing. On her. I'm here. Sober. Clean. And she's letting me be her safe place again.

I let that sink in.

I didn't fuck this up.

I was here for her when she needed me, and the weight of that thought burrows in my chest, swelling my throat until I have to focus on the next breath just to keep it together. It shakes as I inhale through my nose.

She needed me.

And I was here.

I've seen Alley spiral before. A lot. But I was always too far gone to really feel it. To hold it the way I should have. I'd recognize her pain, but it never cut through my own haze the way this does. This hurts.

Because even though I'm the one here holding her now, I'm also the reason this happened in the first place.

Jesus. She thought I had drugs hidden somewhere. Thought I left to get high.

Her fingers dig into my calf, squeezing tight. I bring my left hand around to hers and she latches on like it's the only thing keeping her above water.

"Do you want to go lie down?" I ask, keeping my voice low.

She shakes her head.

Damn. My legs are falling asleep. Couldn't tell you the last time I sat cross-legged on the floor. I shift, careful not to jostle her too much, and straighten the leg she isn't resting on. Pins and needles shoot up my calf, that sharp sting as the blood rushes back in. The other leg's fine... for now.

We stay there, silent, for I don't know how long. Ten minutes at least. Eventually, she relaxes a little. The sharp gasps of air slow into deep, even breaths. The soft whimpers fade. A heaviness replaces the tremors, her body going slack and sinking further into me.

It's *everything.*

Being here for her, and riding it out together. I just hope this doesn't push us back. That it cements her trust in me instead of cracking it. That the fear of this happening again doesn't freeze us in place.

Alley's grip loosens as she slowly pushes herself up. Her eyes find mine, and my heart squeezes in my chest.

God. It's fucking sad—bloodshot eyes, face blotchy and raw, streaked with tears. Hair plastered to her cheek from sweat and saltwater.

I brush a finger along her cheek, freeing the strands and tucking them behind her ear.

"Hey," I murmur, my voice rough, thick like I just woke up.

"Hey." Hers is barely there. Just a quiet breath of sound, but enough to tell me she's still with me. Her gaze searches mine, and moisture wells again. She closes her eyes, letting fresh tears slip down her cheeks.

I cup her face and press a kiss to her forehead. "I'm right here, babe."

She nods, eyes still shut. "I know." Her voice cracks on the words. She swallows. Tears stream down her cheeks as she curls her hands around my wrists, anchoring herself to me. "I know."

A minute later, her hands slide up my arms and fold around my neck. Her lips find mine, soft and barely there, but somehow it lands harder than any kiss we've ever shared.

It's gratitude.

It's appreciation.

It's surrender.

It's trust.

She fucking *trusts* me right now.

She inhales a sharp breath against my mouth, breathing me in like I'm the only oxygen she's got. Then she crushes her lips to mine with the weight of a hundred pounds, pulling me into her like she'll never let go.

Something inside me explodes.

Not in a sexual way.

Not destructively.

In the best way. Like we took every lie, every betrayal, every ounce of hurt between us, shoved it in a box...

...and set that shit on fire.

I kiss her back like I fucking mean it. Like I need her just as much as she needs me. Like this one kiss could heal every splintered piece between us.

I kiss her like I love her.

Because I do.

More than anything.

Her tongue strokes against mine, lips taking what she wants, what she needs. And I let her.

Desire spikes hard, my cock making itself known. I could lose myself in this. But I won't. Not until she's okay. She's too vulnerable right now. Too raw.

So I stifle it.

I break the kiss, tugging gently on her swollen bottom lip.

"Hey," I whisper against her mouth, our breaths mingling. "I got coffee and bagels. How about we go get them?" I pull back just enough to meet her eyes. "We can sit on the couch, talk. I'll hold you while we drink our coffee."

She gives a small nod. "Okay."

Okay.

Chapter Thirty-One

JENSEN

It's been one week since Alley's panic attack. One week since trust was tested. One week since we passed the test.

This couch is deep enough to swallow me whole, but I'm still tense. I'm in Chicago this weekend... at couples therapy. Sophie, our new therapist, has been great so far. I like her. She reminds me a lot of Nina and came highly recommended by Leo. I guess they used to work together.

We're at her house, in her home office. It's cozy and comfortable, way better than the therapy rooms in rehab. Not that those weren't fine. It just feels different. Less clinical. More personal.

I shift in my seat, trying to settle my nerves. "So... I don't know, I guess I just want to be able to be there for her. I want her to trust me. Get back to where we used to be." I lean back, eyes flicking to the clock on the wall before returning to Sophie. "Things have been pretty good, all things considered. But I know we've got a long way to go. And I worry every day I'm gonna fuck it up, or that she'll suddenly decide she doesn't want this." I scrub a hand over my mouth. "I feel like I'm constantly looking over my shoulder, praying my past doesn't catch up, or that she doesn't give up on me."

I blow out a breath, and Sophie offers a small smile. "Thank you for sharing all that, Jensen. And about your addiction. It's hard to be vulnerable and admit our faults and fears."

Sophie turns her attention to Alley. "Alley, why don't you tell me what your goals are and what brought you in?"

She hesitates. This is hard for her. I know it is. She opens up to people she's close to—me, Leo, Scarlett, Matt—but it takes a long time to earn her trust. It's one of her greatest strengths and her biggest downfalls. Once you're in her circle, though, she's loyal as hell. But getting there? That's another story.

She's always hated therapy. She told me that in the first month we were dating, when she opened up about her dad. I guess she had a therapist once who made her feel like shit. I went with it. I'd never done therapy myself, so I had nothing to compare it to. I just knew I wasn't interested. And the way she talked about it made me dread it even more when I ended up in rehab.

But it got easier, and finding the right therapist matters. It has to be a good fit. I got lucky. Nina and Tobias were great, even though I was reluctant to open up at first. But now? I'm here for it. I'm all in.

Here for her. For me. For us.

I just hope Sophie can crack through the fortress she's built. For some reason, Leo's the only one who gets a pass, and even then, it doesn't always last.

She finally speaks, her voice quiet, eyes on the rug in front of her. "I guess I don't really know what I'm doing. I'm here, and I obviously want to make this work, but... I don't know if I can really move forward until we deal with what happened. But I don't want to deal with it because it feels like too much." A smile ghosts her lips, but it's gone in a heartbeat. "But I'm trying."

Sophie's voice stays soft and calm. "Okay. Thank you for your honesty. That's a great start. Being here is a big step for you both. Just to be clear, Alley, when you say you don't want to deal with what happened because it feels like too much, are there specific moments that come to mind? Or a certain timeframe? Or do you mean your entire marriage to Jensen?"

Please don't say the entire marriage. Jesus. I don't know if I could handle that.

I glance at Al. She's chewing on her bottom lip now. *She's so uncomfortable.* She was a nervous wreck the entire drive here, jittery and wound tight, nervous energy ping-ponging in the car.

"I guess there are certain moments that come to mind." Her eyes flick to mine, then drop to her hands, where she fidgets with her fingers in her lap.

"Are you comfortable sharing one of those moments?" Sophie asks gently.

"Not really."

Jesus. It's like trying to peel off wallpaper with your fingernails.

"Why not?"

Alley takes a deep breath, shoulders rising and falling with the exhale.

She picks at her fingernail, then, like she suddenly notices, covers her hand with the other and grips it tight. Her gaze locks on Sophie's. "There's a lot of reasons why."

Sophie nods, encouraging her to continue.

"One, I don't want to relive it. Two, I don't want to make Jensen feel bad or cause him to regress. And three..."

She trails off. My eyes shift to her profile. Her cheeks flush, and her eyes fill with moisture. She's trying so damn hard to keep it together.

"It's okay. You can say it." Sophie gestures toward me. "Jensen, you're okay with Alley being honest here?"

I nod. "Yeah. For sure."

"Alright. Alley, this is a safe space. You can say whatever you're thinking or feeling."

Alley nods, swallowing hard. "Okay." Another pause. "It makes me really angry when I think about these things. *Really* angry. At Jensen. And there's a part of me that hates him for everything he put me through. For making life so hard, when it just didn't need to be." She glances at me, eyes glassy. "For messing everything up." Her voice cracks. "For destroying our trust." She pauses to sniff. "But the thing that makes me the most mad..."

Her voice falters again, and I swear I can hear her heart pounding. My chest locks up, bracing myself for whatever she's about to say.

"...is that he doesn't even know. He doesn't even know how bad it was because he was so messed up. He doesn't remember. He gets to move on and live life with no recollection of half the shit he did."

Whoa. Ho-ly shit. I did not expect her to say anything in the realm of this, and at the same time it makes so much sense. Her reluctance to talk about anything. Her avoidance when I bring up the past. The way she hides her anger. It's like anything that would make her mad gets shoved aside so she can put on a brave front. Best face forward. I appreciate her willingness and need to be positive, but it's almost been hindering us. *God, this is huge.*

Sophie glances at me, then back to Alley. "So, what I'm hearing is that one of the hardest parts for you, Alley, is knowing Jensen doesn't remember a lot of what happened. And that feels unfair."

Alley nods, a soft "Yeah," following.

Meanwhile, I feel like I just took a punch to the face.

Sophie's gaze turns to me again. "Jensen, it looks like you might have some thoughts about this. Do you mind sharing what you're thinking after hearing that?"

My mouth opens, then closes. I don't know where to start. I look at Alley, but she won't meet my eyes. "I do know that," I say finally, my voice rough. "And I know it's unfair. God, it *kills* me." I press my fingers to my forehead, rubbing. "But I promise you, I know exactly how bad I fucked up."

I run a hand over my face. "I try to make it right. Every day. I'm trying to be better. To show you I've changed. And I swear to God, every week, I remember something new. Some moment I hadn't thought about. Some awful thing I said. Some night I locked the door. Some time you cried and I didn't even notice." My throat tightens as my gaze shifts to Alley. "God. The night I let you walk out the door because I was too concerned about my stash? My fucking backpack? Jesus. I was so messed up."

Sophie leans forward slightly. "I can hear how much that still weighs on you, Jensen."

Alley shifts in her seat, arms crossing over her chest. Her eyes flick to me briefly before darting away again. They're red and wet, and I wish I could go back in time. Take it all back. Choose differently. Erase the hurt I caused her.

My lips tremble. "And every time a memory hits, it fucks with me in the worst way. Because you lived it. And I just... forgot. Or numbed it. Or wasn't coherent enough to realize the shit I was doing. And I hate that, Al. I hate that you remember everything. That it haunts you. But it haunts me too, just in a different way."

I suck in a long breath. "Like last weekend? When I found you in the closet?" *Fuck.* My eyes sting just thinking about it, but I keep them on her, the image burned into my head. "Words can't describe what I felt in that moment, watching you. Jesus Christ. The fear in your eyes. The way you were... It's like you were scared of me." I shake my head, trying to regain an ounce of control. "I can't imagine what you were feeling in that moment. But you'll never know what it feels like to be the one who put it there. To be the one you don't trust. The one who broke it all." I rake a hand through my hair, gripping it at the back. My voice catches. "God, I love you so much, and I broke you. That light that used to shine in your eyes—I dimmed it. I sucked the joy out of life. Out of everything. And I'm so sorry. I'm so fucking sorry, babe."

Her hand reaches for mine. *She* holds *my* hand. Yeah. She's that fucking great.

How I have her in my life, I'll never understand. I know I don't deserve her. She's so good. So pure. Deserves the very best. Better than me. But I'm too selfish to let her go.

This whole time she's been carrying all of it alone. The anger. The grief. The fear. I told myself we were okay, that we were making progress, but she was just trying to survive and holding it all in. She didn't trust me with the truth because I hadn't earned it. She's been protecting me and my feelings. And I didn't even know it.

The room is quiet now. Just the faint hum of the white noise machine and the sound of us sniffling. Sophie's eyes move between us, like she's taking a mental inventory of what just happened.

"Okay," she says softly. Her voice is so soothing, so grounding. It almost makes me forget the last five minutes of me unraveling and confessing shit I've never said out loud to anyone but Nina. "Thank you, Jensen. That was really honest, and really important. Alley, is there anything you'd like to say in response? No pressure. Only if you want to."

Alley finally turns to me, her hand tightening around mine. She blinks a few times before meeting my eyes. And fuck... in that moment, it's all there. The history. The pain. The part of her that still loves me, even when she probably wishes she didn't.

I hold her gaze, humbled, imperfect, and so goddamn devoted to her.

"Thank you," she says, her voice raw. "For being here. For owning your shit." Her chin quivers and her shoulders shake as she inhales. "For fighting for me."

My chest constricts, that overwhelming need for her hitting so hard I don't even care that we're in therapy. I cup the back of her head and pull her in, kissing her with renewed conviction. Claiming her all over again. "I love you," I murmur against her salted lips.

When I sit back, Sophie's smiling. "This is good. You both showed up today. You were honest, you listened, and you let each other see what's underneath the surface. That's big. For next time, I'd like you each to think about one moment from what came up today that you want to go deeper into. And between now and then... try talking about one hard thing. Not all of them, just one. Be vulnerable and honest."

She clicks through her calendar, setting us up for a Zoom session next weekend.

Alley doesn't smile. Doesn't say much. But she looks lighter. Happier. A little more at peace.

I feel hopeful. Like maybe we really can get through anything. Jesus, look at us. We've been to hell and back, walked through fire, and we're still standing. We're not done. Not even close. And every time we face something this hard, we come out the other side a little stronger.

I don't know about Alley, but for me? I love her more now than I ever have in my life.

Chapter Thirty-Two

JENSEN

We're on night two in the Berkshires, gathered around the oversized dining table. Alley and I got in late last night. She had to work yesterday, so she caught a six p.m. flight from Chicago, and I picked her up at ten. We drove straight here and didn't roll in until close to one in the morning.

Early 2000s hip-hop pulses through the built-in speakers, and all my siblings are already well on their way to drunk.

Megan stands at the head of the table, pouring herself a generous glass of wine. "Okay, classic rules. Everyone has five five-dollar bills. When it's your turn, say something you've never done. If you *have* done it, throw a five in the middle. You're out when your money's gone. Winner takes the pot."

Alley laughs beside me. "Bets on Matt being out first?"

Matt cocks a brow, grinning. "Hey, this is one game I'll proudly lose. Just means I've lived."

"We all know who's going to win." Megan smirks, eyes sliding straight to Alley.

"Hey! I resent that. I've lived," Alley protests, turning to me. "Babe, tell them. I'm adventurous and dangerous." A wide grin stretches across her lips.

That pulls a laugh from me. "Wild as they come, babe. Matt won't even see you coming." I kiss her mouth and crack open a Liquid Death. Yeah, I know—those never get old.

"I'll start," Megan announces, eyes flicking between me and Matt. "Do I play nice or go straight for the jugular?"

"Do your best," I say.

"Yeah, take your best shot," Matt adds.

"Okay. No offense?"

"None," we echo.

She shrugs, then grins. "Alright. Never have I ever done any drug besides weed or mushrooms."

Matt, Jeff, and I each toss a five into the middle.

"Whoa, wait—Jeff?" Megan turns to him. "What the hell have *you* done?"

"This isn't Truth or Dare, Megan. You don't get answers," Jeff says, sipping his old fashioned with a perfect poker face.

"Oh, come on! Half the fun is hearing the wild stories."

Jeff sighs. "Fine. I did ecstasy once in college."

Megan's eyes widen. "Oh, shit. I forgot about ecstasy. I did that too."

"I'm taking this back, then." Jeff reaches for the five he tossed into the pile.

Amber's up next. "Never have I ever faked an orgasm." She grins, and Jeff practically beams.

Megan and Alley each toss in a five.

Kevin scowls at Megan. "That better not have been with me, babe."

"Please." She rolls her eyes. "Babe. When you're drunk, you need a fucking road map. Honestly, sometimes I wish you'd just stop and ask for directions." She flashes him a teasing grin as the whole table bursts into laughter. "I'm kidding."

I nudge Alley, eyeing the pot. "Babe?"

She feigns offense. "Never! You know my ex was boring in bed. Couldn't even find my clit. Sometimes I faked it just to make it stop."

My brows lift. "Just making sure."

Kevin goes next. "Never have I ever stolen anything."

Matt, Megan, and I each toss in a five. Yeah, the three of us are fucked.

Jeff raises his eyebrows, scanning the table. "Never have I ever had a threesome."

Matt grins and tosses in a five without hesitation.

Megan and I glance at each other.

"Fuck," we both mutter, dropping in a five.

This isn't a story I've ever told Alley. Not because I was hiding it. It just never came up.

She gasps, gaping at me. "What? Holy shit." She smacks my arm. "How do I not know about this?"

"Ow." I laugh. "It was one time. Freshman year of college."

"*Freshman year?*" Her eyes widen.

"Yeah. But I was really drunk. And I'm not sure it even counts. I didn't actually have sex with both of them."

"Oh, well then, sure, that makes it totally fine." Sarcasm drips as she shakes her head in disbelief.

She's smiling though, so I know it's all good.

"And Megan?" Alley whirls to her. "I need stories. *Now.*" Then she swivels back to me. "And *you're* going into full detail on yours later."

Matt frowns, pointing at himself. "Wait—no one's surprised *I've* had a threesome? No one wants to hear *my* stories?"

Everyone snickers.

"You're cute, Matt," Amber says. "We've heard your threesome stories. They're your go-to when you're drunk."

He shrugs. "Well, I've got a new one. But I'm saving it for later, when I'm drunk."

Laughter booms around the table, and warmth spreads through my chest. I glance around and—damn, this is good. All my favorite people, in my favorite place. Laughing. Joking. Having a great time. Just... happy.

A quiet sense of pride settles in.

I did it.

I went to rehab. I did the hard shit. Got clean. Fought like hell for my sobriety and my wife. And here she is, by my side. Relaxed. Smiling. It almost chokes me up. I haven't felt this complete in so long, I hardly know what to do with it. I want to freeze this moment and burn it into my memory.

God, it feels good knowing life doesn't have to stay in the gutter when it's shit. It can always get better. *We* can get better. Do better. I don't know if it's egotistical to admit, but I'm proud. Proud of Alley for giving me another chance. Proud of my family. Proud of myself.

My hand falls to Alley's lap, giving her knee a squeeze. Her eyes meet mine, sparkling with pure joy as she threads our fingers together.

One thing I didn't fully grasp until rehab ended was how much being an addict fucks up everyone else's life, too. They stood by me. They loved me anyway. And right now, I feel like the luckiest bastard alive to be sitting here.

* * *

Alley and I lean back as the ski lift scoops us up.

She laughs when I pull the lap bar down. "Why do I still get nervous I'm gonna fall on my ass every time?"

I glance at her. Her gaze is forward, smile wide, nose red from the cold. Her goggles hang loose around her neck. I slip an arm over her shoulder and pull her in, kissing the top of her head.

"You haven't done this in a long time. You're doing great. Better than ever."

She shoots me a teasing grin. "You have to say that because you love me."

I bark out a laugh. "No. I tell you how shitty you are because I love you. I say you're doing great because you actually are."

"Compared to how shitty I normally am?"

"The why doesn't matter, babe." My arm drops to her knee. "Point is, you've never done a blue run until today. You're getting better."

"Doesn't mean I have to like it. I'm only here for you," she teases.

"Oh, come on. You can't tell me you haven't had fun. You've been laughing all day."

"Yeah, but only because you've been making me laugh. I'd rather be inside by the fire, warm and comfortable, and blowing my nose without having to peel these stupid gloves off." Her grin widens. "Wouldn't you rather be back at the cabin? Maybe a little naked under a blanket together?" Her brows lift, her bottom lip catching between her teeth as her hand slides over my cock. She fumbles against the padding of my snow pants and her gloves. "God, where is that thing?"

A low chuckle rumbles in my chest. "You trying to get me hard on the ski lift? That's a new kind of torture. I can't even adjust myself right now."

"Turning you on is way more fun than skiing."

"I don't know if sliding down the mountain on your ass counts as skiing."

Her head tips back in laughter, and *God, she's beautiful.* It's crazy how easily we fall back into this, like no time's passed. Almost like she never left.

"Hey, you remember this conversation when we *are* naked and you're wanting to get some—"

My lips connect with hers, cutting her off, stealing the heat of her mouth against the chill of the mountain air. She gasps against me, fingers clutching at my coat, and I kiss her deeper, greedy for more.

When we break apart, our eyes lock.

"What was that for?" she asks, her breath visible in the cold.

A corner of my mouth lifts into a smirk. "Only way I could shut you up."

She shoves my shoulder. "Don't be a jerk."

"I'm not." My voice drops to a low growl. "But you're making Clark think about Lola, and that's not very nice when there's nothing we can do about that right now."

"Oh? You don't like it when I tell you how I can't wait to have your"—she leans closer, whispering—"big, hard cock inside me tonight? What if I tell you Lola's *dripping* for you?"

"Shiiiiit." I cock a brow. "You better knock that off, or I'll bend you over right here in the woods."

She just grins, and for half a second I actually entertain the whole woods fantasy. My cock's hard as hell, and there's not a damn thing I can do about it.

* * *

"Ugh! Dammit!" Alley smacks the snow in frustration. She's on her ass again, skis popped off, and if I didn't love her so goddamn much, I probably wouldn't have the patience for it. But she's cute when she's flustered. Too cute.

She flops back dramatically. "I give up!"

I laugh under my breath, pop off my skis, and jog up the hill to where she's sprawled in the trees. She's lucky she didn't go straight into one.

I stab my skis into the snow. "Come on, babe. Hop up. We're almost there." I hold out a hand.

"Uh-uh. Nope. I'm done. Let's fake an injury and call snow patrol."

"Snow Patrol's a band, babe. It's ski patrol."

"Whatever. Tell them I broke my leg and need a ride down."

I step wide, placing her in between my legs, hand still extended. "Can't fake an injury. The unbroken leg's kind of a giveaway."

She purses her lips and reaches for my hand. The second our palms connect, she yanks hard, sending me off balance. I stumble forward, barely catching myself as I topple onto her.

Her laughter bursts out as she wraps her arms around me. "How's it feel to fall down? You like that?"

Oh, she's gonna get it. I grab her forearms, pinning them to her sides, and straddle my knees wide to trap her beneath me. She wriggles, eyes wide with mock horror, laughter spilling between us.

I bend down, my mouth close to her ear. "Oh, I like it," I murmur, skimming a gloved hand over her coat toward her tits. "How do you like getting groped in the snow?"

"This isn't groping. You can't even find my boobs through my coat. They're too small."

I sit back, still holding her pinned, and sweep both hands across her chest in exaggerated arcs.

She shrieks with laughter. "Oh my God, stop! This is not sexy. Nothing about gloved groping and puffy coats is sexy!"

"I'm not trying to be sexy. I'm trying to torture you." I shift, settling my hips lower, letting more of my weight lock her down.

"Do you have a boner? 'Cause I can't feel it through all the padding."

"Why? You horny?"

"Right now?" She shakes her head in the snow, her beanie sliding up past her ears. She grins, little laughs puffing out. "This is anything but turning me on. Lola's dry as the Sahara Desert."

I lift a brow. "The Sahara, huh?" I smother my grin and lean closer, pressing firmly against her. "You're telling me"—my voice drops low at her ear—"that if I took these gloves off and slid my fingers into your pussy, it wouldn't be wet? You wouldn't like that?"

Jesus. The thought of her warm pussy against my cold fingers right now...

My cock throbs against her, agreeing with every word. I kiss her ear, then trail down, leaving heat along her jaw before brushing her mouth. My padded thumb swipes across her cheek.

She bursts out laughing.

Let me tell you what you don't want when you're trying to turn someone on.

Laughing.

"Oh my God, the glove against my skin is like nails on a chalkboard." Her stomach tightens beneath me with giggles.

"Fuck. I give up." Grinning, I roll off her and onto my back beside her, staring up at the blue sky and the towering pines. Each breath leaves a puff of white that vanishes into the air.

She turns her head toward me, and I meet her gaze. "You almost had me. But then that glove..." She winces. "It was like my brother walking in on us in the middle of sex. Cringe."

That makes me laugh. "Jesus. That's not something anyone ever wants to hear."

Her laugh softens, fading into a smile. "I love you for trying, though." Her eyes search mine. "And for bringing me here."

It slams into my chest, knocking the air right out of me. I freeze, my whole body locking. "Say it again. Please. Just once."

She rolls onto her side, glove reaching for mine. She fits her hand into my palm as best she can, and I shift onto my side too.

"I love you, Jensen. Always have." Her eyes roam over my face. "Never didn't," she adds in a whisper.

A grin tugs at my mouth, and I don't think about anything except her as our lips collide.

There's weight in those words—more than I expected. They hit deep, and it feels incredible to hear them. To be loved by her. It feels *earned*. She means it. It's undeniable, the love she has for me.

We kiss in the snow for several minutes. I couldn't tell you how long. Time slows. Everything around us stills until it's just us.

Me and my wife.

The words spread through me like a stiff drink. Burns at first, emotion thick in my throat. Then it warms, spreading through my veins, settling in every limb. Comfort. Confidence. Relief. More relief than any drug or drink ever gave me.

And an overwhelming truth hits me—

Alley's all I'll ever need to be happy.

Could I be happy without her? Sure. But I'd always want more. Always be searching for the next best thing, the next high. Money. Sex. A woman. A thrill.

But with her? Nothing else matters. I could be living in a van down by the river and I'd still be happy. Strip the clothes off my back, I'd only want her. I'd still choose her. Every day.

That's where I was lost before. Yeah, I was in pain. It hurt like hell, but I was chasing some bullshit ideal of being the perfect man. I didn't want Alley to see me as weak, hear me complain, or have to take care of me. That was supposed to be *my* job.

I grin against her lips, deepening our kiss.

I was wrong. I didn't get it.

She loves me. She'd do the same for me that I'd do for her.

I still want to be strong and healthy as I get older, we all do. But what a fucking privilege it would be to have her take care of me. To be in the kind of marriage where *in sickness and in health* isn't just a vow, it's the proof of love itself.

We already have that. She's already proved it.

I was just too fucking blind to see it before.

I pull back, somber, my eyes locking on hers. *Eyes on me.* I told her that the night before we got married. God, she was so nervous. It was me that got her through—my love, my eyes, her trust in me. "I love you, baby. More than life itself. I'm so sorry. For everything."

Her eyes fill with tears, and I take my time memorizing her and every detail of this moment. The soft crease by her eyes from years of laughing. The smile that's almost there but caught on emotion. Her gaze, steady on me.

Fuck. She trusts me.

She presses her lips together, shaking her head with conviction. "I never stopped loving you, Jensen. Not for one second."

"I know, and I took advantage of that. I questioned it. I didn't trust you to love me when I couldn't be strong. I didn't trust you with my weaknesses."

Her voice softens, almost breaking. "You don't have to be strong all the time, you know. You're allowed to be human."

"I know." Then, because it's long overdue, I add, "Thank you. For loving me. For sticking by me when I was at my worst." The words scrape out of me, heavy but freeing. "And thank you for leaving my sorry ass when you did." I shake my head, regret stinging my eyes. "I don't know where I'd be if you hadn't. Passed out somewhere, jobless... maybe dead. You saved me, Alley. I'll never forget it."

Her eyes glisten, and she gives me a soft smile. "You saved yourself." She leans in, pressing her lips to mine. "And I'm really proud of you." A tear slides down her cheek, and I swipe it away with my thumb. She winces, laugh-crying. "God, not the glove!"

I chuckle, kiss her once more, then push up to my feet. "Come on. Let's get you out of the snow and down this hill before ski patrol *actually* comes looking for us."

I brush the snow from my gear and extend a hand. She takes it, and I pull her up. I help her clip back into her skis, and eventually, we make it down the hill, but not without a dozen more falls and even more laughs.

Chapter Thirty-Three

ALLEY

I SET my Kindle on the bath caddy and grab my phone when it vibrates with a text, bubbles fizzing softly around me.

MICHAEL

Hey, how's it going? Dad said you were in the Berkshires this week with Jensen…

My stomach flips. I haven't talked to Michael about Jensen in a while. Only Dad, and a little with Stella. Honestly, I've avoided it. He's been so busy with the restaurant, and while he hasn't said much, I could tell in the beginning he was skeptical—no, maybe that's not the right word. It was more like a quiet, *proceed with caution* vibe.

I hesitate, thumb hovering over the keyboard, unsure how much to share. Michael's opinion has always mattered to me, and part of me is bracing for a response I don't want.

Hi! I'm good. Yes, in the Berkshires with Jensen and the fam. It's been really great. What are you guys up to this weekend?

MICHAEL

The usual. Work. Might take the kids to the aquarium Sunday. When are you both in Chicago next?

> Next weekend. Why?

MICHAEL

You think Jensen could work from Chicago
Thursday? I have it off. You could come for dinner...

Oh. Okay... this is better than expected.

> Idk. I'd have to ask, but I'm sure he could work at
> the Chicago office or remotely for a couple of days.
> His boss is great with that stuff.

MICHAEL

Great. Just lmk when you know.

Happy for you, btw.

A smile slowly spreads across my face. I don't know why I was so
worried. Michael's never been anything but supportive of me.

> Thank you. That means a lot.

> Seriously. A lot.

MICHAEL

Well, I mean it. Have fun.

> Thanks. I'm gonna get back to my book now
> because the slow burn just started burning... 😌
> haha.

MICHAEL

Okay. I know what that means. Oh, and thanks for
getting Stella into those books. It's been very
beneficial for me.

> Hahaha. Not what I ever needed to know, but also...
> you're welcome! Lol. K, love you, bye.

MICHAEL

Love you.

I set my phone down and trade it for my Kindle, sinking deeper
into the hot water. *God, that feels good.*

We got back from skiing about an hour ago. It was a long day. And when I say long, I mean *long*. I keep trying to like it, but I just don't. It's not for me. Of course, I still had a great time. Jensen made sure of that. And my God, the patience he has with me on those hills... I'm not lying when I say I'm terrible. Not kind-of-bad or just new-at-this terrible. Full-on, humiliating, a-toddler-could-out-ski-me terrible. Easily.

We had a lot of laughs, though. And even though I know he'd have a great time with the guys going down harder slopes, he loves taking me. Tomorrow, he gets a full day with Jeff, Kevin and Matt, so he can get his fix then.

Today was crucial. Necessary. It gave us the space to step away from life and just be us. To reconnect without the past, therapy, family, and friends buzzing in the background. To laugh, to joke, to flirt.

It was good—a really great day.

I told him I loved him. I wasn't planning on it, not in the middle of the day, lying in the snow, anyway. Doesn't exactly scream romantic. But it slipped out before I could stop it—three words I'd been holding back like glass in my throat.

It's not like I ever questioned whether I did. I always have. That's why everything the past few years has been so hard. And the second the words were out, I had no regrets. Watching Jensen react—the way his face lit up, the emotion in his eyes, the grin that spread across his lips—and then hearing him ask me to say it again? I haven't seen that kind of joy from him since walking down the aisle. It meant the world to him.

I'd been so cautious to let myself say it. I didn't want to give him false hope, make him think I was further along in this than I was. But it wasn't too soon. And it wasn't too late. It was flawed in all the right ways. Just like us.

After my freak-out last weekend, therapy, and all the late-night talks, he's been there for me. He's showed up when I've needed him most. He's been honest and vulnerable. Open. Humble, too. I've seen parts of him I've never seen, not even before the addiction. He's admitted his faults. Taken responsibility for his actions.

It's made me realize at least this wasn't all for nothing. He's grown. Exponentially. And so have I. Sometimes you just need that silver lining—the thing that makes all the pain and heartbreak make sense. The thing that reminds you why you fought to survive it in the first place.

I sit up, twist the hot-water knob, and paddle my hands through the bath to mix the warmth with what's cooled.

We had another therapy session with Sophie this morning, over Zoom. It went well. She gave us homework, though. She wants us to share something we're afraid to bring up with each other. I've been thinking about it ever since, and I still can't decide.

Do I go with one of the worst memories I have—the one that still knots my stomach and that I'm pretty sure Jensen doesn't even remember? Or do I go with my greatest fear about the future—having kids with him?

That used to be the thing that excited me most, starting a family. But now I can't seem to picture it without the wreckage I grew up with. When I imagine it, it's not quiet mornings, coffee, and sleepy smiles. It's locked doors, hushed arguments, and little faces watching us fall apart. I hate that my brain goes there, but it does.

And honestly, that fear has always been there. It followed me through my entire twenties. Every date, every kiss, every guy I let close, I was already foreshadowing what the future might look like. Was he going to end up like my dad? Would my kids have an absent father? Would they have to watch me juggle the pain of witnessing the destruction of someone I loved?

I can't imagine dealing with what I did the past few years while holding a baby on my hip. It gives me an even greater appreciation for my mom. Some nights, she'd be making dinner and trying to get us out the door for Michael's baseball game—all while Dad was snoring on the couch behind her, an empty beer dangling from his hand.

I didn't understand then, but I felt it. The exhaustion. The quiet resentment.

She was basically a single mother, but with a third child—a rebellious, selfish asshole who happened to be a grown adult. I hate calling him that because he wasn't an asshole. Never really was. Not even when he drank. But what do you call someone who's passing out, disappearing for hours, and leaving Mom with every responsibility? That's not exactly Father of the Year material.

The biggest worry isn't about me, though. It's about what it would do to the kids.

Unfortunately, I know firsthand what that looks like.

And it sucks.

The door creaks open, pulling me from my thoughts, and Jensen pops his head in. "Hey, babe, dinner's ready."

We always take turns with dinner at the Berkshires. Tonight's Amber and Jeff's night, so I took the last hour for myself to soak in the tub, read, and let my mind wander.

I take a moment to drink him in—disheveled hair, T-shirt, joggers. He's so effortlessly hot without even trying. "Alright. I'll be right there. Give me five."

My gaze flicks down to my Kindle. *Dammit.* I didn't get to read the next chapter, and I've been dying for this couple to finally have sex.

I set it down and pull the drain, standing as water drips from my body. Jensen doesn't move. He just stands there, gawking, a smirk tugging at his lips, brow arched, lust burning in his eyes as they roam over me.

"Wanna fuck real quick?"

I'm tempted to say yes—that smirk, those eyes. *God, those eyes.* Heat spreads through me. It would be so easy to give in, to forget dinner, Amber and Jeff, and everyone else waiting outside this bathroom. But I shake my head, forcing a laugh. "Yes. But I'm hungry, and we don't have time."

Wrapping the towel around my chest, I step out of the tub, only to have Jensen meet me halfway with a kiss that could melt ice. His hands slip inside the towel, fingers skimming along my waist.

"You sure?" he murmurs against my lips, fingertips grazing my ass. "We could be fast."

Goddamn him. "Yes, I'm sure. It's rude to keep them waiting." I press a kiss to his lips and step back, dropping my towel and grabbing my clean clothes from the floor.

His gaze burns into me as I step into my underwear. "Save it, babe. It's not happening right now. We can do it after dinner."

He groans, then says, "Hey." I glance up. "What if we were on a first date and I did this?"

Before I can answer, he pushes his joggers down past his ass, pops his dick out, and laughs.

Yes, sometimes he's basically a teenage boy.

I can't help it. A laugh bursts out of me as I pull my shirt over my head. "Why would you whip your dick out on a first date like that?"

"So that you'd wanna have sex with me. Obviously." He chuckles, then glances down at his now raging hard cock and grins. "But seriously... would you be horny once you saw Clark?"

I shake my head, laughing as I step forward. I wrap my fingers around his length, and give him a slow, smooth stroke. "Oh, yeah," I say seductively. "If you did that on a first date, all morals would go out the window. I wouldn't even care if I liked you. You show me Clark?" I let out a soft, deliberate exhale. "I'd be gone. Naked in five seconds."

He just chuckles. "I knew it."

I love a lot of things about Jensen, but the way he can always joke and make me laugh will always be one of my favorites. We lost so many of these moments after we got married—the light ones. I didn't even realize how much I missed them until now.

He leans in, presses a quick peck to my lips, and shoves himself back into his joggers, trying to hide his hard-on as best he can. Then he takes my hand and leads me to the kitchen.

* * *

THE PHONE IS PRESSED to my ear as Dad rambles about seeing me next week.

"Alright, I will. Thanks, Dad." I smile at Jensen as he walks into the bedroom.

"I'll see you next week then. Love you, Alley girl."

"Love you too. Bye."

"Bye."

I end the call, watching Jensen rummage through his suitcase.

We just wrapped up another night of chaos with the Adams crew —his siblings drinking, cracking jokes, trading stories, and laughing until my sides hurt. As the night wound down, I said my goodnights and slipped away a little early to call Dad and invite him to dinner at Michael's next week. I already talked to Jensen about it at dinner, and he wasn't worried about making it work.

Jensen turns to face me, a manila envelope in his hand.

"Hey." His voice is low, expression suddenly serious, brows pulling tight.

"What's up, babe? What's that?" I nod toward the envelope.

He hesitates, then clears his throat. "These are all the letters I wrote you in rehab." His face softens. "I almost tossed one." A corner of his mouth lifts, just slightly. "I was pretty pissed at you in it. But then I figured I didn't want to hide anything from you. And maybe it's okay for you to see that."

My eyebrows lift. "You were pissed... at me?"

"Yeah." He gives a soft chuckle. "It was right after I found out you filed for divorce." *Makes sense.* His hand drags along his neck, tugging. "I raged in a letter about it. I just... had to get it out, and that seemed like the healthiest way. It wasn't really ever meant for you."

He steps closer. "But the rest were. I wanted to send them while I was in rehab, but I never dared. I was too afraid you wouldn't read them. Or maybe I didn't want you to see me as weak or... I don't know. I was feeling a lot of things. I didn't want you to see that, but at the same time, I kind of did." He shrugs. "So I kept them. And I want you to have them now."

He holds the manila envelope out, and I reach for it, fingers pinching the edge. But he doesn't let go. His gaze locks on mine, eyes soft, expression vulnerable. "You don't have to read them. Only if you want to. And when you're ready."

I nod once. "Okay."

His grip stays on the manila. "I want you to know about rehab. About me and where I was. But I don't know exactly what they say. I've only read a few of them, so... please don't leave me for something I wrote months ago."

His thumb drags along the edge of the envelope, over and over, like he's reconsidering. He shifts his weight and swallows, his eyes pleading.

Whoa. He's really nervous.

"You got a secret mistress I'm gonna find out about or something?" I ask, a teasing smile tugging at my lips.

"Al, I'm serious. Promise me."

"Okaaay. I was joking. But now you've got me kinda worried."

His chest rises and falls with a deep breath, eyes never leaving mine. "Al..."

There was a time Jensen would've shoved these feelings so far down I'd never see them. But now? He's standing here, handing me the pieces of himself he's terrified I won't want. Trusting me with the deepest, darkest, most broken parts of him. And God, I want him to know he can. That he always can.

"Alright, alright. I'm not going to leave you. I won't let anything in here sway my feelings. I promise."

His fingers relax instantly. He lets go, combing a hand through his hair with a shaky sigh.

I start to open the manila.

"No! Don't read them now. Not in front of me." He stills. "God, I don't know. Unless you want to? I guess that's fine."

Good Lord, he's a mess.

For a moment, neither of us speaks. The letters feel heavy in my hand, and I can't stop staring at them. Then I force my gaze to his, and my breath hitches. This is a man who fought like hell to get here. To get us here. And it means the world that he's standing here, giving me these.

"I'll wait," I say finally, trying to ease his nerves. But Jesus, the way he's acting has me wanting to run to the closet, shut the door, and devour these right now. Whatever's inside has him in a frenzy, which only makes me more anxious to read them.

I step toward him and press my mouth to his. "Don't worry so much." My fingers slip under the hem of his shirt, brushing lightly over the ridges of his abs. "I love you. I'll always love you," I whisper. "Even when things are hard."

"I love you, too." His eyes lock on mine. "But I don't want loving me to be hard. I don't ever want to hurt you. Ever."

A smile ghosts across my lips. "It doesn't hurt right now," I murmur, sliding my hands higher beneath his shirt. His hand tangles in my hair while the other curls around my waist, pulling me close. He breathes me in with a kiss, lips hitting with force—needy, passionate, intentional. And with every touch, every press of his mouth, the weight of those letters burns away.

My lips part on instinct, ready to be devoured as he backs me toward the bed. I fall onto it, his body folding over mine. There's something primal about him in this moment. It's not just desire. Not just his hard cock pressing against me as he lowers himself closer, finding that perfect angle. It's more than that. It's protective. Fierce. Like his body is a shield and I'm the only thing he's guarding. He'd take a bullet for me, without a second thought.

An awareness of how turned on I am swirls through me, heat pulsing. My legs fall open, hips lifting, wanting more and needing to touch him everywhere—for our bodies to connect in every possible way.

Gratitude floods me, heavy and overwhelming. A lump forms in my throat as Jensen's mouth skims across my neck. *I'm so damn lucky.* To have him. To be loved by him. How many people can say they've found the person they want to spend every day of their life with? Someone to share everything with. Someone who can make them laugh and turn them on in seconds, no matter how many years pass.

Someone who will fight for them, even after everything. I have that. And he comes with blue eyes and a smile that makes women turn their heads in every room he walks into. My life with Jensen is something dreams are made of. It hasn't always felt that way, but it's always had that potential. The love was always there.

Sure, we've lived through nightmares.

But we woke up.

My fingers dip into the waistband of his joggers, just enough to tease him. He sucks in a sharp breath, mutters a *fuck, baby,* and in that moment I know I'm about to be wrecked in the only way I ever want to be: Jensen proving just how much he loves me.

And for once, I'm not thinking about what could break us. I'm just here. In this room. In his arms.

And it *finally* feels so right.

Chapter Thirty-Four

ALLEY

I SMACK the snooze button for the third time before finally forcing myself upright, rubbing the sleep from my eyes. I grab the remote off the nightstand and hit the button for the blackout shades. As they roll up, I stumble to the bathroom like a drunk, still half-asleep. It's not even that early. It's eight. Which means Jensen's probably been up for hours. He doesn't even sleep in on vacation.

After using the bathroom, I shuffle down the hall into the living room and find him sprawled on the couch, coffee in hand, smirk on his face—reading my Kindle.

A laugh slips out as I head toward him, eyeing the espresso machine and wishing for an IV drip of caffeine. Jensen sits up fast, planting the Kindle on his lap like a teenage boy caught with porn.

"Busted," I say. "You reading my smutty book?"

He chuckles low. "Maybe."

I lean over the back of the couch to kiss him. "What part were you reading?"

"I don't know. But the girl just gave the guy a really great blow job, and now I'm horny."

I straighten, my gaze dropping to his crotch and the obvious hard-on. "I can see that," I tease. "I'm making a latte. You want one?"

"Sure, I'll take another." He stands, adjusting himself before following me into the kitchen.

I pull the milk from the fridge and start the espresso machine, tamping the grounds and setting the shots. "What time are you guys leaving today?" I ask as I pour the milk into the frother. My brows knit. "I thought you were heading out at seven-thirty."

He scoffs, sliding onto a stool. "Yeah, that was before Matt, Meg, and Kev got extra drunk last night. I doubt we see any of them before ten."

I finish his latte and slide it across the counter.

He takes a sip. "What time's your spa appointment?"

"Ten-thirty. So I sure hope Meg is up before then."

"What are you having done? The whole works?"

"Yep. Massage, pedicure, facial, some kind of body scrub. It's four and a half hours, and I'm very excited." I pause to steam the milk, then pour the foam over my shots.

Sliding onto the stool beside him, I grin. "I'll miss you, but it's *waaaay* better than freezing my ass off on the mountain."

He wraps both hands around his mug, grinning. "Are we ever going to get you to love skiing?"

"Honestly? Probably not. But you know I love it up here anyway."

His hand drops to my knee, giving it a squeeze. "That's good. And I love you for powering through."

I meet his gaze, his expression soft and genuine. "I love you too."

His fingers drift higher on my thigh as he leans in. His lips brush mine, then curve into a smile. "I want you on your knees later—just like that girl in your book."

I laugh softly as his mouth comes back for seconds. "Later? Why not now?"

His hand finds mine, guiding it to his lap and pressing firmly against his cock. He's hard as a rock, and my thumb trails down his length before he breaks the kiss, grinning as he stands.

"Nope. Not yet. You'll have to be patient." He's fighting a laugh, but I can't hold mine back.

"You literally just put my hand on your dick!"

He arches a brow. "Yeah, but I'm edging you."

I point to myself, my grin widening. "Oh, you're *edging* me? Stop reading my Kindle."

He steps between my legs. "Why? You don't want me to put you on your knees and call you my good girl?"

Butterflies kick low in my stomach. I've always loved when he gets a little filthy, like something out of the darker books I secretly devour. I know he's partly teasing, but it's so fun.

I shrug, a smile ghosting my lips. "I mean, I probably wouldn't complain."

He pulls me up, hands locking around my waist. "Tell you what. You be a good girl today, enjoy your spa day, use *our* credit card—and when you get home I'll let you suck my dick."

"You'll *let* me?"

He leans closer, whispering in my ear. "I promise I'll make it worth your time."

I cock a brow. "Yeah? How so?"

He shakes his head. "Not telling. But I'm gonna send you dirty messages. Edging you. All. Day."

"Can't wait to see what you come up with. I just hope you don't find yourself beating off in a bathroom when I respond."

His chuckle melts into my laugh, both cut off by the warmth of his mouth.

When he finally pulls back, his eyes are soft and full of adoration. "I'm really glad you're here."

"Me too," I whisper.

His hand cradles my face, and we kiss in the kitchen until Matt barges in. He's shirtless, sweats slung low as he slumps toward the espresso machine. He rubs the back of his neck, shooting us a look. "Jesus. Get a room."

So we do.

* * *

I PLOP down on the bed with my phone and the manila envelope Jensen gave me last night.

A missed text from him lights up the screen.

JENSEN

I hope you're ready to be worshipped by my mouth.
I'm going to tease the shit out of you. Lick your
pussy until you're about to cum all over my tongue,
then stop. Finger you until you're begging for more. I
can't wait to watch you lose control.

A grin breaks across my face. He's been sending these every hour, and it's totally turning me on. I can't wait for him to get home and deliver. I text him back, trying to one-up him.

You're the one who's going to lose control. When I
wrap my lips around your cock, I want you to look at
me while I take every inch of you—and when I
swallow every bit of you. I know how much you love
that, watching me take you.

His reply comes instantly.

JENSEN

Damn, baby. I'm hard just thinking about it. That's
one of my favorite things.

I laugh, tossing my phone aside. I'll let him sit with that one for a while. Sorting my pillows, I prop them up behind me and sit cross-legged on the bed. I flip open the manila and tip it over, spilling the contents into my lap. Each letter's neatly labeled: *Week three. Week four. Week seven.*

My fingers hover over week one. My heartbeat quickens, my stomach tightening into knots. I just stare at it.

Part of me is desperate to know. To dig into this side of him—what he went through, what made him into the man I see now, how he came out of rehab stronger than ever.

But the other part craves ignorance. The easy version of us. I already lived my hard; I don't want to shoulder his too. I'm afraid of what it might stir up in me. Afraid it'll make my hard look small in comparison. It's selfish, I know.

Do I really have to go back there? Can't I just stay in the good?

I suck in a breath, then let it out slow, cheeks puffing. *I can do this.*

Erin Cornia

This is what I've wanted—for him to get clean. To do the work. To help me understand why he made my life a living hell.

With shaky hands, I slip my thumb under the seal, tearing it open, and pull out the first letter.

> *Dear Alley,*
>
> *I hate it here. I'm lonely. I'm bitter, and I'm scared as hell.*
>
> *Scared to know things. Scared to remember. Scared to face everything. To face me. To talk about it.*

I tilt my head back. *Oh, God.* My throat tightens. My eyes sting. I take another deep breath, steeling myself.

> *Therapy's the worst of it. Digging into all the shit I've done, dissecting it, talking about all the people I hurt. All the times I made you cry. I fucking hate it.*
>
> *And I hate myself.*
>
> *I'm clean. But the cravings have never been stronger. To numb this. To make it all disappear. To black out and just hope to God I don't wake.*
>
> *I feel like a coward for saying that. And I guess I am. Because when shit got hard, I left. I took the easy way out. I didn't talk to you. I didn't get the help I needed. I lied.*
>
> *I acted strong because I didn't want you to see me as someone who couldn't take care of you.*
>
> *I acted out of fear and desperation, and I turned into the one person you never wanted me to be.*
>
> *Your dad.*

Tears slide hot down my cheeks. There's no stopping them. I inhale slowly through my nose, then look back down.

The one thing you asked of me was to not make you live that hell. And I didn't just put you there... I rolled out the red carpet and walked you straight into it. I'm so fucking sorry.

All I ever wanted was to make you happy. To be the guy who half deserved you. To be someone who you could raise a family with. To be a good dad. Better than yours was. But I failed you.

I missed the mark. I wasn't even close. And I didn't even see it coming. That's the hardest part. That someone like me could end up here. I never thought it possible.

I knew I was addicted long before I could admit I was an addict. It happened fast. By the time I realized, it was too late. You knew. Matt knew. Mom knew. Everyone knew but me. Even though I did. I just lived in denial. It couldn't be me. I wouldn't do that. I'm smarter than that. Stronger than that. Successful. Better.

And why me, Al? Why did this have to happen? I didn't want this. I just wanted the pain gone. I just wanted to be your husband. To show up for you. To work. To avoid another surgery.

I just wanted to be married to my best friend. To travel, to make memories. I wanted to make you a mother, because goddamn, nothing's sexier than the thought of you with our kids. You'll be an amazing mom. I just hope I get to see it. That you'll still be here waiting when I get out.

Ink smears where my tears fall.

I'm going to work hard in here. For you. For me. For our future family. Even though I hate it.

I'll do it this time. I'll stay clean. For good. I'll talk about

*all the shit. I'll do anything to save our marriage. To make you
smile again. To make you proud of me again.*

*That's all I want. For you to stand next to me and be
proud you're mine.*

*But right now you feel so far away. And it makes all this
that much harder.*

I love you. Forever.

Jensen

I don't bother holding it in. I let it all come—the fear, the sadness,
the anger, the hope. And beneath it all, the swell in my chest that's so
damn proud of him.

It's hard, hearing it from his side. Harder than I expected. Just like it
was when he drove me to my dad's a few years ago to finally talk to him.
To hear him out. To let him ask for forgiveness. I'm just glad I didn't
wait a decade to hear Jensen. To *see* him, raw and broken, but trying.

I pull out week two and read.

Dear Alley,

This one's more hopeful. He writes about Max, and how it's vali-
dating to talk with someone who understands.

*Max isn't a bad dude. He just lost his way. Like me. He
didn't go out there one day searching for a way to destroy his
family. He just wanted to forget about some of the crazy shit
he'd seen. He's a good guy.*

The letter makes me cry and smile at the same time.
Week three is longer.

Dear Alley,
God, I miss you. Every second of every day, I miss you so

much. I can't wait to see you again. I've only been here three weeks, and it feels like an eternity without you.

I talked to Matt yesterday. He said you're still in Chicago. He made it sound like you might be moving there... permanently.

Please don't let that be true. I keep trying to talk myself out of it. You wouldn't move. You love New York. Your job. Your friends. You love me. At least, that's what I keep telling myself. I don't really know what's true anymore.

Getting clean has been so fucking hard. Reality and memories blur together. Things I don't even remember. Moments that feel like dreams. It all gets tangled up with the truth. It's confusing, trying to figure out what actually happened, and what's just in my head.

But you moving to Chicago? That can't be real, can it? Because that would mean you're leaving me. Leaving us. And the "us" I remember is so damn good, Al. Too good to walk away from.

I know sorry isn't enough. But I am... down to the marrow in my bones.

I wish I could go back. I wish I could erase all of it. Tell you I was hurting. Go to the doctor. Get another surgery, even. If I could go back, I'd do anything to make it different. I would've never touched that first pill.

I was desperate, babe. I was in so much pain. I tried to power through. I was so worried about you being married to a cripple in ten years, I never stopped to think I could become an addict.

It's not who I am. It's something that happened to me. I picked the pill. But the addiction picked me. I didn't go looking for this. But it found me anyway.

> *And I'll spend the rest of my life regretting what it did to you.*
>
> *I'm working the steps. Taking it seriously this time. Step Four is this week: Make a searching and fearless moral inventory of yourself. It scares the shit out of me. To really look at myself. To look at the harm I've caused. But maybe something good will come out of it. Maybe I'll start to understand why I am the way I am.*
>
> *I've always struggled with AA. The whole "higher power" thing never clicked for me. But here they frame it differently, and it's easier to connect. I've been reading a lot of books on stoicism. The teachings make sense to me, so I'm clinging to them. It helps.*
>
> *I guess I'll let you know how it all goes next week.*
>
> *Love,*
>
> *Jensen*

I close my eyes, chest aching. This was denial wrapped in desperation, but also the first glimpse of Jensen staring hard truths in the face.

Week four felt much the same—hopeful, healing, but still clinging to the fantasy that I'd be waiting for him in New York.

And then I open week five. The tone shifts. It's like something cracked open in him, and things begin to move forward.

> *Babe. I get it now. I finally get it. Today in group we had to name a deal breaker in love. I said cheating. Then they told us to close our eyes and imagine the person we trust most doing it—over and over, lying about it every time.*
>
> *And then I pictured you waiting for me at home, and me not showing up. Jesus, Al, it broke me in a new way. For the first time, I understood what I put you through. I was*

supposed to be your safe place. And I lied. I let you down. I hurt you.

I set the letter down and close my eyes. *God, empathy. Finally.* But then I get to week six. It's crumpled, and I smooth it out best I can before reading.

> Yesterday was the first time I've been clean and thought
> —I'd rather be dead.
> That thought came right after Tobias and Nina told me you'd filed for divorce.

I sniff, wiping at my nose. It kills me to go back here… to when I filed.

> Just when I started to believe in something again, you gave up on me.
> It feels like I was halfway up the fucking mountain, finally breathing, and you shoved me off the edge.
> I'm mad at you, Alley. God, I'm so fucking mad at you.

A sob rips from me. Full-on ugly crying now. This must be the one he almost tossed. His anger slices, and I let it. I don't excuse it. I don't swallow it whole. I just hold it long enough to see his pain. But I still see me.

By the time I finish I can hardly breathe.

> I love you more than this life. More than fucking air.
> More than myself.
> Love,
> Jensen

I press the letter to my chest, shaking.

My sobs eventually fade, and when I finally reach for week seven, I brace myself.

It's short. Numb. Like after he learned about the divorce, he just gave up on us. It's almost like he didn't even want to write me.

Then week eight shifts. A clarity I haven't seen yet. He writes about a session with Nina and a book he read that unlocked something —stoicism, acceptance. Suddenly he isn't in denial. He isn't begging or grasping for a way to fix it. It's like he looked in the mirror, saw the wreckage he caused, and accepted it.

> *I'm not glad this happened. I could never say that because there were far too many casualties. Yours being the worst. But it's hard to say I'd do it different, because I'm grateful for what I'm learning. What's done is done. I may never be forgiven, but I can live with that because I can finally live with me.*

By week nine, confidence creeps back in. Like he's learning to stand again. Determined to be whole—to be great—with or without me.

> *I know I can be happy now no matter what happens. It'd just be a hell of a lot better if I got to share that with you.*

My heart lifts with pride, but fear sneaks in too, along with a little envy. Because if he can be happy without me, *does he even need me? And why can't I have that same confidence—knowing I could be happy without him?* Every time I've imagined a life without Jensen, I can't picture myself being happy. Maybe eventually I could be, but the difference between now and a few months ago is drastic. I was in the pits of despair, and now? Regardless of the fear that still lingers, I'm happy... because of Jensen.

But is that a good thing? It is, and it isn't. Maybe it's time I do the same kind of work he's done. For me. It's not about measuring up to him. It's about finding my own footing. Jensen did. He learned to stand on his own again. Maybe that's the key to all this. Maybe that's how we'll finally stand a chance together.

I continue. Week ten has me melting.

Last night I had a dream about you. A sex dream.

You climbed into my bed, naked, pressing your ass into me like you couldn't get close enough. You're so damn sexy, Al. I woke up aching for you. Yeah, I was horny, but mostly just missing us and the way we connected. That part of me that was lost for a while, it's back now. I feel like me again.

Hot. Honest. Pure Jensen.
Week eleven seals everything up and ties it into a bow.

I'm not done. I'm just steadier. Matt says he hears it in my voice.

I set the letters down and stare at the wall, drained, trying to process. My nose is raw and stuffy, my face blotchy, my thoughts racing. I stumble to the bathroom, splash cold water over my cheeks, and blow my nose.

I climb back into bed, the letters still scattered across the sheets. I pick one up, thumb brushing the ink, lean back against the headboard, and start reading again. His words bleed into me—grief, confusion, clarity, all swirling together.

The way this man holds my entire heart in the palm of his hand... I read it over and over, until nothing has ever been clearer. I see his work. I see mine waiting ahead. I know what I have to do.

I can't snap my fingers and erase the past. I can't pretend trust magically reappears overnight. But I can choose. I can either move forward doubting everything, living in fear—or I can let go, trust my husband, and see him for the man he is now and the man he's becoming.

I choose him.

And through all of it, one truth hits sharper than anything else.

I fucking love him.

Chapter Thirty-Five

JENSEN

My eyes scan the mountain, searching for Matt. The sun glares off the snow, forcing me to squint.

Shit. I lost him.

I finish the section of moguls and push to make up time, crouching low, leaning forward, catching speed. Matt's a way better skier than me. He's been doing this since he could walk. It was the one thing he did with his dad growing up that actually counted as quality time.

At the bottom of the hill, I finally spot him in his red boots, waiting for me.

I skid to a stop. "You're too fucking fast, man. I don't know how you go down those moguls like that."

He grins. "Yeah, well, it was learn to go fast or get left behind crying. I chose the former." He claps my back. "Kev and Jeff are inside grabbing a drink. You wanna hang or head back to the house?"

"I can hang for a bit."

He asks because he can't fathom being at a bar and not drinking. But that's life now. And I'm fine with it. Not that the idea doesn't sound good. There's nothing like an ice-cold beer to warm your belly after a long day on the slopes.

I'm looking forward to spending time with Alley tonight, but I don't want to pass up this much needed time with my brothers. It feels special, and I'm seeing it all through a clearer lens this week.

I follow Matt inside. He drops into a seat next to Kevin, and I slide in beside Jeff. They've already got beers in front of them, and Matt wastes no time, waving the bartender over to order two IPAs on tap.

Jeff glances at me. "You look happy, brother." An awkward chuckle slips out as a grin spreads across my face. Jeff's never been one for deep talks with me. Ever. "It's nice." He clears his throat, voice softening. "To see you happy again."

"Thanks, man. That means a lot. Especially coming from you."

"Yeah? Why's that?"

"'Cause you're my big brother. It always means something when you give a shit." I fold my hands on the bartop, eyes dropping to them. "I've always looked up to you, you know?"

Vulnerability burns through me. Jeff and I don't do this. We stick to surface-level talks. Sports. Work.

"You've always had your shit together. Always knew what you wanted. Never got in trouble. Never fucked up. You just... knew how to navigate life. Amber's lucky to have you. I know I give you shit about being boring, but..." I huff out a laugh. "Truth is, I'm a little envious you didn't need rehab to figure it all out." One corner of my mouth lifts. "You're a great dad too."

My gaze falls on his beer. Not because I want it, but because I realize something. I don't need a drink to have this conversation. Or to laugh. Or to have wild sex with my beautiful wife. Or to live fully. Maybe I'm not as steady by nature as he is, but that makes me a different kind of strong. It hits me right in the chest—I've done some really hard shit. And that alone makes me worthy of the same things he has.

The corners of his mouth pull up. "Thank you for saying that." He takes a sip of his beer, thoughtful. "You know I've always been in awe of you?"

What?

He glances over, sees my surprise, and chuckles. "Don't act so shocked. It's not like you aren't used to being everyone's favorite."

"Yeah, but... I always thought you hated that growing up."

"Oh, I did. Megan too. But you've got something neither of us have."

"What's that? A roster of all the dumb shit I've done?"

He smirks, then shakes his head. "That too, but nah. You've got grit. A determination not to fail that Megan and I didn't get. We're motivated, sure, but not like you. When you set your eye on something, by God, you'll get it. A scholarship, even with all the trouble you got into in high school. Work. Alley." He lifts his beer and nods. "Twice now."

He tips back his glass, taking a long swallow before setting it down. "Even in elementary school—you couldn't spell for shit, but Thomas Sinclair made fun of you, and you came home dead set on winning the spelling bee. Practiced every day after school, made me and Megan quiz you until we wanted to beat you with the dictionary." He leans back, folding his arms across his chest. "And then you won. Took first place. Won the fitness award every year, too. Proved every single person who doubted you wrong."

I chuckle softly. "Well, Thomas Sinclair was a dick, and I lucked out in the physical fitness department. I guess I was fortunate in the gene pool."

Jeff presses his lips into a tight smile, gaze dropping as he shifts in his seat.

When he looks back up, his eyes are glassy—and not from the alcohol. He swallows hard. "I was one of those people. I questioned you. When you relapsed, I treated you like an imbecile. Because you were being one. And I'm sorry. I was secretly praying Alley would leave your sorry ass, because I didn't think you could do it. Not after the relapse." He gives me a small smile, then sniffs. "I should've known better. You always find a way to come out on top. And I'm glad you did."

Jesus Christ. The emotion blindsides me. My chest cinches tight, and I fight not to break down in the middle of this fucking bar. Jeff and I have always been close, but never in the deep, personal way I've always had with Megan. And now here he is, laying it all out.

"I... Christ." My throat works to find words. "You have no idea what that means to me, Jeff."

He lifts a brow. "I have an idea. You do look up to me after all."

A laugh bursts out of me, and he stands, gesturing with his hands. "Come on, get up."

I stand, and he pulls me into a brotherly hug, clapping me on the back. It's stupid, but I've never felt more accepted than I do right now. For so long, he's been the ideal I thought I'd never measure up to. But this? This is everything.

"I love you. And I'm proud of you."

His words clog my throat. For once, I don't feel like the fuck-up little brother. I feel like a man who's finally earned his place. And it feels damn good. "I love you, too."

Chapter Thirty-Six

JENSEN

By the time we get back from skiing, it's close to nine. Alley hasn't answered any of my texts for hours, and the worry's eating at me. Maybe she read my letters and got upset. Maybe I shouldn't have asked her to make a promise she wasn't sure she could keep.

We were flirting earlier—dirty texts, back and forth, laughing—and then suddenly, nothing. Radio silence.

I step inside, eyes sweeping the living room, then the kitchen. No Alley. My gaze lands on Megan and Amber sprawled across the couch, wine glasses in hand. A bottle of red and another of white sit open on the table, and some show's playing in the background. But Alley not being here with them sends my nerves into overdrive. Heat rushes through my chest, every breath heavier than the last.

Megan looks up. "Hey. Did you guys have fun?"

"Where's Al?" The words tumble out before I can even think. My coat and gloves hit the floor, and I kick off my boots in a rush. Panic's rising, and I'm trying not to shit my pants here.

Megan arches a brow. "Wow. Rude. Nice to see you too. We had a great day, by the way, thanks for asking."

I straighten as Matt, Jeff, and Kevin mosey in behind me, stripping off their gear. "Sorry, I need to talk to Al. Is she in our room? Has she seemed okay to you?"

Megan sits up abruptly. "Yeah, why? What's wrong?"

"Meg." Frustration spikes. "Have you seen her?"

"Yeah, she's good. She's in your room. Was a little quiet at dinner, then said she wanted to read. But that's not out of character. What's going on?"

I'm halfway down the hall before she even finishes.

I push the bedroom door open, and Alley's gaze lifts to mine with a soft smile. "Hey, babe. How was your day? You have fun?"

Fuck. Relief rushes through me, loosening every muscle. I step inside and close the door. She's curled up in bed, wearing my favorite jersey—the one I proposed to her in. A lamp casts a warm glow across the room, just enough to read. Her hair's down, one side tucked behind her ear, the other falling across her face, Kindle in hand.

"It was good. Great, actually. Jeff and I even had a heart-to-heart." My eyes land on the manila envelope beside her, and panic flickers again, but I force it down. *She's here. She's talking to me. And she seems... happy.*

"Really? That's unusual. Like a real heart-to-heart?"

I nod. "Yep. He even got emotional."

Her brows shoot up. "No way!" She sets her Kindle on the night-stand and pats my side of the bed. "Come sit. I need all the details."

I unzip my snow pants and shove them down, leaving me in just my thermals. The shower's calling, but so is stripping every layer off and climbing in next to Alley.

I kick my pants aside and slide into bed next to her. She greets me with a kiss. "So? What did Jeff say? How did it even come up?"

I give her the cliff notes from the bar, about Jeff getting emotional. She gasps in all the right places, asks a million questions. She's locked in, and not just about Jeff, but every piece of my day. Which runs I did, which were my favorite, if I beat Matt at any of them. We laugh over all the stupid shit Matt and I joked about. I even tell her about the number he scored from some woman he ditched me mid-run to chase.

It's easy. Natural. Feels like us. But the whole time, my eyes keep drifting to the manila envelope sitting between us, a big-ass elephant in the room just waiting to be recognized.

"Tell me about your day. How was the spa?"

"It was so great. God, it felt amazing. I feel like a new woman." Her grin widens as she leans in, planting a soft kiss on my lips. "Thank you for planning that for me."

"Mmm." I savor the warmth of her mouth and go in for another kiss. "I didn't plan it, Megan and Amber did."

"I know, but you put the deposit down. You made sure I had an appointment before you even knew if I'd come." Her hand finds mine, weaving our fingers together. When she looks back up, there's something in her eyes that's new, something I can't place. "Thank you for that. For not giving up on me."

"I'd never give up on you."

"I know." She pauses, studying me, taking her time. "But I don't know if I deserved that kind of loyalty. I gave up on you." I open my mouth to argue, but she cuts me off. "I know, I know. I had every right to leave you, to do what I did. But you..." Her voice cracks. "You never gave up on us. You just lost your way."

"Babe," I murmur.

She takes a moment to collect herself. "I read your letters." Her lips press together as she swallows, fighting to keep it together. "And I wish I'd read them sooner." Her eyes glisten, and her cheeks flush. "I'm sorry I didn't want to know. That I wouldn't hear you." Her voice is steady, but it's threaded with emotion.

I squeeze her hand. I don't need to say anything. I just want to be here, in this moment with her. I close my eyes and let the weight of her words sink in, settle deep.

She clears her throat. "I have something for you."

My brows pull together, curiosity sparking. Before I can ask, she's reaching for the nightstand. She picks up an envelope and hands it to me.

I take it, cautious, a little nervous.

"Open it," she says, a grin ghosting her lips.

"Alright." I flip it over and slide a finger under the seal.

"Read the letter first."

I open it and pull out the folded piece of paper, glancing up at her. She's sitting cross-legged, leaning toward me, hands pressed into the mattress. Her bottom lip's caught between her teeth, but it doesn't hide the smile tugging at her mouth.

I unfold the paper.

It reads:

I love you, too.

Look inside the envelope.

I tip the envelope and peer inside. Her wedding ring stares back at me, and my heart constricts, chest squeezing tight. I reach inside, letting my fingers curl around it. Emotion floods in, and my eyes sting as I realize she's giving me back more than just a ring. She's giving me us—our marriage, our life together.

"Now look up," she whispers.

I lift my gaze.

Her hand is out in front of me, palm down, fingers spread wide.

"Now ask me to be your wife," she says softly.

God. I can't even speak. My throat burns, thick with everything I wish I could take back. My next breath is forced, years of weight pressing down, then lifting in the same heartbeat. It's the lightest breath I've taken in forever, and still, it nearly breaks me.

I squeeze my eyes shut, clutching the ring so hard it bites into my palm.

"Babe. Look at me."

I draw in a shaky breath, force my eyes open, and lock them on hers. I'm terrified to move. To blink. To speak. To fuck this up.

"Ask me to be your wife," she whispers, softer than before.

I shake my head, my lip trembling. I can't. If I say it, I'll lose it. I'll fucking cry.

Her palm cups my cheek. "Eyes on me, babe. Remember?"

Words fail me. I'm too overwhelmed. *Goddamn.* My chin trembles, and I press my lips tight as I slide the ring onto her finger.

I lace our hands together and crush my mouth against hers. I kiss her like I've never kissed anyone. A fire rips through me, freshly lit, and she's the match that sparked it. She climbs into my lap, her thighs locking around me as our lips collide. We devour each other, pouring everything we feel into this one kiss.

"I love you." Her whisper's soft, breath hot against my skin. She pulls back, eyes locking on mine as her hands slide up my chest. "And I'm so proud of you." Her voice shakes, and a tear slips free. "And I'd be honored to stand next to you." A sob falls from her quivering lip. "And I'm so damn grateful to be your wife."

"Jesus, babe." My voice is rough, choked. "Don't make me cry." I huff out a laugh that's half sob.

She laughs through her own tears.

"Will you be my wife... again?" I ask, lifting the corner of my mouth.

She presses a soft kiss to my lips. "Hell yeah." Then another, and another, before tucking both hands into my shirt and whispering in my ear, "And now I want you to deliver on everything you promised me in those texts today."

A groan rumbles out of me, low and amused. "Oh, you're gonna get it."

"Good." She grinds down, trailing kisses along my jaw and down my neck. I tug at her shirt and she lifts her arms, quick and eager. Mine's off next. I rip it off and toss it. Her warm skin slides against mine, and my greedy hands roam every curve I can touch.

Her fingers toy with the waistband of my thermals, slipping just beneath.

"Shit, babe," I groan, half-laughing. "I need a shower. Been sweating in these all day."

Her mouth skims over my chest, teasing. "Mmm. Guess we better take care of that." Her hand slips inside my underwear, cupping me, soft and torturous.

"Fuuuck," I growl, cock already throbbing. "You're killing me."

She pulls away, grinning as she stands suddenly. "Come on. Let's shower. Your balls are sticky as hell." Her laugh bubbles out, softening the jab, and she tosses me a look over her bare shoulder that nearly undoes me.

"Jesus." I laugh, shaking my head. "Calling me out when I'm this vulnerable?"

She's still laughing when I shove my pants down and stand. She grabs my hand and pulls me toward the bathroom.

I crank the water on but don't wait for it to warm. I pull her in with me.

She shrieks as the icy spray hits her skin, and I swallow the sound with my mouth, teeth scraping her bottom lip. "Told you you were gonna get it."

Her laugh ricochets off the tile as she backs against the wall, arms folding around my neck, leaving the water to pound me instead. It takes fucking forever to heat up, but I don't care, because her fingers just wrapped around the base of my cock. She gives me a slow, firm stroke and moans into my mouth.

"You're so sexy, baby," I murmur. "I love you."

"I love you too."

My hand finds its way between her thighs, and she gasps against my mouth as I touch her—slow, purposeful. By the time she's trembling around me, she's breathless, and so am I. Then she drops to her knees, eyes locked on mine, and takes me in like I'm the only thing she's ever wanted. Every slow drag of her mouth has me bracing against the tile, fighting for control.

When I finally come, she looks up, lips wrapped tight, throat working, and swallows every drop.

Just like she promised she would.

* * *

I SINK into the cold sheets, spent and satisfied. Skiing, sex, laughter, connection. *Damn.* It's been a good day.

Alley curls up against me, nuzzling into the crook of my shoulder. My hand drifts lazily over her back, tracing up and down. Her ear presses firm to my chest, fingers toying with that little trail of hair below my belly button. She loves that hair. I used to shave it, thought she preferred that, until one day she told me she missed it. Said it was sexy. Manly. Haven't touched a razor there since. If Alley likes it, that's how it stays.

She props up onto an elbow, palm sliding over my chest. "Hey," she says softly.

My brows pinch as I meet her gaze.

She hesitates. "I think we should talk about the stuff Sophie told us to talk about."

"The thing we're scared to share?"

"Yeah." Her tone is timid, like she's nervous just mentioning it.

"Okay. You want to go first, or me?"

"I think I want you to."

She presses a quick kiss to my lips, then settles back against the pillow. I roll onto my side so I can look at her. Our fingers weave together, legs tangling under the duvet. The room is dark and quiet.

"Alright. I'll go first..." My pulse kicks up a notch, nerves sparking. "God, I hope this doesn't come out wrong."

"Doesn't matter. Just say it."

I clear my throat and swallow. The words feel heavy in my chest. "I worry," I start, because that's the part I'm sure about, "I worry you'll always be looking over your shoulder, waiting for me to fuck up—to relapse. And I get why. I don't expect you to flip a switch and just trust me again."

My thumb brushes over the back of her hand. "I know trust isn't something you hand over. It's something I have to earn back. But I'm afraid that no matter how much time passes, even as we start a family, you'll just be waiting for shit to hit the fan, for me to be the way your dad was. I can't promise I won't make mistakes, but I promise you I'll show up. Every day. I'll do the boring, ugly, slow stuff—meetings, workouts, whatever it takes. I'll choose you and sobriety, over and over."

My voice drops, softer. "I can't make you forgive me or trust me. Only you can do that. But I will spend the rest of my life trying to earn it, if you let me."

She's quiet for a moment, brows furrowed, lips pressed tight. "I want to trust you again, Jensen. I really do. And I'm trying. So hard." She frees her hand from my grip and slides it up my arm. "I made an appointment today... for hypnotherapy. It's with the same person Cooper went to. Leo referred her. Cooper said it helped her a lot." She takes a deep breath. "I want you to know I'm doing what I can to help myself heal, so I can learn to trust again. Work through all the emotions and trauma. Sooner rather than later." She offers a weak smile.

"That's great, babe. When's your first appointment?"

"Next week. I'm kind of nervous. I don't know what to expect. I've never done anything like that before."

"I get that. But you'll be great. Just show up, do your best." I press a quick kiss to her mouth. "Proud of you. I know you hate therapy."

Her lips twitch.

"Your turn," I whisper.

"Okay." She lets out a shaky exhale. "I'm nervous. Which is crazy because it's you. My heart's racing."

I give her hand a squeeze, chuckling. "It's just me. You don't have to be nervous."

"I know," she says softly. "I couldn't decide what I wanted to tell you. But after reading your letters, it was pretty clear what I needed to say. I just... I don't want it to hurt you."

God, she's so selfless. "Babe, I can handle it. Promise."

She lets out a breathy laugh. "How do you know that? You don't even know what it is."

I kiss the back of her hand. "Because I've got you. As long as I have that, I can handle anything. We're in this together. And we're pretty fucking amazing when we're a team."

Her eyes gloss over. "But we were a team"—she swallows hard, voice cracking—"before."

I let go of her hand and comb my fingers through her hair, letting my palm settle against the side of her head, my thumb brushing her temple. I shake my head. "No, babe. Not like we thought."

Her brows scrunch.

"That's where things went wrong. We were on the same team, but I was playing my own game. I was a selfish teammate. When I needed help, I kept the ball, thinking I could score if I just ran faster. But I didn't. I couldn't."

She smiles. "A football analogy?"

I laugh. "Always." My hand drops to her shoulder, fingers trailing down her arm, brushing her smooth skin. "I won't play that way again. We're in this together. I want you in every part of my life. I'll share the hard stuff. I'll let you be there for me. And I'll be there for you." I kiss her forehead. "But you've got to do the same. And right now is one of those times. You can trust me with this, babe. I can handle it."

Her eyes search mine, the faintest smile tugging at her lips before it slips away. "Alright. I can do that." She exhales, shakier this time. "I'm scared—like, really, really scared—to have kids with you after everything. And that—" Her voice breaks, and a sob rips out, gutting me, shattering something deep in my chest. "That used to be what I looked forward to most. Because I know you'll be such a great dad. But now the possibility of relapse hangs over that dream, casting a shadow I can't seem to shake. I just can't see it. I can't get past these images I have of you... and then these innocent kids caught in it." Her hand slips from mine as she wipes at her tears. "I keep seeing my dad when I was growing up, but now it's you. And it terrifies me."

The words hang like a loaded gun between us. Heavy. Unforgiving.

I want kids more than anything. Always have. But I want them with her. I've been wanting to bring it up, to talk about it, but the timing's never felt right. She's been too fragile, too uncertain.

We haven't exactly been careful, either. Alley's struggled to get pregnant before, and I think she just assumes she can't. Sometimes I catch myself praying she'll get pregnant, while at the same time praying she won't. Because yeah, I want that, but not until she's ready. I don't want her to feel stuck with me. I want her to choose me. To trust me enough to say, *Okay, let's do this. Let's start a family.*

We're close. I can feel it. Tonight's been a huge step, but this? This is the hurdle I don't know how to clear. I'm just glad she made that therapy appointment, that we're still seeing Sophie. That someone can help us figure out all these unknowns.

"It's okay you feel that way," I finally say. "Understandable, even."

Her fingers toy with mine. "I know. It just... sucks. Makes it so hard."

"It does suck," I agree quietly. "And it is hard. But anything worth having usually is." I swallow, the words catching. "And this—us, our future—that's worth it. We can't change the past. All we can do is decide how bad we want it. And I want it, babe. We're going to make an incredible family someday. We're doing the work. We just have to take it one day at a time." My thumb brushes over her knuckles. "Everything else will fall into place if we keep showing up. Be present. Enjoy today. Enjoy each other."

Her eyes are wet, but a smile curves her mouth. "I want that. More than anything."

"Then let's get it, baby." I crash my mouth to hers, letting this kiss say everything I can't.

My lips slide against hers as I roll onto my elbow, leaning over her. Her arms lock tight around my neck, and the next kiss is firmer, hungrier.

"You're so amazing," she whispers into my mouth. "I fucking love you."

A low chuckle rumbles out of me. I love when Alley says fuck. It's rare, vulnerable, real—and it wrecks me every time.

I pull her closer, voice deep and rough. "I fucking love you too."

Chapter Thirty-Seven

ALLEY

I GRAB my toiletry bag and stuff it into my suitcase. I got home from my first hypnotherapy session about thirty minutes ago. My eyes are still red from crying. The moment I closed them, it felt like someone cracked open a vault I'd been keeping sealed for months, and everything came pouring out. I cried through nearly the whole thing. It was raw and vulnerable, but when I walked out, I felt lighter. Like I'd finally dropped a weighted vest I didn't even realize I'd been carrying. I can't wait to tell Jensen about it. I've already got another appointment set two weeks from now.

He's flying in tonight. He'll work in the Chicago office Thursday and Friday so we can go to dinner at Michael's tomorrow. I'm getting ready for another long weekend at Matt's. And honestly? It's getting old. All the back-and-forth, and living out of a suitcase. It's not just New York I pack for—I have to pack for here too. Leo keeps assuring me Jensen can stay here, and maybe I would take him up on it if we didn't have an entire condo available to us. But it's a no-brainer. We have Matt's all to ourselves. But still, I'm over it.

I zip my luggage shut just as my phone dings.

JENSEN

How was the appointment, babe?

> It was good. Different... but so good. Can't wait to tell you all about it. You at the airport?

JENSEN

> Yeah. Can't wait to see you. I was looking at houses today when I was bored. Found this.

He sends me a link for a house.

We haven't talked about our living situation in weeks. Jensen mentioned it in the beginning, but everything was still so new, I couldn't commit. And now... I don't even know where I want to live.

I love New York—family dinners with Jensen's family, Matt's jokes, Scarlett's late-night talks. And don't even get me started on how much I miss Zach. I know my old boss would help me find a job. Maybe not in PACU, but somewhere.

But I love Chicago, too, the friends I've made here, being near Michael and Stella. And then there's my dad. God, I can't give up this time with him, not when his health is so fragile. I already gave up too many years, and that guilt doesn't fade. I don't know if it ever will.

I click the link and gasp. The listing is for a home in Wilmette, just ten minutes from Michael and Stella. Red brick, wide windows, a black door, a yard that seems to go forever. It's beautiful.

What? Jensen's never said a word about moving here. Not once.

My fingers hover at my lips as I swipe through the photos—four bedrooms, hardwood floors, a backyard big enough for kids and a dog. A family. My chest squeezes, then warms until I'm blinking through tears. The thought of him choosing this, moving here for me, hits so hard it steals my breath. He just keeps getting better.

And I feel like the luckiest woman in the world.

Even with all the shit he put me through. Even with the hard we're in now. Even with all the trust still to rebuild. I'll take every second with him, because I'm realizing that being loved by Jensen, even for a day, is being loved harder than some people get in a lifetime. He does it differently. He sees me. He puts me first. And somehow, I know he always will.

And that fear? That poison that lingers in the back of my mind whispering *what if?* I don't have to listen. I don't have to look back. I can be cautious, but I don't have to let it destroy me, my future, or my love for Jensen.

He's here now. And he loves me more than life itself.

I type back.

Is this for real?

I drop my phone in my purse and sling it over my shoulder. Shoving my feet into my tennis shoes, I scan the room, running through a mental checklist so I don't forget anything.

Oh, shit. My razor.

Before I can head to the bathroom, there's a soft knock on the door.

"Come in," I call.

The door creaks open, and I glance over my shoulder as Jensen steps into the room, grinning. "It's for real," he says.

"Oh my God!" I run to him, practically knocking him over. My arms wrap around his neck, and my lips find his before I can even process that he's standing in front of me. "What are you doing here already? You're not supposed to get in for three more hours." My voice is soft, a breath against his skin, my smile stretched wide.

"I lied," he whispers, his grip tightening on my waist, pulling me closer.

"That's no way to earn my trust," I tease.

"Yeah? You mad?"

I shake my head, catching my bottom lip between my teeth. "No." *God, he's the best.* "I'm so happy you're here."

He glances at his watch. "You ready? Because we've got an appointment to get to."

I raise an eyebrow. "What appointment?"

"We're meeting a realtor at this house in thirty minutes. Just to see if we like it." He hesitates, watching my reaction. "Unless... you don't want to."

My smile stretches so wide my cheeks ache, and tears blur my vision—happy tears. Pure, blissful, happy tears. It's been so long since I've had those. "Are you serious? You'd really move here?"

The corner of his mouth pulls up. "Maybe. We'll talk about it." He grabs the handle of my suitcase. "But let's do it in the car so we're not late."

"Alright." A laugh breaks through my tears. "I'm ready."

As we head out, I glance at him. "Cutting it close, don't you think? What if your flight had been delayed?"

He gives me an effortless grin. "I landed at five, babe. I've been killing time at Starbucks so I could surprise you."

"Why didn't you just come over then?"

"I knew you had your appointment, and you'd be packing. Didn't want to distract you." He smirks. "You know damn well you'd be naked right now and not even close to ready if I'd shown up first."

I brush past him, laughing. "True."

* * *

THIS HOUSE IS INCREDIBLE. It's everything I could ever want and more. It's been completely gutted, but the original hardwood floors are still intact, giving it just enough old charm while still leaning into my contemporary style. It's gorgeous.

I fall in love with the kitchen instantly—blonde shaker cabinets, matte-black hardware, ceilings impossibly high for a house this old. The island is incredible. Black quartz waterfalls down both sides, bold and clean. It's exactly what I'd pick if I designed it myself.

The real estate agent lets us wander, which I appreciate. Jensen and I head upstairs to the master bedroom. It's not huge, but the closet is—and it was designed by a genius. Built-in shelves and drawers, the kind you only see on HGTV.

"Oh my God, I might just move into this closet."

Jensen chuckles. "Sold on the closet, huh?"

I glance his way. "And the kitchen. And the original hardwood floors. And the masonry fireplace." I open a drawer and nearly squeal. "There are compartments for all my jewelry!" It's a freaking dream.

"Shit. Hidden compartments? That's like porn for you."

I turn toward him, grinning. "I know!"

We move to the next room, and it stops me cold. It's staged as a baby's room. There's a crib and tiny dresser, zoo animals painted on the walls. My heart clenches, equal parts joy and ache. I grip the doorframe, trying to hold both emotions at once. God, it's adorable. And it hurts.

Jensen steps up behind me, his hands sliding around my waist. "What do you think? You like the house?"

I turn, pressing my palms flat against his chest. "I love it. I love it so much."

He leans down, kissing me softly, and when he pulls back, his eyes meet mine, tender and full of love. "Should we buy it?" His voice is low but eager.

"You'd really move here? And work's not an issue?"

"I told you—already talked to my boss. I can transfer to the Chicago office."

"And what about your family?"

He shrugs. "*You're* my family, babe. They all have their own families, their own lives. They'll be fine without me."

I laugh softly. "I'm not so worried about what they'll do without you as much as what you'll do without them." I arch a brow, lowering my voice. "What about Matt?"

"What about him?" His eyes narrow. "He won't even notice I'm gone."

"That's not true, and you know it."

"It's a good thing he's rich as fuck and has his own plane, then, isn't it? He can visit anytime." A grin tugs at his mouth. "Besides, is he gonna have my babies?"

The words hit me in the gut. In a good way, but they hurt, too. "What if I can't get pregnant?" The fear slips out, ugly and scary.

"Don't go there. We haven't tried in a long time."

"But when we were trying, it wasn't happening."

"We didn't try that long," he says, thumb brushing my temple. "And I was using most of that time. You didn't know it then, but my body was fucked. Who knows what it did to my sperm."

I nod. It *can* do that, but not usually that soon. "But we haven't exactly been careful. Even now."

We really haven't. The first time we had sex again, we didn't use a condom. Sheer stupidity on my part. My brain wasn't anywhere near ready to handle a pregnancy with him then. It had just been so long, and we'd never been all that careful before—I got caught in the moment. Spaced it completely.

And nothing happened.

That's what gnaws at me. *Nothing happened.* Not then, not before. I don't even know if I'm fertile. It's an ache I've carried for years, a quiet worry that never leaves.

"We've been careful enough," he says gently. "Only skipped once, and you even said later you weren't ovulating."

I force a smile and shove the heavy thoughts into a box for later. "Yeah. I guess you're right."

His hand slides over my hip, heat flashing in his eyes, and I let myself lean into the shift. He lets out a soft chuckle, then whispers low in my ear. "All this talk about babies getting your panties wet?"

His lips graze mine, and I grin against them, my arms sliding around him. "That's for me to know, and you to find out." His brows shoot up with excitement.

"Later," I add, laughing.

"Fuck. Is it later yet?" He kisses me, and it feels like he's handing me the world—this house, a future, a family. I want more than anything to believe it's all possible.

I kiss him back, promising him the same things. That I'm here. That we *can* have it all, and so much more. We just have to keep showing up for each other. Trust each other. Love each other.

That's the easy part. Loving him has never been hard. The hard part was pretending I didn't.

And I'm guilty as sin for failing at that.

Chapter Thirty-Eight

ALLEY

I poke my tongue into the side of my cheek, trying to bait a laugh out of Jensen. He just grins, slides two fingers to his mouth, and drags his tongue between them. It's hot—but I crack. Laughter bursts out of me, echoing through the elevator and earning a glare from the elderly couple in front of us. I slap a hand over my mouth, but it's useless.

Immature? Absolutely. But it's our thing. It's something we've always done—try to make each other laugh while in elevators with other people.

The doors slide open, and our laughter spills into the hallway of Matt's complex.

Dinner with Michael and Dad was better than I could have imagined. There was real laughter, forgiveness, even a few tears that felt more healing than painful. For the first time in my adult life, I felt whole with my family. My dad sober. Jensen clean. Both of them sitting at the table with me. The only thing missing was Mom, and I like to think she was there anyway. She would've been proud.

"You better get that sweet ass inside before I tear your clothes off right here," his voice booms behind me, low and warning.

I glance back, still trying to smother my laugh, finger to my lips. "Shh."

The way he's looking at me tells me *shh* isn't happening.

He chuckles, following close behind. "That blow job move got me thinking all the dirty thoughts."

"No!" I gasp in mock shock. "Dirty thoughts? You?"

His chuckle drops deep and wicked. "You better hurry inside. You're about to get it like the good girls in your books do."

"Oh, I'm terrified," I tease, grinning as I punch in the code.

The lock clicks, and Jensen leans in, his breath hot against my ear. "You should be."

Shivers skate up my spine as the door swings open. "Behave yourself—we're almost in."

We barely make it through the door before Jensen's arms wrap around me from behind, hauling me against him. His mouth skims my jaw, playful and teasing, before planting a kiss on the curve of my neck. "Thanks for a great day, babe."

I spin, flattening my palms to his chest. "You're welcome. Not every day you get to have awkward please-forgive-me dinners with your wife's family."

He grins, guiding me backward until my spine meets the wall. "Awkward for maybe five minutes. Michael was great. And your dad always is."

"Still... thank you for coming. I know it probably wasn't something you were looking forward to."

His eyes lock on mine, steady and unflinching. "I look forward to everything with you. Plus, we basically scored a Michelin-star dinner for free."

True. Michael's restaurant earned its star a few months ago. It's a huge achievement. "Well then, in that case, you're welcome for such a fantastic evening."

"It *was* fantastic." His lips brush mine, taunting. "Guess I better repay you now."

"It's only fair. A little quid pro quo."

His brow quirks. "Pretty sure that's not how you use that term."

I shrug, grinning. "Awkward family dinners, you pay me back in sexual services. Feels right to me."

That smirk of his spreads wide. "Babe." His finger presses to my lips. "Stop talking so I can fuck you."

Then his mouth is on mine—hard and hot, swallowing any comeback I had left. Heat sparks low and spreads through every limb, leaving me turned on and already aching for more.

His lips move on mine with the perfect mix of push and pull, his tongue dipping in, teasing, reminding me exactly what it's capable of. I picture it lower, between my thighs, and butterflies stir hard in my stomach.

His hand fists in my hair, tugging just enough to tip my head back. His lips trail up my jaw until they graze my ear. "Is your pussy wet for me?"

Good Lord.

It is now.

"Almost," I lie, breathless.

His tongue flicks the shell of my ear. "Liar." The husk in his voice vibrates down my spine. In a blur, my shirt's gone, and his hands roam greedily across my bare skin.

"Take off your bra."

I do what I'm told, letting it fall to the floor. I've always loved when Jensen slips into Dom mode, telling me what to do, getting a little rough. A *soft* rough.

"Good girl," he murmurs, his voice a slow stroke of heat.

Shit. My knees nearly buckle, a rush of need crashing through me at those two words. My body melts, limbs turning liquid, and I'm desperate—for his hands, his mouth, his skin, his voice. I need it all.

His hand palms my breast as mine slip under his shirt, roaming across his hard abs. My pulse races as I drift lower, but he catches my wrist, pulling it back to his chest. His mouth hovers by my ear. "Don't move."

I freeze, eyes falling shut, surrendering to the path of his touch. His lips trail down, kissing over my breasts, while his hands shove my pants down past my hips. Then he's back at my mouth, hot and claiming.

I reach instinctively for his waistband, desperate to get him naked, but he grabs both wrists and pins them above my head, holding them with one hand. The strength in him only makes me surrender more. I don't fight it. I don't want to.

"I said don't move." His voice vibrates through me—dark velvet, rough. "And don't you dare come. Not until I tell you to. You're mine, baby."

My pulse hammers in my head, breaths shallow. *Holy shit.* He always knows how to turn me on, but this is extra. So hot. Straight-out-of-a-book hot.

His free hand drops between my thighs, fingers teasing lightly, brushing maddening strokes over the fabric of my underwear, a wicked grin curving his mouth. I roll my bottom lip between my teeth, hips arching into his touch, searching for more pressure.

He chuckles. "You just can't help yourself, can you?"

I shake my head as his fingers finally dip inside, sliding smoothly over my slit, stroking slow, lazy circles that have my knees going weak. He keeps his eyes on mine, watching every reaction.

One finger slips inside, then two, his thumb circling my clit. "Oh, God," I breathe. My head tips back on a gasp, and he releases my wrists, his hand gripping my jaw instantly, forcing my gaze to his. "Eyes on me, baby." The words melt through me, and before I can even draw another breath, he crushes his mouth to mine, claiming it with all the possessiveness of a man on a mission—a mission to wreck me completely. A fire builds deep in my core, swirling hot, each thrust pressing deeper until my muscles clench tight around him, desperate for release.

"Come for me, baby. I want you dripping down my fingers."

Jesus. The dirty talk is dialed in tonight, and it's like my body was waiting for those words. Pleasure detonates, rushing through me in waves. He keeps his rhythm steady as I squeeze my eyes shut, pulsing around him, riding it out until I'm nothing but a breathless, trembling mess.

His touch slows, easing me down, and a smirk tugs at his mouth. "You ready to soak my cock with that sweet pussy?" he rasps.

Lordy. What the—? It clicks. The extra dirty talk. The possessiveness. My eyes fly open on a gasp. "Oh my God." I meet his gaze, breathless, stunned. "You read my book!" A laugh slips out of me, helpless and disbelieving.

His grin is sinful, darkly amused. He presses his palm over my mouth, eyes glinting. "Shh."

My laugh muffles against his hand. I can't believe it. *Don't move. Don't come until I say. Dripping. Soak my cock. Sweet pussy.* Straight out of chapter thirty on my Kindle.

He leans in, voice low and taunting. "Maybe I just know exactly how to make that sweet pussy beg."

He releases his hand, and I swat at him. "You're such a jackass."

"Yeah, but a jackass who's crazy about you." He steals a heated kiss, then pulls back, eyes serious now, thumb circling over my nipple. "You gonna be a good girl?"

I nod, my smile fading as his hand trails across my breast and down my stomach, then stops. He strokes and teases, fingertips brushing low—but not low enough.

"Good," he murmurs, kissing me deep before hooking his fingers around my underwear, gripping tight. "Now let's see how long you last this time."

He drags the lace down slow, knuckles grazing my thighs, eyes locked on mine as he sinks to the floor. The heat in his gaze pins me in place, a silent promise, a claim I feel down to my bones.

A kiss lands on my thigh, scruff rasping across my skin. Then his tongue flicks my clit, quick, taunting.

"Wait, babe," I gasp. "Let's move to the couch."

He doesn't argue, just scoops me up in one effortless motion, pulling a squeal from my throat. "Jensen!"

He chuckles, strides to the couch, and drops me onto it. A laugh bursts out of me, cut short when his body pins mine, lips scorching a path across my skin. He brushes a strand of hair from my face, eyes dark with intent, and I fist his shirt, yanking him closer, desperate for more of him pressed against me.

I blink up at him, chest heaving. "Why aren't you naked?" He's been wrecking me so thoroughly I haven't even touched him. And now all I want is his skin on mine—his sculpted abs, that tattoo flexing on his bicep as he hovers over me. I ache for this body. Ache to please him. Ache to connect in a way I can't with anyone else.

My fingers trail down his abdomen. "Take your clothes off," I whisper between kisses, tugging at his shirt. He yanks it over his head and tosses it aside.

God, he's incredible. My hands grip his shoulders, nails dragging down his skin. "You're so fucking hot, babe." I flatten my palm over his chest and slide it lower, pressing against the bulge in his pants. "You do things to me I can't explain."

His groan rumbles deep. "Fuck, baby. You trying to make me lose control?"

I fumble with his button until it pops, then tug the zipper down. "Take these off," I demand, shoving at his pants with one hand.

He props himself on one forearm, shoving his pants and underwear down. Then lowers himself between my thighs again, but I press at his chest. "No. Sit up," I breathe, my pulse racing. He's been worshipping me all night, breaking me apart, and I can't take another second without giving something back.

He obeys, settling back. I swing over, straddling him, nails scraping lightly down his chest. "My turn," I whisper against his ear. Before he can argue, I slide down his body, knees sinking into the carpet.

His cock stands thick and hard, already leaking. Heat pulses low, my thighs clenching, and the ache to please him burns deep and insistent. I lick my lips, desperate to make him unravel the way he's been unraveling me.

He rakes a hand through his hair and leans back, that sinful Jensen smirk tugging at his mouth.

God, I love this man.

I take my time, building it up—kissing his thighs, his hips, every line of muscle, my fingers tracing close behind. I flick my tongue over the tip, lapping at his precum, teasing. My mouth drags down the length of him, slow, deliberate, savoring every inch.

"Jesus Christ. You're my fucking queen."

My nails dig into his hips as I finally wrap my lips around the head, lowering down, torturously slow. I moan around him, letting him feel how much I love it—how much I love him. My hand slides lower, nails softly brushing his balls.

"*God.* You trying to kill me?" he rasps. "Feels so fucking good."

I pull back with a wet pop, wrap my hand around him, and give one slow, deliberate stroke before swirling my tongue over the tip.

"Fuck..." he whispers, like a reverent prayer. His head falls back against the couch, one hand gripping my hair—not guiding, just holding on.

I take him deeper, hollowing my cheeks, thrilled at the twitch against my tongue, the way his breath roughens with every move. Another moan vibrates out of me, and his hips jerk, helpless, like he can't stop himself.

"Jesus..." His voice breaks on a groan, ragged with pleasure. "You're too good at this. I'm gonna come down your throat—and that's not how I want to finish."

He tugs my hair, gentle but firm, pulling me up. "C'mere, baby. I wanna come inside you."

I straddle his lap, his cock hard against my entrance. His hands grip my ass, eyes dark and hungry. He drags my lips into his. It's hot. Desperate. Devouring.

He thrusts up as I sink down, and we groan in unison—the stretch, the pressure, the way we fit together so perfectly.

"Fuck, yes," he rasps against my mouth. "That's it, Al. Ride me."

His hands knead my ass, pushing me deeper, the friction intoxicating.

"Oh, God." It slips out broken, a cry tangled in pleasure.

His mouth curves against mine. "I live for those sounds. So fucking hot."

My body trembles as he drives harder, faster, rocking me into him, his mouth crashing back onto mine, swallowing every moan.

My head tips back, ready to come, but his hand cups the back of my head, bringing my gaze to his.

"I want to watch you come."

The burn builds fast, pleasure winding me tight. I dig my nails into his shoulders, desperate, frantic, every nerve ending screaming.

"Jensen..." My voice is ragged, pleading.

"Come for me," he grunts, driving deeper. "Soak my cock. Show me how good it feels."

And *God*, do I show him. Pleasure rips through me, a guttural moan breaking free as I fall apart. I fight to keep my gaze on his, but my vision blurs, stars sparking until my eyes roll back. Each wave crashes harder than the last, leaving me trembling, clinging to him like he's the only thing anchoring me to earth. My thighs quiver, every nerve alive, carrying the bliss until I'm gasping his name.

He's right there with me, thrusting harder, arms locking tight around me. His eyes squeeze shut, and a raw groan tears from his chest as his release overtakes him.

"Fuuuuuuck."

He freezes, shuddering, before collapsing against the couch. I rest my forehead to his, and the world stills. Just him and me, breathing the same air.

A rush of emotion slams into me, stealing my breath. Tears sting before I can stop them, and I clutch him tighter, gasping for air.

"Shit, babe." His hands comb through my hair. "You okay?"

I nod against him, a shaky smile breaking through the tears. My hand cups his neck, thumb brushing his skin. "Happy tears," I whisper with a laugh-cry. "I just love you. I love you so much."

His hands frame my face. "Look at me."

I do.

"You're so fucking beautiful. I love you."

All the feelings crash over me, too many to name. Pride. Relief. Joy so sharp it almost hurts.

He did it.

I did it.

Somehow, against all the odds, *we did it.*

We're healing. Finding our way back. After everything, we keep choosing each other. Through the hard, through the ugly. We're still here.

Maybe walking away would've been easier. Maybe it would've been harder. I'll never know.

But what I do know is this—

We chose to stay.

To love each other anyway.

Chapter Thirty-Nine

JENSEN

I cross the kitchen of our apartment into the living room, two coffees in hand. Alley reaches for hers before I'm even close, and I pass her the steaming mug.

"Thanks, babe." She's curled up in a chair, blanket draped over her legs like she has no plans of moving.

I drop onto the couch across from her, stretch out a leg, and sink back.

My eyes lock on her. Her hair's piled on top of her head, messy in that sexy way that makes me want to pull it down. No bra. Glasses sliding a little down her nose. Drowning in one of my old T-shirts. She's been sleeping in them for years, but right now it hits me different —like she's claiming me every night she wears one. It's hot and sweet and cute, and God, she's beautiful.

A smile grazes her mouth as she takes a sip. She cups the mug in both hands, peeking at me over the rim. "Do you ever wonder how many people Matt's had sex with on this couch? And then we did it here last night?" She grimaces. "Kinda gross."

A chuckle rumbles out of me, low and easy. She's so fucking cool. "Dozens, no doubt. Thanks for that image."

She lets out a soft laugh. "It crossed my mind last night, but you made me forget about it real quick."

I lift my brows. "I'm down for round two if you are."

She grins, eyes shining with amusement. "Maybe later." She sips again, hiding the curve of her smile behind the mug.

Silence settles between us, easy and comfortable, the kind that's rare and feels like a luxury. Just the morning, coffee, and her.

Then she breaks it. "Hey, can I ask you something?"

"Always," I answer without a beat.

Her fingers toy with the rim of her mug. "What was it like... for you? That night I left and went to Chicago? When you were messed up and asked for your backpack? What was going through your head?"

I still, drawing in a breath and exhaling hard. My stomach knots just thinking about it. "That's heavy for a coffee chat, babe."

Her eyes drop to her mug, her voice soft. "I know. Sorry." She lifts her gaze back to mine. "You don't have to tell me if it's too much. Especially if it's triggering. I just... I've never asked my dad questions like that, and some of it came up in hypnotherapy. Stuff tied to him. To you. And I think I just need to understand. Not the disease. I get that. But you. What it felt like inside your head in that moment."

I stare at her for several seconds, gathering my thoughts. "It's hard to explain." I rub a hand over my face. "Part of me knew exactly what I wanted. *You.*" A soft smile flickers, then fades as guilt cuts through. "And the other part knew what I didn't want. But it's like... your body isn't yours anymore. Like someone else is pulling the strings." I swallow, forcing myself to meet her eyes. "Watching you pack—fuck, that hurt. I hated seeing you cry. Hated knowing I did that. And I hated myself even more."

My throat swells as I keep going. "But then it was like a switch flipped. Like, *oh, shit, she took my lifeline.* The thing that keeps me breathing. And suddenly nothing else mattered. Watching you leave fucking killed me, but when you shoved that backpack into my arms..." I blow out a breath. "It was like drowning and being thrown a life jacket. Pure relief. Even while another part of me was screaming, begging me to fight it. Like watching a demon take over my body while I just stood there."

She swipes at her cheek as a tear falls, then sets her mug down and crawls into my lap. I set mine aside too, my hands finding her ass, fingers brushing soft against her skin.

Her touch comes gentle on my cheek, her gaze burning through me. "Never again," she whispers.

"Never again, baby."

Her lips crush against mine, and I drink her in, letting her fuel me from the outside in. She's my air. My light. My everything.

I kiss her harder, pouring every ounce of me into it, a vow without words: *you're the only fucking thing that matters.*

Because she is.

She's my forever.

* * *

MY KNUCKLES RAP against Matt's bedroom door for the second time. I've been calling out for him ever since I stepped off the elevator. A muffled *I'm coming* drifts from the other side, and seconds later the door swings open, revealing a shirtless Matt. His joggers hang low, and his hair's a mess—like multiple hands have been through it in the past couple hours.

"Hey, man. Sorry, I must've slept in." His voice is gruff and thick with sleep as he presses a palm to his eye and rubs.

It's fucking noon.

"Jesus. You look like hell. Rough night?"

He grips his neck and pulls, a low chuckle escaping. "Something like that. Didn't get to bed until four this morning."

My brows lift. "Wow. She must've been good. Anyone I know?"

"Nah. Met them last night."

"Oh, there's more than one... again." It's not a question.

His mouth twists, eye squinting as he holds up three fingers.

"Jesus Christ. You slept with three women last night?" I shake my head. "What happened—did you see Jordan again?" God. He's got to get this shit figured out.

"Am I that predictable?" He drags both hands down his face and groans. "What the hell is wrong with me? I ran into her at the charity last night. Her and her fucking doctor fiancé."

Erin Cornia

"Did she ignore you again?"

He shakes his head. "She said *hi*. Cordial, I guess. That's it. And then I got drunk." *Of course.* "And I texted her. I'm so fucking stupid. Last time she told me not to text her anymore. And then I go and have one too many and..." He trails off.

"Fuck. Did she respond?"

He scoffs, pulls out his phone, and shoves it at me.

> You look unreal tonight.
>
> I fucking miss you.
>
> Just admit you miss me.
>
> You can't tell me you don't still think about me.

Jesus. It's a car crash I can't look away from—messy, reckless, the complete opposite of the polished ultra-millionaire I know as my best friend.

> Fuck. Ignore me. I shouldn't have texted.
>
> Tell me you don't think about me and I'll leave you alone forever.

Two hours later.

JORDAN

> Matt. Stop. I don't think about you. Please don't text me again. I wish you well, but this isn't fair to me—or my fiancé.

> What happened to never lying to each other?

She left it on read.

I let out a low whistle, handing the phone back. "Christ, man. That's rough."

He groans, tipping his head back against the doorframe. "Tell me about it. It's fucking brutal."

I fight back a laugh. It's not funny. Not really. I don't know all the details of what went down between him and Jordan, but it's fucked with him. He talks to me about everything, but when it comes to her? He's a locked safe, guarded in a way that tells me this goes a hell of a lot deeper than he admits. He loves her. That's clear. And it's been like this for as long as I can remember.

"Guess three women is one way to cope," I mutter with a shake of my head. A smirk tugs at his lip, and I add, "So do they all sign NDAs before or after you sleep with them?"

He laughs, his mood officially lighter. "Before. I might've been drunk and reckless, but I'm not stupid." He exhales. "I need coffee." He brushes past me, heading down the hall. "You want any?" he calls back.

"I'm good. Had mine five hours ago."

"You and Al?" He glances over his shoulder as he rounds the corner.

"Yep." I move to the island and slide onto a stool.

"When's she coming over?"

"She's on her way. She had brunch with Scarlett, but texted me twenty minutes ago that she was just waiting on the check."

Matt makes his coffee, then gestures toward the living room. "Wanna turn on a game?"

I nod, and we make our way to the couch. I sink into the leather, and he flips on a college basketball game.

"Did you end up putting an offer on the house?" Matt asks, sipping his coffee.

"Yeah, we did. On Friday."

"No shit!" His hand claps my back. "Congrats! I'm sad for me, but really fucking happy for you both."

"Thanks, man. It's not final yet. We're supposed to hear back by tomorrow."

"Let me know when you do. You worried?"

"About what?" I ask, side-eyeing him and the game at the same time.

"Moving. Being away from home. New city. New friends." He cocks a brow at me. "Staying clean?"

A flash of heat zips through me, stirring something that feels like worry—but it's not, not exactly. "Not worried. I mean, sure, I'm nervous about parts of it. But that's normal, right? New shit's always a little scary. Al's friends and family are cool, but they're not you. Not Meg and Kev, not Jeff and Amber. Hard to find friends that jive on the level you and I do."

"Yeah, this level's pretty hard to come by."

I grin, because he's right. Friendship like ours is rare. But then my throat tightens. "I guess I am a little worried... Not about staying clean. But about all the other stuff. I'm gonna miss you."

Matt's lips twitch. "No, you won't. Trust me. You've got a beautiful wife and a house." He scoffs. "Hell, you'll probably get a dog. You've got it all, brother." He slaps my back, grinning. "Lucky son of a bitch, too—because you almost lost it. Look at you now. You're like Mr. Rogers." He pauses for half a beat, glancing over. "I'm proud of you. And even happier for you."

Fuck. It lands harder than I expect. Matt's not a guy who throws around words like that. If I get emotional right now over this bromance, I'll kick my own ass.

"Thanks." I nod, a smirk forming. "You gonna admit you'll miss me too?"

He shakes his head, stretching back into the couch. "Nope. Won't even notice you're gone."

I roll my eyes, and his grin cracks wider. "Bullshit."

"You'll be too busy playing house with Alley. You'll forget I even exist. But if you get a golden retriever, name it after me—alright, buddy?"

I snort. "No way Alley's getting on board with that."

He chuckles and takes another sip of coffee, then sets his mug down with a sigh. The grin fades, and his eyes meet mine. "Of course I'll miss you, dumbass. You're my brother."

He stands unexpectedly. "Come on. Let's get this over with now, because we both know if we do this on moving day we're gonna fucking cry." He stretches his arms wide, and I chuckle as I rise. We pull each other in for a brotherly hug, clapping each other's backs hard. "Love you, man. Don't make this weird."

"Wouldn't dream of it." My voice comes out rougher than I want it to.

"Should I come back later, or…?" Alley's voice carries through the foyer as she steps out of the elevator, grinning. "If I'd known you two needed alone time, I would've gone shopping first."

We both chuckle as she sets her purse on a stool and kicks off her shoes.

She starts for the kitchen, but Matt stops her. "Don't think you're getting out of this." He waves her over. "Your turn."

She walks toward us, lips still curved. Damn, that smile. Gets me every time. Matt pulls her into a bone-crushing hug. "Gonna miss the hell out of you, Al."

"Why are we saying goodbyes already? We don't even know if we got the house."

"Because you're moving. If it's not this house, it'll be the next one. And when you leave—I'm not going to be able to take it like a man."

She tightens her grip, cheek pressed to his chest. Then she grins at me, eyes glassy, lips trembling. "I'm gonna miss you too," she whispers.

God, my heart splits in two. Gratitude slams into me, fierce and overwhelming. I don't know where I'd be without these two. They pulled me out of the darkest times. Helped me get my life back.

"So proud of you, Alley. Don't ever stop being too good for him." Matt presses a kiss to the top of her head, and I grin.

Alley shakes her head against him. "Thank you. For everything."

They stay that way for several seconds before her brows furrow. "Um, Matt?"

"Yeah?"

"Why is there a G-string under the coffee table?"

Matt bursts out laughing, letting her go and raking a hand through his hair.

"I mean, who shows up with underwear and leaves without it?" Alley shakes her head, laughter ringing through the penthouse.

"Apparently one of the women from last night."

Her brow shoots up. "One of the women?"

Matt groans. "Oh, God. Here we go." He drops onto the couch, reaching for his coffee like he needs armor.

Alley crosses to me, still smiling, and I wrap my arms around her waist as she leans in for a kiss. "Hi," she says softly.

"Hi, babe. How was brunch?"

"It was good."

"Yeah? What'd you two talk about?"

Her fingers trace up my chest with a teasing grin. That damn dimple deepening. "You."

My brow ticks up.

"Scarlett was so different today, babe. She was so much more open and accepting. Like she could see how happy I am. She wants to come visit us, maybe for my birthday, if we're moved by then."

"That's great." A grin tugs at my lips as hers ghost over mine. "That's really great."

Matt's voice booms from behind us. "You know the back bedroom's fully available if you two need privacy. If not, get the fuck out of the way. You're blocking the game."

Alley laughs, slipping from my arms and heading toward the kitchen. "Want a beer, Matt?"

"Does the Pope pray?" he calls back, eyes glued to the screen.

She rolls her eyes, yanking the fridge open.

I drop onto the couch, leaning back as I watch them, my chest warming with something I don't want to name. Sure, he's a bit of a man slut, and his lifestyle's a wild mess half the time. But he's the best friend a guy could ask for. The kind that'll give you the shirt off his back. The kind that'll be there for your wife when you're too far gone. The kind that'll fly to Switzerland just to make sure you get the help you need.

He's my brother. And the truth is—

I'm gonna really fucking miss him.

Chapter Forty

ALLEY

Five Weeks Later

I TAKE a deep breath as Jensen pulls into his parents' driveway. Knots twist in my stomach, nausea rising. I haven't spoken to Christy in months, and when I did...

Well, I'm not proud of what I said.

Jensen throws the car in park, unclicks his seatbelt, and reaches for the door.

I don't move.

He lets go of the handle, sits back, and drops his hand to my thigh, giving it a squeeze. "You okay?"

"No." I take in a shaky breath. "I'm nervous. Your mom has to hate me. There's no way she doesn't. Not after the things I said and how I left it."

His lips press together. "She doesn't hate you. She made mistakes. You made mistakes. Don't let this hold you back anymore. You used to love my mom. You guys were so close."

"I know. It's just..." Tears spring to my eyes, and I swipe at them fast. "God, I don't know why I'm so emotional." My bottom lip quivers, and I hate not feeling in control right now. Seeing Christy again is a big deal. "I just feel stupid, you know? I lashed out at her." I shake my head hard. "And I've been so stubborn. Like—I get it. My mom did the same shit for my dad that Christy did for you. *I* did the same shit with my dad. For years, I did."

He leans across the console and kisses me—warm, tender—replacing the fear inside me with the calm that always comes with him. Then he takes my hand, pressing a soft kiss to my knuckles. "It's water under the bridge, babe. Just talk to her." His eyes lock on mine, earnest, steady. "She's not mad. Promise."

"Okay," I whisper, nodding, trying to reassure myself. "Let's go then."

I push the door open and step out. We pass Megan and Kevin's car on the way in, and Amber and Jeff's is parked next to the curb. Thank God, we're not the first ones here.

"Where's Matt?" I ask, tugging my jacket tighter as we round the walkway to the porch.

"He had a meeting. He'll be here in a bit."

Jensen pushes the front door open, and I step inside. The smell of garlic and roasted chicken wafts down the hall. Grace, the oldest grandchild, is sprawled out on a sofa staring at her phone. She looks up, eyes going wide.

"Alley!" She springs to her feet and throws her arms around me.

"Hi, beautiful girl," I say through laughter. "It's so good to see you." I pull back, grinning. "Look at you. When did you get taller than me?"

She smiles. "Your hair's longer. It's so pretty."

"Thank you," I say.

She gives Jensen a quick hug, then slumps back into her chair.

We walk through the foyer into the back of the house where everyone's scattered. Jeff, Kevin, and Tom are at the table. Amber and Megan are chopping and stirring alongside Christy.

"Hey, guys," Amber calls out.

Nerves creep up my throat as Christy looks up. She smiles, sets the knife down on the cutting board, and comes straight at me, arms wide. "Alley!" She pulls me into a hug, squeezing like I never left. "It's so good to have you here." Her perfume, the softness of her sweater, the warmth of her arms—it steals the breath right out of me. My arms circle her back, hesitant at first. Suddenly, being held by the only mom I have left hits me hard, and all my stubborn pride feels so petty. *God, she was dealing with the same shit I was.*

Addiction.

Only it was her son and not her husband.

We all deal with it differently. There's no right or wrong way. It's sink or swim, and she tried to swim with Jensen. Tried to keep him afloat. Tried to save him. That's part of it too—the codependency, the enabling.

My grip tightens automatically, and my voice catches as I manage, "Thank you. It's good to be here."

She lets me go and moves to Jensen, giving him a squeeze and a kiss on the cheek. "I hope you're both hungry." Then, to him, "I made plenty of gluten-free options. I know you have dietary restrictions now."

"You didn't have to do that, Mom."

"It was no problem." She gestures back at the counter. "Alley, do you mind making the salad?"

A slow smile spreads across my face, tension melting. "Sure." The simple normalcy of being asked to help is everything. So simple, yet it feels like I belong—again.

Matt's voice echoes over the noise of conversation and knives against cutting boards. "Tell me the hockey game's on. Why the hell isn't the game on?"

"Because no one cares about hockey, Matt," Megan shouts through the chaos.

"Bullshit," Jensen and Matt shoot back in unison.

Megan eyes Matt. "Why are you dressed so stiff? It's Sunday."

"I had a meeting." Matt unbuttons his collar, shrugs off his blazer, and tosses it over a chair before he and Jensen disappear into the living room to watch the hockey game.

I make my way toward the counter where Christy's laid out all the salad fixings.

Megan glances up from the charcuterie board she's arranging. Her voice drops, quiet. "You alright?"

She knows how nervous I was to come today.

I nod, grabbing a cutting board. "Yeah, I'm good. How was your weekend? What'd you guys do?"

"Nothing big. Basketball games and dance performances. The kids ran the show." She smiles faintly, then tilts her head. "Is moving day still Saturday?"

"Yep. Movers are scheduled for the morning."

"And how long am I allowed to stay mad at you?" Megan teases, though her watery eyes give her away.

"Six more days. I'm gonna need you on your A-game come Saturday."

She mulls it over. "Fine. Until then, I'm still kind of mad. No, actually, I'm not mad at you. Only Jensen."

I laugh softly. "Why only Jensen?"

"Because he's the one who found the house." She nudges my elbow, smiling through it. "I'm joking. You know I'm so happy for you. Just... gonna miss you guys."

"I know." My voice dips to a whisper. "I'll miss you too. All of you."

Our offer was accepted on the house five weeks ago. We closed a few days ago, and now we're officially homeowners, in Chicago. It's bittersweet. I've been there for seven months, but these last few I've come back here almost every other weekend. Now it feels final. Like I won't see my friends, this family that's become my own, more than a handful of times a year—holidays, some birthdays, maybe once or twice in between. The thought cuts deep. It sucks.

But I'm excited, too. I love that house. Every time we've gone over, whether to measure for furniture or just stand on the sidewalk and stare at it, the anticipation builds. It feels right, moving forward with my husband, starting this new chapter in a place that's ours. Piece by piece, everything's falling into place.

Jensen's been incredible these past few weeks—months, really. My relationship with him is my number one priority, with my dad a close second. He's been doing well, all things considered, and I pray he stays stable.

By the time I finish the salad, dinner's ready and everyone gathers around the table.

"So what's new with everyone?" Tom asks, glancing around.

"Jensen and Alley are moving in six days. So you'd all better be at their house to say goodbye, and bring booze." Megan pauses, eyes flicking to Jensen. "Or maybe hold off on the booze."

"Meg, you drink around me all the time. It's fine. Just bring it. Everyone knows I love getting fucked up on Liquid Death."

That causes everyone to laugh.

"Liquid Death?" Kevin chimes in. "Damn, Alley, watch out, you're about to get railed Saturday."

I shoot Kev a look, brows furrowed. "You have *no* idea, Kev. When Jensen's had a few?" I pucker my lips and let out an exhale, like it's the hottest thing ever.

Jensen chuckles. "I'm so glad you're all comfortable making my weaknesses the butt of your jokes."

I lean into him. "Ah, babe. We love you. I'm drinking Liquid Death, too. You're not the only one."

"Oh, two Liquid Death drinkers? You're bound to have an unforgettable night," Meg adds.

"Alright, alright. Take it easy, everyone," Tom says loudly. He turns his attention to me and Jensen. "Do you two need any help this week?"

"Nah," Jensen replies. "We hired a moving company, and as you all know," he points to me, "Alley is a control freak. She's boxing up everything that's important, and everything else will be left for the movers."

"Well, I for one am going to miss you both. But I'm very happy for you," Christy announces.

Jensen grins. "Thanks, Mom." He drapes an arm around my shoulder and presses a kiss to my temple. "We'll miss you all too, but we can't wait."

"Your father and I plan to come visit once you're settled."

"That'll be great." Jensen shoves a bite of chicken into his mouth, chews, then says, "Maybe wait until summer when the weather's better. Besides, we'll be back in a month for Jordan's wedding."

Matt's head jerks up. "What? You already got your invitation?"

"Yeah," Jensen says slowly. "A few weeks ago."

Matt turns to Megan. "Did you and Kev get one?"

She hesitates. "Yeah. Same time as Jensen and Al. You didn't?"

Matt's jaw tightens. "No. When were you all planning to tell me?"

"Honestly, man, I just assumed you had one, too. I figured we'd all go together," Jensen says sincerely.

It's a little harsh but not surprising. Jensen told me about his drunken text messages to Jordan last month.

"Fuck," Matt mutters. "I can't believe it." He lets out a bitter laugh. "It's like I never even existed."

"I'm sorry," Megan says softly. "It makes sense, though. You two have a lot of history. She's probably just trying to do right by her fiancé."

"Exactly. We have so much history, that I can't *fathom* not inviting her to my wedding."

"Oh?" Meg cocks a brow. "You getting married any time soon?"

He drags a hand down his face and groans. "Next topic!"

"Alright," Megan smirks, stabbing at her salad. "Did you all see Matt in this month's *Town & Country*? Made Manhattan's Most Eligible Bachelors list."

My fork stills midair. *Whoa.* Matt's on that list? I mean, sure, he's rich, hot, loyal like a golden retriever, but Manhattan's Most Eligible? I stare at him across the table. Sleeves rolled halfway up his forearms, tattoos bold against his skin. Top buttons undone, Rolex gleaming under the light. A thin platinum chain disappears beneath his collar— a cross he never removes.

Yeah... I guess it makes sense.

Matt groans, rolling his eyes as he drops his fork. "Oh, God, don't start."

"What?" Megan grins. "It's an achievement! An impressive one at that."

He shakes his head. "Don't tell me you actually read that crap."

"*Town & Country* isn't crap," Megan fires back.

"It's not crap," Amber and Christy echo almost in unison.

"Al? You read that shit too?" Matt asks, brow raised.

"If it's not in *People,* it didn't happen," I say, grinning.

"Thank God." Matt waves a hand. "One sane woman at the table."

"Hey, don't bite the hand that feeds you," Christy cuts in, her lips curving around her wine glass.

Matt presses a palm to his heart. "You know I would never. Best mother out there." He takes a sip of wine, then licks his lips. "It's not that big of a deal. More of a PR stunt anyway. Alexis Camden's publicist reached out after it ran. Wants me to escort her to some gala."

Megan and Christy both gasp. Even *I* know how big of a deal that is. Alexis Camden is New York elite. Untouchable.

"Holy shit! That's huge!" Megan gapes. "She only dates billionaires."

"Well, apparently not always. Hope I'm not a disappointment."

My brows knit. "Wait, you're not a billionaire?" Honestly, I thought he was. Leo has hundreds of millions, and I know Matt has more.

Jensen turns to me. "Really, babe?"

I shrug. "I don't know. He owns a lot of shit."

Matt chuckles. "Not yet, Al. But this deal I'm working on is a big one. Who knows? Stranger things have happened."

"Like you being on time to dinner?" Megan laughs, lifting her wine glass. "Or not sleeping with Alexis Camden."

"Can we not talk about who I may or may not sleep with at the dinner table?"

I glance at Tom and Christy. This is always my favorite part—when the conversation veers too inappropriate for most families, but they just laugh, poke, and add to the fun.

Tom points his fork at Matt. "Now *that* would be an achievement, Matt."

Laughter echoes around the table.

"Oh my God," Matt mutters into his glass. "Can we please go back to making fun of Jensen?" He sets it down and looks at us. "You two been furniture shopping?"

I shake my head, grinning. "Are you kidding me? You think the new chair we bought is exciting to talk about after that? Matt. This is Alexis Camden. She's *hot*."

Amber calls down the table, "Yeah, when's the gala? Or should I say, when are you adding her to the roster?"

Jensen chimes in, mocking a sports announcer. "Drafting number nine-hundred and eighty-six for the Grayson team, Alexis Camden!"

More laughter erupts around the table, and poor Matt—he just takes it. He pretends it bothers him, but we all know better. He's secretly proud of his *accomplishments*.

"That's a big fucking team, Jensen." Kevin laughs. "But I would've guessed thousands."

Matt stands, feigning offense. "Fuck you all!" He shoots his middle fingers up and leaves... to grab another bottle of wine.

By the time he's back, the conversation has shifted to the grand-children, who are all at the kids table in the front room. Jeff, Amber, Kevin, and Megan fill everyone in on their extracurriculars and how the kids are doing in school.

Jensen's hand finds mine, fingers lacing and squeezing. When I look over, he's watching me, smiling, dimples deep, eyes lit up. *God, he loves me.* Warmth shoots through me, spreading to every limb with his gaze, melting every shred of doubt I've ever carried.

When your husband looks at you like that, you can't help but to soak it up, to drink deep from the well of his all-consuming love.

I haven't forgotten what he's done. I don't think I ever will. But every glance, every kiss, every *I love you* lightens the shadows of the past, until hopefully, one day, all that will be left to look back on will be this. Right here. Me and him. Laughter. Memories.

Love.

* * *

I LAY my head against Jensen's shoulder, sinking into the couch and the comfort of him. My arm loops through his, his hand warm on my thigh. The laughter and chaos hasn't stopped, but it's late, and the night is winding down.

"Alley?" Christy's voice carries through the noise, sharp enough to pull my head around. "Will you come with me?" She nods toward the next room.

Jensen meets my gaze, patting my leg. He plants a kiss on my lips before I stand to follow her. She leads me into the office and closes the door, gesturing to a chair. I sit. She takes the one across from me, her smile warm, almost overflowing with love, and for a moment I wonder why I've been carrying all these ill feelings toward her.

Then I remember. How she went behind my back. Lied to me. Not just a small lie, but deliberate and calculated. A spark of resentment stirs, flipping my stomach. It feels ugly. I can't imagine doing that to someone, and suddenly, the air thickens, heavy and uncomfortable.

"I'll get right to the point," she begins. "I owe you an apology, and probably an explanation. Not that it erases anything I've done, but I want to try. First, I'm sorry, Alley. I'm sorry for going behind your back, for the choices I made that may have hindered Jensen's recovery when all I wanted was to help. And I'm sorry I wasn't honest with you."

Heat burns my cheeks and my eyes. "You weren't just dishonest. You went out of your way to lie to me."

"I know." Her voice is soft, weighted.

"Why?" The word leaves my mouth without a thought. Not that it matters. What's done is done, and I doubt anything she says will make it feel better.

Her gaze flicks to the desk, then back to me, eyes glossy. "I've always babied Jensen. I know that. I've always known that." She swallows hard. "I'm sure you've heard about the car accident when he was three."

I nod.

"He nearly died." Her lip twitches. "You have no idea what it's like, as a mother, to wonder if your baby is going to make it. I sat there day after day, watching as they hooked him up to machines. Tubes fed into every part of his tiny body. The constant beeping, the fear every time a team of doctors rushed in..." Her voice breaks. "I can't—I couldn't..."

She trails off, tears falling fast now, and watching her, seeing her break, cracks the composure I've been clinging to.

I know the story. It was a car accident. Just her and Jensen. He doesn't remember it, but he's seen pictures, heard the stories. From what I know, it was bad. They were driving to the Hamptons to visit his grandmother, and for some reason Christy didn't have his car seat. Things weren't as strict back then. It wasn't unusual for a toddler to ride in the back without one.

My vision blurs. I've never seen Christy like this, vulnerable and raw. It's almost uncomfortable, but also refreshing. She's usually calm, collected, confident, just like Jensen. And I realize she's not telling me this to excuse what she did. She wants me to understand.

She finally continues, her voice cracking through the tears. "We almost lost Jensen. And for so long, when I looked at him, all I could see was my little boy in the hospital. I couldn't yell. I couldn't punish. And when he grew older and pushed boundaries... And *God*, did he push them..." She lets out a watery laugh. "I couldn't stop enabling. The fear of losing him was so strong, and in my head, discipline meant losing him all over again. Like he'd leave or never talk to me."

She sniffs, and I keep listening, a quiet presence. "So when he acted out, when he pushed limits, I just... let him. Because I was grateful he was still here. That he hadn't pushed me away."

Her gaze drops. "When it became clear he was an addict,"—she shakes her head, squeezing her eyes shut, like she's ashamed to admit it —"I was thrown right back into that fear. I was terrified I'd lose him." She reaches for a tissue and dabs at her eyes, forcing herself to meet mine again. "But this time it was worse. I had something else to lose. He had something to lose." Her lips tremble as she whispers, "You."

Dammit. I swipe a finger under my eyes.

"Jensen's always been a happy boy. Always smiling, always making people laugh, always finding the silver lining. But underneath, it felt like he was searching. No matter how much fun he had, how much light he gave off, it never seemed to fill him. He was chasing something deeper, something that lasted. Then you came along. And everything changed. *He* changed."

She pauses to blow her nose, dabbing at the redness before continuing. "I'd never seen him like that before, so alive, when he brought you home the first time." She nods softly. "He loves you. The way

Tom loves me, and I love him. So when he relapsed again, I panicked. I did what I thought was best in the moment. Thought I was saving him from himself. Protecting you from the crash of a relapse. Protecting me from the heartache of losing you both. But it was wrong. It was selfish. I should have been honest with you." Her voice breaks. "You are the best damn thing that's ever happened to my son."

I swallow hard as our eyes meet, both of us crying. Both of us guilty of letting fear drive our choices. Both of us knowing what it feels like to almost lose someone to addiction—someone we love so deeply we'll do things we aren't proud of, just to keep them safe.

That's the irony of it all. I did things in desperation I wish I could undo. I enabled. I let him manipulate. Yet when Christy did the same, I couldn't believe it. Couldn't justify it. Couldn't understand. But she was drowning in her own fears, just like me, grasping for anything that might save her from the sorrow. Save him.

I take a shaky breath, nostrils flaring as I lock eyes with her. "It's not okay," I say, my head shaking. "It'll never be okay. None of it. Not what he did. Not what you did." *God, get it together.* The backs of my hands quiver as I wipe my cheeks. "Not even what I did. But I understand now. Why you did the things you did. And I'm sorry too. I'm sorry I didn't see it then. You were a mother trying to save her son. Just like I was a wife trying to save my husband." A sob tears free. "And we both knew we couldn't."

She pushes up from her chair, rushing to me on the other side of the desk. I stand, and she pulls me tight into her arms. I wrap mine around the woman who had once been like a mom to me. She could never take my mom's place, but she took me under her wing and held me close when I needed a family. Relief floods through me, like a waterfall over a cliff, washing the past away.

I cling tighter. I don't know how long we stand there, hugging, crying, letting old pain melt into something softer: a quiet appreciation and understanding.

I still hate that she lied. I'll never excuse it. But that's the thing about addiction, it twists everyone in its orbit, makes you cross lines you swore you never would.

Erin Cornia

All in the name of love.
And don't they say love makes people do crazy things?
Never has that felt truer.

Chapter Forty-One

JENSEN

I GLANCE around the empty apartment. *Shit.* The nostalgia hits harder than I expected. I've lived here since right out of college, over a decade now. It's where I brought girls back after dates, hoping to get lucky. Where I drank too many beers watching football. Where I once felt alone, searching for the meaning of life and coming up empty.

Until I met her.

I can still hear Alley's laugh bouncing off these walls the morning I asked if she'd just come from another guy's place. Still *feel* the jealousy, that sick pit in my stomach when I thought she might be seeing someone else. That fear of losing something before it was ever mine.

My lip twitches. *Jesus. That was embarrassing.*

My gaze settles on Alley. She's in the kitchen, wiping down the counters... again. I already told her to leave them. The cleaners are coming tomorrow, but she can't help herself. It's who she is. Honestly, they won't even have to do anything. She's scrubbed every surface like she's trying to erase our fingerprints from a murder scene.

I chuckle under my breath, remembering the first time she moved in. Same thing—on her hands and knees, scrubbing cupboards and baseboards, rattling on about how cleaners never touch the little details and how most men wouldn't even notice.

I lean back against the counter. "What can I do to help?"

She glances over her shoulder. "Nothing. The stove just has some grease stains that are hard to get off. I've almost got them."

She's in a tank top and sweats, hair piled on top of her head, and I can't help myself. I step in behind her, arms sliding around her waist. I bury my nose in her hair and breathe her in—that scent I can never place but would know anywhere.

She sinks back against me for a moment, then leans forward again, scrubbing at the stovetop. My hands drift up to her shoulders, fingertips brushing her skin before I press a kiss to her neck. Instead of pulling away, she tilts her head, giving me room.

She stills as my fingers trail down her arms, my lips following, leaving a path of heat along her shoulders.

"Babe." Her voice is laced with caution. "I've got to finish this. I'm almost done."

My arms cinch tight across her chest, pulling her into me, my cock twitching against her. I don't know what's come over me. I'm so ready to leave this apartment behind, ready to start fresh, start new. But holy shit, suddenly I'm slammed with this wave of sadness, like walking away means leaving part of myself here.

Maybe that's a good thing. Hopefully I'm leaving all the fucked-up parts. But this is also where I became who I am. Where Alley and I first had sex. Where she moved in and made me the happiest man on Earth.

It's also where I broke. Where I failed. Where I lost her.

But she found me.

She gave me her whole self. Again.

And that's the piece I'm struggling to leave behind.

My hand slides under her top, and Christ, her skin's so warm. So soft. My thumb circles her nipple and she falls back against me, rag slipping from her hand as she gives in.

"I need you here one last time, baby."

Her grin spreads slow, fingers wrapping around my forearm. "Hmm. On the counter or the floor?"

I chuckle low in her ear, fingers sliding down, dipping below her waistband. "Why don't we see where we end up?"

She spins, and her lips find mine. I kiss her hard, committing this moment to memory—the way her tongue teases mine, the way she melts against me, the little sounds that undo me every damn time. The way her lips make me feel like no matter where we are, I'm home.

Her hands glide up my chest, palms flattening against my pecs before rubbing back and forth, like she can't get enough. Of me. Of us.

She moans into my mouth, and *Jesus*, I'm finished when she does that. The sound vibrates through me like a plucked guitar string, sparking fire in my veins. My next kiss is desperate, met with her gasp. It's pure fucking need. I couldn't stop for anything.

My hand cups her neck as I take her deeper. Her nails dig into my waist, pulling me closer, and suddenly we're moving—me backing her down the hall, mouths fused in wild, clashing heat.

It's carnal, raw, an army of want rising inside me.

As soon as we reach the bedroom, I yank her shirt over her head and shove her sweats down as her fingers claw at mine. We hit the floor in seconds, naked and tangled in each other's arms.

Memories crash through me—a hurricane of joy, laughter, and pain. The tears. The fear. The hollow ache of losing her only to find myself again. I pour every bit of it into this.

And I let myself fall for Alley all over again.

When we're finished, we lie there on the carpet, sweaty and staring at the ceiling. Her hair sticks to my skin, and I can't help the grin that spreads across my face.

I can think of no better way to say goodbye to New York.

Chapter Forty-Two

JENSEN

"Babe!" Alley's voice carries down the stairs of our new house. I'm in the office, knee-deep in boxes, trying to make the space mine. She gave me free rein on this room, with her sign-off, of course. It's the first room you see when you walk in, framed by wide glass double doors. Basically a fish tank, but a hell of a bonus for us, given our history with office doors.

"Yeah?" I call back.

"Can you come here? I need your help!"

I slide the stack of books in my hand onto the shelf and head upstairs. "Where are you?" I ask halfway up.

"The zoo animal room."

I round the corner and find her sitting against the wall, looking wiped out.

"What's up?"

"I hate asking, but... I'm not feeling great, and there are only a few boxes left in this room. You mind?"

My brows pull together. "You don't feel good? What's going on?"

Her palm slides across her stomach. "Just a little nauseous. Kind of a headache too. I know, not a great track record. I'm two for two with moving."

I snicker. "Well, the last move turned out pretty great. Ended with you naked." I waggle my brows. "I'd be fine with a repeat."

She laughs, letting her head fall back. "I bet you would."

I glance around the room. "So what's this space even for? Storage?"

"Mostly. Just stuff we don't use much. These last few are miscellaneous, so I'm not sure what's in them."

"Alright." I shrug, pull the razor from my back pocket, and slice open a box.

"Will you start with that one?" Alley points to another.

"Sure." I move over, stab the blade into the tape, and drag it along the seam. I peel the flaps back, and freeze, confused. "The fuck...?"

Alley tilts her head, pinching her brows. "What is it?"

"Uh..." I rub the back of my neck. "Looks like a bunch of baby shit." My fingers dig through the contents—books, stuffed animals, toys. I push aside a blanket, revealing a tiny Chicago Cubs onesie. I hold it up between two fingers. "Promise me one thing, babe—our kids are not going to be Cubs fans. Yankees, all the way."

She laughs, rolling her eyes, and I toss it back in the box. I dig deeper to see if there's anything else, but nope, just a box full of baby stuff that sure as hell isn't ours. "That's weird." I glance up at Alley. "Think the previous owners left it?"

She shrugs, eyes narrowing. "It's gotta be ours. It was with all our boxes from New York."

I shake my head. It doesn't make sense. "Why would—?"

My brain scrambles, refusing to connect the dots—until she grins, hand on her stomach.

It slams into me all at once. "No. Shut the fuck up."

She just nods, eyes shining.

"You're pregnant?"

She nods again, grin growing wider.

"Holy shit." The words rip out of me as I stagger to my feet, running a hand through my hair. A laugh bursts free, wild and disbelieving. "Holy fucking shit. I'm gonna be a dad?"

"Yes," she laughs, tears spilling over.

"We're gonna be parents?" My hand lingers on my head. I still can't believe it. "Get up here, babe." I pull her into my arms and bury my face in her neck. The emotion hits late but hard, my chest caving and expanding all at once, joy detonating like a bomb. I cup her face and crash my mouth to hers, my voice breaking against her lips. "God, you're amazing. You're everything. I can't believe this is real."

She pulls back just enough to ask, "Are you happy?"

My gaze catches on her dimple, my throat thick. "Are you serious? Look at me. I'm a fucking mess." My vision blurs. "God, I'm feeling so many things."

"So... you're happy?"

"Jesus," I choke out, nodding. "Yeah." My thumb traces her bottom lip. "Yeah, babe. I'm really happy."

I kiss her again, slower this time, letting it sink in. Every ounce of joy, relief, and love spills into her mouth, into us. Into the life we're about to build together.

Her palms glide up my chest, one hand sliding around the back of my neck, fingers gripping tight. She pulls me closer, moaning into my mouth, and *damn*, I want her. The craving hits harder than any high I ever chased. Because in this moment one thing fills every thought:

Us.

It's not just her or me anymore—we're a unit now. Alley. Me. Our baby.

I have everything a man could ever want. A beautiful wife. A home. A family. *God*, I can't believe I almost threw away the chance at all of this. And beneath the joy, there's a flicker of fear. This isn't just about her anymore. It's no longer about just staying clean. I have to provide a stable life for my family. Protect them. Be an example. And I'll never let myself fuck it up.

I drag her bottom lip gently between my teeth, then ease back and rest my forehead against hers. A grin tugs at my mouth as my hands drift to her belly, splaying a palm flat against it. "How far along are you?"

"Not far. Only seven weeks. I don't want to tell people yet. Not until we're farther along."

"How long have you known?"

"Only a few days. It's been *killing* me not to tell you."

"I don't know how you kept it a secret. My family's gonna go nuts over this."

She laughs, soft and sweet. It's fucking music to my ears.

"Do you really not feel well," I murmur, "or was that just a ploy to get me up here?"

She plants her lips on mine. "I really am tired. Exhausted, actually. And I get bouts of nausea. But no." She shakes her head. "I'm not sick." She kisses me again.

And again.

"Why don't you go lie down then." I cock a brow. "You can be my pillow princess." I press a kiss to her forehead. "Let me take care of you."

"Ooh. I do love being a pillow princess." She giggles, her fingers slipping under the hem of my shirt. They trace the grooves of my abs, heat sparking everywhere she touches. My cock jerks, growing harder by the second.

When her thumbs dip below my waistband, I grip her ass and scoop her up into my arms. "Yeah, we're fucking. We have to celebrate."

She laughs as I carry her out of the room and down the hall to the bedroom, where our bed is the only thing put together. I toss her onto it, then cross my arms and pull my shirt over my head.

She sinks into the pillows, settling in, and I dive onto the mattress beside her, making it bounce. My lips find hers, and I let myself get lost. Because if there's ever a time to get lost, it's with Alley.

She's the love of my life. My anchor—my way back, every time.

Chapter Forty-Three

ALLEY

I TIP my head back and close my eyes, letting the sun warm my face. My smile is instant. There's no holding it back. *God, that feels good.*

It's one of those rare spring days in the low sixties, bright blue skies overhead and just enough of a breeze to keep it from feeling too warm. I couldn't ask for better weather on my birthday. It's perfect.

The mulch we spread a few days ago still lingers in the air, and our new patio furniture couldn't be more comfortable.

Matt and Leo are to my right, deep in business talk. To my left, Jensen's bantering with Adam, Michael, and my dad, and Cooper's laugh carries above the buzz of conversation.

I open my eyes and scan the group, squinting against the light. I chose this seat in the sun on purpose—I'm always cold. I live for the heat. Jensen's hand rests on my thigh from his spot at the end of the oversized chaise, his attention on the guys.

Laughter bursts out of him, mixing with Michael's, Adam's, and my dad's. Then his fingers squeeze my knee, his gaze finding mine.

"You remember that, Al?" Michael calls, his voice snapping my head toward him.

I bring a hand to my forehead, shading my eyes. "What?"

"Your Subway prank?"

He and Adam both laugh.

I nod as a grin spreads wide. "Sure do. That was classic. And then you both left Jenny and me to find our own ride home. Dicks."

Jensen turns his head from them to me. "I'm gonna need the whole story."

"Me as well," my dad chimes in. "What would make my responsible teenage son leave my daughter stranded?" He shoots Michael a teasing glare.

"Oh, we're dicks?" Michael points between himself and Adam. "What about you and Jenny? We had a deal."

"It was such a good prank. You could have at least appreciated the cleverness of it." I turn to Jensen, already smiling at the memory. "Jenny and I were fourteen and desperate for Subway. We begged Michael and Adam to drive us and promised we'd buy them a sandwich if they did."

Adam scoffs, chuckling under his breath.

I narrow my eyes at him, my grin only growing. "I wasn't about to spend my hard-earned money on them. So we rolled up socks, wrapped them in Subway paper, and stuffed them in a bag while they waited in the car. It was genius—until they decided to open them right then."

They all crack up, and I shake my head. "Didn't really think that one through. They kicked us out of the car and made us find our own way home. So we ate on the curb and walked. Took ninety minutes."

"Why don't I know about this evil side of you and Michael?" Jensen asks, still chuckling.

"Oh, Michael and Adam were assholes for about two years in high school."

"Only because you were bratty and annoying as hell," Michael fires back.

I scowl. "I was not bratty."

My dad arches a brow at me.

"Fine," I huff. "I was a little bratty. But *you* try balancing hormones while crushing on your brother's best friend"—my eyes flick to Adam—"only to find out he was dating your best friend's older sister. That was torture."

Adam bursts out laughing. "God. I could've shoved your face in a pile of mud and you'd still have liked me."

I nod, lips pressed tight, fighting my grin. I turn to Jensen. "It's true. I liked him a lot. I talked about him all the time."

Jensen pats my knee. "Babe, this isn't news. We all know you liked Adam."

"Yeah, but she never talked about Adam that way she did you, Jensen," Scarlett cuts in, grinning as she shakes her head. "God, when you two first started seeing each other? Borderline obsession."

I roll my eyes, smothering a smile. "Okay, stop." I glance at Jensen. "I wasn't obsessed. I just... really liked you."

He holds up a finger to me. "Shh, babe. I'm listening to Scarlett talk about how obsessed you were with me." That Jensen smirk spreads wide, melting my insides as his hand squeezes my thigh. Honestly, how could I not be obsessed?

Scarlett laughs, curling into Adam, their hands laced together on his thigh. They've been seeing each other since poker night. At first it was just texting and late-night calls, then Adam flew out to New York a few months ago. The rest is history, and I hope it works out. I've never seen her happier.

I swat at Jensen's finger, then turn to Scarlett. "And look how the tables have turned. Who would've thought you'd be dating my childhood crush one day? And now I know things about Adam that are permanently scarred into my brain." I flash them both a teasing grin.

"Whoa. What's that supposed to mean?" Adam asks.

"Means they talk about your sex life, man," Jensen says, perfectly matter-of-fact. "Ninety percent of what you tell Scarlett—you might as well tell Alley."

My eyes land on Adam. "Don't feel special. I know about Ryan and Leo's sex lives too. And unfortunately, way too much about my brother's." I wince, gaze shifting to Stella, sitting beside Michael. Then I glance at my dad. "Sorry, Dad."

He waves a hand, muttering something about us all being adults.

Stella taps a fork against her glass and stands, eyes sparkling as she looks around the group. The chatter fades as heads turn her way.

She lifts her glass. "Since it's Alley's birthday, I thought it'd be fun if we all shared a favorite memory of her."

A mix of cheers and teasing groans ripple through the patio.

"Oh, this'll be good." Michael smirks.

"Careful," Cooper chimes in. "I've got stories."

"I hope they're embarrassing," Adam adds, grinning.

"I'll go first," Stella says, before telling the story of the first time she met me. Michael's next, then my dad.

Then Adam. "Well, there's the socks and Subway, but nothing will ever surpass that riverboat tour when she thought Art Deco was a person." He flashes a grin, and everyone cracks up. I roll my eyes, shaking my head.

Scarlett dives into a story about me making a complete fool of myself at the bar in front of a couple hot guys.

Cooper follows, grinning. "Oh, I've got one. Remember when Viv asked us to babysit for like ten minutes? Neither of us had ever changed a diaper in our lives. We were gagging, shit was everywhere, and just when we finally got him clean"—she throws up a hand, laughing—"little man let loose with the firehose and peed all over you."

Everyone cracks up, Jensen included, while I groan through my laughter. "Oh my God, I've never moved so fast in my life. Fastest way to learn how to change a diaper? Get peed on."

Cooper's wiping tears from her eyes. "When Viv came home, I couldn't even breathe I was laughing so hard. Even Isla was laughing."

Ryan slings an arm over her chair, brows pinched, smirking. "And she says she doesn't want kids."

They all laugh again, but Jensen and I share a look. Mine's mortified, because holy shit, if I can't handle a diaper, how am I supposed to handle a baby? His is steady, almost reassuring—like he's silently telling me, *we'll figure it out.*

Ryan goes next, then Vivian—each sharing a short, funny snippet from the past few months.

Then it's Leo's turn. He's quiet for a moment, and when he looks up, his expression is serious and thoughtful. "Where do I even begin, Al?" He chuckles softly, a glint in his eye. "I've got a lot of great memories with you—family dinners, game nights at mine and Michael's apartment, where you'd flirt with our friends and try to convince them you were in college when you were still in high school."

Jensen side-eyes me, brow cocked, and I flash him a shameless grin.

"You've always filled a special place in my heart. You've been like a sister to me. And maybe this isn't my favorite memory, but it's one that's always stayed with me—when I picked you up from the airport after you started seeing Jensen. All the years before, when you'd visit, you were always your happy-go-lucky self on the surface. But deep down?" His voice dips. "You were sad. After your mum died. When you weren't talking to your dad. When you barely saw Michael." He pauses, smile softening. "But that day... when you got in my car and started talking about Jensen—you lit up. I'd never seen you so excited. So happy. I'll never forget it. That transition? That'll always be a favorite for me. And then, of course, you made fun of me for being incapable of dating."

He chuckles, shooting Vivian a quick wink before his gaze comes back to me. My eyes sting as I hold the tears back and mouth a quiet *thank you.*

He slaps Matt on the back. "You're up, mate."

"Well, shit, how do I follow that?" He chuckles, rubbing the back of his neck. "I don't think I can pick just one. You've tripped over your own feet more times than I can count, and you always have my back when the Adams siblings gang up on me. But honestly?" His smile softens as his gaze locks on mine—pure sincerity. "Just knowing you and having you in my life has been one of the greatest blessings."

He shakes his head, letting out a breath. "You and Jensen have been so inspiring to watch as a couple. I've never known anyone to love as hard as you two do." His eyes turn glassy, and it takes me by surprise. Matt really isn't one to get emotional, not over this kind of thing. And certainly not in front of people. "It's made me realize I want more out of my own life. That I want what you two have." He scoffs, laughing like he can't believe he just admitted it. "Looks like I've missed that boat, though."

I shake my head, the dam of tears about to spill over. "No, you haven't," I whisper.

He glances around at the serious faces—some teary, some smiling—and shifts in his seat. "Ah, fuck." Then he winces when he notices my dad, like he didn't mean to drop an f-bomb. "Sorry to kill the mood. All that to say, I already miss you, Alley. Happy birthday." He clears his throat and looks to Jensen. "Your turn, buddy."

"Thank you, Matt." My smile's soft, warmth spreading through my chest as I fight the rush of emotion.

Jensen leans forward, elbows on his knees, gaze locked on me. "I don't need to dig through memories. Every one with you is my favorite. Even the ones where you're mad at me." He smirks, drawing a few chuckles from the patio. His hand finds mine, squeezing tight. "Because those moments brought us here. To this. You. Me. Our life together. Every day with you is an adventure. And every moment that becomes a favorite is only trumped by another the very next day." His eyes shine. "I love you. And I'm excited for this new chapter with you." He glances around the group. "With all of you." Then his gaze returns to mine. "Happy birthday, baby."

Yep. This is it. It's all I'll ever need. This. Him. Right here.

* * *

I finish bringing the last of the food inside, sorting it into containers and packing them into the fridge. It's late, and I'm wiped—pregnancy's kicking my ass. Matt and Jensen are still outside talking, and everyone else has gone home.

Tonight was perfect. Friends, family, laughter, even a few heated cornhole matches. It filled my birthday cup in every way imaginable.

I tug the overflowing trash bag from the bin, tie it tight, and head for the front door. As I round the corner, I almost collide with my dad.

"Holy shit, Dad! You scared me." A breathless laugh escapes. "I didn't know you were still here."

He chuckles softly. "Sorry." He sets down the framed picture that sits on the console table. His voice is quiet, reverent. "I was just looking at this picture of your mother."

I study him, somber and distant. He forces a smile, but it drops as quickly as it comes, like holding it hurts.

The sight knocks the wind from me. My eyes burn, vision blurring as the ache swells sharp in my chest, stealing my breath. "I... miss her," I whisper, voice thick and shaky.

Dad takes a deep breath, then exhales—slow, cheeks puffed, eyes brimming with tears. "I miss her too, Alley girl." The words break on a strangled cry, and it guts me. She never got to see this. Him, sober. Me, married. The grandkids.

I take a shaky breath. "She'd be so proud of you, Dad." My lips press tight as I try to hold myself together, but it's useless—my birthday, the pregnancy hormones, the exhaustion. It all crashes over me.

He chuckles through his tears, voice rough. "No. It's *you* she'd be proud of. And dammit, it kills me she's not here to see it. It should've been me. You all needed her. And I'll never understand why it was her and not me."

I don't argue. I don't need to. He knows we're grateful he's here. He knows we want her back. He knows he's just giving voice to the thoughts that haunt him.

"I'm pregnant," I whisper, needing to give him something good, something light in this moment, and hoping Jensen won't mind I told him first.

A grin spreads across his face, breaking through the tears. He pulls me into his arms and kisses the top of my head. "That's the best damn news I've heard all year. Congratulations, Alley girl. You're going to be a wonderful mother. I'm so happy for you both."

I press my ear against his chest, squeezing tight. "Thanks, Dad. You're already a wonderful grandpa."

We stand there, wrapped in each other's embrace, the quiet of the house pressing in around us as we stare at my mother's picture. And for the first time in a long time, it feels like enough—even without her. Because I know, wherever she is, she's proud of us.

She's proud of me.

* * *

I WAKE to Jensen in the bathroom and glance at my phone. It's 1:06 a.m. I'd crawled into bed and passed out the minute my dad left.

A few minutes later, the bathroom light flips off and Jensen slides in quietly beside me.

"Did Matt just barely leave?" I murmur.

"Yeah. A few minutes ago." He scoots in close, his arm slipping around my waist and pulling me against him. "Did I wake you?"

"Yes, but it seems like every little thing wakes me lately." I yawn softly. "Guess it's practice for never sleeping again once we have the baby."

A low chuckle rumbles through his chest as his hand finds mine, weaving our fingers together and resting them on my stomach.

"I can't wait to meet the little guy."

"Little guy?"

He laughs. "Well, I don't want to keep saying *the baby*, and it doesn't feel right to call it an *it*. So until we know—he's little guy."

My bottom lip rolls through my teeth as my grin spreads wide. "Whatever you say, babe."

His lips press softly against my neck, trailing down to my shoulder blade. "Did you have a good birthday?" he murmurs, breath warm against my skin.

"Mmhmm." I press back against his sturdy frame, settling into the comfort of his arms.

"That's good."

"I told my dad I'm pregnant," I blurt, and he stills. "I'm sorry. We were having a moment, missing my mom and crying together. I just... needed to give him something good. Something happy." The silence stretches, heavy. My stomach knots. *God, did I ruin it?*

Then his hand slides up my stomach, over my breasts, to my cheek. He cups it gently, turning me toward him. His eyes search mine for a beat before he lays me flat and presses his lips to mine, firm and certain. "Was he excited?"

His mouth moves against mine, tongue teasing.

"Yes," I whisper between kisses. "You're not mad?"

"Nope." He kisses me deeper, his palm closing over my breast. "I could never be mad at you."

I snort, the moment breaking as I grin against his lips. "That's so not true. I could name a dozen things right now that would make you mad at me."

He shakes his head, amused. "Name one."

"Um, okay. What if I sent that dick pic you sent me the other day to the family group text?"

"That wouldn't make me mad. Embarrassed? Maybe. But mad? Nah. That's fucking funny."

"What it I posted it to social media?"

"Wouldn't blame you. It's a good dick."

"Oh my God!" I grin wider. "And if I sold your basketball cards?"

"Okay, you win." He kisses me. "I'd be pissed if you sold my cards." His chuckle vibrates against my mouth as his lips slide down my jaw to my ear, tongue flicking against the shell. His voice drops. "Now will you stop talking so I can give you the best damn birthday orgasm a girl could ask for?"

Butterflies flicker low, heat swirling as his hand slips between my thighs, and I gasp. "Yes. I'll be quiet."

He chuckles against my ear, voice dark and low. "I didn't say anything about being quiet."

He pulls back just enough to meet my eyes, then slides a finger inside me, curling it just right. A moan tears out of me, and his grin turns wicked as his mouth claims mine.

"That's my girl," he murmurs against my lips, smug.

He eases his finger free, slow and deliberate, then pulls my shirt up over my head. His mouth trails down my chest, teasing, lingering, sucking at my nipples until I'm writhing beneath him. Then he shifts lower, kisses skimming down my stomach, heading south—

"Wait, babe."

He stills immediately, eyes flicking up to mine.

"Just kiss me a little longer," I whisper. "I want to make out for a bit first... then you can do whatever you want to me."

A slow grin spreads across his face as he presses a tender kiss to my belly, his palm rubbing gently over it like he's already imagining our baby there. Then he shifts up, hovering over me. His eyes lock with mine, lingering, admiring. "You're my favorite person, Al."

"You're mine too," I whisper.

His lips find mine, slow at first, and I kiss him with everything in me. My arms loop around his neck, anchoring myself to him as his mouth moves over mine—warm, steady, sure. For a heartbeat the noise of the world drops away and it's just us and the thrum of his pulse against my palms.

Memories crash through in a rush, the good and the bad, reminding me of how we got here. Our first kiss. First sleepover. All the times he made me laugh. The times he made me cry. When being with Jensen was the safest thing in the world.

When it wasn't.

When I did everything right and everything went wrong.

When he came back for me...

I never thought I was the one who needed saving, but God, he rescued me. Pulled me from the sad hole I'd buried myself in and showed me how to live again. How to breathe. How to laugh. How to love.

He saved me. Saved us.

And I'll never forget it.

Our kisses turn hot, desperate, full of need for one another.

What we share is rare. A once-in-a-lifetime love.

A love so deep it hurts.

A love that's been shaken to the core.

Battered. Bruised.

A love that felt too good to be true.

A love that broke us.

A love that saved us.

A Note From the Author

Dear Reader,

DAMN. What a journey this was—and thank you for being part of it.

This duet broke me wide open. Writing it forced me to dig into pieces of my past I thought I'd already put to rest. Turns out, I hadn't. I cried... a lot. I lost hair. I booked hypnotherapy sessions after finishing just to process everything that came up.

While I left my first husband, there were many times I left and came back while we were married. The anxiety, the panic attacks, the exhaustion of loving an addict—those are things I knew too well. And after my divorce, I drank to forget. To numb. To have fun. (The irony isn't lost on me.)

It's why I wrote Alley the way I did—her doubt, her trust issues, her drinking to laugh. Writing her in this book was like holding up a mirror. And I remember some of my beta readers being a little upset with me for making Alley such a mess in the beginning.

But, guess what? Being around addiction can fuck you up.

I'm so grateful for the people who walked beside me while I wrote this story. I truly believe people are put in our paths for a reason, and this duet is proof of that.

When I started *A Love That Broke Us*, I actually intended for

Alley to end up with Adam. (I know, I know.) I was ready to take this duet out of the romance genre entirely because I didn't think a happily ever after with Jensen was possible. But somewhere mid-book, everything changed. I fell in love with him, and with *them*. Still, I was scared. Scared I couldn't make it feel real or honest because my own experience told me otherwise.

Enter the people who come into your life when you need them most. My alpha team—Bree, Courtney, and Gina—helped me sort through all of it. My thoughts. My fears. My new path for Alley and Jensen and their happily ever after.

And Courtney... I truly don't know if I could have done it without you.

She and I both experienced marriage with an addict, but she stayed. She made it work. She shared her story with me, and in doing so, she helped me process mine. We cried together, grieved together, and eventually healed a little together too. She reminded me that happily ever afters *can* exist after addiction. That love doesn't always end in leaving. That sometimes, staying is its own kind of strength.

No experience is linear. Like Alley says—there's no one way to deal with addiction. No right or wrong. We all do the best we can with what we know at the time.

After my divorce, I remember having a bit of a pity party. The whole *"Why me? I did everything right,"* story we tell ourselves. Then, one night, my ex-husband called. I was already remarried at the time, and he told me he was getting married too. During that conversation, he said something I'll never forget:

> *"You may wonder why you married me. May even*
> *regret it. But I've never doubted that I was*
> *supposed to marry you—because if I hadn't, I know*
> *I'd be dead."*

Maybe it's true. Maybe it's not. Maybe it doesn't even matter. But that moment changed something in me. It made me realize we never truly know the impact we have on someone else's life. Sometimes, we're exactly where we're meant to be, even when it doesn't make sense. Even when it sucks.

My ex wasn't Jensen—he was much worse. He was a heroin addict, and things got very dark. Honestly, I don't doubt that if I hadn't been there—locking him in a room, babysitting him through detox, taking shifts with family members—he might not have survived.

I've become such a believer in forgiveness. It sets you free in ways nothing else can.

If you take anything from this duet, I hope it's this:

Lead with compassion. Show empathy when you can. And most importantly, choose forgiveness—for yourself, and for others when possible. I've learned that letting go of resentment and shame is the quickest path to peace.

We're all just doing the best we can with what we have and what we know. Until we know better.

Thank you for reading.

Thank you for loving Alley and Jensen.

~ Erin ~

New to my books?

The Broken & Bound Duet is interconnected with my Chicago Series standalones.

You can start anywhere, but most readers begin with *If It Can't Be Us*, the first Chicago book.

Acknowledgments

As always, I owe everything to my husband. Babe, thank you for coming into my life when I needed you most. For being my best friend and helping me grow into the best version of myself—and for inspiring so many of the best parts of not only Jensen but all my MMCs. You are, without a doubt, the best real-life book boyfriend I could ever ask for. Thank you for being my biggest cheerleader.

To my amazing kids—thank you for letting me get away with some questionable mom moments, for manifesting in Target and airport bookstores with me, and for loving me unconditionally. I love you both more than you could ever know.

To my beta readers—thank you for your support, excitement, and friendship, and for always being willing to read just one more chapter.

This duet took us on a whirlwind of emotions, and I loved experiencing them all with each of you. Getting to know you, sharing GIFs, text messages, inside jokes, and taking on the challenge of making you all fall back in love with Jensen have been, hands down, some of my favorite parts of this whole process. In no particular order: Nikole Allred, V.L. Williams, Shauna Haddock, Hannah Wells, Derrian Whetton, Paige O'Neill, Bree Sleater, Kallie Street, Lauren Andrew, and Leah Richmond. And to Kyle Carsey and Tyler Allred, for providing valuable feedback from a male perspective.

To my alpha readers, Bree Dodge and Courtney Summers, and my PA, Gina Rinaldo—thank you for everything. I truly couldn't have written this duet without you. Alley would have ended up with Adam, I'd be emotionally scarred, and chances are—so would readers.

A special thank you to my editor, Celia Killen, who once again worked her magic in perfecting this book. You have a gift, and I'm so grateful for your patience, insight, and the suggestions that helped shape Alley and Jensen's story.

Thank you to my Bookstagram community. Damn, you ladies are the best. Thank you for taking a chance on me, for reading and reviewing my books, for supporting me, posting, sharing—the list goes on and on. I will never forget you and the role you've played in this journey.

A shoutout and thank you to some of my favorite authors who have inspired me in one way or another: Meghan Quinn, Sarah J. Maas, and Colleen Hoover.

And last, but surely not least, to you, the reader. Thank you for picking up my book.

About the Author

Erin Cornia lives in Austin with her husband, two children, and two mini golden doodles. She rediscovered her passion for reading after a long break when *It Ends With Us* by Colleen Hoover fell into her hands. Now, she has a deep love for romance novels—contemporary, fantasy, and historical alike.

Some of her favorite authors include Sarah J. Maas, Colleen Hoover, Meghan Quinn, and Judith McNaught with *Throne of Glass* by Sarah J. Maas holding the spot as her favorite series of all time.

When she's not reading or writing, she enjoys playing pickleball, working out, traveling, and spending time outdoors with her family. You can often find her watching *Schitt's Creek* or *Sex and the City*—with a bowl of homemade popcorn, of course.

For updates on new releases, ARCs, and bonus scenes (or to scream about the book and share your feels) come join Erin's Facebook Reader Group—*Erin Cornia: Romance, Heartbreak, Healing & Hard-Earned HEAs*

Follow Erin on Instagram and TikTok:
https://www.instagram.com/erincornia_author/
www.tiktok.com/@erincornia.author